THE WITCHES OF PLEASANT GROVE

JENNIFER CHIPMAN

THE
WITCHES
OF PLEASANT
GROVE

JENNIFER CHIPMAN

SPOOKILY YOURS

To my spoopy, Halloween loving girlies.

This one's for you.

PLAYLIST

willow - Taylor Swift

Season Of The Witch - Lana Del Rey

Lost - Michael Bublé

I Put A Spell On You - Annie Lennox

Make It To Me - Sam Smith

A Safe Place to Land - Sara Bareilles, John Legend

Wildes Dreams (Taylor's Version) - Taylor Swift

Dancing With The Devil - Demi Lovato

Through the Dark - One Direction

Demons - Imagine Dragons

Mercy - Lewis Capaldi

ivy - Taylor Swift

I Found - Amber Run

Falling - Harry Styles

If Only - Dove Cameron

I Can See You - Taylor Swift

MIDDLE OF THE NIGHT - Elley Duhé

As Long As You're Mine - Stephen Schwartz, Idina Menzel

Take Me To Church - Hozier

I Don't Wanna Live Forever - ZAYN, Taylor Swift

Love In The Dark - Adele

Monster In Me - Little Mix

exile - Taylor Swift, Bon Iver

Graveyard - Halsey

Die For You - The Weeknd

Afterlife - Hailee Steinfeld

Queen Of The Night - Hey Violet
Sweater Weather - The Neighbourhood
Hold Me While You Wait - Lewis Capaldi
peace - Taylor Swift
My Girlfriend Is A Witch - October Country
Timeless - Taylor Swift
In The Next Life - Kim Petras

ONE

WILLOW

I'd always been taught that black cats were a sign of good luck. Maybe that just came with the territory as the daughter of a witch, but every time I'd seen one, life seemed to look up.

A flash of black caught my eye as I winded through the quiet, shady street towards town.

This one was perched on the edge of the brick wall that bordered the path, his flicking tail garnering my attention as he licked his paw, like he didn't have a care in the world.

Though I supposed he didn't. I sighed to myself. *The life of a cat.*

"If only we could all be so lucky to laze around all day like you," I said with a snort.

The little beast didn't have a collar, so I assumed he didn't have an owner. Shaking my head at myself, I adjusted the tote bag on my arm and continued on my way down the path.

Crunchy leaves littered the ground, giving a satisfying *crunch* anytime I stepped on one with my boots. The entire world was lit up with color, all the trees turning the magnificent hues of autumn.

Turning around, I looked back at the brick wall, but the cat was already gone.

I loved every bit of this season—when the air turned crisp and you could pull all the warm sweaters out of the back of your closet. It felt like the equivalent of wrapping yourself up in a warm, cozy blanket with a cup of hot apple cider in your hands.

But there was something extra special about the fall in Pleasant Grove. This town had always been a secret haven for witches, a cozy little town full of covens, where magic was *ordinary*. Long ago, the founding witches had shielded this place from the outside world, putting up protective barriers with magic. Giving us the freedom to be ourselves, not having to hide who we were.

I smiled as I saw a cobweb covered front porch; the lawn decorated with a giant spider. Families had begun putting out their Halloween decorations weeks ago. In our community, it was like a huge competition. We took it as seriously as the humans did their Christmas lights.

It was my favorite month of the year. Ever since I was small, I'd looked forward to my family attending the town's festivities together. There was nothing better than the days where we'd decorate our house for *All Hallows' Eve*, especially when there was a pot of pumpkin juice brewing.

I missed that.

The tantalizing aroma of sugar and baked goods hit me before

I'd even reached for the door handle of the bakery and coffee shop in town—*The Witches' Brew*. My sister and I had opened it several years ago, and it was still crazy to me how popular we were each morning.

But right now, it was quiet, the morning dew still settled across the town as the world only just began to wake up.

The bell rang as I entered the shop, my mouth watering from whatever was currently baking in the back. The sugar cookies were my sister's specialty, iced with such precision. Everything she made was amazing, but I eagerly awaited fall each year, knowing that it meant pumpkin-flavored treats.

Heading into the kitchen, I dropped my bag onto the chair and went to grab my apron, smoothing my light brown hair into a ponytail.

"Will!" Luna's blonde curls popped into view. "Good morning!" Her cheery voice instantly smoothed over my unsettled mood. She'd always done that for me.

We were almost perfect mirrors of each other, my sister and I, except for our hair. We had the same little nose, the same bright green eyes, the same slant to our nose. And while she'd inherited my mom's beautiful honey-blonde hair, I'd gotten the caramel shade from our dad.

"Morning," I replied, tying the apron behind my back, inhaling deeply as if I could absorb the scent in the air. "How was your morning?"

Her dedication to the bakery side of our shop was the reason we had a line out the door most mornings. What skills I had with brewing potions, Luna had gained in her efficiency with breads, muffins, and all things sweet.

"It's been good." Luna's face split into a grin. "I made your favorite."

Mmm. I thought I had scented them in the air. "Are those chocolate chip pumpkin scones?"

"You got it." She flicked her finger, levitating one over to me.

When we were young, our parents had encouraged us not to rely on our magic. Not all witches in our town, or even in our coven, had telekinetic abilities, but we were both lucky. Our powers had gotten us out of quite a few situations in a pinch.

The scone—still warm from the oven—landed into my hand, and I bit into it happily. "Oh. So good," I moaned. "I needed that. This morning has been, well…"

I'd barely been able to drag myself out of bed this morning. And then there was the cat. I blinked.

"I saw a cat," I said, the words slipping out.

Luna raised an eyebrow. "Babe. There are almost as many cats in Pleasant Grove as there are Witches. It's the most common familiar, after all."

Familiars were no secret in this town, and most people bonded for life with theirs. They weren't just pets—they were part of the family.

The special bond you developed went beyond just *pets* and *owners*.

I'd had that once before—with my first cat, Binx—a big fluffy gray thing. The moment they had placed him in my arms at six years old, it was like I *knew*. He understood me, down to my soul. We had a connection that couldn't be replicated. He'd been my familiar, my lifelong companion, and the creature of my heart.

But twenty-two years was a long time for any cat to live.

This summer, we'd dug a tiny grave in our backyard, Luna etching the little stone by hand.

Now my house was empty—quiet.

But it wasn't just that. "This was… different." I shrugged.

"Willow." Her voice was soft—quiet. "I know you miss Binx. But maybe it's time."

To move on.

To accept that I'd have to find a new animal to fill my heart. My potions lacked a certain luster lately. Like something was missing.

Luckily, I could still make a mean mocha, since I ran the coffee shop side of our business.

I took a deep breath. "I know."

Binx had a good life. It was time to let his soul go into the afterworld, to the beyond. He'd earned that right.

But it didn't solve my loneliness. My sister had moved out of our parent's home, the one we grew up in, six months ago, leaving me alone in the creaky old Victorian manor. I kept saying I needed to update it, but I hadn't worked up the courage to go see the twins about renovations. If we weren't witches, I would have sworn ghosts haunted it. Maybe it was.

"I was thinking about going to the shelter. Just to see."

If there was a connection. If one called out to me. I'd been avoiding going for months. What was I scared of? That none of them would bond to me—or that one would?

I sighed, shaking my head. "I just need to get out of this funk."

Luna dipped her finger in her icing bowl. "You know, it's a good thing that the Pumpkin Festival is right around the corner. And Halloween! That always cheers you up." She plopped that finger in her mouth, licking the icing off. "Needs more vanilla," she said, crinkling up her nose.

"Yeah, but…"

I didn't have a good excuse, so I just busied myself by getting the coffee ready.

My sister crossed her arms over her chest, staring at me. "Isn't Eryne working the counter today? Why don't you take the day off? Go *look*. And maybe go do something *fun*. You're acting like your soulmate died, or something."

"Hey!" I frowned. No, that aspect of my life had *long* been dead. When was the last man I'd even dated? Probably before my parent's death.

There was a reason I was twenty-eight and still single. The last few years, I'd hidden away, only leaving my parent's home for work, errands and to see my coven. I was a homebody, I'd admit. I preferred curling up on my couch with a blanket and a bowl of popcorn to going out.

"There's always The Enchanted Cauldron too," she said, a sly smile on her face. "Who knows, Mr. Perfect might just waltz in and sweep you off your broom."

I snorted. "As if."

But my brain couldn't help conjuring an image of a man—tall, dark, and handsome—swooping in to give me the most romantic night of my life. A girl could dream, right?

I shook my head. That wasn't happening. Besides, I'd tried it before. I'd sworn off men, especially human men, for a reason.

"Maybe mom was right," she mused. "When she said we should look into our futures. See who we'd end up with."

I shook my head. "You know better than to meddle in our own lives."

Some witches made a business of it. Even within our community, there were only a few blessed with the sight, putting them in high demand for their skills.

Luna didn't like to call herself a Seer, but she had strong precognition skills. Instead of opening her own fortune telling shop, or moving to the human world to offer her services there, she'd chosen to pursue her passion.

Baking.

On the other hand, I hadn't figured out my true, *genuine* passion yet. I was good at running our business, managing both sides and running the coffee shop, but it had never truly *fulfilled* me. Not like it did Luna. She was only three years younger than me, but she already seemed to have so much more figured out.

Maybe that was why I said what I did. Why I decided I'd stop living my sad little witch life, the one where I practically floated in stasis. Like my hands were holding me up, but not moving. I wanted to move—to *fly*.

To live.

"You know what… Let's do it."

Her mouth dropped open as she stared at me over the bowl of icing. "What?"

"Let's go to the bar. We deserve a night out. You can wear one of those dresses I know you have stashed in the back of your closet, just waiting for the occasion."

She squealed, throwing her arms around me. "Oh, Will! We're going to have so much fun!"

Her eyes dragged over my outfit, from the knee length orange corduroy skirt to the black body suit I'd tucked into it, topping it off with my favorite hat. Sure, it wasn't *sexy*, but it was me. Comfortable. And the skirt had pockets.

Luna frowned. "You're not wearing that, though."

I sighed. "Promise you'll go easy on me?"

Her face lit up. Trust my sister to be the one pastel-loving witch in this town. "I know just the thing." She looked around before making a *shooing* motion with her hands. "Now go! Get out of here! I'll come over once we're all closed up."

Thankfully, running a coffee shop and bakery in a small town meant having set hours, since no one really needed anything after about 4pm. After that, there was the diner, and the bar, and we were all too happy to close up early.

"Fine, fine," I huffed, snagging another scone and levitating it over towards me. "But I'm taking this as collateral."

Luna winked before ushering me out of the kitchen. I had a few things to finish up before I could actually leave, getting things ready to open for the day. Brewing the coffee, I steamed a cup of milk, sighing in satisfaction as the smells mixed.

I might not have had everything figured out, but at least I had coffee.

If nothing else, it kept me going.

* * *

Leaving the shop, I ate one last bite of my second scone, sipping on the coffee I'd made myself before Eryne had arrived. She was my favorite hire of the last year, down from her redheaded bob to the cute witchy earrings she wore to work every day. It was hard not to be festive when you worked in a store like The Witches' Brew. Today's were a pair of brooms.

It wasn't even seven am yet. The morning was still young. I supposed I could go to the library, or maybe pop into my favorite apothecary shop. No doubt my reserves on herbs and supplies were running low at home, though I had plenty of time to restock before the next coven night.

I could go to the pet shop, but… I didn't know if I was ready yet. It might have been months, but I still felt like I needed time.

Rubbing at the back of my neck, I sat on a bench on main street, taking in a deep drink of my pumpkin spice latte. This spot gave me the perfect view of our town, Main Street just beginning to come alive as people began to scurry about town, heading to their jobs and lives. Most of the shops didn't open until nine, so even though the roads were busy, the sidewalks were still quiet.

It was the perfect way to enjoy the morning. Pulling a book out of my tote bag, I opened to the page I'd left off, letting the silence of the morning draw me into the world.

There was nothing quite as magical as getting lost in the pages of a good book. I'd always loved that feeling—looking up, and realizing I'd just spent the last three straight hours reading without a break.

When I finally put my bookmark back in, I checked the time. I'd agreed to meet Luna tonight, but what did I do with my free day? Sure, I'd done my job this morning—prep, but I didn't need to balance the books. I'd already placed the orders for the next two weeks.

That meant… I really was free to do whatever I wanted.

Should I go to the pet shelter like Luna suggested?

I thought about the black cat from this morning, the one with no collar around his neck. No home. Was there a cat there, as lonely and desperate for companionship as I was?

That was what made me pause—the idea that someone else out there needed me too.

I shoved my book back into my bag, turning to go the other way on Main Street.

Towards the animal shelter.

* * *

"If you see anyone who you feel a connection with, or just want to take a closer look at, just call me over. I'm happy to let you visit with them, so you can see if you have a bond." The young witch gave me a smile before leaving me in the room of cages.

It was hard to describe how deep the bond went between a witch and her familiar, but it was the reason I hadn't been ready to replace Binx yet.

But… It was time. I knew it.

I wanted someone to come home to.

Even if that someone was, well… my cat.

Staring at the cages, I walked back and forth. The sweet brown cat stretched out her back, but despite the adorable twitch to her nose, I felt… nothing. Same with the tabby in the kennel next to her, and every one after that. Dozens of cats passed by, and there was no tug, no pull. No connection.

And yet… the black cat in front of me flicked his tail. Locked his bright yellow eyes onto mine, and then licked his paw.

He looked just like the cat from this morning. But that was impossible, wasn't it?

Even familiars weren't actually *magic*.

Lucifer, his little name tag read. He looked like a young cat, though certainly nothing like the little kitten I'd gotten all those years ago. There was something about him, though. Something that screamed, *'Take me home. I'm yours.'*

That was the bond I'd been looking for. He tilted his head at me and blinked.

Who was I to argue with destiny? Hopefully, we would have many years together.

"Excuse me?" I asked the girl working at the shelter. "Can I… hold him?" I gestured to his cage.

Gods, I wanted to get him out of here. He seemed almost… irritated to be stuck in this over glorified glass box.

He deserved a big house to run around where he could chase mice and be petted to his heart's content. And I could give him that. The biggest perk of inheriting the Clarke manor was I had plenty of space for the little beastie.

"Oh, him?" She asked me, wrinkling her nose. "He's not very friendly. Are you sure?"

I nodded my head. "Yes, please."

She shrugged, bringing me into a back room before she returned with the cat.

My cat.

Once the worker left, he padded over to me almost tentatively, cocking his head in an un-catlike manner as he watched me.

Another flick of his tail.

"Hey, kitty," I cooed, holding out a hand towards him as he sat in front of me.

I tilted my head to the side, staring at him. "What's your name, hm?"

The cat seemed to snort, as if the name the humans had given him annoyed him. He didn't look like a Lucifer, even though when the light hit his eyes in a certain way they appeared almost… *red*.

But that couldn't be possible.

I held out my hand, and he brushed against it. "They said you're not friendly, but you're like a little sweetheart, aren't you?" I cooed.

And then he nudged my hand with his head, letting me pet him as he rubbed all over me, before climbing into my lap and laying down.

The purring all but confirmed that this was the one.

"Want to come home with me, huh, little beastie?" I scratched the top of his head.

He meowed, looking up at me.

"I'll take that as a yes."

Scooping him up in my arms, I knocked on the door, summoning back the witch.

"I'll take him," I said, giving an affirmative nod. And if in agreement, the cat cuddled lazily into my arms, not a care in the world to me holding him.

Even my sister's cat didn't let me hold her.

The young witch peered at me skeptically. "You want the demon cat?"

I held him against my chest, frowning. "Yes. And he's not a demon." I scratched between his ears, and he looked up at me. "Are you, beastie?"

If only I had known.

TWO

DAMIEN

The collar jingled around my neck that the damned humans had snapped on me.

Didn't they know I wasn't a cat?

I mean, I looked like a cat in my current form, *sure*.

But that was because I was stuck like this. It certainly wasn't by choice. All thanks to one *godsforsaken* night.

A month. I'd been stuck in this shape for a month, and what did I have to show for it? A collar and practically permanent residency at this shelter.

I didn't belong in a shelter, for crying out loud. Sure, I could escape, but that didn't solve my current predicament.

If only I had my magic, I'd have figured a way out of this mess.

But no. They had confined me to a cage, which forced me to stare at my reflection, wishing I could get out of this damn form. To make matters worse, they'd given me a name. And not one that was benefiting of my caliber. *No.*

I preferred when they called me *Demon Cat* to anything else. At least that one was accurate.

But this human… I'd sensed her.

Something about her scent drew me towards her, and I hadn't even needed to suppress the cat-like urges that grew stronger by the day.

She'd looked into my eyes, and a part of me knew I could trust her.

And maybe… she could help me.

That was why I'd practically crawled into her lap. Why I let her take me.

"What do you think?" The human mumbled, carrying me into her house. "I know it's not in the best of shape, but… it's home."

The outside of the old Victorian mansion was just like I would have imagined it, down to the broom that rested against the siding.

And the inside was *warm*. It was clearly a home. A family's home.

But where was her family? The human didn't seem to have anyone else living with her, and I didn't detect the traces of anyone else. Maybe a faint smell of another human—female, and then some older ones, but nothing else.

It's nice. I thought. *Better than any home I've ever had.* But I couldn't say that.

She'd carried me into the kitchen, setting me onto the floor as she rustled through the fridge, clearly frowning at its contents.

"What do you think, little beastie? Do you want some water? I need to go to the store to get some things…" She bit her lip. "I didn't exactly expect this to happen today." She sighed, her cheeks turning slightly pink as she continued mumbling to herself.

Oh. That was cute.

I cocked my head, staring at her with fervent attention as she filled a bowl with water.

She stopped, staring back at me. "Will you be okay while I go?"

Crouching down to place the water bowl on the floor, she rubbed between my ears, and an involuntary *purr* emitted from my throat.

That was… new.

I'd never really had the occasion to let humans pet me when I was in this form before. It surprised me how much I liked it when *she* did it.

I meowed in response. I hoped that it communicated, *I'll be fine, human.*

But what did I know?

The human stood up, brushing off her orange skirt—cat hair I'd left behind, I was sure—and then nodded at me.

"Okay, boy. I'll be back. Be good and don't get into anything." She winced, looking around the room. "I'll have to clean up when I get back. Geez."

I flicked my ears back in amusement as the human talked to herself.

"Gods, Willow," she muttered to herself. *Willow.* I liked that. "You have got to stop talking to the cat like he's going to respond."

If only she knew.

Heading to the door, the human—Willow, I corrected myself—picked up her phone, hitting a contact before putting it to her ear.

"Yeah, Luna?" she said into the speaker. "I'm going to need a raincheck for tonight…" She winced. "I know. I'm sorry—" And then she was out the door, leaving me all alone to explore my new home.

Flicking my tail, I walked across the human's hardwood floors. I figured if I was stuck here till I figured out how to reverse this damned curse, I might as well get my lay of the land.

What's this? My nose caught a scent and I couldn't help but follow it.

What was that delicious scent? My mouth watered, and I knew it was the feline side of me that had been dominant for too long. That was what guided me through the rooms of the house, searching for the location of the wafting smell.

Pushing open the cracked door, I padded into a room, stopping suddenly as all of my senses were overwhelmed by *her*. Willow. Her scent was all over this room, and I realized with a jolt exactly where I'd entered a moment later. Bedroom.

Darting out of the room, I dashed to the other end of the house—peeking my head into what looked like a library. There was an empty bedroom with lilac walls, and then—there was the source of the twitching to my nose.

It smelled like catnip, rosemary, marigolds—the things my cat side *loved*.

The room itself seemed to be some large storage room, though everything had its place. The back wall was covered in bookshelves, filled with a whole myriad of supplies: essential oils, crystals, plants, herbs, dried flowers, candles, incense and books.

Jumping on the table in the center, I surveyed the crystal ball, a grimoire laying open, plus a stack of books, and more candles that littered the table.

It suddenly occurred to me what exactly she used this room for.

Witch.

And then a thought ran through my mind.

This female—she could *fix* me. She could end this damned curse and turn me back into my proper form.

Maybe luck was on my side when they brought me to the animal shelter here. I'd certainly never have expected to end up in a town with a coven of witches.

Fates.

I needed this undone.

But how…?

* * *

She was back, with a bag of cat toys and treats at her side.

"Here, kitty," the brunette girl cooed, shaking a bag of treats. I sat on the floor in front of her as she held the bag.

Internally, I rolled my eyes, flicking my tail to show my irritation.

"Come on," she said, sighing. "They're good. At least, I think." Willow looked in the bag, as if questioning it now.

Sniffing it, I scrunched up my nose. It was bad enough that I'd had to eat whatever the shelter gave me for the last few weeks. I'd barely survived on the scraps except for when I dared to sneak out.

But this? *No.* I couldn't bring myself so low.

I wasn't a cat, dammit.

Willow frowned. "Do you not like treats?" The expression gave her worry lines on her brows, and I instantly wanted to smooth them out.

Why, Damien? Why was that the thought that had popped into my mind?

I jumped to my feet, padding over in search of *real* food. Something palatable that I'd actually be able to stomach. Not dry kibble or whatever they put in those cat treats everyone tried to feed me.

"Where are you going, little beastie?" The witch murmured, following me as I sauntered through the living room into the kitchen.

Planting myself in front of the fridge, I meowed.

Opening the doors, she looked at the contents. "What do you want, hm? Tuna?" She pulled out a can.

I flicked my ears back in disgust. *No, thank you.* I'd never been a huge fan.

"Hmm." She diverted her attention back to the drawer, bringing out a fresh cut of salmon. "What about this?"

Meow. I brushed up against her legs in approval.

She chuckled to herself. "Picky cat, huh?"

My little witch had no idea.

Willow sighed. "Guess I'm making you dinner, then. I don't think raw salmon is good for cats."

I gave her a chirp of confirmation before curling up in the corner, letting my head rest on my front paws as I watched her cook. She was a natural in the kitchen, which made me wonder about the potions room I'd seen. Despite how easy it would be for disarray, the entire room was meticulous, organized—like everything had its place.

I had a feeling she was equally skilled with whatever concoction she was brewing.

And now I had to brew my plan—one to get her to help me.

How not to startle her when I revealed my true identity.

There was something nagging in my gut—*what was it?* The feeling settled within me, though I couldn't identify it.

"Here you go, beastie," she said, placing a plate at my paws.

My nose twitched as she stared at me, her eyes darting between the cooked salmon and me. *Are you going to watch me eat, little witch?*

Apparently she was. I sniffed the cooked fish, and after deeming it smelled good—she'd grilled it perfectly. I took a bite.

Oh, Hell. I gobbled up the entire piece of fish, tearing through the entire fillet faster than I could blink.

Willow scratched under my chin. "You *were* hungry. Poor little guy, huh? I still have to figure out what to call you."

Demon Cat is fine, I thought, sitting up to stare at her.

She snorted, not breaking eye contact. "I still can't believe they called you a demon cat. You're such a sweet little boy, aren't you?" My witch scratched under my chin, and I let out an involuntary purr.

Damien, I thought, hoping whatever bond she seemed to feel between us would communicate that. *My name is Damien.*

I'd never willingly given my name to a human before, but… I didn't think I minded her knowing it.

Didn't mind being here, even if they'd trapped me in this feline body.

Willow's lips tilted up into a smile. "Damien?"

Yes! I meowed excitedly, brushing back and forth against her legs, nuzzling my head against her skin.

"Damien. I like it, too." She scooped me up into her arms, cradling me like a baby. "What do you say we go sit on the couch and watch a movie, huh, beastie? There's so many good ones for the Halloween season."

Meow.

Yes.

Domesticity was never a part of my life before. I'd never really had the chance to just sit and *be.* There had always been something else for me to do, something my brother needed from me. I was never my own person.

But maybe here, in this town, at this witch's house, everything would be different.

So I let her carry me to the couch. Curled up on her lap, and watched a couple fall in love while they rebuilt an old bed-and-breakfast. Snorted when they were clearly too stupid to admit their own feelings. Watched with rapt attention, until the warmth of the little witch's lap lulled me to sleep. I'd never felt so comforted, so at peace.

Maybe life as a cat wasn't so bad. That was the thought that startled me awake.

I couldn't afford to think like this. I didn't know what was wrong with me, but I had to get out of this body—before the change was permanent. If there was even a chance I had to remain as a cat forever, I needed to do everything I could to fix it.

Willow stood up and yawned, stretching out her arms before turning back to me.

I tried to push the nagging feeling aside and remind myself that it could wait until tomorrow.

Curiously, I angled my head and perked my ear up towards her. Did she expect me to sleep in her room? That felt like a line I shouldn't cross. Especially considering I wasn't *actually* a cat.

And I'd have to break the news to her, eventually. That I wouldn't *be* her cat. That I wasn't a cat at all.

But when she looked at me, tucking her hair behind her ear as I peered at her from the couch, I could sense how vulnerable she was. How alone this little witch was.

And I didn't want her to feel like that.

"Should we go to bed now, Damien?"

Meow. I got up, stretching my back, and hopped off the couch, following her loyally.

Witch's best friend, I thought with a smirk.

Despite my upbringing not to consort with witches, this woman had done everything she could to make me happy. Comfortable.

Even if I was just her cat.

I curled up at the witch's feet, and for the first night in weeks, I slept.

THREE

WILLOW

Good morning, beastie," I murmured to the black ball of fur, who was currently sitting up, licking his front paws as he lounged on my bed.

I'd put on my orange buffalo plaid comforter when I'd decorated the house inside for fall, and he almost looked like the perfect little stuffed animal laying on it. Especially when my decorative pumpkin pillow was against the pillow shams.

Meow. It was crazy to me how even though he was a fairly quiet cat, I almost felt like I could tell what he was thinking. What he was *saying,* even with a simple meow. *Good morning, human.*

I'd slept better than I had in weeks last night. Was it because I'd known there was another being in the house? This old, creaky house could get lonely.

"I have to work today," I said, petting him slowly. "But I won't be gone all day—just for the morning rush—because Luna, my sister, she'll need me. I don't enjoy leaving her alone, you know?"

He chirped in agreement.

"I feel bad leaving you alone too, little beastie. But I'll pick up more salmon on the way home, and then maybe we can watch another movie? Snuggle on the couch?"

Why was I narrating my entire day to the cat I'd just adopted yesterday? I couldn't explain it, but the way he looked up at me with those gigantic eyes told me he understood, too.

Damien brushed up against my hand. Instantly, the contact centered me. Calmed me down. I'd never felt anything that gave me such an immediate sense of rightness, but I guessed that was a sign of good synastry between us.

I sighed. *Time to get going.* I didn't want to leave my warm, cozy bed. Damien was basically a bed warmer with his cozy warmth keeping my feet nice and toasty.

Picking him up, I scratched under his chin before nuzzling at his face. "Who's a cute little boy, huh?" He squirmed as I rubbed my nose against his cheek.

I laughed as he jumped out of my arms, moving to the other side of the bed to lick his paws.

Rejected from any further love, I finally forced myself out of bed. Shucking my shirt off, I whisked it into my dirty clothes hamper, the rest of my clothes following behind, and I headed to the bathroom.

Maybe after I'd had a solid few hours of work in the bakery, this strange feeling in my gut would go away.

I could only hope.

* * *

Luna's hands were kneading a ball of cookie dough when I came into the kitchen area, unwrapping my scarf from around my neck and hanging it up on a hook.

"How was your night?" She narrowed her eyes on me.

I winced. "I'm sorry for canceling our plans. It's just… I took your advice."

"Looking into your future?" Luna perked up.

"No." Snorting, I went to pull my hair back so I could help her with prep. "I went to the shelter."

"Oh. And?"

"And… I got a cat."

She blinked. "That soon?"

"Uh-huh." I whipped around from the fridge, where I'd been grabbing the heavy cream to make some fresh whipped toppings for drinks. "What do you mean, *that soon?* You're the one who told me to *go*."

"Yeah, but I figured you'd avoid it for another few months. That's what you always do."

Always? I cleared my throat, dropping my eyes to the floor. "I do not."

Luna's voice grew quiet. "Willow. You don't have to pretend with me. I know you didn't pick this, either." She indicated around us at the shop.

"But I love—"

"I know." She shook her head. "But that doesn't change the way you've always avoided decisions: What to do after college? Selling mom and dad's house? Building your own life?" She smiled sadly at me.

"I..." But I couldn't exactly deny most of it. "I'm not selling the house." Crossing my arms over my chest, I frowned. "There's no reason to. I told you that. It's my house now." Our house, until she'd chosen to move out.

When did my little sister get so introspective?

"There are other houses," she mumbled.

"I don't want other houses, Lu. We've gone over this."

"I just worry about you, all alone in that creaky old house."

"So move back in." I shrugged, like we hadn't had this discussion multiple times since she'd brought up moving out and into the studio apartment above the bakery. "Besides, I'm not alone now. I have Damien."

"Damien?" She raised an eyebrow.

"*My cat.*"

"Right."

"Luna…"

She shook her head, her bandana that was holding her hair back swishing with the movement. "I'm sorry. I overstepped."

"No. You're right." Luna's eyes shot to mine, the surprise as clear in her eyes as I figured it was on my face. "I need to figure out my life. What I want. If…" I didn't want to say it. I loved working with my sister. "If this is it." Maybe it wasn't?

She nodded. "It's okay, you know. To make your own decisions. Even if it's not this."

I dumped the heavy cream into the blender, along with the flavoring, busying myself so I didn't have to meet her eyes again.

All morning, I pondered that very thought.

Because it felt like there was something out there waiting for me, and I didn't know what it was yet.

But I wanted to find out.

* * *

The entire morning and afternoon passed by in a blur. Saturdays during October were always a hustle and bustle of activity. The crisp autumn air was filled with the sounds of laughter and chatter as most of the town was out enjoying the perfect fall weather. Practically everyone in town had made a pit stop for Luna's famous pumpkin cookies.

I couldn't blame them. I'd snuck three over the course of the day.

Early afternoon, I took off, leaving Luna to close up. I never considered myself a morning person, but I loved getting off early. It was the one perk of going in before the sun rose.

And now, I was probably wearing my footprints into the kitchen floor, walking back and forth as I nibbled on another cookie. Luna's words from earlier were still bouncing around my mind.

Was I always avoiding making the big decisions? Waiting for someone else to make them for me?

Damien was sitting on top of my kitchen table, staring at me, but I didn't have the mental energy to make him get down.

"Are you going to pace like that all day?"

I blinked.

Stared at the black cat as he flicked his tail.

"What? You've never seen a talking cat before?"

"Willow, you're losing your mind," I muttered to myself. "That cat is not talking to you."

"No, I am." He jumped off the table, coming to sit at my feet. "But I'm not *technically* a cat." He tilted his head to the side, those ears pointing up adorably.

I raised my eyebrow. "You have whiskers. And a *tail.*"

And now I'm talking to my cat.

"Well, I'm certainly aware that I *look* like a cat." He licked one of his paws. "But I'm not. I'm just stuck."

"Stuck?" *Did he just narrow his cat-eyes at me?*

I'm going crazy. That was the only logical answer to this. I'd lost it.

"Yes. I can't shift back to my normal form."

"And your normal form is?"

"A man. Mostly."

"*Mostly?* What the hell does that mean?"

"I'm not sure you're ready for that." His eyes flickered red, and I could have sworn the room darkened.

Oh. "Well…" I bit my lip. "How do we get you, um… de-catted? *De-catified?*" I pondered the term, and then shook my head. "Has this happened before?"

"No." He heaved a dramatic sigh. "I was cursed. By a witch."

Oh my gods. "A cursed talking cat? What is this, *Sabrina the Teenage Witch?*"

He blinked his eyes at me. "What?"

"You know… Salem? He's cursed to be a…" I looked at his blank face. Clearly, he'd never watched human television. "Never mind." I crossed my arms over my chest. "How do we fix it?"

"Hmm?" His voice came out scratchy, almost a purr. Which made sense. Since I was talking to a *cat.*

My legs wobbled, and I lowered myself to the ground, sitting on the hardwood floor. I wasn't sure I could keep myself upright if I stayed standing. Not with the events currently unfolding in front of me.

I blinked. What was the proper response in this situation? I'd never dealt with a person-turned-cat before. Of all the weird magical things that had happened in Pleasant Grove, this topped the list.

"How do we turn you back to your proper form, then?"

"Now, now, little witch." His little pink nose wiggled. "What's so wrong with our little arrangement?"

My nostrils flared. "Our little *arrangement?* You mean the one where you bamboozled your way into my home, got me to feed you, and slept on my bed? That one?"

He licked his paw nonchalantly. "Yes."

"Oh my—" *Goddess be.*

Slept on my bed.

"Did you see me naked?"

Damien the cat froze. "What?"

"This morning. When I changed. You were in my room, and I—" I paled, glad I was sitting on the ground. "I'm going to be sick."

"Little witch." He placed a paw on my arm. "I promise, I did not look." *Much*, the little grin on his face seemed to say.

I rolled my eyes. "Willow."

"What?"

"My name. It's Willow."

He flicked his tail. "I know."

"Then why do you keep calling me *little witch?*" I was five-six, a perfectly average height, thank you very much.

"Well, you are, aren't you? A witch?" Damien tilted his head to the side. "Which is why you can help."

I crossed my arms over my chest. "Sure, but I'm not *little*. I'm twenty-eight, and I'm a business owner. Even this house is mine."

"You called me your *little baby boy* three times this morning."

I cleared my throat. "I thought you were a cat."

"As normal people do." He purred.

"*Damien.*" It felt weird addressing him like that—with his name. When it had popped into my head, I'd thought nothing of it, but now—

"Ah, see, you already know my name, *witch.*" His nose twitched.

Goddess help me. You've truly lost your marbles, Willow.

"You're not insane."

"What? Did you just read my mind?" I rubbed at my temples.

"No. I can't access my full powers in this form, unfortunately."

"Full powers?" I raised an eyebrow.

Damien stretched his back before sitting up, like he was drawing up his full cat-height. His eyes flickered red again, and I shivered, even though there wasn't normally a draft in here.

"What are you…?" The words came out barely above a whisper.

His black tail flicked against the floor. "I'm sorry I didn't properly introduce myself before. I didn't want to startle you."

Well, you did a pretty good job of that, anyway.

"My name *is* Damien, though I suppose Demon Cat is also appropriate." His ear twitched. I didn't think I was imagining the chuckle in his voice. "I'm the bastard prince of the Demon King, and that makes me—"

"A demon." I paled. My mom had always warned me about demons and their trickster ways. How they'd steal your soul and condemn you to an eternity in their realm. Hell.

Which meant this cat—my cat—was from *hell.*

'And never, ever, make a deal with the devil.' She'd always warned me of

that, ever since I was a little girl. I sucked in a breath. I had a feeling I'd done something a lot worse by inviting this being into my home.

"You look like you're finally getting it now," Damien the *demon*—the cat, currently sitting next to me—said. "Now, can we get back to the important part?"

I ignored his question, still reeling in my surprise. "How did this happen to you if you're the *son* of the *Demon King?* Aren't you like… *super* powerful?" What little I knew about demons wasn't helping me here.

He narrowed his eyes, and the temperature dropped a few more degrees. "Say that again when I'm not in this form, and you'll see just how powerful I am."

But this black cat glaring at me with red eyes made me burst out laughing. "I'm sorry. I just can't take you seriously. You're so *cute*." I *booped* his nose in demonstration, watching as he wiggled his whiskers.

"Willow." His eyes narrowed into slits. "I'm serious."

"So—" I couldn't stop giggling. "—am I."

He climbed up, putting one paw in the center of my chest so he could put the other one over my mouth.

"Listen to me, little witch. I need your help to reverse this damn curse so I can go back to my proper form. My *life*."

I moved his paw off my face, dangling his cat-self out in front of me. "And you expect me to do this out of the goodness of my heart?"

"Well, a little, yes. But also… You *have* heard of making a deal with a demon, haven't you?"

I narrowed my eyes. "Enough to know I shouldn't make one."

Damien sighed, flicking his tail again in annoyance. "I can give you anything you want in return for helping me. Whatever your heart desires."

"But I—" I blinked. There wasn't anything I needed, but what *did* my heart desire? It was something I'd been thinking about. Not that I was going to tell him that.

"Everybody wants something, Willow." He licked his paw. "Even good little witches like you."

Ignoring his comment, and how it made me feel, I frowned. "So, how do I turn you back? Is it some spell, or potion I need to make, or…"

His eyes focused on mine. Unblinking. "I don't know. If I did, don't you think I would have undone it myself by now?"

Oh. Well. I guessed that would make sense.

"Yeah." I muttered under my breath. "But I have little experience with curses. None of the witches here would ever use them. They're banned in the community. Our coven hardly even discusses them, even though I think Cait would love to hex her ex-boyfriend for good measure. Although…"

My thoughts wandered to the library my parents had spent years amassing. I'd read so many of them, but maybe there was something in there that would tell me how I could break this curse.

"Maybe I have an idea."

I didn't need anything from him, but the sooner I could get him out of my house, out of my life, the better. Because Demons were not to be trifled with.

FOUR
DAMIEN

Do normal people take their familiars to the library?" I asked Willow, following behind her as we walked the path to town.

I could have teleported us if I'd had full use of my magic. But then again, if I'd had full use of my magic, I wouldn't have been here, walking behind the witch.

"No."

Somehow, that wasn't as annoying as it had been before. Especially now that I could actually talk to Willow. I had startled her yesterday, but she seemed to have gotten used to me talking now.

I'd been on this path before, but everything felt new walking beside her. The little bell on my collar jingled when I moved, something I'd been steadily ignoring for weeks.

"So... How exactly did you end up stuck as a cat?"

"I told you. A witch cursed me."

"Mhm." She bit her lip, a motion I'd noticed she seemed to do often when she was deep in thought. "And what did you do, exactly?"

"Who said I did anything?" I walked faster in front of her so I could jump up onto a short wall, sitting on it and staring at her.

Willow rolled her eyes, continuing to walk down the path. "No witch would curse an innocent man."

"But I'm not a man, remember?"

It was her turn to come to a screeching halt. "Are you telling me someone found out you were a demon and then did this to you?" Her eyes looked almost... concerned. I didn't deserve that.

"Something like that." I couldn't explain to her *why* I was in the human realm, why I'd been out where a witch could curse me in the first place, but when you boiled it down, that was what happened.

"And no one's come looking for you? No one's... worried about you?" Her eyes were glassy. And how strange was that? That this little witch was concerned for me?

I shook my head. No one would come looking. My half-brother wouldn't give a second thought to my absence as long as I completed my task.

"Come on," Willow said, scooping me up into her arms. Cuddling me like she had before work yesterday, even though she knew what I was now. "Library is just around the corner."

"Why are you carrying me, little witch?" I muttered, tilting my head up to look at her. "I can walk just fine."

"Shush, beastie. I don't want them to think I've gone completely nuts."

She scratched my head, and I let out an involuntary satisfied meow in response before settling into the hold.

I… didn't hate it. Maybe it was because it was her? I had razor-sharp claws in this form, and yet I was perfectly content letting her carry me into the library, nuzzling my face into the crook of her elbow.

I didn't perk my head up again until the smell of old books entered through my nostrils. The library was dark, densely filled with books. It almost felt like there was an other-worldly presence in here. I wondered how many witches had studied here, learned magic here.

"Willow!" A young man's voice called out, and I felt the hair stand up on my back.

For whatever reason, I didn't like other humans talking to my witch. *Huh.*

"Oh, hi, Simon," Willow said, the warmth clear in her tone. I didn't need to look at her to know a smile curled over her face.

"Who's this?" The redheaded boy—who could have been no older than his early twenties—pushed up the glasses onto the bridge of his nose, looking at me.

I hissed, bearing my teeth at him.

"This is my new cat. I couldn't leave him home," she said, wincing. It surprised me at how easily the lie slipped from her lips.

Though maybe she didn't trust me. I would understand why.

"I see." Simon's lips spread into a fine line as he looked at me, before turning his attention back to my human. "Is there anything you need help with today?"

"No. Just doing some research." She looked down at me, and I chirped, the sound passing through my lips unintentionally. "I promise he'll be on his best behavior."

I meowed in response, narrowing my eyes. *Yeah, as long as you don't keep looking at her like that, young wizard.*

"Damien," she huffed, her voice low as we headed towards a table in the back. "You're going to get me in trouble."

Rows of books surrounded us on either side, keeping us out of eyeshot from the other patrons. And, hopefully, out of hearing range too.

I jumped out of her arms, landing in front of the table. "I didn't like how he was looking at you."

Willow deposited her bag onto a seat, draping her coat over the back. "He's my *friend.* I've known him since I was a toddler. Goddess help me." She rubbed at her temples. "Now, you stay here. I'm going to go see what I can find on curses."

"You don't want me to come?"

I found I didn't like that, either. I wanted to stay by her side. Protect her. Even if I weighed ten pounds, I still had sharp claws. And pointy teeth.

If anyone threatened her…

"You don't think it's going to look weird if I wander around the library *talking to my cat?*"

"Mm. Point taken." Laying down, I curled my body up into a ball, resting my head on my paws so I could still watch her.

"Don't hiss at anyone else," she warned me before taking off in a blur of orange and brown. The hit of her sweet scent—like coffee and vanilla and something *else*—caught my nose.

There was something satisfying about that, just watching her. Every so often, she'd disappear from my line of sight, and then she'd return to our table, depositing another handful of books. I stayed quiet, just a few meows of acknowledgment. I couldn't help but notice how her face lit up when she brushed her hand over my back, and the way her eyes sparkled when she rubbed that spot in between my ears.

I already hated the thought of leaving her. It was strange, the affection I felt for this human. This little witch. Despite having just met her, there was already a sense of familiarity and ease.

And not just because she was so delicate with me, even though she knew now that I wasn't actually a cat.

Willow sat down with another pile in her hands and I perked up. "Anything good?"

"Shhh." She looked around, her eyes widening before turning back to the book. "Don't talk to me. It's bad enough that I brought my cat to the library."

"Not a cat."

She reached over and scratched under my chin, that involuntary purr coming from my chest. Like she was proving to me I was exactly that. I'd been stuck in this form for too long.

I narrowed my eyes. "Don't do that."

"Then let me *focus*." Willow turned back to her pile of books, grabbing a new one out. "I'm trying to help you, after all."

Although I hated to admit it, she was right, and I sat there and watched her work while wishing I could be more useful. I lacked any real understanding of how witchcraft functioned beyond what I learned in the demon realm. Crystals, herbs, candles, potions—that much I knew. Not how their magic worked. Not the things that might actually make a difference here.

"Did you find something?" I asked, peeking over at the book she'd buried her nose into.

She shook her head. "I don't know yet." Looking down at my paws, she sighed. "I'd ask you to help, but…"

"No opposable thumbs," I agreed. "It's probably the worst part of being stuck in this form for the last month. That and being stuck in the shelter with only that horrible kibble for food." I scrunched up my nose, making a disgusted face. I hated that stuff.

She froze. "What?"

I cocked my head to the side.

"A month? You…" Her eyes grew wide. "Gods. Fuck. That's… awful. I'm sorry."

Doing my best cat-equivalent of a shrug, I curled back up on the desk, watching her read a book labeled *The Little Book of Curses and Maledictions for Everyday Use*. She'd already set *Witchcraft: Hexes and Curses* and *Magic Spells To Curse Your Enemies* to the side. There was a pile of books in her discard pile, too, with similar names, that she must have deemed useless, barely taking the time to flick through them.

Something about the names made me want to chuckle. The titles were so on the nose. What else did I expect from a town of witches?

It could have been worse, I reminded myself, *if she hadn't rescued me.*

Because at least now I had a chance. My few experimentations with my magic in the shelter hadn't proved fruitful—except for finding Willow.

Is this better? I said into her mind.

She jolted upright. "How did you—" Willow blinked. "Did you just say something?"

Yes. I kept my eyes focused on her, watching as her green eyes grew rounder.

"But… your lips didn't move." Her voice was a hushed whisper as she leaned down closer to my fuzzy body. "Can you hear what I'm thinking, too?"

I snorted. *No.*

She looked relieved that I couldn't hear into her thoughts, and I wondered what she was hiding underneath her warm smile. What thoughts were so private that she wanted to keep them only to herself?

Besides, the only demons that had that ability were ones who had found their mates. That mind-link between a bonded pair. I wasn't one of the lucky ones who had.

"The problem is," she declared, slamming her book shut, "that I don't know what curse was placed on you. And that's crucial to the undoing of it. Which means…"

Willow took a deep breath. Stood up and paced around the table, deep in thought. The muttering under her breath only intensified as she seemed to work through whatever problem she was having.

"Unless I… No." She pinched in between her brows. "I'm going to have to brute force it. If I untangle the threads…"

You… What? How?

"You really don't know a lot about witches, do you?"

Probably as much as you know about demons, I thought sarcastically.

"Fair point." She sighed. "A lot of these books say the same things. There are a few different methods we could try. But I don't think you're going to like them."

Try me. I'd do just about anything to get out of this form. To stretch my actual legs again.

She flipped back open a book, pointing at the passage on the page. "*Simple Curse Breaking Spells*," Willow read off. "One. Let a source of living water carry it away." She raised an eyebrow, and I shook my head.

"I'd rather not."

"Two. Take a purifying bath with a blend of salt and—"

"I think it's safe to say anything involving water will also involve my claws." I hissed out, retracting them as if in demonstration. "The longer I stay in this form, the more catlike my reflexes become. It's… involuntary."

Willow nodded. "I can try this spell, but for best success, I would need to know who cursed you. Then I could bind them and stop the curse at its source."

"Is it dangerous?"

"What?"

"Going after the witch who cursed me."

What if you get hurt? I didn't like the idea of her risking herself for me.

"I—" Willow's cheeks pinked. "Well, I'd be okay. I can handle myself."

Oh. I hadn't realized I'd projected that last thought into her mind.

She cleared her throat. "Besides, I don't have to find her necessarily, just… know her presence? Even if you just show me your memory, I think that would help."

I hesitated. If she saw the memory, she'd know too much.

The witch who'd cursed me… Fuck. She'd been a seer. I was looking for a powerful one, and yet… I'd almost fucked everything up.

I was just lucky the curse she'd cast on me hadn't *fully* worked. If I'd fully become a cat, losing all access to myself and my powers, I would have lost my mind. I would have been stuck in this form for all of eternity.

"So let's try the spell. What do we need?" I'd do anything to keep her away from that memory.

She scanned the list. "I think I have almost everything—except a belonging of yours. And some black salt. But we need to do it on the full moon, too."

"When's the full moon?"

Willow gulped. "Tomorrow."

Which meant if it failed—I could be stuck as a cat for a whole extra month. Still, it was worth it.

"Let's do it."

My little witch nodded, scooping up the few books she'd selected into her arms. "Let me just check these out with Simon, and then we'll run into town to get the other things for the spell. Do you think you could get something of yours?"

I paused. Something of mine? I barely had anything to my name. Was anything truly *mine?* Not my title, nor my position. Even the clothes on my back weren't my own.

But there was something. I just had to go get it. "Leave it to me, little witch."

She gave me a sad smile, and I instantly wanted to make it better. To soothe her fears.

I couldn't do that as a cat. Couldn't take her beautiful face into my hands and promise her everything would be okay, not yet.

But after she fixed me, I could.

And that was the thought that sent me scurrying in search of the only thing that belonged to me. Something no one else had a claim on.

Something I'd hoped to one day need, but not for this.

FIVE
WILLOW

He'd spent the night sleeping at my feet again, and even though I knew now that he wasn't really a cat, the action still comforted me. It was a small thing, really, to know I wasn't alone, but it made me feel better.

Damien had disappeared during the afternoon, leaving me to work in the study, making sure I had just the right balance of herbs and ingredients for the spell. It was a relatively simple task, but it still required my undivided attention.

He returned, holding something in between his teeth. After hopping up on the table, he unceremoniously dropped it onto the workstation in front of me.

"This is it?" I asked, holding up a small silver ring, the purple amethyst sparkling in the light. The setting was gorgeous—the entire piece was, really.

He cleared his throat. "It was my mother's. It's the only thing I could think of. She gave it to me before she passed away."

So he'd lost a parent, too. I knew firsthand how heartbreaking that was, and I wondered who had been by his side. Who'd helped him through the grief? How long had it been?

"I'm sorry," I whispered, brushing my finger over the stone.

Damien's big yellow cat eyes connected with mine, and I wondered what he would look like if we were successful. What color his eyes would be. If his hair was as dark as his fur. Would he have a strong jaw? His voice was deep, and I imagined—

"Little witch," he murmured, breaking me from my trance. "Shall we prepare?"

"Right." I nodded, setting the ring back down. "We still have a few hours till the sun goes down. I want to have everything ready so I can perform the spell when the moon is at its highest. That way, it's the most powerful moon magic possible. And hopefully…" I snapped my fingers.

"What are these?" Damien said, nudging a bundle of herbs with his nose.

I looked at my chosen selection. We'd talked about doing the spell, but in reality, I was trying *everything*.

"I'm going to burn it," I explained. I'd burn incense—a blend of rue, hyssop, salt, sage, and frankincense. "The smoke should hopefully help to cleanse away the curse from your body."

If it worked. Some of the herbs served specific purposes: hyssop was good for magical self-defense, while frankincense was used to cleanse and purify. Both of them would take part in my spell.

I explained all of that as I worked. Whenever he had a question, that little cat nose of his sniffing at my workstation, I did my best to answer it.

It was weird, because I always worked alone, except for my coven and Luna. But I didn't mind him being there. His presence, while also the cause of my current distress, seemed to soothe some of the jittery feelings running through me.

I couldn't decide if that was a good thing or a bad thing.

"And what about the object you asked me to bring?" He asked, peering at me curiously.

The ring was sitting in the middle of the desk, untouched.

"I'm going to use it as a talisman. Hopefully, it will protect you and keep this from happening again." I swallowed roughly. If it worked. "You can wear it around your neck, I suppose."

I eyed his cat collar, the one with the bell. "How'd they get that on you, anyway?" Reaching over, I took it off of him, setting it on the table next to me. I should have taken it off sooner. The thought hadn't even occurred to me.

"Around the twelfth time of me chewing it off, I realized it was useless. They just kept putting a new one on me. So I just gave up." He peered down at the orange thing. "Strange, to think I might go back to normal soon." He licked a paw.

"Hopefully," I said, giving what I hoped was an optimistic smile. Even though I had no idea if it would work. If any of it would.

Was I strong enough? Powerful enough?

Maybe I was going overboard, but this was all to get the demon out of my house—out of my life. Wasn't it?

"It will," he said, his voice strong with conviction. "I believe in you."

I turned away, not wanting him to see the warmth on my face.

* * *

"What are you doing?"

"Goddess!" I jumped, practically smudging the chalk lines I was drawing on the ground. "Luna! What are you doing here?"

"You didn't respond to my text. It's the full moon—we always spend it together." She pouted.

We did—usually with the coven—but I needed this to work. For Damien's sake. And I couldn't risk them all finding out.

"And also… I brought cupcakes." Luna heaved up the box. My mouth watered at the sight.

"I'm sorry. I just…" I looked down at my partially drawn circle and winced. "Had something I needed to do."

She didn't look surprised. "It's okay, Wil. As long as you're being safe?"

Was I? I was living with a demon in my house, for goodness' sake. Even though he'd been so cute when he'd curled up at my feet last night. When I'd caught him resting his head on my ankle, I'd almost sobbed from how adorable it was.

Sometimes it was hard to remind myself that he wasn't a cat when he snuggled up with me. I'd miss those moments the most.

But maybe he needed it too, that connection—however temporary it was.

As soon as I broke the curse, fixed him, he'd be gone.

"Yeah," I finally said, feeling sadder than I thought I'd feel about that very prospect.

Luna brushed my shoulder. "Do you need anything?"

"I think this is something I have to do alone," I said, straightening my spine. The moment I said the words, the rightness spread through my body.

And I knew I'd spoken the truth. I had to do this alone—for Damien. I couldn't explain why, but it was an undeniable fact.

My sister nodded. "Okay." She looked around the room. "Where's the new cat, anyway? I want to meet him."

I blinked. "He's…" Where was Damien, anyway?

He'd been laying in the patch of sun that came through the library windows earlier. It made me snort, because only this demon could sunbathe, still claim he *wasn't a cat*, and make it endearing.

The worst part of all of this was I was losing another cat.

Meow. He didn't jingle anymore, since I'd taken that damn collar off.

"Oh! Hello there." Luna bent down, extending her hand out to Damien, who tilted his head as he sniffed her unconvincingly.

"This is my sister," I said to my cat, aware that this was only awkward for me. Because my sister had no idea that the cat who was currently rubbing against her was practically royalty in *Hell*.

"He's friendly."

Damien chirped in response, rubbing against Luna's ankles happily.

Except for when a man *is around,* I thought with a snort, and Damien's head whipped around to look at me.

"Oh, yeah," I finally agreed. "Definitely friendly."

You know, I could still bite you, Damien thought into my mind. *I do have teeth.*

I narrowed my eyes at him, unable to say anything back.

"I'll have to bring Selene over for a playdate," Luna gushed, oblivious to the conversation going on in my mind. Selene was her white, fluffy cat she'd gotten at seven years old.

What seven-year-old was *good* at naming their familiar? I'd named mine *Binx*, after all. And Luna—named after the *moon*, well… she'd named her cat after the Goddess of the moon.

That was my sister for you.

I wondered how my sister's familiar would react to my demon cat. Would she feel that something was wrong with him?

How did cats act around demons, anyway?

Especially ones that could turn into cats?

Still not a cat, Damien interjected.

They well warded Pleasant Grove against evil beings and regular humans, so I'd never met a demon before this. Probably why I was so hesitant to accept Damien's status as one. How did he even get through the barrier?

"Well? What do you think?" Luna asked, drawing me back into the conversation, prying my eyes away from Damien's black form.

I resisted rolling my eyes. If I had any luck, well… he wouldn't *be* a cat after tonight. And definitely not my cat. "Maybe." I agreed, not wanting to commit to anything. Especially if I couldn't figure this out by the next coven meeting, I'd probably have to recruit their help.

We're definitely not doing that.

I leveled a look at him. *Get out of my head*, I wanted to say. But it wasn't like he could read my thoughts.

Sighing, I turned back to my chalk. I'd have to redraw the five-pointed star again later, since Luna's arrival had messed up my focus.

Placing the chalk on the big table in the center of the room, I propped my hip against it, leaning back to watch my sister.

It was crazy how fast she'd become her own person. There was only three years between us, but she'd been my little shadow when we were younger—always wanting to help her big sister, to do whatever I was doing.

But before my eyes, she'd transformed, blossoming into herself. The witch who loved pastels and baking and preferred to surround herself with happy, bright things, instead of our sad, old house.

I knew why she moved out, wanting to live closer to the bakery, but still… I missed her. Though—maybe I was glad she wasn't around right now. Not with what was living under my roof. Or who.

"Are you still lonely all alone in this big house without me?" Luna's mind seemed to track the same way mine did, neither one of us having to say anything.

"It's not so bad now." I could feel my cheeks pink, and I knew Damien's stare was on me without even having to look.

How can she be lonely, Damien thought to me, puffing up his fuzzy chest, *when she has me?*

Four days. It had been four days, and already, I felt like I was used to his presence. I'd known he could talk for half of it, and yet, it already felt weird not being able to respond to him.

"It's not like your bedroom isn't still here. You could always move back." I pinned her with a stare. Her old furniture still sat in the room, extra dresses left in the closet. It still smelled like her, too, somehow, like freshly made pastries and icing.

The same scent that greeted me every morning at the bakery. If I was being honest with myself, it was the reason I was still there. Sure, I owned half—we'd started it with what our parents had left us—but I stayed because it was my connection to my sister.

She tugged at her overall dress as she stood up. "I'm twenty-five, Willow. You don't have to keep taking care of me, I promise. I can take care of myself."

"I just…"

"I know." She sighed. "I know what losing our parents did to you. But I'm okay, really." Luna squeezed my shoulder. "Now, I'll let you carry on with your secret spell." She winked at me. "Don't go chasing after your soulmate without me, Wil."

Barking out a laugh, I shook my head. "That's *not* what I'm doing."

"Sure." She shrugged, giving Damien one last pat on the head before turning to head out the door. "Whatever you say, sis."

"That's not what I'm doing," I repeated to Damien after she'd left, who'd curled up on the old wooden rocking chair that sat in the room's corner.

He blinked, his cat-like eyes flashing red for only a moment. "I know that." His voice was smooth, deep, and sent a sudden shudder through my spine.

I nodded, saying nothing else.

Maybe I *was* losing my mind.

* * *

Damien sat in the middle of the magic circle I'd drawn, each tip of the five-pointed star marked with a white candle. The entire thing was ringed in a thick line of black salt, and the bundles of herbs were burning, wafting over the area.

His little cat nose twitched. "Ready?"

Everything was set. The moon was high in the sky.

All that was left was, well… me.

I nodded, stepping up to the circle. I'd donned a more *traditional* outfit for this, complete with my mother's favorite hat and the black cloak that covered the billowing layers of fabric of my dress.

The words ran through my mind, and I visualized what I was attempting to do before I started. Find the curse, break the chains, set the magic free. Nothing like performing a ceremony on the full moon to add pressure to you.

This had to work.

Why was it so important to me? I didn't know the reason, but I could feel it in my soul, the same way I recognized Luna as my twin flame.

Maybe Damien was an evil being, a demon who didn't belong here in our world, but there was an underlying sadness there that I wanted to understand. That I resonated with myself.

Beginning to chant the spell, I closed my eyes as I visualized my magic pouring out of me. It wasn't often that I used it like this, *undoing* what had been done. Hexes and simple spells wore off. But this curse was different.

It was strong.

I squeezed my palm tight around his mother's ring, grounding me to him, to our connection. I'd already blessed it, placing a protection spell on it and adding a chain so he could wear it around his neck, but it wouldn't be enough. That was obvious now.

In my mind's eye, I could see his spirit, trapped inside the form of the cat, staring up at me. Begging to be freed. The curse was complex. Ropes of magic spun around him, keeping him contained, and I slowly worked to untangle them. To free him from the *thing* that plagued him.

This witch had been powerful, that much I knew.

But, I thought with a smirk, I was more powerful. I could outsmart her.

"*Reverse the curse. Break the ties. Let what has come unbidden, be unbound.*" I said in a voice that wasn't quite my own, and when I opened my eyes, I could *see* the magic flowing freely from my hands, wrapping around Damien's body.

And when the magic ran out, when I finally put my hands down, everything faded into black.

I closed my eyes.

Just a minute, I thought to myself.

Before I passed out.

* * *

I was floating on clouds, nestled into a soft, fluffy bed. Warm, comfortable. The feeling of contentment rolled over me. Like everything was peaceful. Happy.

"Willow?" The voice speaking to me sounded so concerned, so… *rough*. At odds with my current senses.

Whimpering, I shook my head. I wanted to stay in this beautiful place. But the voice pulled me in. I peeled my eyes open, blinking back at the dark head of hair looking down at me.

"Damien?" I squeaked out, looking up into a pair of blood-red eyes. "It… worked?"

"Thank fuck."

Of course, he's relieved that it worked.

I sat up, glancing at the bed. Someone had expertly tucked me into the sheets, my favorite fuzzy blanket from the couch wrapped all around me. Oh. I'd—"What happened?" I asked, rubbing my forehead.

The last thing I remembered was unweaving the other witches' curse.

Darkness still flooded in through the window, giving me no indication how long I'd been asleep.

He frowned. "You passed out, Willow. I…" A hand rubbed over his face. "You scared me half to death."

I looked at my hands. "I… did?" Maybe I'd channeled more power than I realized last night, because I'd never passed out from using my magic before. It had always come to me with ease. "I didn't know…" I turned my head to the curtains, using a flick of my hand to close them.

Even that movement was straining. My innate magic was clearly temporarily exhausted. I'd never run so ragged before. Never had a reason to.

Damien made an indistinct sound in his throat, guiding my attention back to him.

"Little witch," he murmured, cupping my jaw with his hand. His voice was rough, like with disuse.

Goddess, help me. I couldn't stop staring at his face. At that jawline, practically sculpted from granite. I'd never imagined my demon cat would look like this. But holy hell, anything I could have imagined paled compared to the actual man sitting in front of me.

My lips tilted up in a small smile.

"I've got you," he promised. "Nothing will happen to you as long as I'm here, Willow. I vow it."

His words sank into my skin.

As long as he was here. But how long would that be?

And why did I not want to see him go?

SIX

DAMIEN

Fuck. That was the first thought that had sprung to mind as Willow released me from the cursed prison I'd been in.

I'd barely been able to make it to her as her body fell to the ground, practically lifeless. If it hadn't been for my demon abilities—that superhuman speed—I would have lost my shit. Maybe I still was.

Because my heart was racing, even as she gave me a small smile from her bed. I couldn't help myself. That was the only explanation for what slipped out of my mouth.

I've got you. Nothing will happen to you as long as I'm here, Willow. I vow it.

Why had I said those words? Maybe I'd been thinking them, but they slipped out before I could stop myself.

The second I'd gotten my form back, when all of my powers had drawn back into my body, the truth had clicked in place.

Her scent hit me like a lightning bolt to my system. *Mine.*

She was—mine.

How did I not see it sooner? How had that curse clouded my thoughts so fully?

Especially when I *knew* what it was like to find your—

"You're really fine?" Willow's question interrupted my thoughts. Her eyes were wide, the green hue so bright.

"For fuck's sake," I muttered, thrusting my head into my hands. Willow was concerned about *me?* Even though I'd been the one to carry her weak body to this room? "You're the one that was hurt, and you're asking me?"

A small smile curled upon her lips. "You're not a cat."

"I told you I wasn't." My lip twitched. It was hard not to give her the same expression back.

"Still, I couldn't be sure. Who *would* believe a talking cat?"

I chuckled. "Nothing gets past you, little witch, hm?"

Willow yawned, stretching her arms out. "What time is it?"

I glanced at the clock that sat on her bedside table. "Three AM."

"I was out for that long? Gods."

"Yes." My head tipped down in a brief nod.

I'd sat by her bedside for hours, terrified that her breaking my curse had caused some irreparable damage to my witch. What I would do if it had, I didn't know, but… I didn't leave. Even though her scent was intoxicating to my system. I wondered if I was already addicted to it. If the way I craved her, down to my being, was normal.

I needed to keep my distance. To stay away. To not let my primal instincts take over.

I cleared my throat. "Now that I know you're awake, I should let you sleep. We can talk more in the morning."

"Mmm." Willow's eyes drifted closed once more, the ghost of a smile still carved onto her lips.

Stay. The voice crept into my mind, soft and sweet. *Hers.*

Rolling my head back, I let out a sigh of relief. Willow was okay. It would be fine.

And… it was good to be back in my proper form. I flexed my hands, staring at my fingers.

Touching her was bad. I knew it as soon as I had picked her up into my arms, carrying her limp body back to her bedroom, laying her under her comforter and making sure she was comfortable.

Because touching her… was going to make me want more.

And I couldn't give her that. I wasn't worthy of it.

What business did I have coming in here, messing up her life, anyway? She'd adopted a cat, expecting a lifelong feline friend.

Instead, she'd gotten *me.*

A tricky, conniving asshole who wasn't even honest with his purpose here. And yet—I couldn't look away. Couldn't force myself to part from her. Fuck, but I didn't want to.

Maybe I didn't need to come to terms with the truths I'd realized today, but I'd think about those later. About what they meant.

Instead, I'd stay here, just like this—watching her sleep.

* * *

"Good morning," Willow said with a yawn, tightening the robe around her waist.

When she saw me standing at her fridge, looking at its contents, she raised an eyebrow. "What are you doing?"

"Making breakfast?" I answered. "What does it look like I'm doing?"

"You… you can cook?"

"Of course I can cook. There's a lot you don't know about me, after all." I smirked.

"Huh." She blinked, as if taking in my form for the first time. Taking in *me*.

I'd never been insecure about my appearance. From a young age, even in the demon realm, they had praised me for my looks. My dark hair and pale skin. But to have Willow's eyes on me, tracing over every inch of my six-foot-six frame, was something completely different.

When I'd shifted back into my form, I'd had half a thought to conjure clothes before scooping her up. I was still wearing that same tight black t-shirt and pants. In all the heyday with making sure she was okay, I hadn't changed this morning. But watching the way her eyes trailed appreciatively down my body, I was almost glad I didn't.

No one had ever looked at me like *that* before. It was a curious stare, like she couldn't believe who stood in her kitchen.

Closing the refrigerator doors so the food wouldn't spoil, I moved to stand in front of her.

"You did it," I confirmed, willing myself not to touch her. To take a step back. I couldn't think straight with her this close to me. Not with her scent invading all of my senses.

How had I not noticed before just how lovely she was? Even with her hair tousled from sleep and in hardly more than pajamas, she was beautiful. I towered over her, and it struck me how much smaller she was than me when I was in this form. *Little* was fitting. In every sense of the word. I had to be at least a foot taller than her.

Maybe it was because it had been so long, but for the first time in my life, I felt like having access to my full powers had completely overwhelmed my senses. Or maybe they were just flooded with *her*. Especially when she was so close to me and looking at me like *that*.

She hummed in response. "I guess I did." Her eyes focused on my face. "How do you feel?"

Even now, Willow was more concerned about me than herself. I didn't know how to feel about that.

"Normal." My powers thrummed through my body again, my access no longer limited. I let a sliver of darkness weave through my fingers before turning my attention back to her. "What about you?"

Her cheeks turned an adorable shade of pink. "I'm okay. Really. I didn't know using that much magic would overwhelm me. But I feel fine this morning. Thank you." She bobbed her head. Shook it. "You didn't have to stay, you know?"

"What do you mean?" I murmured, my hand moving to cup her jaw. *How could I not?*

"Damien…" Her voice was quiet, but—*sweet*.

I removed my hand from her face. Fuck. I couldn't keep touching her like this.

Distance. I needed distance from her. Clearing my throat, I changed the subject. "What do you want to do today, little witch?"

She looked surprised. "Today…?"

I quirked an eyebrow. "Well, after feeding you, I was thinking maybe you could show me around town."

"But… I thought… Don't you have to leave?" She trailed off. There was a hint of sadness in her eyes that I didn't think that I'd imagined. Like maybe she didn't want me to leave, either.

So I'd stay. Of course I'd stay. How could I leave her?

"Not right away."

My body thrummed with the decision. With the *rightness*.

Maybe I was supposed to be here. There was obviously a reason I'd ended up here, in this town. I'd been tracking signatures of magic, looking for *her*. So maybe it was okay that I stayed.

She perked up. "Really?"

"I was thinking about staying for a month or so." Clearing my throat, I finally moved away from her. "There's still some… unfinished business I have here, actually."

Something that started with a *W*.

Now that I was back in my form, I needed to focus on my mission. Not on the witch in front of me. But fuck if she wasn't alluring. I didn't want to part from her.

Willow raised an eyebrow. "Really? Here in Pleasant Grove?"

I nodded. "Yes. So, I'll just stay with you. Lay low while I fi—."

"What? No." Willow interrupted, suddenly flabbergasted. "You can't stay *here*."

But she hadn't wanted me to go before, had she? Yet, she looked flustered; her face an even brighter shade of pink than before.

"It was fine before."

"Yeah, well, before, you were a *cat*."

Smirking, I leaned in closer towards her. "I can go back to being a cat if you want." I didn't want that, but I knew there wasn't a chance I was leaving her. Not like this. Not after last night. "And I still owe you a favor." For helping me. Freeing me from being stuck in that form.

"That's not how this works. We didn't make a deal. You don't owe me anything."

"Willow." I sighed. She was so stubborn, and damn it, I *liked* that. It was joining my ever-growing list of things I liked about my little witch. "I just…" I looked around her house. What was it about this place that made me feel so at *home?* "Just for a few weeks, and then I'll be out of your hair. We can be… roommates."

"Roommates?" She raised an eyebrow. "What's the magic word?"

I grit my teeth. *You've got to be kidding me.* What was I, a five-year-old? "*Please.*"

Her light brown locks framed her face, somehow making that little scowl she was wearing look endearing. I liked it. More than I wanted to admit.

"Okay. You can sleep on the couch," she finally agreed, crossing her arms over her chest, doing her best to look menacing. It failed, because no matter what she did, the little witch managed to look adorable.

The couch. I snorted. "Fine."

Willow's lips widened, her teeth peeking out as she gave me a dazzling grin. "That was easier than I thought."

"What?"

"To have you begging me."

You'd like that, would you? Me on my knees for you.

"All you have to do is ask, witch."

"Mm. You'd like that, would you, demon?"

My hand curled around her bicep. "Be careful what you ask for."

Something passed between us. Her eyes flickered from my hand on her arm, up to my face, and down to my lips. I didn't think I missed the heat there, but as much as I wanted to… *No.*

It was too soon for that.

Prying my fingers from her skin, I turned back to her kitchen. "So… What do you want for breakfast? I've fried up a mean egg or two. As long as it's not seafood. I don't have much of a stomach for that. Not after so long as a cat."

When I looked at her again, she was still standing frozen in the same place, her eyes wide. "You're really staying?" Her words were quiet, barely more than a whisper.

"Do you want me to?"

Maybe that was the more important question.

Her eyes met mine, and she gave me a small, single nod. The movement was almost too slight to catch, but I couldn't miss it. Not when I was so focused on her.

"Okay. It's settled then." I crossed my arms over her shoulders. "I'm staying in Pleasant Grove." *With you,* I didn't say.

Clearly unfazed by my statement, Willow just gave me another dip of her head to acknowledge my response before turning around. "I'm going to shower."

"What about breakfast?" I shouted after her, willing my feet to stay put. Not to follow her into her bathroom. Not to think about Willow in the shower. *Fuck me.*

"We'll eat in town!" She hollered back. "I have to go to the bakery, anyway!"

A moment later, I heard the shower water turn on, and I sank into the chair.

What the hell was I doing?

I had a mission to think about. Except any time I was near her, every thought of that slipped my mind, and it was just *her*.

Long, brown hair tumbling down her back. Bright green eyes staring into mine. There was a lightness in them I'd never felt before. I wanted to experience it, too.

Groaning, I looked down at my rumpled clothes. If we were going into town, I'd probably need more than this. Human temperatures didn't affect me much, but people often looked at you strangely if you didn't match the locals. Although in a town of witches, I wondered if anything would be odd to wear around them.

Was I really doing this? Sauntering into town on the arm of a witch, knowing I absolutely shouldn't? Her kind hated me. And yet… I couldn't imagine letting her out of my sight.

So if she was going to work, I'd follow her. Make sure she was safe. Protect her from anyone who looked her way.

It wasn't the first time she was taking me into town, and yet this time, it was different.

Maybe because I wasn't a cat—I was back on my own two legs, with my wits about me. Or maybe it was the way something had happened, changed between us.

Did she feel it too?

I exited that line of thought as quickly as I'd entered it. I couldn't afford to be distracted from my mission. Not when so much was at stake.

Leave no rock unturned, brother, he'd instructed me.

I'd trekked through dozens of witch towns, but the identity of *her* remained elusive to me.

I snorted with the thought of how mad he'd be when he found out I'd wasted a month stuck in feline form. My brother didn't share the trait, though he had other powers. His mother wasn't a shifter like mine had been.

So deep in thought, it was her scent that startled me out of my stupor instead of the sight of her, her long brown hair down in a loose braid.

"You ready? I'm starving." She asked, still tugging on the bottom of her boot. When her eyes landed on me, she froze. "You changed."

I cleared my throat. "Yes."

"Huh." She peered up at me, a curious expression having settled over her face.

"What, Willow?"

"Do you… know how to glamor yourself?"

SEVEN

WILLOW

There was something about Damien like this that I had a hard time keeping my eyes off of. Where he'd gotten his clothes from, I had no idea. Somehow he looked perfectly natural here in his pair of denim jeans, tight black shirt, and black leather jacket. It was effortlessly *hot*.

When was the last time I'd been this attracted to another person? Years.

Tugging on the bottom of my forest-green sweater dress—one of my favorites, because it made my eyes pop—I attempted to pull it further down my thighs. I'd pulled on a pair of fleece-lined tights with it and my favorite heeled booties, but suddenly I felt completely out of sorts.

Maybe it was his demon magic. There had to be a reason they warned witches to stay away from them, right? That was what was making me feel like this.

Like I was seconds from coming out of my skin.

"What's on your mind, little witch?" Damien asked, catching me staring.

"Oh." My cheeks practically flushed pink. "Nothing."

Except I could smell his cologne from where I stood by his side, wafting into my nostrils like the most intoxicating smell on the planet. I couldn't even pin down the scent: some mixture of pine, musk, and smoke, but it seemed to envelop my entire being.

There was a part of me that wanted to pretend that everything was as usual—I came this way every day to go to the bakery, after all.

Except today was anything but ordinary. And Damien was a constant reminder of that.

His soothing voice shook me from my inane thoughts. "So, you normally walk into town?"

"Huh?" I wasn't expecting the question. Or, rather, I wasn't expecting small talk at all. Once I'd processed his question, I nodded. "When the weather's nice. It's not very far, and I always love walking this path."

It was one perk of living in such a small community—being able to walk almost everywhere. I *had* a car, but I didn't use it unless I had to drive all the way to the other end of town. Mainly, I drove when I needed to go into the closest human city for something, like getting our coffee machines repaired.

Today, the air was crisp and clear, just a hint of rain that clung around, and it relaxed me. That and the crunch of the leaves littered on the ground made for the perfect fall day.

"I see." Damien shoved his hands in his pockets, and I turned away, not wanting to look like I was still staring at his face. Even if I was obsessed with it.

I hummed in response, thinking about what I was going to say to Luna when I stopped at the bakery. *'I'm sorry'* didn't quite cut it, but I owed my sister an apology after I'd ditched her so much these past few days.

Besides, I still owed her that trip to the bar.

"So you like it here, living in this town?" He looked around, surveying the houses that sat right at the edge of downtown. Main Street, full of small businesses and cornerstone witchy establishments, was only a block away.

Nodding, I tried to look at the town through the eyes of a stranger. Wondering what this place might look like to someone new. "I've lived here all my life. My coven and I grew up together. Most of us only left for college, and even then, we moved back. It's hard being a witch and not living in the community."

There was too much at stake. And no one would understand—except I thought Damien might. Not being able to practice magic, for fear of someone seeing you—that was the true curse of the outside world. Maybe a higher education wasn't *necessary*—several of the witches I'd grown up with had simply learned their family's trade and never left town.

But I'd appreciated the world-view I'd gained by going into the human world for those years. It was before my parents had died, so I hadn't felt as bad about leaving Luna. But now… I couldn't imagine not being by her side.

"All my best friends are in the coven," I continued. "There's thirteen of us, and they're practically family."

It was a perfect number: thirteen. My mom and her friends had all belonged to a smaller coven, and all ended up having kids during the same few years. There had never been another idea when it came time to form ours.

The humans had Girl Scout Troops, and we had our coven. We learned magic together, practiced together, discovered what our innate gifts were together. I'd never once taken them for granted. And I'd always had my sister—even with the three years between us, she was still my best friend—by my side.

"What about your parents? Where are they at?"

I cast my gaze to my feet, my voice growing smaller. "They're gone." Sometimes, I wished I could imagine that they were just off on vacation. Seeing the world. Enjoying themselves. That was easier than the reality.

"Oh. I'm sorry to hear that."

Shaking my head, I willed myself not to look at him. If I did, I'd probably cry. And I didn't want to mourn my parents. Not today. I just wanted to enjoy myself for once.

Pasting a somber smile on my face, I watched as my town came into full view. And I let the jack-o'-lanterns, paper ghosts, and string lights distract me from the rest of the thoughts rattling around in my mind.

Like the subject of my once-cat-turned-demon, followed by the man himself. The stranger, I tried to remind myself—who was currently walking beside me.

I kept my eyes pinned to the ground, trying to force myself not to keep from staring at his face. At the eyes I knew he'd changed to a deep-chocolate brown, which somehow seemed endless. Like if I stared into them long enough, I could find answers to questions I hadn't even thought to ask yet.

At least he didn't look like a demon, even if he still stood taller than any human man I'd ever seen, and the physique his body sported was *unreal.* He was a foot taller than me, and even with my heeled boots, I still felt impossibly short.

Something I was trying very hard not to focus on. There was no reason for me to think about it—how good he looked, simply strolling down the street beside me.

But even as I crunched over leaves in my heeled booties—I knew there was no way to ignore the way I could *feel* him next to me.

How was it possible that I could find his very nearness so comforting after only a few days? He was a stranger to me, in every way, and yet it felt like there was nowhere else I would rather be.

I cleared my throat. "After I help out at the bakery for a bit, I was thinking I could show you around town. And then tonight, if you wanted to go… there's the Pumpkin Festival." I looked up at him under my lashes.

"The Pumpkin Festival?" Damien raised an eyebrow, shaking his head in amusement.

"Mhm. We normally have a booth, serving pumpkin hot chocolate, pumpkin coffee, and Luna's famous cookies."

"Let me guess, they're pumpkin too?"

I couldn't help the giggle that slipped out. "Yes. But also, she makes regular sugar cookies too—those are just pumpkin shaped." I was almost drooling, just thinking about her cookies. Not a single person in town could bake like my sister. "There's also a pumpkin patch, hayrides, a pie-eating contest, and at the end of the night there's a…"

Looking over, I expected to find Damien watching our surroundings, but I found him hanging on my every word. "There's a what?"

He brushed a piece of hair back behind my ear, and I suddenly wished I'd worn my hat, if only so I could hide my face behind the brim. I wasn't used to this much scrutiny or attention from... anyone. Let alone from a handsome man.

"A dance. Old Mrs. Whittle lets the town use her barn, and The Enchanted Cauldron sets up a bar, and... What?"

Damien's lips curled up into a smile. "Has anyone ever told you how your face lights up when you're excited about something?"

"Oh." Was my whole face on fire? It had to be.

Oh my god. I felt like I had bats fluttering around in my stomach. When was the last time a gorgeous stranger flirted with me?

Never. The answer was never.

"Anyway, I, uh... Do you want to go?"

He frowned. "To the dance?"

"Mhm. And the festival."

"I don't really..." Was it me, or did he look almost... embarrassed? "Do stuff like that."

"Dance?" I asked.

Damien shook his head. "I, uh..." Oh, he was *definitely* embarrassed. It made me feel strangely at ease. Maybe because he felt as out of his element as I did with him. "I'm not very good at socializing. I've never been around that many humans before."

"I can teach you." I peeked over my shoulder at him, wanting to gauge his reaction. "If you want." It surprised me how easily the offer slipped out of my mouth, but even more so how easily he agreed.

"Okay. Show me around your town, and then to this pumpkin festival. You just have to promise me something."

"Anything." There was no part of me that didn't beam at his

agreement. About getting to show someone else this place that I loved so much.

He leaned in close, his mouth inches away from my ear. "Don't leave me alone."

"I won't." I gave him a shy nod as the bakery came into view.

It suddenly occurred to me that I still had no idea what to tell my sister. Or anyone else.

What would people think when they saw the two of us together? It was a small town, and people talked. Gossip would spread, especially when I hadn't been with anyone since college. And even then—I'd never brought a boyfriend home. Even when my parents were alive.

I cleared my throat. "So, what's the story here?"

"What story?" Damien raised an eyebrow at me as I gestured between us.

"How we met. Why I'm wandering around town with a handsome stranger that no one's ever seen before."

His voice popped into my mind. *You think I'm handsome?*

"Stop doing that."

Damien shrugged. "I wasn't aware we needed a cover story. We can't just be two people strolling down Main Street, looking at the decor?"

"My sister will ask questions." *Everyone* would ask questions. Questions I didn't have answers to yet.

"Mmm."

"Damien." I rubbed my temples. "This is serious."

"You worry too much, little witch."

Yeah, well, maybe you don't worry enough.

Nonsense. I just worry about the important things.

I stopped in the middle of the sidewalk, and Damien turned around to face me, raising an eyebrow. "What?"

I crossed my arms over my chest. "I… thought you said you couldn't read my mind."

"I can't." He looked confused for a moment. "What do you mean?"

"You're joking, right?" *I didn't say that out loud.* "And you answered me."

He searched my face, and I wondered if he found whatever answer he was looking for there.

How come we can communicate with our minds? Silence was my only answer.

"Why did I think you were actually going to answer me?" I grumbled to myself. There were some witches who had… abilities, but nothing like this. It certainly wasn't anything *I'd* experienced before. Even with Luna, sometimes it felt like I could anticipate what she was going to say before she said it. But she was my sister—my *Twin Flame.* Of course, I was in tune with her feelings.

None of that explained this.

I started moving again, my demon-cat-turned-human matching my pace, stride for stride.

"No one's ever come with me to the festival before," I admitted, my voice low. "I don't know what they'll think."

"Your friends?"

I nodded. "And my coven."

"Right." He winced, as if it was a sudden reminder of our standings in this town. That I was a witch, and he was a *demon.* "And why can't we tell them the truth?"

My jaw fell open in shock. "No one's going to believe that." Watching to make sure I didn't step on any cracks on the pavement—definitely not because I was avoiding watching his face—I continued on. "Besides. One witch already cursed you. My kind… they don't trust demons. I'm not sure I'll be able to fix it if it happens again. Do you really want to advertise who you are?"

"You're not going to tell your sister?"

"No."

"But aren't you… close? She even came over to check on you yesterday." He frowned.

She normally came over a few times throughout the week. It was her old house too, after all. And we worked together.

What would I say when she inevitably asked me why *Damien* the cat was gone and *Damien* the not-human was strolling around our town with me?

"We can be close and still keep secrets from each other. Important secrets. Don't you have them with your siblings?"

His voice was quiet, withdrawn. "I've never really had anything to hide. My brother…" Damien shook his head. "It's not like that. My life's never really been *my own*." When I looked over at him, he'd focused his eyes on a distant spot in the background.

"Oh." That sounded… sad. And lonely. Suddenly, a lot of things made sense to me about him. Why he didn't seem to want to leave my side, and why he was in no rush to go back to the demon realm. He said he had unfinished business here, didn't he? Was it presumptuous of me to hope that it was just *me?*

Was I the first friend he'd ever had? It seemed strange to call him that, since I'd known him less than a week, but it felt right. Better than strangers.

A thought occurred to me, and I let it slip out before thinking better of it. "How old are you?"

"Two hundred and eighty-seven."

"*What?*" I hadn't expected that.

"Aging works differently in the demon realm." He shrugged. "In human terms, I'm not even close to middle-aged yet."

"Wow. I can't even imagine living that long."

What kind of existence had he been living for the past almost three centuries? I hardly knew anything about him as a being, but I got the idea his years weren't full of happiness, love, laughter—*life*. And for whatever reason, I wanted to show him what that was like. What it was like to grow up here in Pleasant Grove.

I let the quiet blanket over us, save for the leaves crunching under our feet and the wind blowing through the trees. At least I could appreciate the decorations this way. It was the reason I still enjoyed walking into town, even when the air was nippy. Most of the residents had decorated their houses, lights and fake cobwebs and carved pumpkins that sat on their stoops. I still needed to get my own—Luna and I normally went to the pumpkin patch the first day it opened, but we hadn't yet this year.

Luna. I let loose a long sigh.

"Never mind," I mumbled. "How we met doesn't matter, anyway."

"Why not?"

"Because my sister… She's a seer. And is *incredibly* perceptive. I can't get anything past her."

There really was no point in trying to hide who he was to her. Maybe for the rest of the town's sake, I could pretend he was just a friend, but my sister wouldn't buy that. My coven would know that I hadn't met him at a bar—though I wasn't sure I wanted the implication of *that*, anyway.

Even if he was handsome. I peeked at him again, catching a wistful look on his face.

I was trying to imagine what my life would have looked like if he'd always been here. A part of this town. If we'd spent the last few Halloweens carving pumpkins together and sipping hot apple cider as we walked through the corn maze.

My heart ached, and that was what startled me out of those thoughts. I had no business thinking about Damien like that.

Like he was *mine*.

He wasn't even my cat anymore, after all.

That left a sour taste in my mouth. I ran my arms over my shoulders.

"Willow." His voice was low, soothing, as his hand wrapped around my wrist. "Where'd you go?"

"What?" I looked up into his eyes, full of concern. For me? Or for himself?

The warmth of his grip flowed through me, grounding me in the moment. I hated that I liked it so much. I wasn't supposed to like *him*. He was a demon, after all.

Every witch's mortal enemy. What did I think was going to happen, bringing him into town?

"This is a mistake." I pulled away, loosening his grip from my arm. "You should go. That way you don't put yourself in danger again just to…"

I froze, looking up at him. All six and a half feet of him. He was looking at me with an emotion I couldn't read in his eyes. And for the first time, I so badly wanted to hear his thoughts. To know what he was thinking.

Maybe it didn't work that way, but I couldn't help wanting more of him.

"No." He moved startlingly fast, and then his hands were on my face. Cupping my cheeks. Holding me, so reverently. I wasn't sure I'd ever been touched like that before. "I'm not leaving. Not yet."

"Okay." The breath I released was quiet, almost inconsequential. Except…

My lips parted as I stared up at Damien. There was no way I could stop my gaze from dropping to his lips. Full and *pouty* and begging for attention. They looked soft, and I wondered what they'd feel like on mine.

Why was I lusting after this man who was practically a stranger to me? I moved to step back, and his hands slipped from my face, severing whatever connection we'd shared.

"Come on. Luna's expecting me." I'd been a shitty co-owner this week. I needed to make it up to her somehow.

And I needed to distance myself from the demon at my side before I got attached. Or worse.

Because he'd be leaving eventually.

✷ ✷ ✷

The bell jingled as I pulled open the door to the shop, the scent of cookies baking instantly hitting my nose.

"Willow!" My little sister's face lit up in a bright smile when she saw me, making me feel even guiltier for the past few days.

"Hi, Luna."

She had a little dusting of flour on her cheek, and more covering the pink pastel apron she was wearing covered in little cartoon ghosts. Her honey blonde hair, a trait inherited from our mom, was pulled up into a messy bun with one of her signature printed bandanas, but her smile quickly faded when she noticed the dark shadow that was still glued to my side.

Damien was frozen, his face drained of all color as he stared at my sister.

I frowned. What was wrong with both of them? "Damien, this is my sister, Luna." I elbowed him in the stomach, hoping he would resemble more of a human, settling my face into a small smile as I turned back to Luna. "Luna, this is Damien. My… friend."

Stepping closer to us, she held out her hand over the counter, schooling her expression into a smile. "It's very nice to meet you, Damien."

He stiffened, only staring at her hand and making no move to offer his own. After a moment of silence, he looked away.

"I have to go," he muttered, turning around.

Walking out without another word to me. Luna's hand was still in the air.

"But…" I frowned, the bell chiming once more.

Leaving the two of us standing in silence.

"What was that about?" Luna asked, turning her head.

"I don't…" I shook my head. "I don't know. He's…"

We were supposed to spend the day together. And now he was just… gone?

Maybe *he* didn't want to be here with me, after all. Maybe I was just a means to an end, and whatever. All those questions earlier…

I shook my head, dislodging the thoughts. At least I had my sister by my side.

"Come on," Luna said, pulling me into the back. She filled a bowl with ingredients for frosting as I hopped up on a counter. I needed to start working, and I hadn't even eaten breakfast yet, but I was too confused to focus on any of that.

Instead, I watched her work.

"So, did it work?"

"Hm?"

"Your spell." She raised an eyebrow. "From last night?"

"Oh." I was glad I couldn't see out the window, because I knew I'd just be looking for him. "Yeah."

"Can't help but notice your new... *friend* has the same name as your new cat." She smirked, starting up the stand mixer to beat the bowl of frosting.

I busied myself by tying my apron and ignoring her question.

I didn't have an answer for her anyway.

Because how on earth was I going to explain to her that I was spending time with a *demon?*

EIGHT
DAMIEN

What the fuck.

I shut my eyes, trying to process everything. The woman I'd come here to find—it couldn't be Willow's *sister*. Not after everything we'd already gone through. And yet… I'd taken one look at her and felt the power radiating off of her, and I *knew*.

Dammit. I needed more time.

To get to know Willow, to get to experience all the things I'd never imagined I would ever get to do. It was so simple, and yet…

My hands raked through my hair as I paced in the back alley, trying to make sense of everything.

Why had I headed here in the first place? I'd felt like something had pulled me here, and once she'd found me, I thought maybe that something was Willow.

But… *Luna?* Her sister?

I hadn't been able to detect it in cat form—thanks to my senses being cloudy, but it was clear as day now.

Growing up in the demon realm, I'd always heard about what it was like when you found *the one*. But I'd never imagined I'd actually experience it for myself, to find my—

"Shit."

Pain tugged at the tether between me and Zain, and I knew I could only ignore his call for so long. But to go back to the demon realm, to reveal everything I knew to him… how could I ever do that?

Willow would never forgive me.

And any chance I had with her… It would be over before it started.

She needed some time with her sister. And I needed space to think.

And… A trip to the demon realm.

To see my brother.

I groaned. Today was not going at all like I'd wanted it to.

For starters, I hadn't even made sure Willow had gotten food. And then I'd ran out of there without even explaining to her *why*.

Brushing aside those strange instincts, I made my way down the alley, trying to ignore the tug in my blood as long as I could.

Gritting my teeth, I cursed out. "You just don't know when to stop, do you?"

Looking around to make sure no one was watching me, I stepped into the shadows—transporting myself back home for the first time in months.

"Brother. You've returned." Zain, the crown prince of the demon realm, was perched atop his throne. My brother. He looked so much like me—down to his dark hair and tall stature—but we couldn't have been more different. Especially in our temperaments.

We'd grown up as half-brothers, but sometimes I still felt like a stranger looking at him. He wore a coat of black, adorned with gold and all the finest trimmings befitting a prince, whereas I stood in my human clothes—a t-shirt, leather jacket, and jeans.

Standing in front of him, I crossed my arms over my chest. "You summoned me?"

Our blood tied us together in ways I couldn't even begin to explain.

"Where have you been? We were worried."

Sure, they were.

"You could say I've been a little… tied up." In a cage. By humans.

But I wouldn't expand on where I'd been, or how *exactly* I'd ended up stuck in my other form. If he wanted those memories, he could pry them from my head himself.

His eyes flashed with amusement. "Ah, yes. I trust you had an… enjoyable time?"

If only you knew the half of it. I raised an eyebrow. "Sure. You could say that."

"It's good to see you, you know," Zain said. "It's not the same here without you."

"You're the one who sent me out into the human world to do your bidding. If you wanted to see me, there were easier ways."

Chuckling, my brother settled back into his chair—three steps up on the dais, perched in front of me. Reminding me exactly where I factored in this equation of ours.

Below him.

Never mind how powerful I was, how much control I had over the darkness—power I'd inherited from my father. The shadows were like a second nature to me, the way I could manipulate and create from nothing.

I was the bastard child, and not the chosen one to rule.

Not that I wanted it, anyway. This place hadn't felt like home in a long time.

If I was being honest, I preferred the animal shelter I'd been living at for the past month to my brother's palace in the demon realm.

And I liked Willow's home a thousand times more than both of them.

"And? Was your mission successful? Or have you been *enjoying* yourself a little too much?"

"I need more time," I grit out, not answering him. I needed that time with Willow.

Zain's eyes narrowed. "Damien. Did you find her?"

I couldn't lie to him—but I didn't want this to be the end of my time in Pleasant Grove, either. Instead, I simply nodded.

The worst part was that I *had* found her. And he knew it.

Damn demon magic. I hated that I'd ever had to connect myself to him in that way.

"So, what's the problem?"

There was no easy way around it. "I can't do it." Deliver her to this place like some sort of prized trophy—it felt more like bringing a lamb to the slaughter. An innocent, adorable little lamb.

"It's your sworn duty." To him.

I scoffed. "I liked you better when you weren't an insufferable crown prince."

"Ah, brother. That's where you're wrong—because I've *always* been the insufferable crown prince.”

"Nice to see you, too." I rolled my eyes

He stood up, walking down the steps, and slapping a hand against my shoulder. All pretenses gone, *there* was the brother I had grown up with. When we were both still young, and things hadn't been so… tense.

But that was what a few hundred years did to you. You grew apart. Or you were forced to serve your younger brother for eternity.

You know—*semantics*.

"One month."

I blinked. "What?" It was eerie how that was the same time frame I'd given Willow this morning. Narrowing my eyes, I stared at my brother.

"Whatever you're doing that's distracting you… You can have one more month. And then I expect you to bring her here, to me, and return to my side."

"But—"

Zain tilted his head to the side. "Does some part of that not work for you, brother?"

I ground my teeth together in an effort to not speak back to him. "Fine."

His sharp canine teeth peeked out of his smile this time as he settled back into the chair.

"Don't get distracted this time, Damien. I'll be waiting." There was a strange look in his eye as I turned away, giving him only the wave of my hand as a goodbye, before I created another portal—back to the human world.

Back to my little witch.

* * *

I let the shadows cloak around me, hiding me from view as I watched her flit around the shop Willow and her sister owned. This time, I could fully

take in the front of their shop. The sign above the door read *The Witches'
Brew* and featured an intricately carved cauldron of bubbling coffee.

One of them had taped little bats to the inside of the windows, with
the entire storefront fully decked out in Halloween decor. Fake cobwebs,
little orange lights that lined the door frame, and even the sandwich
board out front read *'stop by for a brew!'*

It was clear they didn't need the advertising. Downtown Pleasant
Grove was small and bustling, and it felt like half of the town must have
popped inside since we'd first arrived this morning.

Letting my darkness dissipate, I opened the door, shoving my hands
in my pockets as I stood, watching them talk behind the counter.

"Olivia, I have your pumpkin scone and Witch's Cold Brew!"
Willow called out as she handed a small paper bag and a cup of coffee
to a customer at the counter with a smile. Tucking a brown lock of hair
behind her ear, she turned to the next person in line.

She hadn't noticed me yet, and I liked that I could study her like this.
Unabashedly, without worrying about what anyone else thought.

There was a pull to her I couldn't explain, a kind of magnetism that
drew me in.

I rubbed a hand over my face. This was crazy. There was no way.

Even from here, her sweet scent wafted into my nostrils, and it was
all I could do to resist burying my face in her hair and inhaling it.

I wanted her. With every fiber of my being.

But I didn't deserve her. How could I ever deserve someone as
perfect, as untouched by hatred and destruction?

She was *mine*, and I knew that down to the depths of my soul—
whatever part of it still existed—but she didn't need me.

Fuck.

Willow's gaze connected with mine, and I could feel my face softening as she walked over to me, the irritation clear on her face.

I had to fix this. I had to make her understand I hadn't *wanted* to go. Even if I couldn't tell her the truth yet. No matter how badly I wanted to.

"I'm sorry."

NINE

WILLOW

Throwing myself into the bakery was my best course of action after Damien's sudden disappearance. Once the morning rush was over, I took the time to sweep the entire storefront, leaving no corner untouched. Not only had I finished all the dishes, but I had also wiped down all the tables.

I'd given up on pretending that I wasn't staring out the window for him to come back.

The worst part was I felt like a lovesick fool, consumed by emotions I couldn't control. His vow to stay echoed in my mind, but a small voice inside me wondered if it was true.

Sighing, I turned back to the counter, brewing a fresh pot of coffee while I made an apple cider latte for one of our regulars.

"Is everything ready for tonight?" I asked Luna, who was sliding another tray of freshly baked cookies into the rack to cool. I checked the time. It was almost noon, which meant more than half of our day was already over.

She wiped her hands on her apron. "That's the last of the cookies I had to make. Everything else should be ready to go. You're still going to make the hot chocolate, right?"

The bell on the door chimed, as I called out another customer's order, handing them their drink and pastry.

I nodded. "Of course. And I'm sorry for bailing so much this last week." I'd already prepped everything I'd need for tonight, so when everything was set up, it would just need to be stirred and heated up.

Luna rested her head against my shoulder. "It's okay. I know you've had your hands full with that one."

That one? I looked over at her, and she raised her eyebrows, tilting her head towards the door.

Damien was standing there, looking sheepish and a little guilty.

Walking over to him, I crossed my arms over my chest, ready to tell him off for ditching me, but his expression was full of so much pain that it stopped me in my tracks.

"I'm sorry."

I blinked, not expecting that. "For what?"

"Disappearing." He shook his head. "I had to go… back."

Even though I'd told him so much about my life, and my love for this town, I didn't know the first thing about his home. The demon realm. If he'd had to go back, that must have meant something was seriously wrong.

"Is everything okay?"

Damien's eyes drifted over to Luna in the background, before he turned his attention back to me. "It will be. I'll explain everything later, I promise." He wove our fingers together. "But first, I owe you a date."

"A date?" My cheeks pinked. "I mean, breakfast, yes, but…"

He nodded, kissing my knuckles. "Yes. A date."

Oh. "Oh." I turned back to look at Luna, but she just shook her head with a smile, turning back to her tray of cookies. A silent permission. "Okay. Let me just…"

I looked down at my apron, thanking the Goddess that I hadn't covered it in coffee or flour. Quickly pulling it off over my head, I returned it to my hook, stopping to let Eryne know I'd be heading out before waving goodbye to Luna.

"Shall we?" Damien offered me his hand once again. I ignored the rush of warmth to my face at taking it.

"Where to?"

"How about we finally get to that tour now?"

I nodded, happily pulling him out of the store—our hands still intertwined.

And for whatever reason, even knowing it would probably lead to disappointment, I didn't want to let go.

We spent the rest of the afternoon wandering through all of downtown. I showed Damien some of my favorite shops, including my favorite bookshop—*Broomsticks and Books.* It had mostly stopped carrying the former, leaving the shop full of magical tombs and regular books alike. Luna loved the romance section, while I loved looking for new recipes tucked amongst the cookbooks here.

Hardly anyone needed broomsticks for transportation anymore. Most of us witches had one sitting in our house, regardless. You never knew when you might need a magical flying broom, after all.

Damien had given me a snort when I told him that.

Next was the ever-changing *Magical Curiosities:* a shop that sold just that, though I'd found quite my share of trinkets there over the years. It was like a thrift store for magical artifacts and witchy goods. My trusty hat had come from there, as well as my black boots with little buttons up the side.

As we walked down Main, we passed by a few more shops: *Dark Moon Fashions*, where I got all my favorite dresses; *Pleasant Grove Realty*, where any witch could find a perfect home; and *Hexed Home Renos*— newly opened and run by two twin witches, Tammy and Talley. They'd been toying with the idea for years, and finally opened it after the rest of our coven told them they'd stop speaking to them if they didn't.

Tough love worked.

My demon companion scratched his head, standing in front of the last one on the street. "What's with the name?"

It'd been Grey's Supermarket for as long as I'd been alive—run by the Grey's, now an older couple whose kids had grown and moved away.

"It's so… normal."

"What?" I laughed. "It's just a supermarket. Do you think we come up with puns for every business here?"

Sure—most of the businesses downtown had cute, kitschy names, but they also catered to the witches that came to visit. We were only an hour outside of Salem, after all. Even if horrible things had happened there, the legacy was strong. Still, there were plenty of normally named establishments in town.

Damien shrugged. "Witches are weird." And wasn't that the understatement of the century?

"This is my favorite spot down here," I murmured, staring at the town gazebo, complete with its own decorations.

His eyes swept across the view before settling back on me. "It's nice."

"When I was younger, I used to come out here and just people watch. It was nice, even when things got busy, to come here and just… slow down. Appreciate life."

Tilting my head, I watched him. I wondered what sort of life he'd led. If he'd ever experienced any moments like that. Blissful peace— quiet happiness. It was a strange thing to ponder, but the tortured look in his eye made me think maybe he hadn't.

Maybe that was one reason he talked little about himself or his life.

"Are you hungry?" I finally asked, breaking the silence.

* * *

That was how we ended up sitting at the bar of *The Enchanted Cauldron* for lunch. We'd both ordered burgers, and if I was being honest… it surprised me at how normal it felt with him by my side. Even in college, I'd never felt this comfortable with another person besides Luna or the other members of my coven.

Maybe it was because of the way he'd watched over me all night when I'd passed out. He could have just left. Instead, he didn't leave my side.

I happily chowed down on my burger, noting the look of satisfaction on Damien's face as I ate.

He finished his before mine, though that was partially due to how many people came over to say hi to me. I'd always been a chatty person, and knowing almost everyone in this town didn't help with that.

They were all curious about the man seated by my side, even if they hadn't said it straight out.

"Do you want me to scare them all away so you can eat?" He grunted, taking a sip of his drink.

"No, it's okay. They'll stop eventually. They're just curious about you."

My cheeks warmed at the thought that he cared enough to do that. That he seemed to want to take care of me.

I *was* starving, though, even though I'd definitely eaten a muffin and a few scones while I'd been at the bakery. Even I had to admit that Damien's glares at the other patrons helped to stave them off.

"Thanks," I finally said after I'd finished the last bite of my burger, sucking the extra ketchup that had spilled onto my fingers. "That hit the spot."

Damien looked at his empty tray. I still had a bunch of fries left, but he'd already eaten it all.

"That was… surprisingly good."

I scrunched up my nose. "Were you doubting it would be?"

He chuckled. "No. It's just… the other communities I've been in weren't like this. And they didn't have food nearly this good."

"That's Pleasant Grove for you," I beamed. "It might not be much, but… It's home."

I looked around the bar. The Enchanted Cauldron had been around for generations. Despite the foot traffic this place saw—on account of it being one of the few restaurants in our little community, let alone our only bar—it was still in good shape.

They'd hung all sorts of witchy paraphernalia in here over the years, some as gags, and some that dated back to the Salem Witch Trials themselves. The low lighting from the various lanterns created a cozy atmosphere, and the old-timey portraits on the back walls added a touch of history to the room. There were candles on the shelves that looked like they'd burned and had melted into place—like no one had ever bothered to clean up the wax. But my favorite part was the Morgans, who'd bought the bar last year and spruced it up, had even added little cauldrons filled with succulents to each table.

"I can see why you love it." His words brought a smile to my face, and I couldn't stop myself from beaming. "Thank you for showing it to me today." Damien said it like he knew what it meant to me.

"It was my pleasure," I said, blushing. "So, what do you think? Still want to stick around?" I nudged him with my shoulder, scooting my barstool closer to his.

Part of me was hoping he'd say yes. That he didn't want to leave, either. That for the first time I could go to the festival with someone at my side.

Maybe it was too soon to be thinking that way, but when he slipped his hand into mine, squeezing it slightly, I knew I wasn't imagining things.

"Yes, Willow," he said, a slight chuckle accompanying his words. "I still want to stay here." *With you.* He didn't say it, but I liked to think I could hear it in the tone of his voice. In the depth of his eyes. Even if he'd glamored them at my insistence.

"Okay." I turned my attention back to my fries, shoving a few in my mouth to hide my smile. "Just making sure," I mumbled under my breath.

We had some time to kill before we headed out to the farm for the festival. I needed to help Luna set up our table, but I already couldn't wait for everything.

There was no way I was holding back at the festival tonight. After all, pumpkin pie was my *favorite*. Luna was an amazing baker, but she'd never quite nailed pie, and Wendy—another member of our coven—made the best I'd ever tasted. Plus, topped with homemade whipped cream? I was in heaven. I practically moaned at the thought.

Damien gave me a strange look, and I flushed. "Sorry. Just thinking about pie." I gave a dreamy sigh.

"Pie?" His face scrunched up.

"You have *had* pie before, right?"

"Willow. I'm a demon. I wasn't born yesterday." He narrowed his eyes, stealing a fry from my basket.

"Mhm. Just wait until you taste it. It's the best pumpkin pie I've ever had." Popping another fry in my mouth, I couldn't resist it. "So good."

The idea of introducing all of my favorite foods to the man sitting beside me warmed my insides. Showing him my town, my home—my life—it felt *good*.

He gave me a stare, his jaw tight as he stopped chewing.

Tilting my head back, I smiled up at the ceiling as I finished the rest of my fries. I hadn't considered how fun it might be to tease him. Sure, he had limited knowledge of human things—probably because he'd lived in the demon realm for over two hundred years—but his reaction was the fun part.

"So… where to next?"

TEN
DAMIEN

There were pumpkins everywhere.

Literally.

Willow had insisted we go back to her house and change before the evening's festivities. I'd pulled on a soft, dark gray henley and a flannel jacket with my jeans. The temperatures started to drop in the evening, and even if the cold didn't bother me much, I'd watched Willow shiver on the couch multiple times this week.

There was a reason that there was always a blanket handy next to us on the couch.

My mouth went dry when she walked out of her bedroom. Her body was wrapped in a long-sleeved pumpkin orange (because of course it was) dress that seemed to accentuate every curve, making her look like the embodiment of sin.

She was always beautiful, but this was—*wow*. The tan boots she'd pulled on gave her a few extra inches, making me that much closer to her mouth, and—

There was something seriously wrong with me.

A fuck-ton of pumpkins surrounded me, but all I could think about was her lips. Soft, pink, and ever so sweet. I wondered what she'd taste like. If the taste of pumpkin would overpower the vanilla-and-coffee scent that always followed her around.

I'd never wondered what anyone *tasted like* before, but I couldn't get it out of my mind.

Her eyes lit up as soon as she stepped out of her car. Even though I'd told her I knew how to drive—how uncivilized did she think we demons were, anyway?—she insisted on it.

I'd let her do it a thousand times, though, just to see that look on her face again.

"I have to go help Luna set up," Willow said. "But then I'm all yours."

Yours. Why did I like the way that word slipped off her tongue? Especially when it set off my *instincts*, the ones that wanted *everything*.

"Okay." My voice was thick, and I tried to push the thought away as I followed her through the crowd, towards the blonde girl setting up a tented stall.

Luna's cookies, individually wrapped in cute little bags with ghost prints, filled one table, while the other boasted a drink station.

"And you do this every year?" I asked, not sure what to do as I watched Willow stir her hot chocolate.

Luna gave me a smile, and I tried not to grimace as her powers hit my senses. It was insane to me that no one else could feel it. All of that magical potential, and she baked *cookies* for a living.

"Yep. Ever since we opened the shop." Happiness radiated off of her, which further cemented just how much she loved her job.

And you're going to ruin that for her, my brain took the time to remind me.

But Willow… She didn't have the same spark in her eye that Luna did. I could tell she loved her sister, and loved the shop, but it wasn't her *passion.*

"I'm done!" She said, popping back up at my side. "Luna, you don't mind if we take off, right?"

The smell of chocolate and sweets wafted over to where I was standing.

Her sister shook her head. "Nah, go ahead. Cait's coming to keep me company, anyway."

I thought Willow had mentioned her to me—their cousin. Was she the one who wanted to hex her ex?

"Great." Willow turned back to me with a smile. "What should we do first?"

I cleared my throat. "This is your thing. Why don't you pick?"

My witch bit her lip, looking around at the festival. She'd really undersold the event when she'd told me about it earlier. I expected a few food stalls and some low-key small town attractions, but this place looked like a big carnival. There were tons of games set up and even some small rides they'd brought in.

I recognized one of them: the Spider. I'd been on that before. It'd almost made me throw up, so I had no desire to do it again. Really, I was content just following her around. I'd gladly let her eat her pie, while possibly feeding me copious amounts of sugar. I wasn't sure if I'd ever have another opportunity like this, after all. To be normal. To feel like a human and not a demon who wasn't even close to being in the middle of his life.

"Well… Do you want to take a ride?" Willow asked, forcing me out of my stupor.

I turned my attention back to her eyes. If I kept looking at her lips, I was going to do something stupid.

Like kiss her.

"What?"

She pointed at the little red tractor pulling a cart with an open back full of hay bales. "It's practically tradition."

I raised an eyebrow. "That doesn't look very comfortable."

My witch giggled. "Maybe not, but you drink a cup of hot cider and cuddle up under a blanket, so it's not so bad. Plus, the view is amazing."

I looked around, trying to see it through her eyes. Strings of lights adorned the farm, adding a touch of magic that perfectly complemented the changing leaves and the sunset in the background.

The world was a blanket of orange, and she was at the center.

"It is," I murmured in agreement. It was nice, but she was the most beautiful thing here.

Willow laced her fingers through my hand, beaming up at me. I loved her smile. It made me wonder what lengths I would go to earn it, over and over again.

* * *

"Come on, try it!" Willow said, offering me up a forkful of pie. "I promise, it's *to die* for."

I raised an eyebrow. "Really?"

She pouted. "Just try it. Please? For me?"

"Okay," I agreed, bending down to her level. I couldn't say no when she looked at me with that face, anyway. "Feed it to me."

Willow's cheeks pinked as she held up the fork to my mouth, and I held her eye contact as I slowly took the bite off the fork.

"Mmm." I licked my lips. I hadn't known quite what to expect, but the texture was incredible, and the whipped topping must have been homemade, because it was rich and delicious.

It could rival a feast in the Demon King's palace.

"You have a bit of—" She giggled, pointing at my upper lip.

"What?"

"—Whipped cream. Right there."

Her thumb brushed over the top of my lip, capturing the bit of cream.

"Oh." I looked away, clearing my throat. "Thank you."

She was staring at her thumb, and I bent down, licking it off with my tongue.

"Damien!" Willow turned pink. "You can't just do that here. What if someone sees us?"

And what if they do, little witch?

A little scowl formed on her face. *Do you want people to know who you are? What if something happens to you again?*

Then it's a good thing I have a fearsome witch on my side this time, isn't it? I wove my fingers back through hers, kissing her knuckles. *Besides, look around. Everyone is enjoying themselves, too.*

No one was paying any attention to us. All around us, there were families laughing, the parents holding their kids' hands with blissful smiles on their faces as they ate bucketfuls of sugar. Older couples quietly strolled along as they likely reminisced about the past. Even the teens looked like they were enjoying themselves, playing the carnival games, determined to win.

I could see the Witches' Brew booth from here. Luna was flitting around, helping customers as she handed out bags of cookies and cups of hot chocolate. Frowning, I turned to Willow, about to ask if we should help, when—

"Willow?" A voice called, and a female, dressed in all black, rushed to catch up with us. "Who's your friend?"

"Oh." My witch peeked over at me. "This is Damien. My…" she trailed off, looking at me. I hated how she didn't have a label for me.

But what was I? I'd known her for a week and a half, and most of that, I'd been stuck as a cat for. A fact that never failed to raise my hackles. *Roommate? Friend?* Something more? I desperately wanted to know how she was going to answer it.

I caught her eye, answering it when she failed to. "Friend," I confirmed. I liked when she'd called me that before.

"Damien, this is Cait. She's my cousin."

The orange-haired witch stuck out her hand for me to shake it. "It's nice to meet you," she beamed. I'd never met a witch quite like her before. She had a nose ring and beautiful tattoos that went up the sides of her arms, and her tights looked like snakes.

"Cousins, huh?" If I looked really closely between the two of them, I could see the similarities. They had the same shape of their nose and structure to their jaw. But her cousin had dyed her hair, and her eyes were nothing like the bright green of Willow's—that reminded me of Granny Smith apples.

"Yup. Our moms were sisters." Cait gave me a warm smile.

"We're in the same coven," Willow added as her cousin threw an arm around her shoulder, hugging Willow tight.

"Ah," I said, nodding. "Of course."

It was a sobering reminder—these people would be in Willow's life forever.

And me? Maybe we'd have a month. One *good* month. I wanted to make sure it counted.

"Come on," Willow said, tugging my hand. "Let's go find pumpkins."

We said our goodbyes to her cousin, and I completely forgot about mentioning helping Luna as she pulled me toward the pumpkin patch.

I frowned, looking at a sea of endless pumpkins. "What exactly am I looking for? I've never exactly done this before."

She looked surprised for a moment before smoothing her expression out, bending down to look at the orange squash at her feet. "You want one that's a good shape, medium to large size, and a smooth surface." Willow pointed out a few examples on the ground. "Though I suppose it all depends on what you want to carve into it, anyway." She bit her lip, and I couldn't help but stare at her teeth digging into those sweet, pink lips.

I blinked away the thought of what it would be like to do that to her.

"Was I supposed to think of something before this?" Because I definitely hadn't.

"Oh. Well. I suppose not." Willow brushed her hands on the skirt of her dress before standing up, leaning against me. "But you will… carve one with me, right?" Her eyes were pleading, practically begging. But she didn't have to ask.

"Of course," I chuckled. "Anything you want, Wil." Wrapping an arm around her waist, I pulled her in tighter to me, inhaling the smell of her sweetness. I couldn't get enough of it.

"Oh!" she squealed, pulling away from me. "I found them!" She rushed farther down the row, where two pumpkins were sitting side by side. They were almost equal in color and shape, despite one being slightly smaller than the other. "What do you think?" She looked up at me, and I nodded.

"Perfect." But I wasn't talking about the pumpkins.

Hefting them into my arms, I took them over to the weigh station so Willow could pay for them before depositing them in the car.

On our way back, Willow stopped at a few food booths, continuing to feed me different sweets. I'd lost how many forms of pumpkin I'd tried. Fudge, bread, muffins, scones…

"How are you still eating?" I asked her, watching her plop another bite of pumpkin spice cake in her mouth.

She stopped chewing to stare at me. "I have a bottomless stomach for sweets." Willow's voice was so matter-of-fact. "Obviously."

I wiped a smudge of frosting from the corner of her lip before she handed me a small bag of candy.

"What is this?"

Picking one out, I held up the strange multicolored candy—yellow, orange, and white in a triangle shape.

She giggled. "It's candy corn. Try it. It's one of my favorites." *Corn?* I made a skeptical face before popping it into my mouth.

Sweet. I made a face. It tasted like frosting and sugar, all rolled into one.

"What?" She laughed. "You don't like it?"

"It's too sweet. Are you sure you aren't just eating pure sugar?"

Willow stuck her tongue out at me, grabbing a few pieces from my bag. "More for me, thank you."

I didn't mind at all as she finished it, entranced by watching her happily munch on the candy.

"Should we go through the maze now?" She asked, looking towards the stacks of straw bales stacked on top of each other.

We promptly deposited our food wrappers in the trash before she dragged me over to it.

The witch working the front handed us a map of the maze, so we could apparently find our way out of it. I stared at the diagram, showing the view from above. They'd made the damn thing the shape of a jack-o'-lantern, complete with the eyes and mouth in the middle.

"One year, they made it so hard that old Granny Crowley couldn't figure out how to get out of it. They had to send in a search party," she giggled.

"It's a pumpkin," I stated plainly.

"Last year it was a ghost." She pretended to look contemplative. "Should I see if next year they'll make it a cat?"

I rolled my eyes, pulling her into the opening of the maze. "Let's do this."

But when I turned around, she couldn't see the ghost of a smile that spread over my lips.

How much straw could be in one fucking place? Hell. This place was *actual* hell. We'd been going through it for fifteen minutes already, but it felt like hours. The tall walls of straw made me feel trapped, like I couldn't get out—even though I knew it would only take a moment, one use of my power to get out.

Letting my shadows curl through my fingers, I breathed out, calming down slightly.

I turned around to ask my witch a question, but she wasn't behind me.

"Willow?" I spun around. Where'd she go? "Willow!" I shouted, backtracking slightly, checking the other branches of the path before going back to where we hadn't walked yet.

"Fuck," I cursed, rubbing my forehead.

How had I managed to lose her?

This place was claustrophobic, and despite the map, I still felt completely turned around.

"Got you!" She said, popping up behind me.

"Willow. For fuck's sake. Don't do that." I rubbed my forehead.

"What?" She frowned.

"I thought—" *You were lost. That something had happened to you.* "Never mind." I shook my head.

"I was just—" Willow started, moving towards me, but there was a patch of mud on the ground in between us, and her foot slipped, launching her forward.

As she stumbled, I quickly reached out and wrapped my arms around her waist to prevent her from falling.

"Oh." Willow breathed, and I was vividly aware of the fact that the hay bales hid us from view, secluded in the maze.

She smelled so sweet; I had to stop myself from leaning over to find the source of the scent. Was it her shampoo? Or just something uniquely her?

Fuck.

"Little witch…" I groaned.

I was losing control.

If I wasn't careful, I was going to take her.

ELEVEN
WILLOW

My lips parted, and the slightest breath of air escaped them as I stared at his face. Into those dark eyes, which I never failed to get lost in. No matter if they were red or deep chocolate brown, there was something so captivating about them. About him, really.

I let my gaze linger down to his lips.

There was no mistaking the way he did the same.

We were so close together, barely an inch left between our bodies, and I was struck with the sudden realization that I *wanted* him. More than I ever could have imagined.

Maybe I shouldn't have—he was a demon, after all, and my whole life I'd been taught to stay away from them—but I couldn't help it anymore.

Not when I'd spent the entire day in his presence, and he'd let me drag him wherever I'd wanted to go. When we'd been sitting together on the hayride, our thighs touching, sharing the same blanket… I wondered, *was he feeling the same way?*

"Willow," his voice rasped out. "Don't look at me like that."

"Like what?" Mine was hardly a whisper against the wind, but I hadn't needed to say it at all.

My tongue ran over my lips, moistening them as we stared at each other. If we moved just a fraction of an inch, we'd be kissing. All I had to do was lean up, and—

"Like you want me to kiss you."

His hand tightened on my waist, keeping me pinned firmly to him. The other spread across my back, and the heat from his palm was practically burning me, but I didn't want it to stop.

"But…" I looked up at him through my eyelashes. "What if I do?"

"Little witch…" He warned, a pained expression forming over his features, even as I gripped his jacket tighter. "I don't think you know what you're getting yourself into."

I did. But… *I don't care.* The realization struck me, hard and fast. I didn't care what I got into with this man, this demon, as long as he kissed me.

"Kiss me," I whispered. "Please."

He exhaled roughly before that hand holding my back threaded through my hair, and he bent down and—Damien's lips were on mine.

Soft, like he was gauging my response. Making sure I was okay with it. Wrapping my hands around his neck, I curled my fingers into his hair, tugging him down more forcefully against my mouth.

The first stroke of his tongue against mine had me gasping. The sudden surety—the rightness I felt—I'd never felt like this kissing *anyone* before.

Magic, my brain wanted to say. But I knew magic, and this was nothing like my powers.

Not when every movement of his tongue in my mouth, every press of his lips against mine had me dizzy, my mind blurring.

I wanted *more*.

I wanted him to kiss me like this forever.

Sighing into his mouth, I wrapped my arms around his neck.

That was all the invitation he needed to pick me up, spinning me around to pin me against the straw bales as he explored my mouth with his tongue, not letting go.

"Fuck, Willow," he murmured, awe in his voice as his eyes traced over every inch of my face. Lingering, memorizing. I tugged on the back of his hair, pulling his mouth back to mine.

Bringing our lips together. Now that I'd felt it, I didn't want to stop.

By the time we made it out of the maze, the sun was gone from the sky.

* * *

"Look!" They'd fully decked the barn out for the festival, the string of lights on the ceiling illuminating the dance floor. "It's beautiful." I emitted a dreamy sigh.

I'd always dreamed of having a wedding like this one day. If I met the right person. Lately, that had seemed less and less likely. Except...

The man by my side was making me think of things like that again. Which I couldn't afford to do. He'd only said he'd stay for a month. I couldn't expect a lifetime from a demon, of all people.

He wasn't from here. Didn't belong in Pleasant Grove. I let loose a deep sigh.

Damien rubbed his thumb over the crease in between my brows. "What are you thinking, little witch?"

I shook my head. "Nothing." Forcing a smile on my face, I refocused my attention on the barn. "It doesn't matter."

He looked skeptical, but I ignored that. "Do you want to get a drink? They have pumpkin beer."

Damien groaned. "You and pumpkin. Is there anything in the flavor that you don't like?"

"Nope!" I beamed. "I even have pumpkin cupcake scented body wash."

Grumbling under his breath, he said something that I was pretty sure sounded like, *Of course you do.* But I couldn't be sure.

Still, I pulled him over to the bar, ordering a beer for him and a pumpkin hard cider for me.

Damien's eyes trailed over the room as he sipped his drink. He made a face after swallowing. "That is… truly something."

I laughed. "It's okay if you don't like it. I won't be offended if you don't finish it."

He grunted, taking another sip.

My eyes tracked the movement as his tongue slid over his bottom lip, catching the extra drops of liquid. I could practically feel my body heating as I thought about that kiss earlier—feeling his tongue against mine. Wondering what else it could do.

You're losing it, Willow, I told myself, awkwardly avoiding eye contact as I chugged my cider. I should have picked something with a higher alcohol content—maybe it would have given me the courage to be more bold.

Instead, I was standing and watching the couples on the dance floor twirling their partners in their arms. They were doing some sort of upbeat, country two-step dance I ought to have known by now. I wasn't much for dancing, though. Maybe I just hadn't found the right partner.

"Come here," Damien whispered, holding his hand out to me.

I took it, surprised when he spun me into his arms.

"Oh, you have moves, do you?" Maybe part of me was just surprised he knew how to dance. Especially as he spun me around, his feet moving faster than my eyes could seem to keep up with.

"It's the demon realm, not hell," he said, his deep voice rough against my ear. "I learned how to dance when I was young." Why did that make him even more endearing?

He shut his eyes, a warm smile curling on his lips. "My mother loved to dance."

"Damien…" I murmured. That was the sweetest thing he'd ever said. "What happened to her?" I'd lost my own parents, but hearing him talk about her in the past tense made my heart ache.

He shook his head. "My father… the palace… even with all the guards, it wasn't the safest place for her." A distant look filled his eyes, like he was thinking about the past. "She died protecting me."

I knew what it was like—losing a parent—but not like that. "Mine passed in a boating accident," I said in a whisper. "I'm sorry you had to go through that alone."

His eyes connected with mine, and the pain evident in them… It made me want to kiss him again, just to take it away for a little while. Or maybe give him a hug. I wasn't sure which one. But given that we were in the middle of a crowded dance floor, I just kept letting him lead me.

"It's been a long time." His grip on my back tightened. "It doesn't hurt as much anymore."

I rested my head on his shoulder. "That pain… It never really leaves you, though."

"No," he agreed. "It doesn't."

We were quiet for awhile after that, just losing ourselves in the music's flow.

"Can I ask what happened to them?" Damien's voice was quiet, resigned. Like he thought I wouldn't answer.

"I don't talk about it much," I said, honestly. "Most people in town know what happened, and my coven, well… You're the first person who's asked about them in a long time." I fiddled with his shirt with my hand that wasn't still holding onto his. "They've been gone for years. I still miss them, of course, but I stopped crying ages ago. I had to be strong for Luna. Keep it together for her."

"How old were you?" He murmured.

"21. I was in college when I got a call. There was a freak accident. And Luna, she… She'd barely graduated high school."

He rubbed my back. "So you came back?"

I nodded. "So I came back. Finished a semester early, got my degree, and then kept our house from falling apart as Luna went to pastry school. She knew what she wanted and I…" Didn't. Hadn't had a dream.

"Did everything for your sister."

"Yup."

He made a noise of agreement. "I know what that's like. To feel you've given up your life for your sibling."

"It's not that I don't think it was worth it. I love Luna. I love working together, the business we've grown. The Witches' Brew is my baby as much as it is hers. It's just…"

"Not your dream."

I looked up at him. "Yeah," I whispered. "It's not my dream."

He cleared his throat. "So what is?"

"You know, I think I'm still figuring it out."

"Me too."

I laughed. "What, two hundred and eighty-seven years wasn't enough to figure out what you wanted to do with your life?"

Damien brushed a hair behind my ear. "It didn't feel like much of a life until I met you."

Our eyes connected again, and this time—I held his gaze. Drank it in. Reveled in it.

Knew that something about it was going to change my life.

Maybe in all the ways I'd always dreamed it would.

TWELVE
DAMIEN

I was in more trouble than I'd thought. I was letting myself get distracted with pumpkin patches and dances and the intoxicating presence of Willow. Thinking that maybe this could last. That there was some way I could make it work.

Like I wasn't a demon with responsibilities that didn't involve getting entangled with a witch.

But that *kiss*.

I hadn't been planning on kissing her. I was trying so fucking hard to be good. To not tarnish her sunshine with my darkness. But I couldn't help it. When she'd looked up at me with those big green eyes—I'd lost any semblance of self control.

Looking over at the passenger seat, I watched Willow sleep, her head turned towards me even with her eyes closed.

I wanted this. Wanted her. But I couldn't have her.

"Fuck," I muttered, turning back to stare at the house. It was a miracle she'd let me drive home. I'd had to prove to her that I did, in fact, have a driver's license—even though it had been faked by the demon realm, since I wasn't exactly a human with real ID—and that I could drive her car before she relented.

But she'd been exhausted. After hours of swaying on the dance floor, her eyes had been closing on their own.

And now, I couldn't bring myself to wake her up. So instead I was staring at her, tracing the lines of her face with my eyes.

But I couldn't help myself, and I reached out, brushing over her cheekbone with my thumb.

"Hmm?" Willow gave a small groan as she stirred from her nap.

"We're here," I said, looking up at her house.

"Oh." My witch yawned, stretching out her arms. "Thanks again for driving."

"No problem." I cleared my throat, avoiding looking at her dress, or the way it had ridden up, exposing more of her thighs.

My mouth went dry.

"We should go inside," I whispered.

"Yeah." Her voice was quiet, low. "We should."

Padding into her guest bathroom, I looked at myself in the mirror.

You need to get it together, Damien, I scolded myself. *She's not yours to touch.*

But our kiss was replaying in my mind.

The way her soft, smooth lips moved over mine. The way she'd sighed so sweetly into my mouth. How she tasted so fucking good. I wanted more.

But—no.

Stripping off my clothes, I stayed in my boxers, leaving the rest folded neatly on the counter.

When I'd come out, Willow had left a pillow and blanket on the couch. It was strange to think that this was only our first night sleeping under the same roof with me in this form. That every other night, I'd slept on her feet.

I chuckled, looking at the pile of bedding. *The couch.*

Because even if she'd kissed me back—I was still a stranger. This wasn't serious. It wasn't like she was going to invite me to her bed.

Not again. Not yet, at least.

But…

Turning back into my cat form, I waited until she'd turned her lights off and gone to sleep, and then I slipped into her room, curling up at her feet.

Where I could protect her—my small, little witch—from harm.

THIRTEEN
WILLOW

I woke up in a panic. There was something on top of me, something warm, and—I kicked, trying to get it off of me.

"Willow!" A smooth, rich, *angry* voice grit out. Oh no.

"Damien?" I peeked over the bed and instantly regretted it.

"What the *fuck* was that for?"

"I… I can't…" I blinked.

He was naked. Completely nude, and gloriously bare, and—"I told you to sleep on the couch!" I practically yelled. "And can you put some clothes on, *please?*"

I was trying not to stare. Luckily, it was dark, and I could only see the outline of his chest and… other regions. There was no mistaking that.

Damien's voice was full of humor. "Why, like what you see?"

I threw a pillow at his face. "No!" *Yes.* I was glad it was dark enough in here to hide the flush on my face.

Damien placed the pillow over the lower half of his body, and I swallowed roughly. I was trying not to think about the shape of it. He was a large male, and even the impressive size of his package... *Woah.*

This was not good for my health.

"Why didn't this happen before?"

"Because I wasn't asleep when I transformed before." He narrowed his eyes at me. "And I certainly didn't expect to be kicked off the bed while I was sleeping."

"You were *supposed* to be on the couch."

"Maybe I don't like the couch," he huffed, a lock of dark hair falling onto his forehead. "Besides, perhaps I just wanted to keep an eye on you."

"To what? Make sure I don't curse you too?" I rolled my eyes. "You can relax, Damien. I'm not going to do anything to you."

He ground his teeth. "Maybe I'm not worried about myself."

I blinked. *Me?* He was worried about... *me?* "*Why?*" I asked, nothing more than a whisper in the night.

"There are worse things out there than me, little witch. Things you can't even imagine."

There was more he wasn't saying—it was obvious in his tone, in the fear that crept into his voice. Was that why he'd been so freaked out when I'd lost him in the maze?

What could such a powerful demon like him be afraid of?

I frowned. "Nothing's going to happen to me. This is Pleasant Grove." The name was fitting for our town. It was a happy, friendly place. *Pleasant.* "Not here. Our wards and spells are exceptional."

Except… if they were so good, how did Damien get here in the first place? They should have warded off other magical species as much as they did non-magical beings. If a regular human *did* somehow end up in our town, then they would see whatever their brain would make them believe.

Normally, it was people who thought we were putting on a show, living some recreation of a witch town in the 1700s.

But there was a reason I'd never seen a demon before him. They had taught us they were bad. To fear them.

Yet I knew Damien wasn't like that. He'd given me little peeks into his life, his mind—his heart. He wasn't a bad person. Nor was he out here trying to get me to sign over my soul to him, or agree to some other contract.

And then… there was the way he'd kissed me.

So softly, and then with such intensity.

There'd been no mistaking the way he wanted me. Right? I'd felt it when he'd had me pinned up against the straw. Except we'd come home, and he'd… stayed away from me. Waited until I fell asleep to come in here—in cat form—and do the same.

So he might have wanted me, but he didn't want to act on those impulses.

Which was worse?

"Damien…" I breathed, but I didn't know what to ask. What to say.

I just turned over, facing the other wall. "I'm going back to sleep," I murmured, not looking back at him as I heard him clamber up off of the floor.

As he padded away into the other room.

There was one thing I knew for sure: Damien might not have been a dangerous demon, but he was dangerous for my heart.

Because I *wanted* him.

Despite my best efforts, I couldn't get back to sleep, and the rest of the night was spent tossing and turning. As the first light of dawn appeared, I quickly showered and dressed before rushing out of the house.

Maybe I didn't know what was going on with Damien, why I was feeling this way, but it was okay—I had my sister, and she always had good advice for me. Sometimes I forgot I was the older sister, because she seemed wise beyond her years. Damn precognition skills.

It was a windy, rainy day, so I took my car, pulling into a spot right off Main Street and bundling my raincoat tighter to me as I walked to the bakery.

The moment I stepped inside, I could hear the familiar sound of my sister's mixing bowl clattering against the counter. She normally beat me here since she rented out the apartment overtop of the bakery.

She'd piled her blonde hair high in a bun, with a pretty pink scrunchie holding it all together, matching her overall dress and turtleneck perfectly.

One of these days, I was going to find it in me to be annoyed that she always looked this cute so early in the morning. It had taken all of my energy to throw on a pair of jeans

"Mmm. Smells good in here." It always did, without fail.

"I hope so," she smiled. "I made doughnuts."

My mouth watered. "Doughnuts? What's the special occasion?" I was always trying to get her to add them to the regular menu, but Luna insisted they were too much work. Despite that, our customers loved them.

"No special occasion," she shrugged. "I just felt like it."

Using my magic, I moved my hand like I was going to levitate one out of the pan, but she smacked my hand away. "Later. They're still too warm. Let the icing set." She raised an eyebrow at me. "Why are you here so early this morning, anyway?"

Damn, I thought as I braided my hair back and tied my apron around my waist. *Busted.*

"No reason," I said, busying myself with prep for the day. "I was awake, so I thought I'd come spend time with my sister."

"Mmm. *Sure.*" She said it like she didn't believe me, but at least most of that was true. I *did* want to spend time with her.

"Yup," I said, popping the *p* as I got everything out to make myself a coffee.

"So, how's your cat?" Luna asked, looking up from her bowl of dough she was working on.

"He, uh… Ran away?" I could already feel my cheeks pinking, thinking about Damien and how glad I was that he *wasn't* a cat.

My sister gave me a knowing smile. "Sure. And that has nothing to do with your new mystery man, hm?"

I ignored her question, instead voicing one that had been bouncing around my mind all morning. Or maybe it had been longer than that, something I didn't want to admit. "Luna, I… Do you believe in fate? In destiny?"

Luna blinked. "Where is this coming from?" She moved over to the mixer, where she was mixing up more frosting.

I shook my head. "No reason. Just…" I sighed.

How did I explain to her how I was feeling? Or maybe that was the problem itself—that I didn't want to put these thoughts into words. To verbalize my fears and hopes, because then they'd be real.

"I believe the Goddess gives us the paths we can follow, but the rest is up to us."

Biting my lip, I turned to face my sister fully. "But like…Twin Flames, Kindred Spirits, *Soul Mates*. That stuff. Do you believe there's someone out there who you're fated to be with? To fall in love with?"

She tilted her head. "You've always told me not to look into your future. That you didn't want to know. But now…" Luna raised an eyebrow.

"No!" I exclaimed a little too quickly, the question clear in her face. "I still don't want to know." My voice was barely audible as I lowered it to a murmur. "I was just wondering."

Luna turned off the mixer, setting the bowl on the counter in between the two of us, and leveled a stare at me. "Willow, what are you really asking me?"

"When Mom met Dad, she *knew*, right? Do you think that's possible?"

She blinked and then nodded her head. "I think *anything's* possible, Willow." Luna moved the spoon in her frosting bowl with her magic. "Especially in a world where magic exists."

Maybe she was right. Nevertheless, that didn't explain why these thoughts were running through my head.

Even if it was real, it wasn't *Damien*. It couldn't be. He was an immortal demon prince, and I was just a witch.

"Hm." I swiped a finger through the rim of the bowl of frosting, getting a glob of the cream cheese mixture she'd made. "Yum. My favorite."

"Probably why I make it so much," Luna said with a smile. "There's a fresh batch of spice cake cupcakes to frost."

"You're the best sister ever." I wrapped my arms around her, pulling her into a tight hug.

"And *you* still owe me that bar date soon. I bought a new dress that I'm dying to wear out." She poked me in the arm.

"Okay," I agreed. Because we both deserved to have fun. And maybe it was time I finally *lived* my life, like she kept telling me. And maybe just a small piece of that had to do with Damien. The man who had been sleeping on my couch when I snuck out. "This weekend?"

"You're on. And not just because Friday is *Ghoul's* night at the bar." She wiggled her eyebrows.

"Attire?"

"Spooky. Naturally."

Gods, I loved Halloween time in Pleasant Grove. The way everyone got so into it, with themed nights and decor. Somehow we stretched All Hallows' Eve into an entire month of festivities.

"I'll be there."

✳ ✳ ✳

"Where are you going?" Damien asked, leaning against the doorframe as I attempted to zip up my dress. It was Friday night, Luna and I's big night out at The Enchanted Cauldron.

I turned to look at him, and my mouth dropped open.

Abs. Muscles. Towel around his waist.

Oh, Goddess.

My mouth went dry. I'd seen him shirtless before, even if it was in the cover of darkness and *mostly* just an outline of the ridges to his body. But this was… I shut my eyes.

"Did I adopt a demon, or a damn God?" I muttered under my breath, eyes still focused on his muscles. Those abs I wanted to trace my tongue over—multiple times, if I had my way. Especially after that kiss last week. It wasn't enough—I wanted more.

No being should be allowed to look like *that*. Especially when I was trying so hard to be good. There was a part of me that felt like a sex-crazed beast every time I saw him. One look from him was all it took, and I was wet. *Dripping*. It was unfair, really.

But he was basically my roommate, my *friend*, and he was leaving. He'd only promised me a month, and how much of that did I even have left?

But I couldn't ask him to stay.

Sure, we'd settled into some sort of normal routine over the last week. I'd go to work, stay at the bakery until the late afternoon before coming home and making dinner.

Damien—well, who knew what Damien did during the day.

But at night, we'd sit on the couch, a cushion between us, watching whatever Halloween movie was on the TV.

I still wasn't sure what to make out of my unexpected houseguest in a lot of ways, after all. Especially after he'd kissed me.

But nothing else had happened.

Damien hadn't kissed me again. We'd barely even touched since coming home from the festival. He hadn't made another move.

Sometimes, when he was looking at me, I'd catch his gaze dropping to my lips. Or the heat in his eyes.

Yet the complete rest of this week we just… hadn't talked about it. I was tired of dancing around the subject. Pretending there wasn't some heat between us that I couldn't explain.

"Out," I said with a huff, giving up on the zipper. It might have been a themed night, but I still wanted to look good. *Feel* good. For no one else but myself. Definitely not for the man who currently stood behind me.

"Here," he murmured, coming up behind me. "Let me."

Our eyes connected in the mirror as he slowly zipped up my dress, his breath ghosting on the back of my neck. The whole encounter probably took only seconds, but it felt private—intimate—and I didn't know what to make of that.

"Um." I smoothed my hands over the tight black dress. "Thank you."

His voice was rough. "Of course."

Looping my dangly ghost earrings through my ears, I looked over my appearance. It was casually spooky for sure, but I felt cute. I'd add my favorite hat and a pair of heels and call it good.

Damien leaned against the door frame. "Should I be worried about where you're going dressed like that?"

My eyes lifted in the mirror to his. "The bar. Luna wanted to go out." I bit my lip. "Why? Worried someone else is going to sweep me off my feet?"

The way his eyes lit up… Maybe that was exactly what he'd been worried about. And for some reason, I liked that I'd riled him up with just the one comment.

"I'm going with you," he said, his tone offering no room for argument.

I raised an eyebrow at his still naked body.

Maybe some clothes first?

He dressed in a flash—literally, with one snap of his fingers, and he was in a button-up shirt and a pair of slacks. One day, I needed to ask him how he did that. Where he stored his belongings that he could just retrieve them without blinking an eye.

I pondered that for a while, trying to ignore the truth bouncing around in my brain.

Somehow, he was even more handsome in dress clothes than just in the towel.

* * *

My eyes flickered over to Damien, who was sitting at the bar as my sister and I danced.

Maybe it was a little *too* on the nose to play *The Monster Mash* during Ghoul's Night, but it was fitting.

"You know… He's *hot*!" Luna shouted over the music. "Why don't you see where that goes?"

I shook my head. "He's not here forever. We're just friends! Roommates!" I hated that thought. *It's just temporary.* "And I… don't want to start something that will end." I hadn't realized that was how I felt until I uttered the words, but maybe that was why I'd let the wall form between us this last week. Sure, he had stayed, but for how long?

Distancing myself was safe.

Kissing him again… That was not.

"Okay, but the way he's watching you? Damn." She fanned herself.

I was pretty sure she had some inkling of who he *was*, especially after her comment earlier this week at the coffee shop, but I wondered if she knew the full story. That he was the cat she'd let brush up against her legs just a few days ago. That he was living under my roof.

Sleeping curled up on the edge of my bed every night, even though I'd find him back on the couch every morning. Like he didn't want me to find out.

"Luna, I should probably tell you—" I started, getting interrupted by the music changing. The crowd cheered around us.

"You just need to let loose, Willow! Get *laid!*" My sister said the last word with a singsong voice, and my body flushed.

"I… Luna." I groaned, even as we moved to the beat.

"What?" She frowned, giving me a little shrug as she shimmied on the floor. "I can't have my older sister trying to take care of me forever. You have to live your own life, too, Wil."

My own life… My eyes wandered up, connecting with Damien's, who was still sitting at the bar, sipping his drink. Watching me dance.

But the heat in his eyes… I wasn't mistaking it this time. Definitely not.

"Do you want to dance?"

The words were ones I wanted to hear—but they weren't from the right person.

I turned around, and there was Simon from the library, his auburn hair combed back, and a bowtie that looked like a bat tied around his neck.

"Oh, I…" I looked back to the bar, but Damien was gone, his empty drink sitting on the counter. "I actually came here with someone. Sorry." I winced involuntarily.

"Yeah," my demon agreed, pulling my back flush against his chest. "With me."

I turned my head to look up at him, my cheeks heating at the determination I saw there.

FOURTEEN

DAMIEN

You're beautiful. The words I should have said to Willow earlier, when I saw her standing in her bathroom, the black dress showing off the creamy smooth skin of her back. Instead, I'd practically forced her to bring me along tonight.

Dammit. How hard was it to say the words?

All week, I'd had them on the tip of my tongue.

But everything faded away whenever she was around.

The light brown strands of her hair caught the light as she danced with Luna, and I scowled at the thought of someone else touching her. I shouldn't have been this possessive, but watching her sway her hips, thinking about anyone else having what was *mine…*

It was enough to make my lips curl over my teeth.

"Fuck," I muttered to myself as I watched the two of them dance.

"Can I get you another one, sir?" The bartender asked me, and I shook my head.

I'd been nursing the same one all night, and I had no plans of getting drunk. There was no way I'd risk something happening to Willow—or her sister.

I took another sip as the two girls danced. They'd been playing popular Halloween songs all night. Some I recognized, and others I had never heard before. While I wasn't well versed in a lot of human culture—especially with their holidays—I'd spent my fair share of time while on this mission in bars. That, at least, wasn't all that different from the demon realm.

And it was the reason I didn't take my eyes off of them. Not for a second.

Part of me had hoped to find the girl I was looking for in one, but that had only led to me being cursed. The damn witch who took one look at me, talking to her sister, and decided I was bad news. Well, I deserved that.

Especially when the girl I'd been searching for was currently by Willow's side. She'd been here all along, like destiny was just waiting for me to find both of them.

Gods. Her sister.

How was I going to explain everything to her? I rubbed my thumb over the top of my glass. I'd been doing so good all week, trying to build a relationship with her. Getting to know *her*.

I watched her human movies and then she told me about her past. What growing up here was like. About her relationship with her coven and her sister. How she'd thought about moving somewhere else after college. I couldn't listen to her talk about the human boys she'd been with, not without my veins filling with rage. The jealousy was almost suffocating, the way it hit me out of nowhere.

There was no prying my eyes away from her.

The redheaded boy from the library was moving closer to my witch, making my hair practically stand up on my arms. My body sang for me to defend her, to claim her publicly.

To make it known that she was *mine*.

I was out of my chair before I knew what I was doing, pulling Willow's body into mine. Covering her in my scent.

Her head tilted back to look at me, and I watched as her cheeks pinked. Fuck, I liked that. How had I gone this whole week without touching her? Without taking her lips in mine again?

"She's here with me," I repeated, as the young wizard looked between the two of us.

"I'm sorry, Willow." He looked embarrassed. "I didn't know you were seeing anyone."

"We're just…" My witch looked up at me as she said, "It's still new." She offered him a small shrug.

"Hey, no worries." He gave a sad smile before turning around, going to the other side of the packed dance floor.

"Do you want to get a drink?" I murmured into her ear, my lips brushing against her neck as I pulled away.

She nodded, mumbling, "Mhm," in response. Even the tips of her ears were a little pink as she slipped her hand into mine and led me back across the room.

Willow slid onto a barstool, her hand staying intertwined in mine even as I took the one next to her. Watching her, my eyes traced her flushed cheeks, her eyes twinkling as she ordered another drink. If only I could commit it to memory, so I'd never have to forget this moment. Or her.

Once she had the cocktail in her hands, she spun around to look at me, her eyes bright. "Hi."

"Hey," I practically grunted back.

I was still struggling with the possession I'd felt earlier, the need to claim her as mine in front of everyone. Her smell was in my nostrils, and I wanted it deeper. In my lungs, maybe. Burrowed underneath my skin. My innate nature was hard to deny.

"Sorry if this is boring for you," my witch frowned.

It wasn't. Not when I'd been unable to take my eyes off of her all fucking night.

"You could never bore me," I said. Fuck it all. I didn't like the distance we'd had in the past week, so maybe it was time for honesty. "Besides, this is... enlightening."

Watching her. Seeing how she let loose.

"Hm? Can demons get drunk, anyway?" Willow wondered out loud, sucking on the straw of her drink, her eyes wide as she watched me.

"Of course we can." I looked around the room. Luckily, no one was paying attention to us or her words, or else we could be in trouble.

Not because I was worried about something happening to me. The last thing I wanted was for someone to confront Willow about *me*. The idea that I could make problems for her just because of who I was... I didn't like that. But I was already here, being a selfish bastard, all because

I couldn't seem to walk away from her—but I didn't want to affect her reputation.

Because it was clear, any time she was around other people, whether it was flitting around the bar or in her coffee shop, just how beloved she was.

I'd experienced nothing like this town in the demon realm. Not that there weren't communities or towns of our own—demons, living in their true forms, free to live their lives—but my life had been cold. Emotionless. Sometimes it felt almost meaningless. I'd lost my mom at a young age. My father… Well, the Demon King had his own set of worries, and it wasn't about me. No, that distinction went to my older brother. The *Heir*.

I scrubbed a hand over my face. She'd lost her parents, but she was still so kind, caring, and generous. In all my years, I'd never met a woman who enchanted me the way Willow did. I couldn't stop. Couldn't keep my eyes off of her, or my body from wanting to touch her. Wrap her soft brown curls around my fist and—

Willow's hand landed on my thigh, causing me to startle out of my thoughts.

"What?" My eyes flickered to the counter, to her finished drink. Mine was gone now too, meaning I had no more excuse to be a grumpy asshole tonight.

"Should we dance?" She held out her hand to me. The music had slowed—no longer one of those poppy hits she had been moving her hips to.

I thought about how good it had felt the other day—holding her in my arms, dancing with her. Even though I knew it was dangerous, that nothing good would come out of it, I couldn't say no. Couldn't bring myself to turn her down.

"Of course," I murmured, giving her my hand. It always amazed me how much smaller hers were than mine. How I could wrap my entire hand around hers. And yet, when she laced her fingers through mine, nothing had ever fit so perfectly.

Yes, my body screamed as my hand wrapped around her waist, pulling her in closer to me.

"You look beautiful tonight," I murmured against her ear, finally saying what I'd been dying to for hours.

"Thank you." She bobbed her head, a pretty blush spreading over her cheeks. "You clean up pretty nicely yourself."

I'd hardly noticed what I'd thrown on when she told me about her plans. I'd just focused on her bare back as I zipped up her dress, and the way it hugged her curves. So fucking perfect.

Begging to have my hands all over them.

A dark shadow caught my eye in the back of the bar. Some alarm bell went off inside my mind, that I should investigate—to see what was going on.

But then Willow wrapped her arms around me, and nothing else mattered.

Unlike at the festival, when I twirled and spun her around the room, in a dance of intricate steps, we just held each other, swaying to the music. I liked it too much.

Which was why I needed to come clean.

"Willow…" I sighed, opting for honesty. "I'm sorry for this week."

She looked confused. "Why? I thought we were having a good time."

She tilted her head to the side. "Getting to know each other. You know."

"We were. And I liked it. Watching your human movies. Listening to your stories." Too much. I liked it way too much. "But I've been avoiding… *this*, and it's not fair to you." I swallowed roughly, fingers itching to dig into her skin. "To either of us."

"No," she agreed, "it's not."

"But…" I tightened my grip on her hip. Held her closer to my body. Let my breath brush against her ear, and watched the way she shuddered from it.

Her eyes were closed as she murmured a quiet, "But?"

"But I'm tired of holding back. Pretending I don't want you. Pretending I don't know what your mouth tastes like. Pretending I don't want to do it again."

Willow's eyes flew open, her hand on my shoulder moving to grip my jacket instead. "You do?"

My lips ghosted against her neck, the faintest press of a kiss to her perfect skin. "I do."

When I stared back down at her, there was a spellbound look in her eyes. "Oh, good." She let loose a giggle. "Because I do as well."

I looked into her eyes. They were big, but not overly dilated. And she didn't seem drunk to me. Which meant…

She wanted me as badly as I wanted her.

"Should we go home?" Willow whispered, her eyes bright. "Because I really want to kiss you right now."

"Yes." And fuck, I liked the sound of that. *Home*. Her place felt more like home than anywhere I'd ever been before.

I was so close to losing control. To giving in to every thought, every desire.

What the hell were we still doing here?

"Will Luna be okay?" I asked, looking at her sister, currently chatting with another witch at the bar.

Willow nodded. "She's a big girl. She can take care of herself."

And before either of us could utter another word, her hand was in mine, and I was pulling her towards the door.

FIFTEEN

WILLOW

"Willow." His voice was a caress over my skin, and my eyes fluttered open, taking him in.

How much did I have to drink tonight? Not enough that it would impact my judgment. Not enough to keep me from wanting this.

Him.

He'd been watching me all night.

Just like I'd been watching him.

I dropped my purse on the kitchen table, keys and all. I wondered if he could hear how fast my heart was beating from there with those demon senses of his. If it was any faster, I thought it would beat out of my chest.

From where I was standing, I could see out the large windows into the backyard, illuminated only by the light from the front entryway.

Even without looking at him, I could *feel* his presence behind me.

Damien's shadows wrapped around my arm, the tendril dancing over my skin in an intimate motion, like he was trailing a finger across my bare skin—

I closed my eyes, shuddering just from the small contact.

"Little witch…" He started, but before he could finish his thought, I turned around, bringing our bodies together.

He was so much taller than me, so bringing our mouths together was a challenge. Damien leaned down, taking my lips in his. And everything felt right again.

The kiss quickly turned deeper, more frantic. *Gods.* Kissing anybody else could never come close to my demon. He knew how to use his tongue, making me practically mewl against him. The way he could coax my mouth open for him, licking inside, those playful little bites against my lip…

And wasn't that the most unfair thing? He'd lived so much longer than me. Of course, he'd had his fair share of kissing other women. An idea that made me want to put a hex of my own on someone, because I didn't like the idea of anyone else touching him. Of his lips on anyone else.

But then his hands wrapped around my ass, lifting me up against his body, and it drained me of all rational thought.

My voice betrayed me, letting out a small moan when his erection brushed against my core as he pinned me against the wall. Taking me with his mouth again, he explored every inch—like he was trying to commit it to memory. Every swipe of his tongue against mine only spurred me on more.

My fingers brushed over his hardened length.

For *me*. This man—this demon—wanted *me*.

Maybe that was the thought that made me more brazen, bolder, but I didn't have it in me to care. I just wanted more. Needed it.

A low rumbling sound emitted from his throat when I moved my hand up, attempting to flick open the button on his pants.

I blinked. "Did you just… *growl* at me?"

"Little witch," he gritted out through his teeth. "I suggest you stop if you don't want to take this further."

I hummed in response, cupping him fully. "And what if I don't want to stop?" I ran a finger up his impressive bulge.

Fuck, I'd never wanted to have someone inside me so badly.

Damien leaned in close, enough for his lips to brush against my ear. For the rush of his warm breath to tickle my neck. "Then I'm going to take you to bed, Willow. And I'm not going to be able to hold back." He buried his nose in the crook of my neck. "Not when you smell this good."

He kissed the skin there, trailing a line up to my jaw with his lips, each touch like a brand against my skin.

I wanted it. Wanted him to mark me, for people to know I was *his*.

Wanted to not have to hide who this man was to me, because I was starting to wonder if I'd ever truly lived before he'd come into my life.

"I don't want you to hold back," I murmured, running my hands down the planes of his back as he sucked on my pulse point. "I want *you*," I moaned.

I couldn't keep it in any longer.

When he pulled away, his red eyes flared with need.

"*Fuck.*" Any pretense of who he was gone—left behind in the bar, I assumed—and he looked down at me, perhaps more demon than man, but I *liked it.* "You want me to fuck you, Willow?"

"*Yes,*" I agreed, and then I was back on my feet, spun around, his breath against my neck.

Damien stepped forward, pulling the zipper down slowly on my dress. If I was being honest, I'd only worn it for him—I liked to dress up, of course, but the way he'd looked at me when I walked downstairs… I'd never felt more beautiful, or desired.

I was finding I liked that with him. The way he could light up my body with just a kiss or a small touch.

He kissed my bare shoulder as he pushed the dress down my back, leaving me in my bra and the hip hugging lace panties I'd pulled on at the last minute. Damien's nimble fingers quickly made work of my bra clasp, and my nipples tightened as the cool air hit them.

Normally, I would have tried to hide myself, but how could I with the way he was looking at me? Like I was something to be treasured, worshiped.

"Fuck. You're perfect." He brought his hands up, cupping my breasts. When he ran his thumb over my nipple, I shuddered at how good it felt.

The lust was burning me alive. I'd never felt like this with anyone before—not this soul-encompassing need that I felt for him.

"Spread your legs for me," Damien murmured, bending down to capture my lips once more as his fingers dipped below the band of my panties—seeking, searching.

I was happy to comply. When was it last? *Months*. Maybe years.

"So wet, baby," he crooned, rubbing his fingers against my slit. "Did I do this to you?"

The only response I gave was a hum in agreement as he slipped a finger inside of me. He'd been driving me wild all night, teasing me with all of his lingering touches and heated glances.

I couldn't hold back my voice as he added another finger, exploring my folds. Trying to find that spot that he knew would drive me wild.

"Damien," I pleaded, my breaths growing heavy as I gave into the growing pleasure. There was a part of me that was vaguely aware of how tightly I was grasping his shoulders, my legs growing unsteady underneath me.

I pulled away from him slightly, my eyes growing with awareness. He was still fully clothed, and we were standing in the hallway. Despite how eager I was, I didn't want our first time to be against the wall. Or on the floor.

"Bedroom," I panted, resting my forehead against his chest.

Is this my invitation? He thought, and I could almost feel the smirk on his face.

He could sleep in my bed for the rest of eternity if he kept up that movement with his fingers. I gasped. *Yes. Please.* I didn't want him on the couch anymore, anyway.

I could feel the loss as he pulled his fingers out of me, my juices coating them.

"I can't fucking wait to taste you," he murmured, putting them into his mouth, sucking my taste off of his digits as he maintained eye contact with me.

"*Oh.*" I squeaked out, as he gave one last lick of his lips.

"So sweet," he murmured, and then I was being lifted into his arms and carried towards my bedroom.

I was aching, squirming with need after he worked me up without letting me come.

Damien playfully swatted my ass. "Be still."

I'd never found getting spanked hot before, but the look in his eyes… *Damn.*

The demon's long legs quickly devoured up the space, and he kicked in the door before dropping me down on the bed.

His eyes were only slits as they traced over my naked body, from the line of my bare neck down to my tits and then to the panties that still covered me.

"What did I do to deserve you?" he mumbled, quickly stripping out of his clothes. Damien's eyes never left me as he dropped each article on the floor—until the only thing that remained was his briefs. The outline of his hardened length pressed against them, begging to be freed.

I sat up, reaching for his waistband, ready to give him the same treatment he had me. Sliding my thumbs into either side of his boxers, I pushed them down, eagerly freeing his cock.

Feeling him through his pants earlier had given me some idea of his size, but… My eyes widened. He was bigger than anyone I'd ever been with before, and I suddenly wondered what he would taste like. I ran a finger up his hardened length, watching him shudder at my touch.

Oh. I really liked that.

Only Damien clicked his tongue to the roof of his mouth, grabbing my hands before I could play with him any further. "Easy, witch. I have more plans for you."

I frowned. "But—"

Damien clicked his tongue, silencing me by pushing me down to the bed and threading his hand through my underwear. I expected him to roll them down, or slowly drag them off of my body, but instead, in a quick motion that left me dizzy, he ripped them off with a devilish grin.

"I liked those," I said with a frown.

He shook his head mischievously. "I'll get you new ones. Now, be a good girl and let me lick your pussy, Willow."

My cheeks flushed as he pulled me to the edge of the bed, positioning me so he could kneel in front of me. Placing his head level with my opening, he gripped the insides of my thighs, spreading them apart roughly.

Burying his head in between my legs, the first swipe of his tongue against my clit made me shudder. He groaned as his tongue lapped against me, like he couldn't get enough of my taste.

So sweet, his voice said into my mind.

"Damien," I begged, as he swirled and licked and drove me wild, not giving me the pressure that I needed. "I need—"

"Shhh, baby," he soothed, slipping his fingers back inside of me. Those apt fingers moved against my walls while he continued giving my clit attention with his mouth. "Gonna take care of you."

I didn't hold back my voice, the little noises he made me emit with each movement, or the moan when he sucked my clit into his mouth. There was no stopping the sensations unfurling inside of me, how close I was getting—

Damien looked up, his gaze connecting with mine even as he kneeled between my thighs. "Want you to come for me, Willow. Let me feel it on my tongue."

This time, his tongue darted inside of me, tasting me directly, and he brought his thumb to my clit, rubbing it in circles as his tongue explored my insides.

"Oh, *Gods*."

He gave me a wicked grin. "No Gods here. Just your Demon."

My demon. I didn't care what anyone thought—he was. *Mine.*

That was the thought that I tipped over the edge with, with his tongue inside of me and those talented fingers making me come harder than I thought I ever had in my life.

Damien pulled back, his lips swollen, traces of me still glistening on them. I blushed. "Fuck, little witch. That was…" He placed a kiss on the inside of my thighs before standing up.

My heart was still racing. "Yeah." I didn't have the words, still panting from the exertion of my orgasm. No one had ever made me come so fast before, and I thought maybe it was all him. That the knowledge that he was the one playing with my body, lighting me on fire…

Sitting up, I looked between us, my finger reaching out to swipe the pre-cum from the head of his cock. I wanted him inside of me, wanted to know what it felt like to be joined together. He was so hard, his tip practically weeping, begging for a release of his own.

"Shit." I blurted out, a thought suddenly occurring to me. "I don't have any—" Protection.

When was the last time I'd needed it? I'd been too busy to date in forever, and even the thought of bringing home a man hadn't been in my mind in ages.

Damien looked pained, one hand wrapping around his length, squeezing slightly. "We don't have to do this."

"I'm on the pill," I murmured, reaching up to thread my fingers through his hair, wanting to be closer to him. "And I'm clean. So…" My eyes focused on his hand, how he was slowly working himself with it.

I'd never gone without condoms before—especially not with any humans I'd been with. But there was something about being with *him*—that it was us—that I didn't mind.

He groaned. "I don't want anything between us. Not the first time. Not when—" Giving a grunt of agreement, he dropped his forehead to my mine, kissing me roughly, our tongues tangling together. I could taste myself on his tongue.

"Please, Damien," I begged. "Need you."

Laying me down against the pillows, I wiggled my hips impatiently as he notched himself at my entrance, not giving me what I wanted. His entire body engulfed my frame, and I could barely take the time to revel in it, I was so eager.

"Patience, baby." He shook his head, the motion causing his hair to fall onto his forehead. "I don't want to hurt you."

I brushed some of the sweaty strands back with my fingers, reveling in the feel of his soft hair against my skin. "You won't," I promised. "You couldn't." Even in the short time I'd known him, I knew it to be true.

He closed his eyes, and when he opened them, the ring of red was almost entirely black. "You're sure?"

I nodded, wrapping my arms around his neck.

That was all it took before he pushed inside of me, slowly—inch by torturous inch.

"Fuck," he gritted out. "You're so tight."

"Only—" I moaned, "—because you're so *big*." *Fuck*. He'd basically stuffed me full, and he wasn't even fully inside of me yet.

More. Even with the fullness, I wanted more. My hips rocked against his involuntarily, pushing him in deeper. I could feel myself stretching around him, that feeling of fullness increasing as he worked his way inside of me.

"Look, how well you're taking me," he praised, as his eyes fixed on the spot where our bodies were connected. My body spread around him, greedily taking in his cock.

He stilled, letting me adjust to his size. As the slight pain faded away, a growing sense of pleasure replaced it.

"Willow." His voice was deep—raspy—in my ear. "I'm going to move now."

Damien kissed me before pulling out, almost all the way to the tip, before plunging back inside of me, burying himself to the hilt. I was so wet, his ministrations from earlier providing all the lubrication we needed.

Yes, Yes, Yes. I chanted, unsure if I was even forming verbal cohesive words at this point.

All I knew was it had never been like *this.*

Filthy. And yet I loved every moment of it.

The only sound in the room was our skin slapping against each other, my moans each time he hit *that* spot inside of me, and his small grunts as he focused on my body.

The delicious slide of his cock moving in and out of my body was too much, and yet…

"I need—" I said, vaguely aware that I didn't know what I needed, just that *more,* and I was losing my mind, but *more, more, more*—

He didn't stop, thrusting into me as his hands gripped the outside of my thighs tight enough I thought they might bruise. But then his shadows brushed against my skin, dancing across my nipples, almost like his tongue. When he did the same to my clit, my back arched off of the bed. The stimulation to every part of me was going to make me lose it.

Holy gods—"Don't stop," I moaned.

It was everything. It was too much. *"Damien,"* I moaned his name, loudly, thankful that we were alone in this house. That there was no fear of getting caught or being too loud.

Wrapping my legs around his hips, I intertwined them behind his back, forcing him in deeper.

My demon gave me another smirk—one that had no right being as sexy as it was—before bringing our mouths back together. His shadows were a caress around my entire body, only adding to how he was touching me.

"You feel so good inside of me," I encouraged, feeling him growing harder inside of me, knowing he must be close.

I wanted him to let go, to lose himself. Tightening my muscles, I clenched myself around him, squeezing his cock.

"Willow. Shit." He grimaced. *"Fuck.* I'm going to come if you don't stop that."

"Do it." I wasn't above begging for it. His cum—I licked my lips, rocking my hips in time with his movement. "Fill me up, Damien."

But—he shook his head, taking my lips in his, biting my lip slightly as he pulled away. "Need you to come again first."

His lips moved down to a nipple, sucking it into his mouth as he massaged the other one, letting that tendril of darkness take over rubbing circles on my clit. It felt like his hands were *everywhere*, those shadows working as extensions of himself.

I'd already been close, but this time, I let go, burying my fingers into his shoulders, not even caring if I left marks from my fingernails as I came, crying out his name.

Damien kept up his thorough torture, switching his attention to my other nipple as he continued that glorious movement in and out of me.

My insides clenched around him, and he stilled, his mouth sliding off my breast with a wet *pop* as he gripped my hips, hardening even further inside of me.

"Fuck," he murmured, his eyes focused solely where we were joined together. Damien grit his teeth, burying himself to the hilt before letting go. I could feel the warmth spilling through my insides as he came, pouring inside of me on a shaky breath.

After he'd finished, he collapsed on top of me, holding me to his body before rolling both of us onto our sides as his cock softened inside of me.

"I didn't hurt you, right?" He asked, the concern evident in his voice. "I wasn't too rough?"

"No." I snuggled my head into his chest. "I liked it."

I'd never felt better. I was floating on air; the rightness surging through my body.

He kissed my forehead before shifting, like he was going to pull away.

I whined. "Don't. Not yet. I just wanna stay like this."

Tucking me back against his body, I wound my arms around his back, inhaling his spicy scent. Something about it calmed me—soothed me.

I wasn't going to evaluate why I liked it so much. Not yet.

"Willow," he whispered, and I realized my eyes had shut, so warm and comforted by his presence that it had almost lulled me to sleep. "I'm going to get up now."

He pulled out, and I whimpered from the loss. I knew I needed to get up, to clean up, to take care of things, but I was boneless. Totally spent. I wasn't sure my legs had any strength left in them.

"Fuck, that's hot," he murmured, pushing his cum back inside of me.

Oh. Gods. That greedy little possessive side of me, the one that didn't want to imagine him with anyone else, liked that *very* much.

Damien came back to the bed a few moments later, and my eyes peeked open to find him holding a washcloth, wiping in between my thighs. He'd pulled on a pair of boxers, but left his chest bare.

After he seemed satisfied, he handed me a glass of water, getting me to drink it before slipping back under the covers.

Damien's arms wrapped around me, and I snuggled into his chest, letting my eyes close as I drifted off to sleep.

Some part of me recognized I shouldn't trust him, shouldn't let him into my heart—but I wasn't sure I cared anymore. Not when he was so gentle with me, especially when it mattered. When he'd shown, over and over, how he was here for me.

And if I wasn't careful—I was going to fall for him completely.

SIXTEEN

DAMIEN

I kissed her forehead, watching her sleep.

She looked so peaceful, so… calm like this. With the morning light bathing her face in gold, a serene smile spread across her face. She was an angel, a goddess. A gift I didn't deserve.

I'd never known how good it would feel—to wake up like this. To spend a night in each other's arms. I was no stranger to sex, but last night… It felt like a first for me.

Brushing a hair out of her face, I held my breath as she stirred slightly.

"Hi," she murmured, voice rough from sleep.

"Good morning." I kissed her cheek, because even if I was trying to be good, it was hard to keep my hands off of her.

"What's the plan for today?" I asked, curling an arm around my witch.

Willow stretched her arms, the sheet moving back from the motion, exposing her cute pink tits. My mouth watered.

"Mmm." Her groggy voice groaned. "I'm hungry. Should we have breakfast?" Her body cuddled closer to me, pressing her nipples against my chest.

I held in the groan I felt from the feeling, trying to focus on the woman in front of me. On her priorities—instead of how I was already half hard, just from the feel of her body against mine. "What about the bakery? Do we need to go help Luna?"

She waved me off. "No, she's got it. She told me to take the day off." Willow sat up, wincing slightly as she moved. "Maybe she knew I'd be sore."

A devilish grin spread over my face. "I think I know just the thing that will help."

I wanted to make her feel better, since I was the reason for it. She'd taken all of me so well, and I couldn't help how much of a satisfied male that made me.

Ripping the sheets off our bodies, I picked her up in my arms. Her still naked form made my current plan much easier. Willow's soft curves pressed against my body, and I couldn't help but appreciate her figure. How lucky I was that she'd picked me. Setting her on the bathroom counter, I got everything ready for her.

Moving to her giant claw-foot tub, I started the water running, adding some soothing oils and sea salt to help her muscles relax. As it filled, I went and grabbed a few candles, leaving them on various surfaces in the room. It created a beautiful ambiance, illuminating both of us in candlelight when I flicked the light off.

"Wow," she said sleepily. "Such service."

"Have to take care of my little witch," I said, kissing her forehead as I held out a hand, helping her into the tub.

"Ohhh," she moaned as she slid into the warm water, closing her eyes and tipping her head back against the rim. "If you're going to spoil me like this, I won't be able to let you go."

"Willow—" I hated that she thought this thing between us was temporary. That there was any doubt in her mind about what I was feeling. But I couldn't tell her that. It was too soon.

"Not now," my witch whispered. "Please."

Stripping off my boxers, I slowly slid into the water behind her, wrapping my arms around her waist. I couldn't stop touching her. I needed to, if only to calm that instinct inside of me. The one that screamed *Mine*. I wanted to claim her, to mark her, for the world to know exactly who she belonged to.

Later. It wasn't time for that yet. There was still so much she didn't know.

"Better?" I asked, massaging her thighs.

Willow hummed in agreement, leaning her head back to rest against my shoulder. She shut her eyes, looking totally at ease.

After I'd washed her hair, we stayed in the bath until the water ran cold, neither one of us wanting to break this perfect bubble.

She was right. We could talk about everything later. I just wanted to enjoy my time with her for now.

* * *

Her eyes widened as she entered the kitchen. "You weren't kidding when you said you know how to make breakfast."

I'd fried eggs, cooked some bacon, and even made pumpkin pancakes after leaving Willow to get ready, knowing we'd never leave her bedroom if I stayed in there.

My eyes trailed over her body in an obvious perusal. She'd pulled on a cozy white sweater and a tan overall dress, tying her hair up into a ponytail with an orange and white polka dot scrunchie.

"Hi," I said, giving her a small smile before she slid in behind me, wrapping her arms around my torso.

"Hi," she responded to my back. "I like you in my kitchen," she murmured.

"Oh?" I felt smug. *Me too.* Mainly because I liked being here too. It was crazy how quickly I'd become comfortable in this house. How little I wanted to leave. But I owed all of that to the witch hugging me from behind.

I'd be here as long as she wanted me to. A month wouldn't be enough time with her. I knew it now. Especially after last night. The bond I'd felt strengthening between us with each movement…

Rubbing my hand over my heart, I gave a deep, contented sigh. I'd never felt more peaceful than I did here, with her in my arms.

"Hmm?" Willow asked, but I just shook my head.

"Shall we eat?"

She grinned, grabbing my hand and leading me over to the table. "Gods yes."

Willow sat down at one end of the table, guiding me into the seat directly next to her. Part of me liked that I was close enough to press my knee into hers, that I didn't have to lose contact for even a moment. It made my body purr, the prolonged connection between us.

Willow quickly devoured the pumpkin pancakes, barely taking a break between bites. I finished my plate fast as well, having worked up quite an appetite from last night's events. If we were going to keep *that* up, I needed to feed her properly.

"*Ohmygods,*" she moaned, her mouth full of pancake. "This is so good. *Whatthehell.*" She swallowed, taking a deep drink of milk before speaking again. "Where did you learn to do this?"

I shrugged. "When you've lived as long as me, it's hard not to get bored." I propped my chin on my hands, watching her dig in. "Every decade, I picked up a new hobby to keep things interesting. I learned to play the piano. Dance. How to paint—though I'm not very good at that." He wrinkled up his nose. "I just ended up with more paint on *me* than on the canvas."

She giggled. "I'd love to have seen that."

"Most things from the human world make their way over to ours. Your culture. The demons who are working here bring it back, and, well…" Running my hands through my hair, I stared down at my empty plate. "Cooking was enjoyable. I was good at it. Never quite got the hang of baking, though."

Willow's mouth was hanging open before she recovered. "That's okay. You don't like sweets anyway, right?"

Leaning over, I took her mouth into mine, slipping my tongue inside. She tasted like pancakes and syrup and *Willow*. I practically groaned at the way she exploded onto my taste buds.

She blinked as I pulled away, her eyes glazed over in a haze. "What was that for?"

I licked my lip before running my thumb over the corner of her mouth. "So sweet." I smirked. "Maybe I do like it, after all."

Her cheeks flushed as she took another bite.

Part of me knew I should get up and start cleaning, but I just kept watching my witch eat instead. Satisfied, I let my chest rumble as she shoveled another bite into her mouth.

"What should we do today? I've been wondering what else you have left on your *fall must-dos* list. How much education do I have left?"

Willow stared up at me, and I rubbed my chest again.

Fuck. Was it that loud? I couldn't control it. Part of my shape-shifting abilities was being able to change forms at will, but the instincts came with the territory. The purring came whenever I felt especially content or fulfilled. I'd hardly ever experienced that level of satisfaction before this, though. Before Willow.

"Well, what do you think?"

She blinked. "Sorry, about what?"

"About our plans for the day. I was thinking we still had those pumpkins…" I grinned, pointing at the two perfect pumpkins waiting to be carved. They'd been sitting on the counter staring at me over the last few days, and I felt taunted.

Sure, I'd experienced a lot of things from human culture, but we didn't carve pumpkins in the demon realm. And if it meant more time with Willow, I'd gladly take it.

Even if I was ignoring Zain's *summons*. My mission seemed less important now, knowing who exactly sat at my side. My brother could wait a little longer.

"Oh." Willow's green eyes lit up with excitement. "*Yes!*" She clapped her hands. "We definitely need to do that. I have to go dig out the box with the tools from the attic."

"I'll come with you," I said instantly

"No, it's okay." She shook her head, wincing. "It's pretty messy up there. All of my parent's stuff, well… I'll get it." She kissed the side of my head as she rose from her chair.

"Okay." I sighed, wanting to help her but not wanting to push too hard. "I'll clean up from breakfast."

"Perfect." Willow gave me a smile, setting her dishes in the sink before promptly disappearing.

There was nothing that could ruin my mood today. Not with Willow by my side.

* * *

There were pumpkin guts everywhere.

On every conceivable surface.

In Willow's hair.

"What did you do?" I asked, wiping a drip off of her cheek. "Blow the damn thing up?"

She giggled. "Luna likes to use the seeds and the insides for the bakery. I might have… overestimated my magic." There was a sheepish grin on her face, and I couldn't help cupping her cheeks with my hands.

I enjoyed how they engulfed her face, much like my hands did with her tits. They were the perfect size, considering I could practically cup them in my hands.

"Do you need me to clean you up again, little witch?"

She gave me a wicked smile. "Are you going to dirty me up first?"

Swallowing roughly, I willed myself not to think those thoughts. We were supposed to be carving pumpkins, not christening the kitchen table.

"Later," I agreed, picking up the tool. "First, we're going to carve these things."

"Right." Willow nodded, moving to stand behind me. "So… what are you doing?"

I shook my head. "It's a surprise."

Carving pumpkins was much harder than it looked, and I was pretty sure mine looked like absolute shit, but at least I'd done it. I was grateful for the opportunity to try new activities here, things that I never had the chance to do in the demon realm.

We certainly didn't have pumpkins lying around in wait for being carved.

"Ta-da!" Willow turned around her pumpkin, showing me the opposite side. "It's you!" She'd carved a cat out, complete with a tail and glowing eyes.

I laughed. "That's… amazing."

"What'd you do?" She asked, coming around to see mine.

Sheepishly, I stepped away, revealing my design. "I know it's not very good, but…"

"A tree?" She made a face. "Why?"

"It's… supposed to be a willow tree." I winced.

"Oh." Our eyes connected, and I could detect a faint blush on her cheekbones. "That's… *Damien.*" She clasped her hands over her heart. "No one's ever done anything like that for me before."

I pulled her into my arms, placing a kiss on the top of her head. How did I tell her I felt the same way? No one had ever cared for me before like she did. No one had made me feel like she did.

It was crazy, since we'd known each other for two weeks, but I already felt closer to her than I did to anyone else in my life. My brother was the only person who came close, but we weren't really *friends*. Sometimes it just felt like a business relationship between us.

"You deserve it," I said instead. "Besides, you did the same for me."

Her cheeks deepened in color. "Yeah. I guess I did."

Leaning down, I took her lips in mine, a gentle peck to convey my gratitude, but it slowly deepened into more. Running my fingers through her hair, I reveled in the way the silky strands slipped through them.

"Damien," she mumbled against my lips. "I want—"

"I know," I agreed, lifting her up by the hips, reveling in the feeling of her as she wrapped her legs around my back, holding on.

I carried her to the bedroom, my ever hardening erection pressed against her center.

And then I stripped her down, and we got lost in each other.

In these feelings I couldn't quite acknowledge.

We were both insatiable, like last night had only lit a fire in us we couldn't quell. Once wouldn't be enough.

It would never be enough.

* * *

"I need more time." I hated bringing myself this low, begging him for this, but I had no other choice. I needed more time with Willow. I couldn't let her go yet.

And that was why I was here, on my knees, bringing myself to a position I'd sworn never to be for my brother.

Zain crossed his arms over his chest, raising an eyebrow. "Why? What exactly are you afraid of, little brother?"

I grit my teeth. "You know exactly what I'm afraid of."

"I need her." He sighed. "You can't keep me away forever."

160

"Just… give me until Halloween, at least. Please. Willow needs her sister."

"Very well." My brother waved his hand, dismissing me. "You have until then."

I closed my eyes, letting the shadows take me home.

To Willow.

The only place I wanted to be.

SEVENTEEN
WILLOW

There was something about knowing I had someone at home waiting for me that made me giddier to leave the shop each day than I ever had before. Maybe that was what made the time pass quicker than it felt like it ever had before.

Damien.

I smiled to myself as I wiped down the counter, eyes focused on the clock, waiting for Eryne to come in for her shift. I'd been cleaning for the last hour, and as soon as she took over, I'd be free.

To head home to my demon, and whatever festive activity we'd choose for tonight. In the last week, we'd watched countless Halloween movies—I had to educate him, after all—as well as tried all my favorite kinds of candy. I was determined to find something he liked. I wasn't below resorting to black licorice, if that was what it took.

I especially liked it when he'd give up halfway through and pin me to the couch, kissing me roughly with that mouth I'd grown so fond of. Sometimes it felt like he was trying to commit every inch of me to memory, like if he kissed me enough, I would never fade from his thoughts.

Thinking about him leaving—my house, my bed, my life—hurt, so I tried not to. To just appreciate this thing between us, no matter how short-lived it would be.

We hadn't talked about our feelings, though. Every time he brought it up, I brushed him off. Everything was so good, and I didn't want to ruin it by talking about the future.

I had to remind myself that no matter how he made me feel—when he was so tender and caring with me—that this wasn't a relationship.

But October was coming to a close faster than I'd have liked.

So was the month he'd promised me. The town's big Halloween party was only a few days away.

Our pumpkins we'd carved were now sitting on my front porch, complete with flickering lights I enchanted to never burn out. Sure, I could have used electric LED candles, but where was the fun in that?

Some nights, we would sit on the porch swing outside as the sun set, hardly speaking a word. It was almost like we didn't need to.

And losing ourselves in each other's bodies every night… I was pretty sure Damien had turned me into some sort of sex demon, because I couldn't get enough of him. He'd leave me exhausted, totally boneless, and I would fall asleep as soon as my head hit the pillow.

I grinned, just thinking about whatever he had planned for me tonight. Even as I taught him human things, I was learning new things about myself too—my preferences. How he could key up my body and turn me on with just the faintest of touches. The whisper of a touch, the brush of his powers against me, or the feeling of his sharp canines brushing against my throat.

I shivered at the thought.

"You look smitten," Luna murmured as I spun into the kitchen.

"What?" I came to a stop, attempting not to drop my armful of dishes that I'd brought with me, using my free time to tidy up the front of the bakery. Were my cheeks pink? "N-no." How vehemently could I deny it?

Especially when it was true.

Okay, I *was* smitten. Too smitten. It was a problem. "I… I like him, okay?" I dropped my shoulders in defeat as I dumped the dirty pitchers and spoons into the sink. "It's never been like this for me before."

"And he feels the same way?" Luna asked. I could tell she was skeptical of Damien—and maybe that was fair. It wasn't like I'd really told her what was happening between us. Who he was.

"I mean, I haven't asked him for sure, but I think so." It felt like he did.

"What are you afraid of?" She probed, and I folded, just like always.

I didn't want to say it, but I couldn't stop the words that slipped from my lips. My deepest fears, brought to life. "That he'll leave. Decide I'm not worth it and walk away."

"Willow." Luna's voice was soft. Reassuring. And yet filled with so much care and compassion, my heart nearly broke at the love pouring out of her. "You don't even know how amazing you are, do you?"

"You *have* to say that." I shook my head. "You're my little sister."

"No." She shook her head. "I mean it. You always take care of everyone but yourself. Even me. It's time to put yourself first. Besides, if that man really leaves, he's not who I thought he was, anyway."

"He's a demon," I murmured, turning around and facing the sink.

"What?"

"Nothing." Turning on the sink, I let the dishes fill up with water before washing them.

When I finally turned back around, Luna rolled her eyes at me. "I'm just saying. I've seen the way he looks at you."

"Like what?" I was almost too afraid to say it.

"Like you're his entire world."

"Oh."

"Yeah. *Oh.*" She pinched my arm. "If you don't tell that man how you feel about him, I'll do it myself."

"*Luna,*" I complained, drawing out her name. "It's still new. I don't want to ruin it."

She raised an eyebrow, and I held up my arms. "Fine, fine! I'm going home now."

Luna raised her fingers, giving me a little wave. "Tell your man I say hello."

I rolled my eyes as I grabbed my stuff, heaving my bag over my shoulder. "Don't stay too long yourself," I added. "Goddess knows you could use some time away from this place. You practically live here, I swear."

She didn't dignify *that* with a response.

Waving goodbye to Eryne at the counter on my way out, I headed home.

To the demon waiting for me.

* * *

"Damien!" I shouted, tossing my keys on the front table and my tote bag onto my designated stuff chair. "I'm home!"

Part of me liked being able to say that to someone. Sure, I used to say it to my sister—and to my cat—but now, knowing that the being in this house was mine, even if it was just for now, made me giddy.

"I brought home some of the extra scones Luna made today," I added, carrying the box into the kitchen. "They're pumpkin and chocolate chip." I was watering just thinking about the contents. As if I hadn't had two this morning.

"What are we doing tonight?" His arms wrapped around my shoulders as he placed a kiss on my temple. "Does this town have any other fun festivities I should know about?"

"Have you ever gone bobbing for apples before?"

Damien looked horrified. "Willow. What?"

I laughed, unable to keep a straight face. "I'm kidding. Though you wouldn't believe what some of the kids here can do. They're champs." I brushed a hair back from my face, grabbing the other bag of supplies I'd brought home with me. "I thought maybe we could make caramel apples and then just watch a movie. There's a new one on tonight."

Slowly, I was going to convert him to like my silly Halloween romance movies. I had no idea what he watched before meeting me, but I'd watch them all year long if people let me. We'd already watched Halloweentown and Hocus Pocus, two of my favorites, but I had an entire cabinet full of options.

"Mmm. Sounds good. But I have an idea before that."

"You do?"

He nodded, taking my hand and guiding me outside to the back patio.

"Is this…" I looked back at him. "Did you do all of this?"

Damien gave me another nod. Not only had he strung a canopy of lights over the backyard, but he'd laid out a blanket—laid out with a complete picnic and a glass of wine. The last rays of sunset showed through the trees, lighting up their orange and yellow leaves. I loved New England in the fall. Truly, even though I could have moved anywhere, I couldn't imagine being anywhere but here.

"It's probably not as good as the one at the festival, but…" He pulled the lid off of a dish, exposing a freshly made pumpkin pie.

"Damien…" My eyes watered. "You made me my favorite pie?"

"Of course." He kissed my forehead as we both settled onto the blanket. "Anything for my little witch."

"You gotta stop spoiling me," I murmured, staring up at his chiseled jaw as I settled against him. "Or I'm never going to let you go."

My admission was too close to the truth, and I promptly shut my mouth. I didn't want to ruin this moment with that conversation. It could wait.

He gave me a lopsided grin before starting to unveil the rest of the dishes. It must have taken him all day to do this. Damien placed a glass of wine in my hands, and I took a sip, enjoying the flavors as they blossomed on my tongue.

The lighting, the ambiance, it was all simply perfect. He was perfect. How could he be anything but? He'd come into my life in the most unexpected of ways, but he fit so perfectly.

Fit with *me* so perfectly.

I gave a happy sigh, leaning my head against his shoulder. The aroma of the food wafted towards my nose, and I was suddenly starving. I couldn't wait to try everything he'd made for us.

"Oh. And one more thing." He pressed a button, and a low, soothing melody started playing. "Now it really is perfect."

I shook my head in disbelief. He'd really thought of everything, hadn't he?

Which led me to the question I'd been asking myself for the last week…

How was I going to let him go?

* * *

"I'm so full," I bemoaned, talking to the black cat who laid at my feet.

I didn't know why he still insisted on sleeping in cat form some nights, but part of me didn't want to complain, either. As much as I preferred falling asleep wrapped in his arms, I enjoyed having his little bundle of weight at my feet.

His little vampire teeth were visible as he laid on his back, all sprawled out in cat form on my bed. One paw was dangling over the edge. Damien in cat form was simply adorable.

Moving my hand to scratch his head, he nuzzled against my palm. I stifled a giggle. "You're pretty cute like this, you know?"

Damien shifted in a flash, lying on his arm on top of my comforter, his fangs still poking out over his bottom lip. "And what about now, little witch?"

Much like that first night where I'd kicked him off the bed, he'd shifted completely naked. I was wearing my favorite nightgown, which wasn't particularly sexy. And with him draped on top of my bed like *that*…

"Damien!" I flushed red, throwing my arm over my face. "You can't just—"

Nuzzling his face into my neck, he ran his sharp canines over the sensitive skin of my throat. "Can't what?"

I wondered what it would feel like if he were to bite me. He didn't need to drink blood, as far as I was aware. At least, I'd never seen him do it—but did those sharp teeth serve another purpose? Every time they touched my skin, they sent sensations straight to my clit. Like I could explode with one touch.

"Do *that*." Not looking, I gestured at his body.

Not that I needed to look at him to know what his body looked like. I'd memorized every line, traced every one of his abs with my tongue. I'd gotten more comfortable with him than I had with any human who I'd ever slept with in the past.

They all paled compared to Damien, anyway. My passionate, caring, thorough lover, who knew exactly how to use his tongue and fingers.

And don't get me started on when he used his magic on me.

In a flash, he'd moved, pinning me to the bed, his muscular arms positioned over me. "What about now?"

"*Please*," I moaned, not sure what I was begging for. Him to stop, or him to keep going?

He kissed at my throat, his talented tongue making me squirm within a matter of minutes.

More. I needed him brushing his shadows over my nipples and my clit.

I wondered to what extent he could use his powers—how *else* he might use those tendrils of darkness on me. Inside of me—

Damien's nostrils flared, like he could smell my growing arousal. Sense how wet I was getting, just from his teeth and my lewd thoughts. "What are you thinking about, little witch?"

"Nothing." I blushed, shaking my head.

He raised an eyebrow. "Willow." He pressed his hips into mine, and

I let out a small moan. "Tell me, baby."

I shook my head as he started working my nightgown up my hips, exposing my purple underwear covered in ghosts.

He rocked into me, pressing up against that thin fabric, as his lips connected with the pulse point on my neck. Damien's fangs dragged over the sensitive skin—not enough to pierce it, but to send shudders of pleasure through me. "Tell me," he murmured, "and I'll give you what you want."

"I-I was thinking about how else you could use your shadows." I knew my cheeks were as pink as ever. "Besides just... *you know.*"

He chuckled roughly, nibbling on my ear. "Do you want me to fill you up, baby? Stuff you so full of me you can barely breathe?"

"*Yes,*" I choked out. "I want that."

Who was this girl, and what had she done with Willow? I'd never had the courage to ask for what I wanted before. Even if I was still embarrassed. Even if he had to encourage the words.

It was like I'd come to life completely from just his one touch.

And I wanted more, and more, and more.

The question was... would I ever stop wanting him?

EIGHTEEN
DAMIEN

This girl. My little witch.

"Willow," I rasped out, already out of my mind just from her suggestion. I'd never done *that*, not with anyone. But what she was asking me… "Are you sure?"

Her eyelids fluttered hazily as I pressed myself against her again.

"Mhm. Please, Damien. I need you inside of me."

Pulling her cute little nightdress off her body, I took my time to kiss down her collarbone and stomach before coming to her hips.

Purple ghosts. "Fuck me, these are so adorable." Her collection of Halloween undergarments never failed to make me smile. I kissed one of her hip bones, and then the other. "You drive me crazy, Willow."

She hummed in response as I slowly peeled her panties off, nipping her inner thighs as I went.

"Come here," I said, laying down and patting my chest. "I want you to sit on my face."

Willow scrambled to sit on my chest, her thighs parted around me.

"Are you sure?" She looked concerned, like she didn't know that I would die without this. That I'd been thirsty for her taste only.

"Mhm. Let me taste that sweet pussy, baby. I want you to come all over my mouth."

"O-kay," she said, and I helped guide her up to my mouth, my hands on the outside of her thighs as she settled her cunt over my lips.

With the first slide of my tongue against her wet folds, her hands darted out to hold on to the headboard.

"*Oh*," she cried. Her legs were squeezing against my head, my nose pressed against her clit as she rode my face, and with each flick of my tongue inside of her, she moved in earnest, rocking her hips as I licked up every drop of her.

I kept up my pace, those slow languid licks, even as her hips moved faster, and I could feel how close she was getting, the tiny tremors of pleasure that ran through her.

There was nothing I wanted more than to feel her orgasm on my tongue, so I didn't stop. Even as she cried my name. As her thighs tightened their grip.

Let go, I coaxed her. *Come for me, little witch*. I added my thumb to her clit, rubbing it in circles as I kept fucking her with my tongue.

My girl didn't hold back. And when she came, body shuddering, her insides squeezing around my tongue, it was better than anything I'd ever imagined.

And so was the realization that I didn't want to do this with anyone else. Never again. Because Willow was mine. Her intoxicating coffee and vanilla scent had crept into my veins, and I couldn't get her out. Didn't want to get her out.

I wanted to feast on her taste for the rest of my life. One human lifetime wasn't enough. I needed more.

This may have started because of the bond I sensed between us, but I knew the truth now. I'd felt it creeping up on me over the last week, but there was no doubt in my mind as she let go for me.

I was an idiot to think anything else could have been the cause.

Guiding her body off of my face after the aftershocks of her orgasm had subsided, I gave her a smirk. "You taste so damn good, baby."

Her cheeks were pink—maybe from her orgasm—but I liked how my words affected her.

Willow leaned down to kiss me, not hesitating, even knowing that she'd taste herself on my lips.

Fuck, but that was hot.

She perched herself on my torso, each one of her strong thighs positioned against my legs, and I could feel her wetness pooling there as her tongue battled mine.

It made me even more eager to bury myself in her. Feeling how ready she was. How eager she was to take my cock.

"Fuck," I muttered as she pulled away, biting my lower lip as she disconnected our lips. I was painfully hard—something she'd be aware of soon, if she couldn't already feel my hardness pressed against her ass. "Need you," I panted. My hands went to her hips, loving the way her body felt in my hands.

Would I ever be able to get over it? How perfectly we fit together? How each one of her curves felt like they were made for my hands?

She rocked backwards, rubbing her cute little ass against my cock, and I let out a deep moan.

"Willow—" I warned, but clearly, I hadn't needed to at all.

Because she picked her hips up, even as I kept my hands on her waist, and positioned herself over me. Ready to spear herself on my cock.

And when Willow guided me inside of her, it was all I could do to squeeze my eyes shut, trying not to blow my load too soon. Being inside of her—*fuck*, nothing compared.

She splayed her hand over her stomach. "Gods. I can feel you *everywhere.*"

"Feels like you were made for me, little witch." The truth came spilling out from my lips. It was true—even if I hadn't meant to say it yet. But the pieces fit. We… fit.

I let Willow set the pace, moving back and forth on my cock, feeling the way her body jolted each time her clit hit the base of my shaft.

"Damien, I—I can't," she cried. "I'm going to come."

Yes. Yes. Give me everything, I agreed, watching her tits bounce as she lost herself in the sensations.

"Tell me you're mine," I commanded, needing to hear the words. Needing to know that what I felt was true—real.

"I'm yours," she agreed, rolling her hips as she rode me. "All yours. Only yours."

"Mine," I repeated, grabbing her neck to bring it down to me so I could fuse our mouths together. My hips thrust up to meet hers, and I could feel the way she was clenching down around me. So close.

Fuck, I loved kissing her. I didn't think I'd ever tire of taking her mouth. She tasted sweet, and I could still detect a hint of the pumpkin pie she'd eaten earlier.

I fucking loved her addiction to pumpkin.

Maybe I just plain loved *her*.

But it was too soon to tell her that. This was too new. And I certainly wasn't some fool of a human who would blurt it out during sex.

"Damien," she cried. "I need—"

That was what unleashed the beast inside of me, and I couldn't hold back any longer. I used my hold on her waist to help her move—up and down, up and down, each slide of her against my cock, providing me with another moan.

My shadows curled possessively around her body, pressing up against practically every erogenous zone. Her throat, a light squeeze. Her nipples, that sucking sensation I knew drove her crazy. And one pressed against her back hole, nothing more than a finger's press, but she cried out. I used my powers like hands, cupping her breasts, squeezing them, even as I helped her ride me, watching her bounce on my cock. Her breasts moved with the motion, and I was in awe as I watched her.

Willow's head fell back as her eyes shut. *It's too much,* she sobbed into my mind.

You can take it, I soothed, my hips moving in time with hers as we worked together. Giving her everything she'd asked for—everything she needed. *Eyes open,* I added, nuzzling my forehead against hers. "Want to watch you come," I murmured.

She came without warning, a squeeze around my cock, like she wanted to milk me dry. I was so deep—basically pressed up against her womb, and somehow, the idea of that made me tip over the edge.

Of painting her insides with my cum. Filling her up.

She'd asked me to that first night, and, like a fool, I couldn't resist. Something about knowing she would fall asleep with my cum dripping out of her made me feral. Weak. Uncontrollable.

I could feel the telltale signs of my own release—my balls tightened, and I held Willow in place, with me buried to the hilt inside of her—as I spilled every last drop.

And even when we'd collapsed on the bed—boneless and spent—I didn't pull out of her.

"Mmm," Willow murmured sleepily, curling against me. "I think you've ruined me for anyone else, Damien."

That was the idea, baby, I thought, but I didn't say it out loud.

I just wrapped my arms around her and fell into a deep sleep.

* * *

I woke up with sweat dripping down my back, pulse racing. Willow laid next to me, the sheets tugged up her body as she dozed peacefully.

Ripping the sheets from my body, I launched myself out of the bed, silently slipping out of the room. Something was suffocating me, and all I knew was I needed to get out of there, needed air, needed space, needed—

In the kitchen, I guzzled down a glass of water.

Why was it bothering me so much? But I knew why. Even if it wasn't real.

Closing my eyes, all I could see was *red*. Blood. They'd…

"Are you okay?" Willow wrapped her arms around my bare torso. "I heard you get up." She'd pulled a robe on, the soft fabric brushing against my skin in a warm embrace.

No. No, I wasn't okay. When I turned to her, I knew my face looked pained.

"Just a bad dream," I murmured, burying my face in her hair. Inhaling her scent.

Reminding myself that she was here.

And nothing was going to happen to her. I'd make sure of that.

"What happened?" Her voice was quiet as she rubbed the muscles in my back—soothing, like she could get rid of all my tension just from her touch. My magical fucking girl.

I shook my head against her hair. "I don't want to talk about it."

"Damien…" Her hands moved down to my lower back. "You can talk to me, you know. I'm here for you."

I heaved out a sigh. "It's not…"

How would she understand? I couldn't even figure out my own irrational fears and worries, and trying to explain them to her? Impossible.

Especially when there was so much I was still keeping from her. But I'd tell her soon. All of it. The truth about us.

Right now, I just wanted to hold her. To remind myself that she was here. That *this* was real. No matter what would come in the future, I had this.

When I made eye contact with her, she looked up at me with such bright eyes. So hopeful. So curious.

Why wasn't I letting her in?

"I'm scared," I said, my voice so low it was essentially a whisper.

"Of what?" Her arms tightened around my back as she hugged my chest.

Losing you. I couldn't say it out loud, so I said it into her mind instead.

"Oh." Willow's sweet voice slipped out.

Not wanting to go another minute without holding her, I wrapped my arms around her thighs, lifting her up so I could carry her back into the bedroom, just like that. Willow wrapped her legs around me, clinging on like a baby bear.

She didn't unwrap her arms from around my back even as I sat on the bed.

"Little witch," I murmured, running my hands through the silky strands of her hair. "You have to let go now."

"Uh-uh." Her lips curled up into a smile. "You're always taking care of me. Let me take care of you for once. Till your dream goes away."

I didn't think it ever would, but I wouldn't tell her that.

"Okay." I wouldn't argue with her when I loved the way she snuggled against me.

Like she was *mine*.

After we'd gotten comfortable on the bed, Willow curled up next to my body once again.

Laying her head on my shoulder, she traced circles over my bare chest. "Why don't you tell me about your family?"

"Hm?"

Of everything she could have asked… Did she even know how close that hit to home?

"You never talk about them," she said sadly. "Or your mom. Not really. I want to know everything about you, Damien."

I'd opened my mouth to tell her that wasn't true, that I talked about them, but I couldn't deny it. And knowing what was between us, what I felt for her… I didn't want to hold it in anymore.

So I started talking. I told her about my mom, and how she'd been my favorite person in the entire world. How when she'd died, leaving me alone with my father and half-brother, there had been a vacancy that could never quite be filled. A hole in my heart.

One she'd filled.

How I wished my mom could have met Willow. Seen what an amazing woman she was.

I left out the blood.

I could still feel it against my fingers. Hear my voice screaming out for help. But the memory of my mother's death was being overwritten with my dream about Willow's.

And even so… I didn't stop. I told her about growing up in the demon realm. Training to fight in my father's battles. Serving as his right-hand man. King of the Demons.

And, later, being relegated to an over-glorified errands boy. Serving my brother, the Crown Prince. Who'd take over for our father one day, after he found his bride.

Long after she'd fallen asleep, I still kept holding her, stroking her hair, mystified that out of every person in this world, she was the one chosen for me.

I love you, I thought to myself alone, cradling her body into mine.

* * *

I tugged at the collar of my costume for the town's Halloween party. The damn thing itched my neck, and I still couldn't figure out how I'd let Willow convince me to dress up like this.

The truth was, all it took was one flash of those green eyes, and I'd cave every time.

So she'd dressed us up—in Victorian-style costumes, as a Vampire and a Witch.

"You can put those pointy teeth to use," my witch teased me, her thumb running over a sharp canine.

"I think you just want to find out what it feels like when I bite you," I teased her back.

Her cheeks pinked. "Maybe."

I purred in response. I wanted to claim her. To see my mark on her neck.

Everything felt so right. I knew I could no longer keep denying the truth. How much I loved her. Why we fit together so perfectly. Why everything with her was *more*.

But it also terrified me to admit it. To say the words. What if she didn't want *that?* Every time I'd tried to bring up what we were, she'd brushed me off. Had she only ever been looking for this? Something casual?

My deadline was looming. I'd asked my brother for an extra month. Not even being the son of the Demon King could deny what was next.

The fates had foretold that the next demon king would marry a great witch. I was sent here to do just that. To find Zain's consort—his fated *mate*—not a woman to call my own. Perks of being the illegitimate son of the current Demon King, I supposed. I was forced to serve Zain's bidding. Like finding him a wife in this accursed place was anything short of easy. But of all the demons, I had the easiest time blending in. Being unnoticed.

Passing as human. Four months had passed since my brother had sent me to the human realm searching for *his bride.*

Despite my little roadblock—I'd found her, to my worst horror.

Because the witch who was fated to sit by my brother's side… was none other than Willow's sister. *Luna.*

Time was running out.

The worst part was I knew Willow didn't belong with me, anyway. She was too bright and beautiful to go back to my world of darkness. This place—this town of witches—it was where she belonged. I could feel it. Though that didn't stop me from wanting her.

I couldn't believe that she'd been here for twenty-eight years and I hadn't known that she was here. That she existed at all. But… in all my years of life, I'd hardly come to the human realm. I'd never expected to find my mate here.

"There's my handsome demon," my girl beamed, coming to stand by my side and sliding her arm around my waist.

"Hi, Wil," I murmured before dropping a kiss on the top of her head.

"Hi." Her eyes lit up. She'd curled her hair, letting it fall down around her in waves, and an old-fashioned witch hat sat on top. My witch looked perfect, down to the little star earrings and her striped stockings.

I was obsessed. I couldn't wait to take them off of her later.

"You look beautiful. I love this." I fiddled with the cape that was tied around her neck.

She giggled. "It's not too much?"

I groaned. "That would be impossible. Nothing you do could ever be too much."

"Oh." Her cheeks pinked.

How did I get her to understand I meant every word? I brushed a hair away from her face before playing with her earring. "You look stunning. It's so you. I can't imagine you being anything less than that." I dragged a finger down her throat. "I almost don't want anyone else to see you like this."

She kissed my cheek. "You're the sweetest demon I've ever met."

"I'm the *only* demon you've ever met," I grunted.

"That you know of."

"And we're going to keep it that way," I growled, pinning her in my arms as she laughed.

Kissing her, because if this was all the time we had left, I wanted to savor every bit of it.

Especially if it was all we'd have left.

NINETEEN

WILLOW

All Hallows' Eve. My favorite night of the year was here.

The air was filled with children laughing, candy wrappers tearing, and the smell of sugar in the air. Damien was at my side, his hand curled around mine, hardly an inch left between us.

It was the perfect Halloween night, the moon high in the sky, shining down on us.

The entire town was abuzz with life, and for once, everything felt right. The loneliness that had plagued me just over a month ago was gone, and it all had to do with the demon who had chosen me.

My heart was full. Lighter.

It was too soon, wasn't it? A month was hardly enough time to get to know someone. Let alone to fall in love with them. And yet… I had.

I loved him.

Dammit, I'd fallen in love with my demon, all else be damned.

And I knew in my heart—I wanted him to stay. I didn't want this to end.

"Why?" I stopped, staring at the ground. "Why are you still here?" I'd avoided this conversation for too long. But I needed to hear it now. Needed to say the things I'd avoided out of fear of him leaving.

Because I wanted him to *stay*.

"You know why." He narrowed his eyes. "You can't tell me you don't feel this too. This thing between us."

"But…" I couldn't say that, because I *did* feel it. The golden thread, tied between us, that tether that was always pulling me to him. Like the fates had intertwined our lives together.

"Say it," he murmured. "It's the reason we can communicate with each other's minds. Why just being in your presence calms me. How everything always feels so right. There's a word for it between your people, too."

But there was a part of me that was scared to utter the words. Because if I did, that would make it *real*.

And if it was real, and he still chose to leave…

Then I'd be opening myself up for heartbreak. Because everyone always left me. Everyone but Luna. And even she'd chosen to move out instead of staying with me in our parents' old house.

But that string of fate… *Soulmates*.

We couldn't be. It wasn't *possible*. Right? I hadn't even believed in soulmates when we first met. The idea that there was someone out there meant for me felt like a truth that I couldn't deny, no matter how hard I tried. Not anymore.

There was a rightness when we were together, a peace I felt anytime I was in his arms.

Soulmates. It clicked in place. And I knew it was true. That this was *real.*

That I couldn't deny it anymore.

"You're…" I stared up at him in shock. "How is that possible? Demons don't have souls."

How could we be destined for each other? Of all the people the fates could have chosen for me… Why was it the demon who stood in front of me now?

How could it have been anyone else?

Damien frowned. "Where'd you get the idea that we don't have souls?"

"W-what?" I stuttered. "That's what they taught us growing up. Why you make deals to take our souls—"

He huffed out a response. "Whoever's been teaching you about demons needs to get their facts straight, little witch." My demon smoothed down my hair. "Your education has been thoroughly lacking."

Though he was right. The witches' deep hatred of demonkind had given me multiple pauses throughout our relationship.

Our *relationship.* Gods. We'd ignored the word, hadn't given it a term, but that's what we'd been doing all along, hadn't we?

I'd been falling in love with him, and I had hardly given him a label besides *roommate* or friend.

"Don't change the subject, Damien," I said, crossing my arms over my chest. I wanted to be giddy over this realization—the idea that we were fated for each other—but all I could see was doubts and fears. "This still doesn't make any sense."

Besides, he *was* leaving. It wasn't like this changed anything. I was mortal, and he would live hundreds more years. He had to go back to the demon realm. To the brother he served.

"You're—why not?"

"Do you really think anyone is going to believe it?"

"You're my mate, Willow." He cupped my cheeks. "The fates—they made you for me. It doesn't matter what anyone else thinks. Just what we think."

"But I'm nothing special. And you're…" I gestured at him. "You."

"Willow. Look at you." He cleared his throat. "I… I'm the one who's not worthy of you." He got down on his knees, dressed in his silly costume, holding both of my hands in his. "I've been in awe of you every single day since I first saw you. Your kindness, generosity… The way everyone loves you, because how could they not?" Damien shook his head. "You deserve better than me. But I want you, anyway. When I picture you with someone else, I want to tear them limb from limb. The thought of someone else touching you… No."

"Damien…" My heart stuttered in my chest. No one had ever said anything like that to me before. No one had ever made me feel so cared for—worshiped.

Even if this thing between us was the reason, if he only cared for me because we were mates, I still had him.

And I'd never felt so loved before.

Even if he hadn't said the words.

I hadn't either, after all.

* * *

After our little confession, we went to my cousin Cait's Halloween Party. She'd decked out the entire house, from lights and a fake skeleton on her porch to cobwebs hanging in every corner.

She popped out wearing a pair of fishnet tights, a ruffled top and a corset tied over her skirt. The bandana she'd tied around her forehead and her chunky jewelry just added to the pirate vibes.

"Willow!" Cait grinned, her orange hair glinting in the light. "You made it!" She looked at my demon. "And you brought your man, too."

"You look incredible," I said, blushing at her comment. *My man.* It was true, but even then, it was still so new. "Thanks for inviting us."

"Of course! The rest of the girls are all here." Cait's familiar, a Russian blue cat, jumped on her shoulder, nuzzling at her cheek. "Hey, Thunder." She scratched underneath the cat's chin before it jumped down, coming to stand in front of Damien.

The gray cat sat, staring up at my demon, letting out a small meow.

Damien raised an eyebrow before bending down, holding out his hand. Thunder sniffed at his hand before brushing against it, back and forth, beginning to purr.

My cousin's eyes were wide. "He doesn't do this with anyone but me."

Damien rubbed the top of the cat's head before standing back up, sliding back against my side. "What can I say?" His voice was rough. "Cats love me."

Says the cat. I chuckled. Cait didn't know how loaded that statement was.

"This is nice," he murmured a few minutes later at my side, drinking a beer from a plastic cup. They'd gotten orange ones and doodled fake jack-o'-lantern faces on them. It made me smile seeing my demon holding something so silly.

"Sure," I agreed. "Until the coven descends."

"What?"

I raised an eyebrow. "Are you ready for the interrogation?"

Like clockwork, the other ten members of our coven appeared in front of us.

Rina. Wendy. The twins who ran the renovation and construction business, Tammy and Talley. Olive. Constance. Celeste. Iris. Sophie. Gretchen. All witches of different shapes and sizes, a sea of different hair colors between them. Lavender, light blue, even neon green. And yet one thing united all of us. Our coven. The only one missing was Luna.

Cait stood sheepishly in the back. *Sorry,* she mouthed.

I shrugged. It was what our coven did. We had each other's backs, and they were going to make sure he had only the noblest of intentions.

As long as they didn't know what happened behind closed doors, I was fine with that. I wanted to keep my sex life private, thank you very much.

I loved all of them, but these girls could *gossip.*

"We heard you brought your man," Wendy offered, smiling as she sipped on her drink, her blonde hair bobbing with the motion. She'd worn a red costume with a hood, even carrying a broom along with her. "I'm Wendy," she told Damien.

He looked her up and down before turning to me. "The Good Witch?" We'd watched *Casper Meets Wendy* the other night.

I laughed. "It's a little on the nose, isn't it?"

He wiggled his, and I could almost see the motion of him in cat form, his whiskers moving.

Rina, standing at Wendy's side, just laughed. Her short brown bob somehow further complemented her tanned skin tone, as if she was striving to look as far from her namesake—Sabrina—as possible.

"Damien, this is my coven." I gave a small sigh as I gestured to all of them, giving him each of their names as he shook hands and said hello.

I had to give him credit for not turning and running at the sheer sight of them. Eleven witches would have made anyone nervous, but he just took it all in stride.

The rest of them launched into their questions.

Maybe I'd made a mistake keeping them away from him so far. I didn't think so, though. I was glad we'd had this month practically to ourselves. To get to know each other. For those feelings to grow naturally between us. Sure, we were *soulmates*—fated to be together before we'd even been born, but it was deeper than that.

And maybe I just enjoyed having him to myself.

"So, Damien, how long are you sticking around Pleasant Grove?" I heard Rina ask as I tuned back into the conversation. They'd all been rapid firing, and Damien had been answering all of their questions patiently.

He looked at me, an eyebrow raised. "I haven't exactly decided yet."

Maybe that was what triggered my fears. He was my soulmate, but he wouldn't stay?

"I think that's it for questions now." I tugged at his arm, pulling him away from the group. I didn't even apologize to my coven for leaving so abruptly.

"Can we talk?"

Damien nodded. Maybe he sensed the discontent I felt inside of me. The dread I felt at his eventual departure.

Maybe it was time we had that long overdue conversation. About what we *were* and my *feelings*. Luna was right. She always was.

I loved him, and he was leaving.

I loved him, and I hadn't told him.

TWENTY
DAMIEN

"Wil. What's wrong?" I rubbed my thumb over her knuckles, back and forth, as we stood in the backyard of her cousin's party.

I could feel the anxiety pulsing through her veins. I thought I'd reassured her earlier, but clearly it hadn't been enough.

"It's nothing. But it's just… been a month." She looked down at the ground, avoiding my eyesight.

"A month?" I raised an eyebrow. "What does that have to do with anything?"

Willow frowned. "You said you'd stay for a month."

Oh. I hadn't promised her any longer. "Fuck. Baby. That was before…" *Us.* Before I'd realized I was in love with her. Before everything had changed.

"Don't go. Please." Willow's green eyes filled with unshed tears, sparkling in the light. "I couldn't..." She swallowed roughly. "I couldn't bear it if you were gone."

"Willow..." I pulled her into my body, letting her bury her face in my chest as I flattened my palms against her back. "I'd never leave you, my little witch."

"You promise?" She looked up at me, and I almost dropped to my knees right there.

Fuck, but I loved her.

"With everything that I am, I'm yours." I kissed her forehead. "Forever."

She slumped against me, giving me her full weight. "I didn't want to lose you, but I felt so guilty asking you to stay, too." Her head stayed buried in my chest, her words slightly muffled through my t-shirt. "I know you have responsibilities and things, and that's your home, but..."

"You're my home now," I said, meaning it with every fiber of my being. "My mate." I kissed her forehead.

Willow pulled away, and I reached out to grab her wrist. There was still more I needed to say. Things I had to explain. "Listen, there's something I should tell you—"

"Have you seen Luna?" She interrupted, looking around with a frown on her face at her cousin's backyard, and then into the house. "She said she was going to meet us hours ago."

I shook my head. "Maybe something's keeping her?"

She whipped out her phone, sending a quick message to her sister. Pacing back and forth, she waited for a response.

It didn't come.

Worry crept into my veins.

"I'm going to try tracking her," she said, pressing a few more buttons on the screen. "It says she's… still at the bakery. But…"

"Why don't we go check on her?" I offered.

If it gave her the peace of mind, then that was worth it. Especially so we could get back to enjoying the festivities. Not that I cared one bit about spending time with the witches in town, but I knew what it meant to Willow. How much these people meant to her.

Luna was probably fine, in her apartment, getting ready. Or maybe she'd chosen to make another batch of sweets at the bakery. I'd lost count of how many times my witch had come home with a box of something her sister had made.

Willow nodded, heading out the back fence. Following the streets to downtown, she pulled me towards their shop.

The windows were dark except for the soft glow of the lights strung across the counter. No one was inside. The whole place was silent.

"Maybe she's getting ready upstairs." Willow rushed around to the side door, rushing up the stairs two at a time. She reached for the handle, pausing to look at me. "It's… unlocked."

"Get behind me," I said. What if someone had broken in? Or were still inside?

But when I opened the door, Willow peeking around my arm, the apartment was deathly still. Dark. Quiet.

Empty.

We looked through all the rooms, but she was gone—without a trace—her cell phone sitting on the kitchen island.

Even her cat, Selene, wasn't there.

The bad feeling in my gut was slowly getting worse. If she wasn't here—in town—then there was only one place she could be. Which meant that…

I closed my eyes, detecting faint traces of two different smells in the apartment. Luna's, and… my brother's. Fuck.

"Damien. Where's my sister?" She looked around the apartment frantically. "What happened to her? And Selene…"

Both of them.

"I… *Shit.*" Shaking my head, I pinched the bridge of my nose. "I thought I had more time. He came early."

"What?"

"There's something I haven't told you." My eyes connected with hers, those beautiful green showing complete concern for her sister. And hurt. Because I hadn't let her in. "It's about my brother."

"*Where. Is. Luna?*" She emphasized each word with a pause, poking at my chest. "What are you not telling me?" Those green eyes that I loved narrowed.

I was glad she didn't have gifts of fire, or I would have worried about her burning the entire building down.

I grimaced, looking over at Willow. "I think maybe… my brother took her."

"Your… Brother." She stood frozen, perfectly still in the dim lighting of the apartment's kitchen. "The half brother, the fucking *Prince of Hell?* Why would he take my sister?"

"Not hell," I said, cursing internally. *Not the time.* "But yes, that's the one. He took her back to the demon realm to…" I didn't think my witch would appreciate the whole *make her his queen* thing. "You know how demons believe in mates?" *Like we are.*

Willow nodded. "Luna's always had a knack for setting people up. I never really believed in them until…" She trailed off. *You,* the implication was clear.

"Right. Well… I haven't told you everything about why I came to your world."

She cocked her head. "What?"

"Maybe you should sit down."

The anger in her eyes flared. "I don't want to sit down. I want my *baby* sister to be sitting on her couch, safe and sound. Not in the *fucking demon realm!*"

"I know."

"She's my little sister, Damien. I was supposed to protect her. Make sure she was okay." Her voice choked up as she finally slumped onto the couch. "I can't believe your brother would kidnap her."

"He believes that, well…" I shook my head. "That she's *his* fated mate."

Surprise, Willow, I thought to myself bitterly. *My brother's a giant asshole who couldn't keep his filthy paws off your sister!*

Yeah, I was royally screwed.

"Luna?" Her jaw dropped open. "Like… he wants to…" Her brain must have been running a million miles an hour. "How long have you known about this?"

I sighed, sinking onto the floor next to her. "A while. It's why I was here."

"In Pleasant Grove?"

I nodded. Whatever had called me here when I was still in cat form, it had been right. "And the human realm. He sent me to look for her."

"And you found…" *Me.*

"Yes. Finding you, Willow… That was the happiest coincidence of my life. But I never thought Zain would be looking for your sister."

"Why didn't you tell me?" Her voice was almost a whimper. "We could have done something. Stopped this."

I shook my head. "I didn't want to lose you. And if he made me go back—"

"But now I've lost her, Damien. She's my only family. My best friend."

I pulled her into my arms as the first tears fell, holding her upright so she didn't fall onto the floor. "I know, baby. I know."

I held her as she cried in my arms, rubbing a soothing hand over her back.

"We'll get her back," I promised. "We can go tonight."

She blinked. "To the Demon Realm?"

Yes. I offered her my hand, pulling her off from the couch. "We'll go make sure she's okay. No harm will come to her, I promise you that."

Okay. Her sweet voice slipped into my mind, clutching my hand tight.

I brushed away her tears with my free hand, rubbing over her jawbone with my thumb.

I'm so sorry, I murmured into her mind.

Leading her back down the stairs, I moved to the back alley. The same one I'd opened a portal in weeks ago. The day I'd realized who Luna was.

I was thankful that most everyone in the town was currently in the town square, or milling about downtown, because no one was back here to witness this.

Opening up a portal, I commanded the shadows to do my bidding.

"Are you sure this is a good idea?" Willow murmured, clutching onto my arm as I commanded the shadows to open a portal to my brother.

"Me going there?" Her eyes were still red, and full of worry. "What about the demons?"

"I'll protect you, I promise."

"I know." Her voice didn't falter. "I'm *really* pissed at you, but I know you will." Her hand slid up my chest. "Now, let's go get my sister."

I nodded.

"Hold on tight," I instructed her, curling my arm around her wrist to hold her tight to me.

And we stepped through the darkness.

* * *

"This is... nothing like what I expected." Willow's eyes trailed over the outside of the palace, catching on all the ornate details. The polished stone shone, even with the moon high in the sky.

"What did you expect?"

"Hm. Darker. More black and red." She looked up at the sky. "An endless darkness. Blood. I don't know. Stuff like that."

"Ah." I couldn't exactly fault her for that.

I'd grown up here, so the gray palace walls didn't phase me, but I could see how they might have differed from what she expected.

The palace itself rivaled any in the human world, that much I knew. It was lavish—unrivaled in its magnificence.

"What do I call him?"

"Him?"

"Your brother."

"Ah. Well, Zain would prefer *Your Majesty* or *Your Highness*, I'm sure. But you can just call him his given name. That's what I do." I flashed her a grin. "You're not his citizen. He can't touch you."

196

"I've never met royalty before," she said, tugging down her dress.

I couldn't help but laugh when I realized we were still wearing our Halloween costumes. She really looked like a witch in her garb. Thankfully, we didn't stand out very much in them around here. The demon realm fashions hadn't changed too much over the last few centuries.

"What?" she asked, tilting her head at my chuckle.

"You realize *I'm* a prince as well, right?"

"Oh." Willow flushed. "Well…" She looked at me out of the corner of her eye. "You're different."

"Why?" I paused, tugging on her arm to bring her face to face with me. "What if I wanted you to call me *Your Majesty?*"

"Damien," she groaned, her cheeks growing even pinker. "That's not who you are to me. You're just…"

"Just what?"

My Damien.

I kissed her cheek before I guided her in through the palace doors, nodding to the guards standing at attention. *I like that even better, little witch.*

I thought you might, came her response.

The throne room's just ahead. I could feel her trembling, so I tightened my grip on her hand to reassure her. *I've got you.*

She tried to force her face into a smile, but even that couldn't mask the worry I felt pulsing through her body. *I know.*

Zain sat on his throne. Cool, calm—too calm.

"Ah, Damien. How nice to see you! I see you brought your witch."

I bared my teeth. "Where is she?"

"Who?" He cocked his head.

"My sister," Willow said, narrowing her eyes.

"Ah." Zain gave a lazy smile. "She's right here. Come on out, moonbeam." Luna walked out next to my brother, dressed in a white gossamer gown—looking pale, but not in anguish like I might have expected.

Willow choked out a sob. "Oh, thank god."

My brother whispered something into Luna's ear, and then she was down the stairs—colliding into Willow's arms for a hug.

"Are you okay?" Willow tightened her arms around her sister, like if she held tight enough, she could pretend this never happened. But it had. And it was my fault. I could have prevented all of it.

"Brother." I turned to him, face stone cold as I stepped up in front of him. "We had an agreement."

He rolled his eyes, somehow managing to look both annoyed and amused. "We had no such thing."

"I said—"

Zain shook his head. "Damien. I don't want to fight. I…" His eyes slid over to Luna, and for the first time, there seemed to be a sparkle there.

"She's her *sister*, Zain." I spat the words.

A sliver of remorse showed on his face, only for a moment. "And you're…" He looked between my witch and I.

"Yes. Willow's my mate." I chuckled. "Funny that you sent me to find *your* Queen, and it led to me finding mine as well."

He raised his eyebrows and said, "You're not planning on returning, are you?"

My muscles tensed. I wanted to stay with Willow, but I still had a vow to my brother. And yet…

"No. I want to stay with her."

"You love her."

I nodded. "Yes." With everything I was. Even if I hadn't told her that yet. I hadn't earned hearing the words from her lips. Not yet.

"Will you be staying, brother? I'd love to get to know your mate."

"I don't—"

We cut our conversation short as Willow came back to my side, sliding her arm around my waist. I wanted to bury my head in her hair, inhaling her scent. She looked up at me, and then back to her sister.

Should we go? I asked her.

Not without Luna, she replied, her voice sweet in my mind.

Of course. I nodded at my mate.

"Let's go home, Luna," Willow said, offering a hand to her sister.

But Luna shook her head, looking over at my brother. "I…" She walked back to Zain's side, standing next to him in front of the throne.

Let my brother take her hand in his.

"I know it's crazy, Wil," Luna told her sister. "But… I feel like I have to do this. To see where it goes."

"Are you sure?"

Luna nodded, the action loosening her blonde curls, bringing them down over the silky white dress. All she needed was a tiara, and she would look like a princess. "I want to do this. We made a deal."

Willow's gasp echoed through the hall. What had they bargained for? I wasn't sure I wanted to know.

"We're having a ball tonight," my brother announced. "You two are welcome to attend if you want to stay. I'll be announcing my betrothal to my *fiancee.*"

That was when I noticed the gemstone that sat on Luna's ring finger.

Willow's eyes darted to her sister.

She's really going to do it, Willow thought bitterly. *She said* yes.

It's her choice, little witch.

I know, it's just—

"Well?"

Willow's face smoothed out into a pleasant smile. Anything to hide the thoughts I felt warring in her mind. "We'd love to attend your ball, Prince Zain."

His face flattened out into a smooth smile. "Brother?"

"My witch's will is my command," I promised. I'd stay by her side, no matter what. Wherever she wanted to be; wherever she wanted to go—I'd be there. "I live to fulfill her every wish."

Zain's face curled up into a knowing smirk. *Whipped already, brother?* His face seemed to say.

If only he knew the half of it. How far gone I was for her. How much I loved her.

"We'll see you tonight then," he said.

What had we just gotten ourselves into? And what the hell had I been thinking, bringing her here? I *hadn't.*

It was just that she'd been so concerned about Luna, and I wanted to make sure she was okay. That Luna wasn't being kept against her will.

And now, I'd roped us into a party where hundreds, if not thousands, of demons would be present.

Instead of being safe and comfortable in Willow's house, enjoying the rest of her favorite holiday.

"Let's go to my rooms, little witch," I murmured into her ear.

At least we'd be safe there.

TWENTY-ONE
WILLOW

There was a first time for everything, and mine was attending a freaking *ball* in *Hell*. Okay, the demon realm might not have exactly been what I imagined, but I'd never pictured this.

Especially not the plush *giant* bed with the softest pillows I'd ever laid my head on.

"I'm never leaving this bed ever again," I groaned, laying out like a starfish and closing my eyes as I sunk into the mattress. It still smelled faintly of my demon, even if he'd been occupying my bed for the last few weeks instead of his own. I inhaled that spicy smell, loving the way it invaded my senses.

When I opened them, it was to a pair of red eyes looking down into mine. Damien had perched himself over top of me, his lips curled up into a smirk. "I'd be okay with that," he purred.

"Hm?"

"You never leaving my bed." He leaned down, pressing a kiss to my forehead.

I stretched my arms out, moving my hands in a grabby motion. "Come here."

He climbed on top of me, pinning me in place with his powerful arms.

"Are you still mad at me?"

"A little." I sighed, running my hands over the slight stubble on his jaw. I wondered what it would be like if he let it grow out. He'd kept his face and neck shaved so far, but… what about the future? "Mostly that you didn't tell me."

"I should have. But I didn't know how to tell you without telling you that you were my mate, and that was why I couldn't let you go. Couldn't leave you."

I leaned up to press a soft kiss against his lips. "I understand."

"You do?"

Nodding, I closed my eyes for a moment. "I was scared, too. That if I told you how I felt, you'd still leave."

"Never." He kissed my cheek. "You know that now, right?"

I nodded. "Yes."

The heat was pooling in my veins from the way he held his body over top of me, a desire for him to pin me down, to feel that delicious weight over mine.

"Damien," I mumbled. "What are you doing?"

"Earning my forgiveness." Kissing my neck, he worked his way up till he found my lips. "While I'd love to take my time with you—" he paused to kiss the side of my lips, "I'd need all night—" another kiss to the other side. "And we have to get ready for the party."

"Mmm." I pouted as he interlocked our lips once more before pulling away. "Not fair."

Damien gave me a little smirk before getting off the bed, pulling me up into a sitting position. "Tonight," he promised. And I knew in my heart that I'd already forgiven him. Luna was safe. He'd brought me here to give me that peace of mine. And I loved him. So much.

I heaved a sigh. "Fine."

"Besides, don't you want to see your dress?"

Perking up, I repeated, "My dress?"

He nodded. "Mhm."

Quirking an eyebrow, I clambered off the bed. "When did you have time to get me a dress?"

Damien's lips curled into a small smile as he took my hand. "I have my ways."

He tugged me into the giant dressing rooms that adjoined his room, and the sound of the door closing behind us echoed off the walls.

My jaw dropped as I saw what was hanging on the rack.

They'd detailed the dress with hundreds of tiny diamonds, which made it sparkle like the stars in the night sky. The midnight blue color blended into a deep purple as it rippled to the floor. Even more crystals detailed the sweetheart neckline of the silky gown.

"Oh. Damien." I gasped. "It's beautiful." Spinning around, I threw my arms around his neck, bringing my lips to his. "Thank you. I love it." Giggling, I kissed him again.

I love you. The words were on the tip of my tongue. But I swallowed them down. Even if he said he wouldn't leave, that he'd stay with me…

Admitting how I felt still scared me.

What if it was still too soon? I swallowed it down, refocusing on my demon's handsome face. I traced his jaw with my hand.

He nuzzled his nose against mine. "Do you want to take a bath before we get ready?"

My eyes lit up. "Together?"

Damien laughed. "Little witch. You're going to kill me." He kissed the side of my cheek. Whispered in my ear. "If we get in there together, we're not getting out. Not until you're covered in my scent and look freshly fucked, so everyone knows exactly whose you are."

"Yours," I said, burying my face in his throat. Inhaling his smell like he always did mine. "I'm yours."

He kissed me one more time, his tongue slipping into my mouth as I let out a contented sigh. I didn't want to let go, but Damien set me down, guiding me into the lavish bathroom.

After two lesser demons who appeared from nowhere had cleaned and pampered me, my hair was curled and they tied me into my gown.

The soft silky fabric was smooth against my fingers, slipping through like liquid metal.

"Wow." Damien's voice brought me out of my trance. When I looked up, I was struck by the sight of him in a stunning tuxedo. "Just… Wow."

I blushed.

"You look incredible, Willow." His voice choked up, speechless.

"You look pretty great yourself, demon." I tugged on his lapel.

He pulled away before I could kiss him, his thumb rubbing over the sparkles they'd brushed onto my cheeks. Like he knew what I wanted.

"Shall we?" He offered me an arm, and I slid mine into his.

"Yes."

And my *mate* took me to the first ball of my life.

* * *

I glanced back and forth, trying to get a glimpse of my sister.

"Relax," Damien murmured into my ear, running his hand down my spine. "I'm sure she's okay."

"I know, but…"

We didn't get to talk properly earlier. Away from prying eyes and ears.

I was sure I could trust Damien, but his brother?

There were waiters making their way through the crowded ballroom, dressed in simple black suits, distracting from their innate demon-ness. Some of them had horns, or solid black eyes that felt like they could stare right through you. There were even beings with dark black feathered wings and some with barbed tails.

"They'll want to make a grand entrance, most likely," he said as he handed me a glass of a shimmering gold liquid.

"What is this?" I asked, swirling it around.

"Demon wine."

I blinked at him. *What?*

"Just try it," he encouraged, picking up a flute of his own. "You'll like it. It's sweet."

I took a sip, and—*woah*. I'd never tasted anything like it. All the regular wine paled in comparison to the smooth liquid sliding down my throat. "*Oh.*"

"Don't drink too much of it. Gives you a bitch of a hangover." He chuckled.

I giggled, taking another drink. "It's good." My head was already feeling light after just a few sips of the drink. It would be too easy to get drunk off of it.

Another waiter passed by us, this time with a tray of food, multiple pairs of horns curling away from his forehead. A thought popped into my head.

I looked up at Damien. "What do you really look like?"

"What do you mean?" He raised a dark eyebrow.

I squinted my eyes. "Isn't this form of yours some sort of glamor? To look like a human?" If so, he'd accomplished it. The only feature on him that wasn't human-like were those piercing red eyes.

"What are you expecting?" He scoffed. "Cat ears? A tail?"

I shrugged. "I don't know. You don't have horns?" I poked at his forehead, where his dark black hair rested.

He laughed. "No. My dad does, but my mom was a regular shifter. I got her features." Damien wrapped an arm around my waist, pulling our bodies against each other's. "Why? Do you like the horns, baby?"

I shook my head, sliding a hand against the side of his face. "I like you just the way you are."

But I'm not saying no to the cat ears, either.

He laughed, brushing his lips over my pulse point, the tip of his tooth brushing over my skin. "You're cute."

Taking another sip of my wine, I couldn't help my smile.

"Look!" I exclaimed suddenly, catching a blur of white in the corner of my eye. "They're here."

The ballroom practically came to a standstill as Zain came to the top of the stairs, my sister standing at his side. The demon holding my sister's hand was not what I expected when I thought of Damien's brother.

Damien and him looked almost identical with their jet black hair, sharp nose, and chiseled jawline, but there was a distinct difference in his presence.

Zain was less rugged, and more… *Princely*. His whole demeanor screamed royalty. He was handsome, perfectly polished, and just as tall as my demon, but in the place of Damien's blood-red eyes sat two golden ones. They were almost piercing, and though I'd always thought of gold as a warm color, his gaze felt cold.

Until it fell upon my sister, and I saw some of that cold facade melting away.

Huh.

"Now presenting, the Crown Prince and his fiancée, our Princess-to-be. Prince Zain and Lady Luna!" The room erupted into cheers as the demon finished his proclamation, stepping back into the shadows.

Luna, at his side, was wearing a ballgown that looked like hundreds of tiny stars interwoven together, and every time she caught the light, she sparkled. It was gorgeous—she was impossible to take your eyes off of. When you combined it with the tiara of crystals sitting on her head, she looked every bit the title she was about to undertake.

Princess of the Demons. I shook my head. I still had no idea what she was thinking.

They glided down the stairs, heading towards the front of the ballroom together.

Finishing my flute of wine, I turned to Damien, ready to go talk to Luna, but a voice interrupted me.

"Who's this pretty little thing you have with you, Damien?"

My demon stiffened, his arm coming around my front. Guarding me against whatever danger he thought this male posed.

Could other demons sense a mating bond? Ours was still so new—precious, precariously settled between us. And how had I not realized it sooner? Now that I knew, it was so obvious.

With my magic, I could see the gold threads that intertwined between us. There was no doubt in my mind that they'd grow stronger—thicker—with time.

The demon gave him an evil grin, one that instantly made my stomach drop. "Did you bring us a new plaything, *Prince?*" He said the last word with a sneer. Unlike Damien, who appeared mostly human, this demon wore his true form—horns curving up his forehead, and a sickly gray pallor to his skin.

My jaw dropped. Even though Damien had told me about how he did Zain's bidding, I couldn't believe people talked about him like this.

"How dare you—" I started, but my demon tugged me tighter against him. This demon should have been terrifying, and yet—I felt perfectly safe. Because I knew he would protect me.

Damien growled, practically guarding me with his body. "She's *mine*." His lips curled up over his teeth, and I could see the exposed fangs there. "No one else will ever touch her except me." You could hear the snarl in his voice. "And if anyone tries, they'll find out exactly how it feels to really be in *Hell*." His red eyes were smoldering, like fire inside his irises as he turned back to me.

The other demon backed away slightly, holding up his hands in surrender.

I frowned, tugging at his jacket to bring his face into view. "Why do they talk to you like that? You're a prince too."

He sighed. "I'm the bastard son of the King. They've never let me forget it."

"Oh." I ran my fingers through his hair. "Do you really think they'd try to hurt me?"

He shook his head. "I would never risk finding out." I felt weightless as he scooped me up into his arms and carried me away.

"Damien," I murmured, rubbing my hand over his jaw. "You don't have to do this."

"What?" He spoke through clenched teeth.

"Try to protect me." I leaned in, nibbling on his ear. "I'm a big girl. I can protect myself." I wiggled my fingers. "Witch, remember?" A few sparks emitted from my fingertips.

"You're so little," he muttered. "Fragile. I don't... I can't... My instincts are going crazy right now." He sighed in frustration, setting me down in a dark corner before rubbing his face against my throat.

"What are you doing?" I laughed.

"Trying to make you smell like me."

I raised an eyebrow. "What?"

"If you smell like me, the other demons will leave you alone. Know that you're mine."

"And..." I swallowed. "That's the best way to do it?"

His eyes connected with mine, and he gave a slow shake of his head as his fangs popped out of his lips. "No."

Heat flared in his eyes, his voice like gravel, rasping out. "There's another way. But I don't want to hurt you, Wil." His thumb brushed over my cheek.

"You can't." I shook my head. "You won't." I believed in him fully. I knew that no matter what happened, he would protect me.

"You don't understand. If I claim you, I could lose control. My demon senses would take over."

He cupped my face, and I closed my eyes, leaning into his warm palm. "It's okay, Damien. I trust you. I… want you to claim me." My cheeks flushed with warmth. "Please." My voice was a whisper in the night.

Shadows had fallen all around us, like a comfortable blanket, but I didn't mind. I knew they were his doing. That they were keeping us wrapped up in each other, even in the middle of the busy ballroom.

"Willow, I…" His lips crashed against mine. "Fuck."

I was lost in the moment as he kissed me, his breath mingling with mine. The kiss was rough, but I couldn't get enough as he claimed my mouth again and again.

His fangs brushed against my bottom lip, and I moaned from the sensation, even as his tongue explored every inch of my mouth.

My body was on fire, alight from every little touch. I whimpered softly as the sensation washed over me.

It was too much. It wasn't enough.

"Gonna take you here, so they all know that you're mine." His lips connected with my neck, kissing a line down to my chest. "Claim my pretty mate in public, hm?"

I whimpered. "Damien…"

I knew the dark surrounded us, but even the idea that someone could see us—even in a place like this, full of demons—shouldn't have turned me on more, but somehow, it did. When his fingers trailed over my slit, I knew exactly what he'd find. I was soaking wet. Thank the Goddess there was a slit in my ballgown, giving him access.

"My little witch. So good for me," he murmured against my neck as he pushed my lace panties aside. "So wet."

I moaned, baring my neck to him further.

He sank his teeth into me, those fangs piercing the skin of my throat. I'd expected pain, but pure pleasure exploded across the bite, and I moaned deeply from the sensation.

"Fuck, Willow," he groaned. "You taste so good." He didn't drink from me, but the claiming bite tingled, ripples of ecstasy flowing through my body.

"Damien. Please." I mewled, needing more. "I need—"

He dipped his fingers inside of me, working me higher while his tongue gently brushed against my bite. With each stroke of his tongue over the teeth marks, my body trembled with pleasure.

"I've got you, baby," he soothed. "My mate. My beautiful mate."

The moment his thumb connected with my clit, I slumped against him, my knees going weak.

"You need to come, hm?"

"Y-yes." I buried my face in his neck, inhaling his spicy scent.

"What do you want?" He asked, crooking his fingers inside of me. "My fingers or my cock?"

Inside me, I begged, hardly coherent enough to know if I'd said the words out loud or not. I didn't care that we were up against a wall, with the only thing keeping anyone from seeing us being Damien's shadows.

I longed for him, knowing that only his presence could ease the burning sensation inside of me. Damien's playful fingers kept teasing me while my dress remained bunched up around my waist, and I clung to him.

"You're going to have to be quiet, little witch." He rumbled against my ear, his breath tickling my skin. "My shadows will keep anyone from seeing us, but I can't say the same thing about them *hearing* us."

Were we about to fuck in the middle of the crowded ballroom? *Yes.*

I nodded in agreement as Damien unzipped his pants, pulling himself out, revealing his hardening length to me. If we were somewhere else, I would have dropped to my knees right there and begged to taste him.

But this fire in me, this burning, maddening emptiness, wasn't going away without help. Only his touch could soothe it. Was that the mating bond? Did demons feel this too?

Fisting his cock, he roughly tugged on it a few times before bringing his tip to my entrance, running it through my wetness.

Teasing me, over and over, without letting the tip slip inside.

Please.

Are you gonna be quiet, baby?

Yes. I nodded into his jacket. *Now fuck me.*

I didn't care about anything else as he finally pushed inside of me, burying himself to the hilt. Neither of us said a word as he braced us against a wall, giving it to me with everything he had. Damien wrapped his free hand—the one not currently holding me in place against him—over my mouth, keeping me from making a sound.

We both lost ourselves in the sensation as he drove us higher and higher. His shadows joined in, a cool press against my skin, and I was *gone*.

Exploding, just like that.

He wasn't far behind me, and I squeezed my insides around him, feeling him growing even harder inside.

"Willow," he groaned as he came, spilling rope after rope of cum inside of me.

Every warring emotion inside me calmed as the warmth spread through my insides, leaving me feeling peaceful and content. It was like a balm to my soul, and I felt the beast within me finally relax and let go. Damien placed a kiss on my lips before pulling out, re-situating my underwear in place before letting my dress fall back down to the ground.

"Damien," I whispered as I took a step, fully aware of the way the shadows were dissipating from around us.

"What, baby?"

Grabbing my hand, he interlaced our fingers, giving me a guilty smile.

"Your cum is dripping out of me."

He flashed me a devilish smile as his shadows danced up my thighs before pushing it back inside of me. "I know." Leaning into my ear, he said to me, "At least you smell like me now."

I hummed in response, still not having enough words for what we'd just done.

And how much I'd *liked it*.

Loved it, even.

Like I loved him.

TWENTY-TWO
WILLOW

"Luna!" I exclaimed, finally coming within an arm's reach of my sister for the first time all night.

She was so popular with the demons, I'd barely been able to keep track of her all night. Plus, when you added Damien thoroughly distracting me with that show in the shadows… this was my first opportunity to actually talk to her.

When I made it to her side, I instantly wrapped my arms around her, hugging her tight before pulling away.

Her dress was even more intricate and beautiful now that I was seeing it close up. It sparkled every time it caught the light under the chandeliers. "Wow. This is beautiful." She exuded an air of elegance, with every detail on her expertly curated. Not a strand of hair was out of place, and her makeup was flawlessly applied. The work of demons, I was sure.

"Thank you." She messed with the skirts. "Did Damien give you yours?"

I nodded. I still had no idea how he'd been able to procure it in time.

But that wasn't what was important.

I just wanted to spend the little time I had with my sister talking about her. To know what was going on inside her head.

"Can we talk?" I asked, pointing to the outside balcony with my head. My hand was occupied with another glass of the sparkly gold beverage. I was a little addicted.

Luna nodded.

The breeze was cool against my balmy skin as we stepped out into the night. Luna rested against the railing as I propped my arms against it, looking out. "This place is… Wow. Definitely not in Pleasant Grove anymore."

"Mhm," she agreed.

"Luna." My voice was stern. "Talk to me."

She turned, looking into my eyes as she emitted a deep sigh. "I am, aren't I?"

I sighed. "You were right."

"About what?"

"Damien. Telling him how I felt."

"And you told him you love him?"

"Er… Well… No." My cheeks went pink. "I only realized that *today*."

"*Willow.*"

"Hey. Don't sister me while I'm sistering *you*." I crossed my arms over my chest. "Are you sure this is what you want?"

"So, you get to fall in love with a demon and be with him, but I can't?"

"Do you?" I asked softly. "Love him?"

Luna shook her head. "No." It was a whisper of an omission. "But…" When her eyes connected with mine, they were watery. "I can't explain it, Wil. But when I saw him, my heart knew."

"Knew…?"

"That he was mine. That I was his." She used her hands to indicate everything around us. "Maybe I'm supposed to be *here*, you know?"

"But… Your bakery. Our lives. You're leaving everything behind."

She fidgeted with the ring that sat on her finger. "Lately, I've been thinking, well… I don't know how to describe it. Like I was missing something. And when he asked me to come with him, I didn't even have to stop to think about it. I just… said yes."

"But he's a stranger. You don't even know him."

Luna blinked. "Well… That's not entirely true."

"What?"

But… Damien had told me he'd been sent to the human world to find her. When would Zain have had the time to meet her?

"We've met before. At the bar." She shrugged. "And a few other times."

"You didn't think to tell me you *met someone?*" I dropped my voice, hoping she couldn't hear the hurt. "I'm your sister, Luna."

She sighed. "I know. But you were all wrapped up in Damien, and I didn't want to pop your bubble. Plus, it's not like you were one hundred percent truthful with me, either."

"Right. Well, *maybe* I should have told you about his, er… *demon-ness*. In my defense, I thought I was doing the right thing. Keeping him safe." I didn't think I'd needed to keep her safe too.

Luna laughed. "I don't think he needs you for that." She stared off into the distance at the palace gardens, the silence growing between us.

"A witch cursed him," I offered. "That's the spell I did. Reversing it."

"I thought I would hate it here," she admitted. "This place. I thought it would be *hell*. But it's not. People are free to be whoever they are here. Monster and demon alike. It's nothing like Pleasant Grove."

"No, it isn't," I murmured. The moon was high in the sky, and the sky was scattered with stars—constellations I didn't know, didn't have the names for.

Luna picked up my hand, squeezing it tightly. "I don't know what will happen, but I can promise you I'm safe here. I'm not here against my will. I chose this... I choose *him*."

"Okay," I whispered, squeezing back. "And if you decide this isn't what you want anymore?"

"Then I'll come back."

Back, she said. Not home. Because maybe Pleasant Grove wasn't her home anymore. Not when her soulmate was here.

"Okay," I agreed as we dropped hands, still staring out at the palace's surroundings. I still couldn't believe a place like this could exist in the demon realm. How much that we'd been taught was wrong.

But maybe… hiding Damien had never been the right thing to do from the beginning. Maybe I needed to show the other witches that demons weren't all bad. That they were capable of love. Life.

"There you two are," Zain said, wrapping an arm around Luna's shoulders. "We've been looking for you."

Damien stepped to my side, and I instantly wanted to bury myself in his warmth. It hadn't been that long since he'd touched me last, but I'd already missed it.

"Hi," I murmured, slipping an arm around his middle.

"We were just getting some air," Luna responded. "It's a little stuffy in there." She tugged at one sleeve of her dress.

My sister's demon prince—her *fiancé*, I had to remind myself—chuckled. "They're just fascinated by you, my bride. Give it time." He kissed her cheek.

I was surprised at how tender and loving he seemed to be. Was it all an act?

She sighed. "I know."

He turned his attention to Damien and I. "Did you two enjoy the party?"

"Oh, yes," I said, thinking about the demon wine. Definitely not what we'd done in the shadows. "It's been lovely."

Zain laughed. "She smells like you now."

My cheeks were on fire, like he'd caught us red-handed, and Damien nuzzled his nose against my neck.

"I had to keep the other demons away from my mate somehow."

Zain looked down at Luna, humming slightly in response.

"I can take care of myself," she muttered, rolling her eyes as she stared out at the gardens.

Sounds a lot like someone else I know, Damien muttered into my mind.

Shut it. I'm pretty sure your brother knows what we did earlier.

So?

So, I'm mortified.

He laughed. *So you don't want to do it again?*

I narrowed my eyes at him. "I didn't say that."

Luna raised an eyebrow at me, but I just shook my head.

I'd have time in the future where I could explain our weird telepathy thing to her. Who knows, maybe she had it too? We hadn't exactly had a lot of time to compare our *demons* with each other.

Resting my head against Damien's chest, I shivered. The cool air had felt nice before, but now it was getting chillier.

Plus, I was exhausted. I'd been up since this morning, and Halloween felt like yesterday. It was weird to remind myself that it had been tonight. It must have been close to two in the morning already.

He scooped me up into his arms for the second time tonight. "Come on, my mate. Let's get you to bed."

I yawned. Nothing sounded better.

"Goodnight, you two," Luna said, offering me a smile.

I gave her a wave. "Night." I looked at Zain. "Don't hurt my baby sister, or I'll tear your heart out." I looked at Damien. "Or turn you into a cat. Might be just as effective."

My demon laughed. "I think you had too much demon wine, baby."

"Uh-uh," I argued, feeling myself get sleepier as we walked away. But it was hard to deny the fact when I'd had a glass in my hand most of the night. I didn't feel drunk, though. Just a warm, pleasant buzz.

"Sleep, little witch," he soothed. "We'll talk more in the morning."

I nodded into his chest.

Yes. In the morning, I'd tell him everything I'd left unsaid.

Starting with those three words.

✳ ✳ ✳

Stretching my arms, I sat up, clutching the sheet around my naked body. Damien was sprawled out at my side, one arm possessively over my stomach.

I'd passed out in his arms the night before as he carried me. He roused me from my half-sleep to help me out of my dress before we took a brief shower together. The day had left me feeling completely depleted.

I watched him sleep, curling my fingers through his dark hair.

"I'm so glad I adopted you," I murmured. "Thanks for being my not-cat, Demon."

He stirred at my touch, grabbing my hand and kissing my knuckles as he woke.

"Good morning, Willow," he said, voice groggy from sleep. But he didn't give me my arm back—no, he placed gentle kisses all the way up my arm before pausing at the mark he'd left yesterday on my neck.

"I like my mark on you." The sound of his voice was like a deep, rumbling growl. "Fuck. What it does to me…" He kissed the mark before tracing his tongue over it.

"Damien." I ran my fingers through his hair once more. "I need to tell you something—"

"I still owe you a favor, you know."

I kissed him to shut him up. "You *are* my favor, demon."

He laughed against my mouth.

I sat up, not caring about bringing the sheet with me. "I mean it. You… I never could have imagined this. You. Us. And I l—"

He shook his head. "Don't say it. Not yet." The fangs popped out from his upper lip. *I want to say it first.*

I shook my head, even though I loved his possessiveness. "Why did you stay?" I let the words slip out. I'd asked him something similar before, but this time, it was different. "Besides me being your mate."

"Isn't it obvious?"

"Maybe I need to hear it. The words."

"Willow." Damien's forehead rested against mine. "I stayed for *you*, little witch. Because I couldn't bear to be apart from you. Because you're mine." The corner of his lip tilted up, exposing a canine tooth. "I've never had somebody of my own. Somebody to…" His voice choked up. "Love."

"You…?" My eyes filled with tears. Maybe I'd thought it was too soon to say the words myself. Even then, I'd been seconds away admitting the same thing to him. How could I not, after letting him claim me yesterday? My fingers fluttered up to the bite, tracing the puncture wounds.

"I love you." He took my hands in his, intertwining our fingers together. I marveled at how perfectly we fit, just like always. "I think I've loved you since I first laid eyes on you, Willow."

"But you…" My eyes widened. *You were a cat.*

Damien sucked in a breath. Nodded. I didn't need to say the words, because he knew what I was thinking. Our bond gave us that, always. "Even then, I think I knew what you were to me. But it wasn't until you helped me get back into this form that I *knew*. But it's more than that."

I blinked. "It is?"

"You're *mine*, but that's not why I fell in love with you, little witch." He brushed his fingers over my chin. "I fell in love with you because you're clever, and kind, and you never give up on people." Damien gave me a small smile. "Especially not on me. And I've never had anything that was mine before. Really, truly *mine*. Never had somewhere that felt like home before you. But fuck, Willow. I'd give up anything for you. Do anything for you. Burn down hell just for a chance—just for a moment with you."

"I love you too," I said, unable to contain all of the emotions flowing through me. "I have for a while. I wanted to tell you, but I was just… scared."

"Of what?" Tucking a strand of hair behind my ear, gently, he looked more vulnerable than I'd ever seen him before. More open, too. "I'd never leave you."

"I know that now." I sighed, burying my head against his pecs. "But before… I thought you'd have to go back here. That you wouldn't be able to stay."

"You were something I never expected, never hoped for, but… I'd never trade you for the world, Willow. My mate," he murmured. "My beautiful mate."

"Damien…" My eyes filled with tears. "I love you. So much." I wrapped my arms around him, letting our lips connect.

Kissing the man I loved.

Kissing the man who loved *me*.

"Do you want to go home?" He tilted his head up to look at me, pausing all of the little touches I loved. I wanted them—craved *him*, but there were more important things right now.

"You don't want to… stay?" I asked, surprised. We had each other, but I hadn't known what our plans were. If he'd have to stay here, because of his brother. "This is your home." I would have hated every minute of it, even if he'd asked me to stay with him. But I would have understood. Even more so after Luna had decided to marry his brother.

He shook his head. "This isn't my home."

"What?" I laughed. "Isn't it?" I gestured to the room around us. These giant suites we'd occupied for only a night.

He cocked his head to the side. "That's not what I meant."

"Oh."

"I do though. Have my own house, away from the palace." He laid his head on my lap. "I'll take you there sometime."

I traced a finger over his jaw. "I'd love that."

"You're my home, Willow," he said, taking my hands in his. "I told you that. And wherever you want to be… I want to be there, too."

"Okay." I liked the sound of that.

"Home?" He asked again, his voice quiet.

"Home," I agreed.

* * *

After we'd finally extracted ourselves from the bed, washing up in the giant bathtub once again, we'd put on fresh clothes. I didn't ask where he'd gotten my clothes from. How his magic worked, exactly.

"I'm sorry," he offered as we walked back outside of the palace. Despite my initial reservations of the place, I was surprised how beautiful it was.

Damien and I had talked about Luna earlier while we were getting ready. My conversation with her.

"It's hard to rescue someone who doesn't want to be rescued." But if she wanted to be here—if she would be happy—then I'd let her go.

"No." He took my hand. "I mean, for not telling you. I should have told you that Luna was destined. That my brother would come for her. I'd spent weeks trying to figure out how to get around it. But…"

"I know." I cupped his cheek with my palm. "But as long as she wants to be there, then… It's her choice. She's an adult. If she wants to be with her…" My voice choked on the words. "*Fated mate,* then who am

I to say anything? After all, I found you."

"Willow…"

My body tensed. "He won't hurt her, right?"

"No. Fuck. No, never." He took my hands in his. "He might be the heir to the demon throne, but he'd… He'd never harm your sister. Or force her to do anything she didn't want to do."

"Okay." I paused, looking back at the glittering tops of the palace. "We can come back, right?"

"Any time you want."

Still holding hands, I watched as Damien opened a portal back to my world with his magic. He used the darkness to walk between realms, and it was mesmerizing, almost. How beautiful it was. His magic might have frightened people—but not me. Never me.

"Home," he murmured, the sound low under his breath.

I love you. I almost missed it, but I knew in my heart that he said it. Could feel the way he felt it, too.

The shadows wrapped around us, taking us back.

Taking us home.

I love you too, I sent back through our tether.

* * *

I felt defeated, like I'd lost something today. It hurt to think about Luna not being here whenever I needed her. She was my little sister, my twin flame—but more than that, she was my best friend. The one who knew me better than anyone else. The sister I'd do anything for.

But looking up at Damien as we stood in front of the old Victorian manor I called home, I realized I hadn't lost everything at all.

Because he was still here.

And we were home.

And… he loved me. I loved him.

I stared at the pumpkins sitting on the front porch. They'd lasted through the end of Halloween, the tree he'd carved for me and the cat I'd carved for him.

I didn't know what would happen next, what was coming for us in the future, but at least we'd be together.

Where we belonged.

TWENTY-THREE

DAMIEN

Home. Pleasant Grove was my home now. Officially.

I stared up at Willow's family house. Our house now, I supposed.

As long as she wanted to stay here, I'd be here. She didn't know it yet, but I had a long future planned for us. An eternity together.

Picking her up in my arms—one of my hands on her back, and the other under her knees, I carried her over the threshold of the house.

Our house.

But when I turned to my witch, expecting happiness, she had a frown on her face.

"What is it, little witch?" I asked her, brushing the hair out of her face. Cupping her cheeks as she turned to face me. "I thought you'd be happy to be home. Together."

"I am, it's just…" Her eyes were glassy. "I didn't think about it till now. I don't want you to watch me grow old. To die. You'll live…" Willow's voice stuttered.

A long time. I knew it. A long lifespan was just one of the many things that came with being a demon.

"Willow," I murmured. "I don't have to watch you grow old." I interlaced one of her hands in mine, kissing her knuckles.

"We don't?" She blinked. "But I'm *mortal*. Practically human. I won't live as long as you."

"We can tether your life force to mine. Ensure that when we take our last breaths, it's together."

"Really?" She blinked away her tears. "So I'd live…"

"As long as I do, yes."

Willow wandered over to look out the window, like she was looking at the town. I wondered if she was thinking about the people here that she loved.

"You wouldn't age. At least, not normally. But we… could stay here. For as long as you'd want."

"We could?"

"I know what this place means to you. How much you love these people. It's your home."

"And Luna…" Her words trailed off, but I knew what she meant.

When Luna married my brother, she'd go through something similar. As the future Queen of the Demon realm, she would live by my brother's side for an eternity. "Yes."

"What about… kids?"

I blinked. "What?"

"I don't even know if you *want* to have kids, but would they…"

"Live as long as us?" I asked her. Sure, children of demons and witches weren't the most common, but they weren't rare. Plenty of demons had mated with humans and brought them back to our world. She gave a slight nod. "They would. They'd inherit magic from both of us."

We'd never had a chance to talk about having kids, about the little witch that had been in my dreams.

"I want that," I murmured, directly into her hair. "A family, with you."

"You do?" The tears were back, only this time—they were happy.

"Yes. Fuck yes, Willow. I want to do it all with you. Every little thing I've never experienced—I want to try it all with you. I want to see your world. To take you everywhere possible. And then show you mine." I squeezed her hands.

"I want that, too," she said, letting the tears fall. "An eternity with you."

"Thank fuck," I responded, taking her mouth. Kissing her, showing her how much I loved her with one simple action. "I love you."

She laughed. "I'm never going to get tired of hearing you say that."

"We don't have to do the ceremony now. We can wait." I thought about the jeweled ring in my back pocket. The one that had been my mom's. The same one she'd enchanted to protect me. "Do it at the same time as our wedding."

"Our wedding?" This time, she looked confused.

I laughed, bringing our foreheads together. "I know it hasn't been very long. That we still have so much to learn about each other. But, when the time comes…. I want to make you my wife. I want you to be mine in every way possible."

I could feel her smile against my mouth as we kissed again.

"Yes," she said as she pulled away, "Yes, I want to be your wife. All of it."

"I love you, Willow."

"I love you too, Damien."

I rubbed my fingers over her mark. "Mine," I murmured.

"Yours," she agreed.

Throwing her over my shoulder unceremoniously, I carted her from the living room into her bedroom.

"Damien!" Willow shrieked, dangling down my back. "You're ridiculous."

I dropped her on the bed, enjoying the way her eyes widened as I stood over her, stripping off my clothes.

"I've wanted you again since yesterday. Since I put my mark on you." Fuck, I'd never imagined how much I'd like it to see those two little imprints on her bare neck. Knowing that I put them there. "We didn't have enough time this morning."

The ballroom had eased the urge that the claiming had brought on, but it wasn't enough. Some males fucked for practically a week straight afterwards.

She bit her lip, watching me from lidded eyes.

"Like what you see?" I asked, smirking, knowing my full chest was on display as I unbuttoned my pants.

Her cheeks pinked, her hands moving to cover her eyes. "I wasn't watching."

"Willow." Grasping her fingers, I pulled them away from her face before pinning them to the bed, our hands intertwined. "Baby, you're allowed to look." Placing a kiss underneath her ear, I slipped my hands under her top, cupping her tits even through her lacy bra. I brushed my finger over a nipple, enjoying the shudder her body made from the sensation. "Because I'm *yours*."

Willow squirmed underneath me. "*Please*," she pleaded, even if she didn't know what for. I was happy to oblige. But first—

"You're wearing too many clothes," I muttered, fumbling with the hem of the sage green sweater she'd pulled on this morning.

"Take them off then," she agreed, before bringing her mouth back to mine.

We pulled apart long enough for me to whip her sweater off, dropping it on the floor behind me before rolling her leggings off of her legs. Stripped down to her orange polka dot panties and black lace bra, she'd never looked so much like *mine*.

I chuckled, kissing the top of each hip bone. "Cute panties." Her cheeks pinked, turning almost the same color as her little pink nipples. "I'm fucking obsessed with them." Hooking my thumbs into the waistband, I dragged them down her skin, not stopping until she was bare for me, exposing that perfect mound. "Obsessed with *you*."

When I'd gotten her back to my room last night, my cum had still been dripping out of her, and I'd almost lost it right then and there. But she'd been so tired, and all I'd wanted to do was take care of her. So I'd gotten her cleaned up and tucked her into bed.

But tonight, I was going to take my time. Maybe start working towards that eventual witchling. Whenever she decided to go off birth control, I couldn't fucking wait.

Unsnapping her bra, I took a moment to enjoy the view of her tits and that creamy skin.

"Can't get over how fucking perfect these are," I said. They were just begging for my mouth, and I couldn't resist tasting her. Moving my head down, I sucked one into my mouth. Lavishing it with attention, I swirled my tongue in circles over and over before switching to the other breast.

"Damien," she whined. "I need—"

I ran my fingers over the soft skin of her thighs, leaving a trail of goosebumps in their wake. Her sweet smell lingered in the air as I leaned back, taking in the sight of her. "I know what you need, baby." I kissed the swell of her breasts.

Standing up, I pushed my pants and briefs off in one clean motion, and my cock sprang to attention. I'd never get over the way Willow's eyes widened every time she saw me.

I eased inside of her without preamble—no foreplay. Still, she was soaked for me, and I squeezed my eyes at the sensation of being inside her bare. Somehow, it got better every time. I was fucking lost in her, and I knew it.

"I love you," I murmured, capturing her lips as she wound her arms around my neck.

She moaned my name as I pulled out slightly, pushing in deeper.

This time, I'd go slow. I'd savor it. There was time for the rest, later.

I wanted her to know how much I loved her. Cherished her.

I kept up that pace, slow slides inside of her, until she was trembling against me, begging me for more.

"Tell me you're mine," I murmured again, kissing her bite.

"I'm yours," she agreed, her hips rocking in time to meet my shallow thrusts. Each time I hit her cervix, I felt a shudder run through her entire body. She was close, and I just needed her to let go.

I'd be right behind her, always.

"Come for me, baby."

"Damien," she cried. "I love you."

Bringing our mouths together, I kissed her deeply, letting go of everything else. "I love you," I murmured.

I used my shadows to apply pressure to her clit, and that was all it took. She came, squeezing around my cock, her insides milking me.

That was what tipped me over the edge, and I came on a cry of her name. Every last drop was spilled inside of her, leaving me boneless.

I buried my head against her breasts as I held her, feeling myself growing soft inside of her.

And even then, we remained connected.

"I can't wait for a lifetime of *that*," she laughed.

I pinched her cute little bare ass. "An eternity."

"Mmm. Forever sounds perfect with you."

It really did.

I couldn't wait to start the rest of our forever—together.

EPILOGUE
WILLOW

Two years later…

A little tiny hand tugged at a black tail. Because, for whatever reason, my *husband* thought it was absolutely adorable to continue shifting into his cat form even when we had things to do.

"Damien." I narrowed my eyes at him.

Meow. He wiggled his butt, tail swishing back and forth as he prevented the chubby little fingers from grabbing it.

"Opal." I sighed, scooping our nine-month-old daughter into my arms. "We don't play with Daddy."

I heard a chuckling sound and the padding of feet coming from our room.

"What—" I looked at Damien, and then at the black cat at our daughter's feet. "If you're not… Then…"

Opal giggled as the cat brushed against her legs, her dark curls bouncing from the motion. She'd gotten his hair, long and thick and black as night. But she had my bright green eyes, and of course—my fondness for cats.

I'd never gotten around to getting another familiar after Damien turned out to *not* be a cat, but I didn't mind. The two-for-one special I'd gotten with my feline companion also being my mate, had worked out pretty well.

And when our little bundle of joy had come, I'd knew our family was perfect.

The spring after we'd met, I'd spent a week unable to keep anything down, and when Luna had come for a visit, she'd taken one look at me and she *knew*. Even before I did. A fact that never ceased to irritate me.

Leveling a glare at my husband, I crossed my arms over my chest. I might have loved him, but I was also peeved at him. "Why, exactly, is there a strange cat in my house?"

He leaned down, kissing me on the lips gently. "Hello to you too, Wil."

I ran my fingers over the wedding band on his left hand. We'd gotten married a year ago, in a small ceremony held in the town's gazebo. I'd been six months pregnant at the time, but we hadn't wanted to wait.

After Opal had been born, we'd had a second ceremony—this time in the demon realm, but with a lot more fanfare.

All I'd cared about was the man at the end of the aisle and the tiny baby who'd slept in her aunt's arms. The rest of it didn't matter.

"Are we just… ignoring that?" I waved at the strange cat.

"Oh, Zain just wanted to drop in and say hello," he said, grinning. "He brought Opal a friend."

"Zain's here?" My eyes lit up. "Did he bring Luna with him?"

Damien brushed his nose against mine. "Of course he did."

But before I could let myself relax into the gesture, I raised an eyebrow, looking back at the cat.

"Relax." He placed a kiss on my forehead. "She's *just* a cat, I promise."

Better be, I sent the thought through our bond. *Or you're on the couch tonight.* I didn't need any more demons masquerading as cats in our lives.

Damien was enough. He was more than enough. He was everything.

He smirked, holding out a hand. "Shall we?"

"What do you think, Opal? Want to go visit Auntie Luna?"

My baby girl gave me a big, toothy grin, and I happily scooped her up into my arms, placing kisses all over her soft skin.

I didn't get to see my sister as much these days—mostly on account of her marriage to the literal Demon King. Another advancement of the last two years, after the death of Damien's father.

We'd both stepped back from the bakery, hiring on a new head baker and a manager.

I hadn't realized that while I was wondering what my path was in life, so was Luna. But she seemed happy, and I couldn't judge. Not when I'd fallen in love with a demon myself.

I hadn't quite decided what was next in life. I'd planned on getting another job after stepping back from the bakery, but then I'd gotten pregnant with Opal. And I decided I liked the role of Mom better than anything else I could have ever dreamed of.

I still dabbled in potions, and these days, I had a whole slew of witches requesting different cures for their ailments. It felt like they had a newfound awe for me after they'd found out about me breaking my demon's curse.

He'd settled into his role as a resident of Pleasant Grove, but more importantly, into being a father. Even though he sometimes still shapeshifted into cat form and let our toddler play with him.

Damien still rolled his eyes when I called it *Hell*—but after visiting quite a few times, I had to admit it had its own charms.

Like the *giant* bathtub that took up almost an entire room, or the king sized bed that was so decadent I never wanted to get out of it. Damien's *suites* were lavish and lush and the perfect escape from life.

And then there was his house—the one that barely deserved to be called that. It was basically a mansion, built onto a large piece of property outside of the demon capital.

When you live a long time, you have a lot of money saved up. He'd shrugged. *I figured it would be an excellent investment.*

And one day, it would be our home. After we'd raised Opal with the witches, let her choose her path—then we'd retire to the demon realm for the rest of our eternity.

I liked the sound of it more and more every day.

Forever with the man—the demon—that I loved.

And the baby girl who'd brought so much joy into my life.

With the sister I'd given up everything for, who'd found her own path.

My family was complete. Mine. Perfect.

My demon smiled up at me, taking Opal from my arms. "Come to daddy, baby girl." He brushed a hand over her little black curls.

Part of me—part of him. She'd gotten my eyes. And a tiny splattering of freckles on her cheeks. The rest, though, was all Damien. His complexion, the onyx hue of her hair.

We could always make another one, you know, he said, watching me watch them. *It might be fun.*

She's not even a year old yet. What's the rush?

He gave me a little smirk. *What? I like seeing you pregnant.*

"Mommy and Daddy need to give you a little sister, huh, Opal?" He grinned, bouncing our little girl up in the air.

"How are you so sure it won't be a boy?" I furrowed my brow.

He laughed. "I just have this feeling."

I rubbed over my wedding ring—the ring that used to be his mother's—thinking about our family. Not yet, but… I liked the idea of adding another member to our family soon.

After Halloween was over, maybe we could start thinking about it. But I wanted to enjoy my baby girl's first Halloween. I'd already bought the cutest costume, and we were all going to match.

Besides, what were the odds he'd knock me up on the first try, anyway?

I adjusted her little jumper.

"Shall we?" He asked.

But I know he didn't just mean going to see Luna and Zain.

"Yes," I agreed.

To the future. To our life. To our family.

To every blissfully perfect moment that would come, and every single one in between.

I'd never expected to find my perfect man, let alone a demon. Never imagined that the cat I'd adopted would have been the male the fates picked for me. My mate.

And yet, here I was. Living my perfect life. It was everything I'd ever wanted, and everything I'd never known how to wish for.

"I love you," I murmured, pressing a soft kiss to his lips, before leaning in to kiss our daughter's cheek.

"I love you, too, little witch," he agreed, returning one back. "Both of you."

EXTENDED EPILOGUE

Damien

"Don't put that in your mouth," I said to my four-month-old daughter, prying the little bow out of her mouth that was *supposed* to be on her head. "Your mommy isn't going to be very happy with me if I let you mess up your hair."

Opal cooed, her big green eyes—just like Willow's—staring up at me. I nuzzled my nose against her cheek before tickling her soft tummy. She giggled and I couldn't help the grin that split my face.

Repositioning the bow, I ran my fingers over her short black hair. She was like the perfect combination of Willow and I, and I soaked up every moment of Daddy time I could with her. I liked to think I was making up for all the moments my dad hadn't spent with me.

Hence, why I was holed up in our room in the palace as Willow got pampered in preparation for our *wedding*. Never mind that it was technically our second one—we'd tied the knot in her hometown while she'd been pregnant with Opal, but this one was bigger.

We didn't do anything halfway in the demon realm, after all.

"How's she doing?" Luna popped her head in the door, finding the two of us lounging on the couch. Me, in my wedding tuxedo—if you could even call it that—and my little witching in her lavender dress.

I kissed the top of her head. "Good. She'll probably want Wil soon, though."

Luna laughed. "I was sent in here for that exact reason."

Willow was still nursing, and even though she pumped, our daughter still preferred her breasts to a bottle.

"Want to go see Auntie Luna, baby girl?" I asked her, taking the excited bubbles that came out of her mouth as a resounding *yes*.

Willow's sister scooped her up out of my arms. "You love your Auntie Luna, don't you?" She babbled as she walked out of the room.

I sighed. The notion that we couldn't see each other on our wedding day—our *second* wedding day, specifically, was a ridiculous and antiquated notion, especially when we were already married. Never mind the fact that we also already had a daughter together.

The door opened again, and a familiar face peeked in. "How are you feeling, brother? You ready for this?"

I smoothed a hand over my face, resisting rolling my eyes at my brother. "We're already married."

"Still. You'll remember this night forever." He grinned. His own marriage had made him softer, even though he was still an asshole at times. "I know I do."

This time I did roll my eyes. "You're ridiculous."

"I'm happy for you, you know." His eyes flashed a brilliant gold, such stark contrast from the red of mine. "I don't think I tell you that enough."

I shook my head. "I didn't do much." I'd found Willow by chance—circumstance. We might have been fated, but still: if I hadn't been out looking for Luna, I never would have found my little witch.

"No. That's where you're wrong. You made a choice. To stay. To love her. To be there."

I knew I was thinking what he was thinking: that was more than either one of us had gotten.

"Thanks, Z."

He reached over, ruffling my hair. He might have been three centuries old, but he still treated me like the little kid I'd been when we'd first met—when I'd first come to live at the palace.

"Should we go get you married now?"

I laughed, fiddling with the ring on my finger. "Married again."

"You can consider it a vow renewal, then. Maybe use it as an excuse to freshen up your mate mark." He wiggled his eyes suggestively.

As if I didn't think about that every time someone else looked at her. Especially with all the visits to the demon realm we'd made since that first one. I ran my tongue over my canines, thinking about how it had felt the first time—when I'd sunk my teeth into her as I'd buried myself inside of her at the same time.

Oh, yeah. That sounded like a great idea.

"The girls are all together?" I asked my brother as he headed for the door, catching the slight tip of his lips.

"Yeah." My girls—and his.

"I never imagined this would be our lives, you know. Mates. Wives. The whole thing." I waved my hands. "I kinda thought we'd end up doing Dad's bidding until we turned to dust."

He chuckled, but the sound was rough. "We deserve this, you know that."

"Do we?" I adjusted the bowtie around my neck. I loved her, and I'd promised Willow forever, but that didn't mean I felt like I'd earned her. There were countless terrible things I'd done, and I'd spend the rest of my life atoning for them if it meant I got to keep her. My precious witch, who filled my life up with so much love and happiness.

I closed my eyes, taking a deep breath as Zain slapped a hand on my shoulder. "You got this."

And then he disappeared, leaving me in front of the two big closed doors that entered the ballroom.

"Hi there, demon," came my favorite voice in the world, and I whirled around to find Willow standing in a beautiful white wedding dress with billowy sleeves and sparkly star accents, plus what seemed like a thousand diamonds threaded in her silky brown tresses.

"Hey, little witch." I held out a hand for her, letting the rightness flow through my body as she interlaced our fingers. "You look beautiful." That was an understatement, but they hadn't invented words to describe how lovely Willow was, so that was what I was sticking with.

Her cheeks pinked. "Thank you. Luna said I had to go with the same demon who'd made her dress, and I wasn't sure it would fit since my body has changed so much after the pregnancy, but…"

"But it's perfect."

Willow nodded. "Yeah. I love it."

I leaned close, cupping her chin with my free hand. "I love you."

She giggled. "That's kind of why we're here today, isn't it?"

"Mhmm," I agreed, kissing her nose lightly. "How was Opal doing?"

"Good." Her eyes lit up when I mentioned our daughter. "I nursed her right before Luna took her to sit down. Hopefully I have a few hours till she needs to eat again."

Luna had reassured me that she would take care of our daughter tonight, so I could have my wife all to myself—a special surprise. Her first treat would be a long, luxurious bath in the giant tub she loved so much.

"She'll be fine," I reassured her.

"I know." Willow squeezed my hand, and then looked at the doors. "Should we do this, then?"

I cleared my throat, getting choked up thinking about the last time. "Yes."

Our first wedding, Luna had walked Willow down the aisle. Luna and Zain had come back to Pleasant Grove for it, and even if the townspeople had been a little hesitant around us at first, I was glad we'd had our siblings there. Of course, Willow's whole coven had showed up as well as we tied the knot.

Seeing her round and growing, knowing she was carrying my baby inside of her. We weren't ready for another one, not yet, but I couldn't wait for the day that we were. Trying to make another one sounded like a *lot* of fun.

"We're just… walking in?" Willow bit her lip. "And everyone's going to be there?"

"Mhm. Just hold my hand, Wil. I'll be by your side the whole time."

"I'm not nervous," she whispered, even as she squeezed my hand again. "I just never thought I'd willingly be entering a room full of hundreds of demons."

I laughed. "This isn't the first time." And it wouldn't be the last.

She looked at me, pointedly. "You know what I mean."

Bending down, I kissed her softly, being careful not to ruin her makeup. "There's nothing I wouldn't do for you, Willow. Even if you want to turn around and go home right now, and not do this."

"No. I want to be married to you." I raised an eyebrow at the ring on her finger. "*Here,*" she clarified. "There. Everywhere. I want everyone to know that you're mine, and I'm yours."

"That's my girl," I replied, moving us closer to the doors.

They flew open upon our approach, enchanted to open for us. Open to see the crowd of demons waiting for us. Beings that had become our friends over the last year as we'd come back to visit Luna and Zain. Not that they didn't have the threat of being eliminated if they so much as looked at her wrong.

"Ready, wife?"

"Ready, husband," she replied.

"I love you," I whispered as we made the first few steps.

"I love you too," she murmured, her eyes fixated at the end of the aisle. At our baby girl, sitting on her Aunt Luna's lap.

I'd have given up an eternity for this moment alone.

* * *

Willow

My cheeks hurt from smiling as I swayed back and forth with Opal in my arms—her in her pretty purple dress, me still in my gorgeous wedding dress. It was more than I'd ever imagined, especially since I'd been perfectly content with our little gazebo wedding back in Pleasant Grove. But I had to admit—I was having *fun*.

Opal giggled as I spun us around in a circle, and a hand pressed against my lower back—a warm, soothing presence. I didn't have to look up to know it was Damien.

"Hi." I tilted my chin up so he could press a small kiss against my lips, and then he placed a kiss against Opal's forehead as well. Her dark hair had a little bow on the top of it, even if it was slightly askew—she'd been trying to eat the thing all evening. I'd watched Luna take it out of her mouth during the ceremony.

"There's my girls," Damien said, sliding his other arm around our daughter so he could hold both of us.

I hummed into his hold, leaning my head against his shoulder.

"Are you having fun?" He whispered against my ear, my whole body shuddering from the brush of his skin against mine.

I was, but also… "Is it bad if I say I want to go home?" I looked down at our daughter, nuzzled into my arms with her eyes drooping closed.

"Home home?" He asked, his eyes flashing bright red. "Or here home?"

I shrugged. "Either." I loved his rooms in the palace, but the one he'd built in the demon realm was even better.

"Luna said she'd watch Opal tonight," he murmured, brushing my hair back to place a kiss against my neck. Against the mark he'd made all those months ago. "So I can have you all to myself."

"Oh, did she?" I made a mental note to thank my sister later. I didn't like spending the night away from my baby, but Damien and I hadn't been alone since I'd given birth, and I *really* missed my husband.

He nipped at my ear. "It's our wedding night, Wil."

I looked down at our daughter, making my decision quickly. Cupping her head, I buried my nose in her hair, inhaling her sweet baby smell. She didn't have that newborn smell anymore, but I was still in love with the way she smelled.

I hadn't told Damien yet, but I wanted another one. Not now—I was only four months postpartum, and even though my doctor had assured me everything was healed down there, I still wanted to wait a bit. To enjoy the time with *just Opal.*

"Let me go find Auntie Luna," I said in a soft whisper to Opal's head. "And then you get to have a little sleepover." She'd be in good hands.

Damien leaned down, whispering in Opal's ear before kissing the crown of her head. "Love you, my little witching," I was pretty sure. His nickname for her made me swoon. It was so sweet, seeing him be a daddy. He was a natural with her, and it was obvious every time he held her or played with her just how much he loved her.

It was doing unfair things to my ovaries.

Damien chuckled as I weaved through the crowds—through the hoards of demons, who weren't as scary looking as they'd been the first time I'd come here. Maybe it was the shock factor rubbing off, but most of them were honestly *nice.* Especially the ones who weren't trying to sign contracts and steal souls. But no matter what, I knew my demon would protect me—just as much as I could protect myself.

Thank you, magic.

"Luna!" I exclaimed, finding my younger sister at the edge of the dance floor, sipping on a glass of demon wine. Normally, I would have had some myself, but I'd planned on feeding Opal tonight, so I'd abstained.

"Hey, Wil." Her lips split in a knowing smile. "Damien tell you are plan?"

I nodded. "You're really okay with taking her?" I switched Opal from one hip to the other, trying to absorb all her baby-cuteness before I gave her up.

"Of course. What's one more?" She reached out, doing the grabby hands motion. "Now gimme my niece so I can cuddle her."

"If anything happens, just let us know. We'll come back."

"She'll be *fine*," my sister promised. It was weird to see her like this—all grown up. So fiercely independent, and happy in her own right. She was a queen now, after all. "It's just one night."

"I know." I sighed, handing over my daughter to Luna's waiting arms. She instantly snuggled her against her chest, cooing sweet words at Opal.

Luna waggled her eyebrows. "Now go let your demon husband ravish you, girl. That dress doesn't stand a chance."

I winced. "But it's so nice! I don't want it destroyed."

"Says the girl who picked the lace-up back."

"Well, it seemed prettier than a zipper." I shrugged.

"It's okay—Zain practically popped all the buttons trying to get mine off." She giggled, and then sighed happily. "Sometimes this still doesn't feel real."

"Kidnapped by a demon prince and carted off to be his wife? I bet."

Luna rolled her eyes, and I knew she would have swatted me on the shoulder if she didn't have a baby in her arms. "Go on then. Go get laid. Maybe make another one of these."

A laugh burst from my lips. "Luna! She's only four months old."

"What?" She shrugged. "I'm just saying, you two made a cute kid."

"Thanks, Lu. I love you." I pulled her in close, giving her a hug before plopping one last kiss on my baby girl's head. "Love you too, Opal. Be a good girl for Auntie Luna."

"She's an angel," Luna reassured me—before shooing me away so she could have my baby all to herself.

Trudging back over to Damien, I sighed, letting him wrap his arms around me. "That was harder than I thought it would be," I mumbled, resting my forehead against his strong chest.

"Want me to take your mind off of it?" He asked, curling a hand around my shoulder. His voice held the promise of delicious sex and countless orgasms—and who was I to turn that down?

"Yes. Please."

He teleported us out of there, wrapping us in his shadow magic before I could even blink.

* * *

"Damien." I gasped. "What's all this?" I whirled, staring at my demon. When did he have the time to do all of this? I'd expected—well, I hadn't expected anything, because we still had an infant at home. But he'd taken us straight to the giant bathroom I loved in the house he built. There were dozens of candles—still unlit, though between the two of us that would only take a moment—and a trail of purple petals that led to the bedroom.

"I snuck out earlier," he responded, resting his forehead against mine. "Wanted to make this night special for you."

"Oh, my love." I cupped his face, holding my world in my hands. My husband. My mate. My demon. "It already is."

He grinned, his fangs popping loose from his mouth. "You deserve the world, Willow. And I intend to give it to you."

Didn't he know he'd already given me that?

Running my fingers down his chest, I admired my husband's body. Even if he wore them so infrequently, he looked damn good in a tux. I untied his bowtie, getting ready to pull it off, and he took a deep breath.

"Turn around," Damien said, his voice almost a purr.

Obeying his command, I turned away from him, and felt as his fingers swept my hair off the back of my neck. He placed a kiss to my shoulder before those deft fingers started tugging at the laces of my dress.

Luna was right.

"What?" He growled.

I giggled. "She said you were going to rip it off of me when you couldn't get the laces undone."

"Fuck the laces," Damien muttered, before giving up and slicing them open. I *supposed* those shapeshifting abilities did come in handy every once in awhile. Even if I'd randomly wake up and find him curled across my feet in cat form some nights, and I'd roll my eyes and go back to bed.

My beautiful dress slid down my hips, and with just a few tugs, Damien had gotten it off of me, leaving me in just the little white bridal lingerie set I'd bought for the occasion.

It might have been our second wedding, but when I'd been hugely pregnant I hadn't gotten to wear anything cute under my wedding dress, so I was making up for lost time.

I turned around to face him, and the way his eyes flared when they trailed down my body made me feel sexy. *Wanted.*

My cheeks were warm, and my eyes dropped to his lips as I ran my tongue over mine.

"Your turn," I whispered, stepping closer to him and reaching up to push the jacket off his shoulders. "I don't think I ever told you how handsome you looked today."

He smirked as I tugged on the loose strap of his bowtie, pulling it off, before I started on the buttons of his shirt. I placed a kiss to his open chest as it became exposed, torturing him by going slowly down the front.

Damien groaned as I loosened the final one, whipping the shirt off in a flash.

"Bath?" He asked, flicking his eyes over the tub.

I shook my head. "Later. Bed now."

He chuckled, scooping me up into his arms. "I like what you're thinking, Willow." My voice was a rasp as he nuzzled his face into the crook of my neck. Inhaling my scent.

It had been so long since I'd had my mate's hands on me, for anything other than a quick kiss. Nothing like before. But I wouldn't trade our lives now for anything.

"What's running through that mind of yours?" He purred, as if he could scent my arousal. Maybe he could. I never really knew the extent of his demon abilities.

Damien set me down on the bed, and I fiddled with the little bow between my white lacy bra.

"That I want you inside of me. That I need to feel you."

He smirked, leaning down to kiss me. "That can be arranged, little witch." Then his pants were discarded on the floor, and he joined me on the bed, not hiding his breath of surprise when I straddled him, guiding his length into my entrance with no warning—no foreplay. I needed him to take me, *hard*. Needed to feel him pulsing inside of me.

Needed him to give me everything, just like he'd promised me so long ago.

My hands clutched at his shoulders as I slid down his cock, relishing in each inch as he stretched me, as I moved to accommodate his size.

"I love you," I gasped as I settled onto his lap, taking in every inch of him.

Damien's hands clutched at my waist as he helped me find my rhythm, riding him with careless abandon.

"I love you," he groaned. "*Wife.*" He nipped at my ear. "Gods, the fates really did make you for me."

I dug my fingers into the hair at the base of his skull as I worked my hips harder against him, the pace getting me maddeningly close—but not enough.

"Damien," I whined. "I need—"

"I know." He leaned in, pressing his lips to mine. Taking them in a dizzying kiss. "I've got you, Willow."

He always knew what I needed. Knew my thoughts—my mind, my heart, my very soul. As if all of those things spoke to him.

And when he unleashed his shadow powers, letting those tendrils brush over my nipples, giving my clit added stimulation—I saw stars.

"Fuck." He nipped at my neck, sinking those sharp canines of his into my mark—the one marking me as *his*. And after the sting passed, all that I felt was bliss, the feeling of our very essences tangling together as he thrust up inside of me. His hands grasping my body tightly to keep me in place as he fucked me. Another orgasm pulsed through me, pleasure flowing through every inch of my body as he hardened even further inside of me.

"*Husband,*" I said, letting out a deep moan.

Damien's roar of release was his only reply as he poured his seed inside of me. Filling me up with his cum.

"My mate," he said, brushing a hair off of my face as we slumped against each other.

I hummed sleepily, sated and happy as I let his scent fill my lungs.

Without slipping out of me, he guided us backwards onto the bed, his cock still half-hard inside of me. I was sure it would only be a few moments it'll he'd be ready to go again.

I didn't mind. We had all night, after all. And I'd needed this, too—just as much as he had. I nestled further into his side, kissing his pecs. Appreciating his bare chest for all that it was—the hard plane of his body that he kept finely toned.

Damien's hand rested on top of my abdomen. There were unshed words in his eyes, but I didn't need to be able to speak with him mind to mind to know what he was thinking.

I slid my hand on top of his.

"I can't wait to see you swell with our child again," he murmured, staring at the stretch marks and skin there with awe. I was sure magic could have removed them, but I didn't want to be ashamed of the body that had let me bring Opal into this world. That would bring another child into it. Not yet, but soon.

Resting my forehead with his, I kissed him lightly. Smiled. My heart clenched at how happy he looked. How normal this had become for us.

A reminder that we'd gotten the life I could only ever have dreamed about.

And who would have guessed that I'd be doing it all with a demon by my side?

253

BONUS EPILOGUE

Damien

I stared down at the little kitten on the floor whose tail was swishing back and forth happily. Crossing my arms over my chest, the leather jacket on my back stretched with the movement.

"Willow?" I called, figuring this was just another prank. She didn't *actually* get a new cat, right? That seemed like a decision she would have consulted with me first about.

Besides, I liked being the *cat* of the house. And the man of the house. Even if being a demon meant I wasn't really a human *man*. Still, my senses weren't tingling. No unusual scents were in our home, which meant there wasn't an intruder.

No unusual scent, except… One of my mate's delicious smelling brews must have been cooking, because the whole house smelled the way she did. Sweet, *alluring*. Desire flooded my body, and I resisted a groan.

Even when she didn't work in the bakery anymore, the smell of coffee lingered. Though these days, that was limited to one cup a day.

"Hm?" My wife said as she padded into the living room, her hand resting on her stomach. She looked as beautiful as ever, with her long, flowing golden-brown locks tumbled down her shoulders and back.

Willow was wearing a dark green sweater dress that hugged her curves and showed off her pregnant belly. I wouldn't be the only male in the house for much longer. I looked forward to welcoming our son into the world.

Even if I'd been so sure we would have another girl. *Next time,* I thought, the idea making my cock thicken in my pants. Shaking my head, I turned my thoughts away from my pregnant wife, and back to the tiny thing sitting on our floor.

"When did we get a kitten?" I asked her, staring at the creature. "I didn't think we'd agreed to get a cat." I blinked. The tiny cat blinked back, it's large yellow-green eyes staring up at me.

Her eyes tracked to where I was looking. "Um." Those bright green eyes widened. "We didn't."

"So who's this then? We got a little stray in our house?" The little thing was a dark gray color, and I crouched down, making clicking noises with my tongue as it started to purr, rubbing against my hand.

"Damien—" Willow started to say, warning evident in her tone.

I scratched the kitten's tummy. "She's just a little sweetie, huh?"

Picking her up, I rubbed at the top of her head, my witch's eyes sparkling with delight as I cradled the tiny thing against my large body.

A giggle ripped through the room, and then the kitten in my arms was Opal. Our daughter. Who was stark naked. I chuckled.

She threw up her hands. "Again, Daddy!"

"I didn't know she could do that." Willow's eyes widened as I walked towards her bedroom to grab her a new pair of clothes.

"Me either." I grinned, sliding the hand not holding Opal into hers and squeezing. "We have a little shapeshifter on our hands, baby." I suspected we'd be seeing a lot more repeats of today. If she was half as mischievous as I had been growing up, we'd have our hands full.

Willow tugged on a dark curl on our daughter's head. "That's my little witchling, huh?" She kissed our daughter's cheek.

"*Our* little witchling," I agreed as Opal squirmed to get down.

Waddling over to the closet, my wife pulled out a new pair of clothes for her, letting out a small laugh. "I guess what did we expect from a half demon, half witch, right?"

I took the dress and undies, wrangling up our two-year old until she was wearing the polka dotted garment and free to run around the house again.

Leaning against me, Willow murmured, "Maybe you should show her the ropes, huh?"

I arched an eyebrow. "The ropes?"

"Of being a cat." Her eyes twinkled with humor.

Rolling my eyes, I wrapped my arms around her belly. "What are we going to do if we end up with a whole clutter of cats, hm?"

She tilted her head to glare up at me. "How many kids do you think I'm having? There isn't a litter of kittens in here."

"No." I rubbed my nose against her neck. "Just one."

"Our perfect little boy." She sighed happily, resting her hand over mine. "Just a few more months."

Humming against her skin, I took a deep pull of her scent. "And then we can have another one. Or two."

"Damien!" She shrieked as I pressed my lips to her soft skin.

Spinning her in my arms, I scooped her up, carrying her out of Opal's room.

"Put me down," she said, poking at my chest. "I'm heavy."

"You're not," I said, quirking an eyebrow. "Don't forget, I'm an all-powerful demon, little witch. I could lift two of you."

"I liked you better when you were a cat," Willow muttered, rolling her eyes.

"That's not what you said last night when I had my tongue buried in your—" I flirted, flashing her a grin, a sharp canine tooth popping out over my lip.

Willow's hand clasped over my mouth. "Damien!" She scolded me as I carried her to the living room.

Nipping the palm of her hand, she pulled back, rubbing her fingers over my jaw. "Opal's not going to remember, my mate."

Still, she pouted until I deposited her on the couch, grabbing her ankles and massaging them. "Now, what's that delicious smell that's brewing in the kitchen?"

"Oh." She sighed, shutting her eyes. "That feels so good." A small moan slipped from her lips.

After a few minutes, her body relaxed, and she looked back up at me. I still had her feet in my lap.

She tucked a lock of hair behind her ear. "I'm just… trying some new recipes. Thought maybe I'd get back into potion making again. I'd always been good at it, and pleasant grove doesn't have an apothecary right now, so…" She looked hopeful. "People were always coming to me for different brews, even when I worked at the bakery. I feel like I've struggled with my place here, in life, and I've just been thinking about what's next." Her fingers traced circles over her belly.

"I think that sounds great."

"You do?"

A hum came from my throat. "Of course. Whatever makes you happy." I wanted her to feel fulfilled. Wanted her by my side always, but I did my best not to become a feral, possessive animal whenever she left my side.

Her having my scent all over her helped some. So did her carrying my child, the sight of her swollen belly that soothed my instincts. She was mine, and that would never change. No other male would dare to touch her.

"What about you?" Willow asked, nudging me with her foot. "What makes *you* happy?"

"Ah." I paused. What made me happy? She did. This life here, with her, Opal and our unborn child. "You are all I could have ever asked for. This life of peace. I don't know that I ever imagined what my life would be like if it was my own. I expected to serve my father until the ends of my days." A frown slipped over my lips. "What more could I want?"

I had helped with things around town. Her coven had been wary of me, but they'd warmed up to me. But maybe that was because I tended to be volunteered first for manual labor and I was good with my hands.

"You're allowed to dream of more, though." She sounded… sad.

Didn't she know this was all I'd ever dreamed of? But then again… There was more.

"I do." I cleared my throat. "Now that my father is gone, and my brother is King, I'd like to spend more time in the demon realm. In that house I built with my own two hands. I'd like to teach our children about who they are. Witch and demon both." Willow's eyes were shining with unshed tears when I looked back at her. "But we have time for that. Many, many years. I want to enjoy this time, too. In the human realm. With your witches."

Because I knew that this time was fleeting for her. I'd lived almost three hundred years before she came into my life, and who knew how many we'd have together now that our life-forces were tied? But here, now… I liked this cozy little home.

"Damien."

"Hmm?" I looked up at her, and she tilted her chin. "Look."

There was a little black fluffball sleeping on the arm of the couch. I scooped up our daughter in kitten form and placed her on her mother's tummy.

Willow ran a finger between her little ears. "How old were you when you shifted for the first time?"

"I'm not sure," I murmured, feeling in awe as I watched them. "Most shifters can't control their transformations when they're this young. Strong emotions—or states of exhaustion—can trigger it."

"Hmm."

"What?" I raised an eyebrow.

"Just thinking that explains some things." She gave me a little smirk. "So on nights where I need a foot warmer, all I need to do is wear you out, huh?"

"For *kids*." I crossed my arms over my chest. "Fully grown males aren't susceptible to that." *Much.* Though sometimes I still reverted to cat form and slept on her feet just because I liked to.

It made me feel needed.

The same way I felt needed when I tied her up with my shadows and buried myself inside her tight heat. I'd always be there to satisfy her every whim, after all.

I slid my hand up her calf. "Maybe it's you who needs to be worn out, mate," I purred.

She bit her lip, looking up at me through half-lidded eyes. "Later," she murmured.

"Later," I promised, knowing I'd hold true to every word.

Only the best for the witch I loved more than life.

* * *

Willow

I watched as the tiny gray kitten ran around in our living room, being chased by a much larger black cat.

Damien was having too much fun with our discovery that our little girl could also shape-shift, and my hormones were weeping every time I watched him be so gentle with our daughter. He was such a good dad. Though I knew he had his own fears, they were completely unfounded.

I couldn't wait to watch him raise our son, too. Heat flooded my core when I thought about his words from earlier. *Another one or two.* God, was it insane? Maybe. But the way he worshipped my pregnant body... Yeah, I wasn't complaining.

Thankfully, we had plenty of time. Forever was still a daunting concept, even if I'd had over three years to get used to it. It was hard to imagine not aging. That everything would change around us, but we'd be frozen in time. So, I just wasn't thinking about it. A problem for later.

I rubbed at my belly, feeling a kick. I could already tell he was strong.

Hopefully, he'd be just like his daddy. Even his blood red eyes didn't phase me anymore. I'd stopped making him glamor himself when we went out into town. The witches who knew us wouldn't say anything, and those who didn't, well… they could mind their own business.

My sister was the Queen of the demons, and I was damn proud I was married to one. Besides, we'd become a lot more accepting of other paranormal creatures over the last two years. Turns out, Pleasant Grove had been shutting ourselves off from a lot more than the human world, and meeting Damien had helped us realize that. Now, we were a thriving city full of many other species.

And it helped that Eryne and many of my coven, including my cousin, had found love of their own. Though those were their stories to tell.

"I think she's out," Damien said, shifting from cat form to human form in a flash. It used to startle me, but these days I was used to it.

Most of the time. When he shifted with clothes on. Sometimes he still caught me off guard in the middle of the night. Though the sex that usually resulted from that was… *hot,* to say the least.

Sure enough, our daughter was asleep. *And,* she'd shifted back to her toddler form, that polka dot dress from earlier still on her body this time. Well, that was something.

I took a step towards her so I could pick her up, but Damien stopped me. "I got this. You just relax."

A sigh slipped from my lips, but I knew there was no arguing with him. Not while I was heavy with his child.

He pressed his lips to mine once Opal was in his arms. "Meet you in bed? I believe I have some earlier promises to keep." Damien waggled his eyebrows. My demon certainly loved to indulge me, even when hormones were driving me crazy with need.

Turns out that pregnancy sex was somehow even hotter than when he used his shadow powers on me, so no complaints here.

"I like the sound of that, husband," I said, a seductive lilt to my voice. I liked it a *lot*.

* * *

He laid me on the bed carefully, and Damien's fangs poked out over his lips as he seemed to drink me in.

"What are you doing?" I murmured, reaching out to pull him down over top of me, but he stood in place. Adjusting the pillow behind me, I stared up into his deep red eyes. At the messy dark hair I loved to run my fingers through.

How had I gotten so lucky?

"Admiring my wife," he said with a hum. "My mate."

I ran my tongue over my lower lip. "Why look when you can have me?"

His shadows caressed my skin with a teasing touch, brushing over my already hardened nipples and making a small moan slip from my lips.

"Please," I said, willing to resort to begging. Arousal already pooled between my thighs, and I was eager for him.

"Does my little witch need me to touch her?" A devious smirk curled over his lips as he wrapped a tendril of his power around my ankle, letting it wander up my leg before his power pried my legs apart.

All the while, he stood over me, fully clothed, not moving. Meanwhile, my sweater was forgotten on the floor, since he'd pounced on me as soon as we'd both slipped inside of our room.

"Not fair," I whined as I felt a brush over my clit. Needy. I tried to rub my thighs together, but he held them apart. *"Damien."*

"No?" He ran his tongue over his lower lip, over those canine teeth that he loved to sink into me at the height of pleasure. "You don't want to feel my shadows inside of you?"

Oh. Damien teased my entrance before plunging inside of me. It felt like his hands were everywhere. Like he was touching each spot he knew would drive me crazy.

"*Yes,*" I agreed, knowing I'd surrender to the pleasure. Always. Because when he touched me like this, he knew exactly what he was doing. "Give it to me," I cried out. Needing this. Needing everything.

His power filled me, *deep,* and I didn't bother trying to hold in my gasp. He circled my clit as his shadows played with my nipples, and it wasn't long until I was already close to the edge, crying out with each brush of his power against my body. Tilting my head back as I came, I rode out the bursts of pleasure, all too aware of how empty I was, how desperate I was to have him inside of me.

"I need you," I begged, my eyes connecting with his. Seeing the heat, the lust swirling inside of them, I knew it wouldn't take much. "Come here, my demon."

In the flash of an eye, he shed his clothes, and then he was on top of me, lips claiming mine in a searing kiss. Damien's hands cupped my cheeks, and I let him take my lips, my mouth, devouring me with each pass of his tongue over mine.

"My mate," he murmured, nipping at my lower lip. "So beautiful and needy for me." He ground his hardened length over my entrance, and I practically saw stars.

"Yes," I said with a gasp.

He lined up his cock with my entrance, burying himself inside of me in one deep thrust.

"*Fuck*," he groaned, bringing one hand to rest on my belly and the other angling my hips. "You feel so good. Like you were made for me." His eyes were dark, his irises barely visible as he rocked his hips into mine.

My only response was a moan, and I could feel him *everywhere*. He was so deep inside of me, each thrust making my muscles contract around him.

I'm gonna— I said into his mind, losing my ability to speak. Wrapping my arms around his neck, I couldn't stop the movements of my hips, the way they were rising in time to meet his thrusts.

Damien lowered his head, brushing his fangs over my mate mark. "Come for me, Willow. Let me feel you gush all over my cock, baby." He groaned.

His teeth sunk into my neck without warning, and I came instantly, the pleasure bursting inside my veins as he kept fucking me through it.

Pulling his mouth away from my neck, he licked at the mark, before lifting up to take my lips with his. I could feel him hardening further inside of me, and it was maddening how good it felt. Our mouths pressed together, sharing each breath, his tongue intertwining with mine as he pumped into me.

I knew he was close, but the telltale signs of another orgasm were already creeping in. My magic was swirling just under the surface of my body, and I knew it was right there—desperate to come out.

His words were only a rasp when he asked, "Do you think you can give me another?"

"It's too much," I cried, shaking my head as I dug my fingers into his back.

He resumed his explorations with his shadows—brushing over my clit, teasing my nipples, and driving me wild before he kissed me again.

"So sensitive," he murmured, dipping his head down to take one of my tender breasts into his mouth. He licked and sucked at my nipple, and that was when I realized the bastard was prolonging this, torturing me with pleasure while taking none for himself.

I squeezed my internal muscles around him, and he groaned.

"Willow." His voice was low, a warning. But I wanted him to unleash himself. "Fuck."

"Let go," I murmured, brushing my nose over his as he repositioned us, grabbing one of my legs so he could reach deeper inside of me. "Fuck me, Damien."

His demon side took over, and he buried himself inside of me. "Gonna come in this tight pussy," he groaned, his words causing a moan to slip from my lips. "Already full of my child. Fuck, I love seeing you like this. Going to get you pregnant again after this. Over and over, so I can watch you swell with my child. So fucking beautiful."

His shadows dipped inside of me, fucking me the same way he was with his cock.

My magic unleashed as I came once again, my hair floating in the air, and random objects levitating around us. I barely noticed, too lost in him. In the way he was looking at me, because even when he was rough with me I could see the love on his face.

He came with a growl, burying his head in my neck and wrapping his arms around my body, keeping me pressed tightly against him as he filled me with his cum. I relaxed in his arms, sighing happily, even as everything I'd been holding afloat with magic fell to the ground.

We rolled onto our sides, Damien content to stay just like this, not pulling out even as he eventually softened inside of me. I ran my fingers through his hair, listening as his breathing evened out.

"How are you feeling?" He asked, his eyes back to their normal shade of brilliant red. His hands cupped my belly, no doubt feeling our child moving inside of me. I'd never quite get used to that, even if it was our second.

"Good." I yawned, feeling content. "Great, actually." I reached down to let one of my hands rest over his. "Even if your child likes to sit on my bladder and kick me in the ribs."

He winced, kissing my collarbone. "I am sorry, my love."

A small price to pay, I thought. Because I already loved this baby so much, just like I loved Opal more than life itself.

I wiggled against him to get comfortable, and he groaned. "*Willow—*"

"Already?" I giggled, feeling him hardening once again. "You really are insatiable. That demon stamina of yours."

"I can't help it," he muttered, brushing a few strands of hair off my sweaty skin. "You're everything, my mate."

"And you're mine," I agreed, intertwining our fingers. "I love you, demon."

"I love you, witch," he murmured, taking the moment to kiss me softly. "There's nothing in this world that I would trade you for. This life with you… I'm grateful for it. Even if you wish to have a job and spend less time in our home."

I wrinkled my nose, and he leaned forward to kiss the tip of it.

"I just mean that I want you to be happy. And I'll do whatever I can to ensure that happens. For the rest of eternity."

"I know." I snuggled my face into his bare chest. "Do you think we can go visit Luna and Zain in the demon realm?"

"You know there's no way I could ever say no to you, Willow."

I hummed, happiness filling my chest. "I know." Tilting my head, I looked up at him. "Thank you."

"For what?" He asked, a strange expression forming over his face.

"For being my home." The love of my life. The reason I woke up with a smile on my face each morning.

"Only if I can thank you for the same thing," he said, his free hand playing with a strand of my hair, our intertwined hands still resting against my pregnant belly. "For just as I am yours, you are mine."

"Forever," I promised. That was the truth of it.

I was his little witch and he was my demon, and I was more than grateful for this lifetime we would get to spend together.

Resting my forehead against his, I didn't say anything else. Instead, we let our bodies fill in the words, showing each other just how much we loved each other with each touch, each caress, each kiss.

"Forever," he murmured in agreement.

THE END

WICKEDLY YOURS

For all the girls who want a six and a half foot tall winged man to swoop in and tell them that they're fated mates.

(Me too.)

PLAYLIST

Make It To Me - Sam Smith

Haunted - Taylor Swift

Lavender Haze - Taylor Swift

I Knew You Were Trouble - Taylor Swift

Moonlight - Ariana Grande

Wicked Games - The Weeknd

I Can See You - Taylor Swift

Don't You Know - Jaymes Young

sex - EDEN

Mercy - Lewis Capaldi

gold rush - Taylor Swift

I Wanna Be Yours - Arctic Monkeys

Locked Eyes - Casual Sex

i can't breathe - Bea Miller

this is me trying - Taylor Swift

Gravity - Sara Bareilles

Labyrinth - Taylor Swift

Bedroom Hymns - Florence + The Machine

Fallin' All In You - Shawn Mendes

So It Goes… - Taylor Swift

Power Over Me - Dermot Kennedy

Be My Queen - Seafret

Queen Of The Night - Hey Violet

False God - Taylor Swift

2 die 4 - Addison Rae, Charli XCX

As Long As You're Mine - Stephen Schwartz, Irina Menzel

Die For You - The Weeknd
Starving - Hailee Steinfeld, Grey, Zedd
Dark Blue - Jack's Mannequin
Can't Help Falling In Love DARK - Tommee Profitt, brooke
What Was I Made For? - Billie Eilish
Tears of Gold - Faouzia
Hesitate - Jonas Brothers
A Safe Place to Land - Sara Bareilles, John Legend
So Close - Jon McLaughlin
If I Could Fly - One Direction
Call It What You Want - Taylor Swift
Until I Found You - Stephen Sanchez
King Of My Heart - Taylor Swift
Golden Hour - Kacey Musgraves

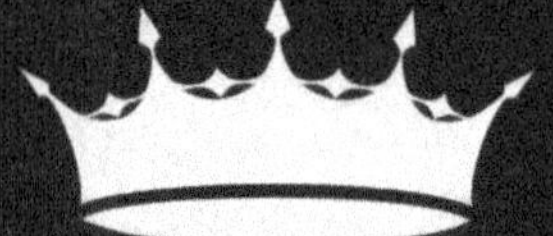

PROLOGUE
ZAIN

Damn Bastard. Couldn't he do the one thing I'd sent him to the human world to do?

Find *her*. My queen. The woman who would sit by my side and rule with me.

I could smell her on my brother—his mate.

He'd found his while I was beholden to this place. Ruling in my father's stead, even though he wouldn't concede full control to me. Not yet.

There was only one thing that stood between me and taking my rightful place on the throne: the witch destined for me.

I'd waited almost three hundred years for her, and yet I'd sent someone else out looking for her.

"I need more time," my brother Damien said from down on his knees.

Kneeling in front of me was a show, and we both knew it.

Crossing my arms over my chest, I raised an eyebrow. "Why? What exactly are you afraid of, little brother?"

As the second son of the Demon King, he'd endured our father's wrath growing up but none of the expectations of being the Crown Prince. And yet, no matter our own choices in the matter, we were both bound by roles we never asked for.

I'd grown into mine. Had to become whatever wicked thing I needed to be to survive here. In a palace of demons, there were very few who you could trust.

He grits his teeth. "You know exactly what I'm afraid of."

"I need her." I sighed, wishing it didn't have to be this way. That the fate of my kingdom didn't ride on one witch. "You can't keep me away forever." My eyes flared as lightning crackled outside.

"Just… give me until Halloween, at least. Please. Willow needs her sister." There was a desperation in his voice that I hadn't heard before. Maybe finding his fated pairing had changed that. Made him softer.

I couldn't afford for that to happen to me.

"Very well." Waving my hand, I dismissed my brother. "You have until then."

He disappeared into the shadows without another word.

I watched him go, contemplating my actions as my powers swirled around me. The darkness threatened to swallow me whole, and for a moment, I considered letting it. If only to be free from this torment, this constant *longing*.

But maybe it was time to take matters into my own hands. If he wouldn't bring her to me—fine. I'd go get her myself.

ONE
LUNA

Let's pumpkin spice things up a bit, read the sandwich board out front, complete with a drawing of a coffee cup and a scone. I smiled, knowing my sister would love it. Girl was obsessed with all things pumpkin.

Flicking on the lights, I took in the space, inhaling the smell of sweets and coffee beans.

It was a smell that instantly made me feel like home.

But maybe that was just from all the hours I'd spent here, whipping up new confections. After all, it was my bakery—*the Witches' Brew.* Years ago, I'd started it with the help of my sister. We had a pretty good thing going: I baked, and she did, well… everything else. I was probably biased, but she was the best barista in town. Willow never had to ask me twice when offering me a drink.

I loved this place. It was mid-October, and the entire storefront was decked out with Halloween decor. As soon as the air chilled, I'd started decorating. Pastels, because who said Halloween couldn't be cute? Bats were taped to the front windows, little paper ghosts hung from the ceiling, and orange string lights lit up the outside. Those barely scratched the surface of how in-depth my theming went.

Though once the season got in full swing, decorations were the last thing on my mind. I'd barely been able to keep my sugar cookies in stock the last few weeks. The Pleasant Grove townsfolk were constantly selling me out of the adorably frosted, spooky designs. Pumpkins, bats, black cats… the only limit was my imagination.

Luckily, in a town of witches, that wasn't too hard.

The sun hadn't even risen yet, but like always, I was here, ready to turn the ovens on and lose myself in a batch of cookie dough and a bowl of frosting. The refrigerated display case was empty, ready for me to fill it.

Of course, it helped that my commute to work was a whopping one minute since I lived in the one-bedroom apartment over the bakery in downtown Pleasant Grove. This morning, I'd pulled on a pair of jeans and a pink t-shirt that said *Boo, You Whore* with an adorable ghost on it. My pale blonde hair was pulled back and braided into two French braids. I'd only applied a light application of makeup on this morning to cover the dark circles under my eyes.

Even with the nippy October air, I hadn't bothered with a coat—one of the biggest perks of living right downstairs. Plus, I tended to overheat being in the kitchens all morning.

Grabbing my apron and sliding it over my head, I started my prep work in the kitchen. With the flick of a wrist, drawers and cabinets were opened, objects flying around me and settling onto the countertops.

I let myself get lost in a flurry of flour, sugar, and butter as the aroma of freshly baked goods slowly filled the air. Thank god for industrial mixers—they were practically better than magic. Maybe. It was close.

By the time I'd looked at the clock again, it was almost seven, and the bakery case out front was full. While I made fresh baked goods every day, I also kept a stock of popular items in our large fridges.

The tinkling of keys in the door alerted me to my sister's presence, and I attempted to brush some of the flour off my apron.

Willow finally shuffled into the kitchen, blinking back a yawn. "She's alive," I said with a hand flourish that made the air whoosh past her.

"Coffee," she muttered, dropping her stuff. "I need coffee." My sister was wearing a green sweater dress with tan heeled booties, and had left her light brown hair down, letting it fall in loose waves around her face.

I'd always loved her hair, given my own was stick-straight. Even with copious amounts of product, it would never hold a curl. Still, I hadn't given up yet. One day, *something* would work, right? Until then, I'd just be jealous of hers.

Willow went out front, fumbling with the coffee machines. When she came back into the kitchen, it was with two steaming mugs in her hand. She handed me one, and I took a small sip, careful not to burn myself.

The floral tang of the lavender latte exploded on my tongue, the sweet flavor overriding my taste buds. Delicious. Swiping my tongue over my lips, I caught the leftover foam before setting the mug down.

"That's better," she groaned, eyes shut as she took a long drink from the mug.

"Not getting much sleep, Wil?" I asked, teasing her.

"Shut up, Luna," my sister muttered, though there was no bite to her tone.

"Is your new houseguest keeping you up?"

She looked into the cup of coffee, her cheeks pink as I grinned.

At the beginning of the month, Willow had adopted a black cat named Damien. I'd encouraged it since she'd seemed lonely lately, living in our childhood home all alone. Only later the next week, she'd surprised me by showing up with a dark-haired man with the same name on her arm to our town's annual Pumpkin Festival.

I wasn't dumb. I could put two and two together. Clearly, there was magic behind it. *But why hadn't she asked me for help?* The idea still stung, though she hadn't approached the coven, either. But that was Willow. Headstrong and determined. A trait the Clarke girls both shared.

Even if she'd been avoiding the topic of conversation about what had happened altogether, something was happening between them. I could feel the change in her heart.

She cared about him. And wasn't that the most dangerous thing of all?

My sister was quiet, so I just carried on. "I'm just happy you finally agreed to go to the bar with me."

I'd bought a new dress recently, and I desperately needed to let loose. I loved my job—loved my life—but I wanted to forget about everything for one night. Wanted to get happy drunk and dance my ass off in the Enchanted Cauldron.

That way, I didn't think about the dreams haunting my sleep—the vision of those golden eyes that I just couldn't shake off.

But mostly, deep down, the feeling that something was missing in my life.

Willow relaxed at the subject change, running her fingers through her hair. "Me too. It'll be fun. Sorry I've been so MIA lately."

I waved her off. She'd given up everything to help me start my dream. We'd bought it together, but she'd taken on both running the storefront *and* playing barista until we'd been making enough to hire staff. So, I didn't blame her for taking some time for herself.

Sometimes I still felt bad for moving out and leaving her in the big house that our parents had left us, but I'd wanted to feel like an actual adult instead of letting her take care of me. And I didn't mind living alone much, especially considering that I saw most of our little town's residents every day. The Pleasant Grove residents couldn't resist one of my scones, and I'd happily take their money to do what I loved.

"I'm okay here. Plus, I have Eryne." We'd hired the short-haired ginger last year as a barista. She was an enormous help, especially when Willow was busy with ordering supplies and bookkeeping. Lately, she'd been closing the bakery down on her own, letting me head upstairs since I'd been up before the sun.

Secretly, I thrived in the night. I always felt like I had my best ideas when the moon was still high in the sky.

Like it somehow *called* to me.

To the magic in my veins.

Or maybe it was just the only time I felt comfortable letting it free.

I'd always been different. For as long as I could remember, I'd always had strange dreams. Hazy visions of moments that hadn't happened yet. Things that didn't quite make sense.

And I *knew* things. Things I couldn't explain.

What sort of witch didn't even understand her true magic?

A sorry excuse for one. One who could have become a powerful seer but had chosen something safe instead. Something comfortable. Something that felt like home.

That was how I'd chosen to become a baker.

Flicking my fingers to pull a cookbook off the shelf with magic, I moved my finger in the air to swipe through pages till I landed on the recipe that I was looking for.

"What are you doing?" Willow asked, watching me rumble through cupboards, using my powers to pull out bowls and then the flour, sugar, and everything else I needed.

"Making another batch of scones."

I didn't normally make lemon lavender scones—my favorite—during October, but Willow's coffee had inspired me, and maybe it would settle the restlessness in my gut.

That, and drinking a lot of alcohol tonight.

Shrugging, Willow left me to it, tying on her apron before heading back out to the front to serve the citizens of Pleasant Grove, who'd be arriving as soon as we opened the door at eight sharp.

After dumping all the dry ingredients in my bowl, I tried not to think about my dream from last night. The one that always started the same way. A flash of dark hair. Golden eyes. Mighty wings that unfurled in front of me. A palace that I was sure I'd never seen before.

A shiver ran down my spine. Those eyes had always followed me. Sometimes, in the darkness or when I was alone, I thought I'd see them looking back at me.

And yet, when I looked again—they were gone.

I had a feeling I'd see them again. I always did.

282

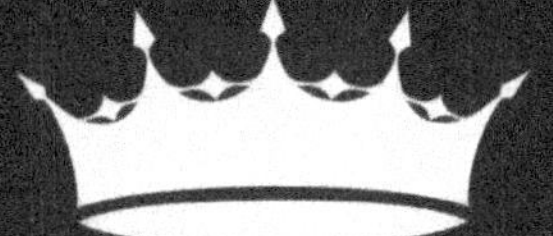

TWO
ZAIN

Crossing my arms over my chest, I stared down at the group of demons who were *supposed* to serve as my advisors. Not that they were doing much in the way of *advising* right now. Instead, they were all *telling* me what to do, ignoring my thoughts completely.

We were gathered in my study, standing around the large, scaled map I had of the demon realm. With magic, we'd overlaid a map of the human world. Thanks to my brother using his powers to teleport in and out of the place, I knew exactly where to look.

"I'm going to go get her," I declared. "Surely, that would be easier than this *nonsense*." Lowering my brow, I waved my hand at the five of them.

I was tired of debating it. Tired of ignoring the pull I felt towards her.

Lilith frowned at me. "And you think *that* will work?" Her dark hair framed a pair of curved onyx horns, and the pair of leathery wings she used to fly—making her my perfect spy—sat closed on her back.

I'd recruited her two centuries ago, rescuing her when a group of much larger demons had been intent on beating her into a bloody pulp in an alley.

All because she'd been looking for work—and refused their advances.

Sometimes, I still saw her as that small teenager, not the woman she'd become.

The weapon I'd honed her to be.

Lightning cracked outside. "Why wouldn't it?" I tried to temper down my annoyance.

The group didn't even flinch, used to my outbursts by now.

Of course they were. Like Lilith, I'd picked them all up off the streets. They'd all had a fight in their eyes, perseverance that didn't quit. So I'd convinced them each to work for me and earned their loyalty until I knew they would never betray me.

"You really know *nothing* about women." Asura snorted, picking at a few of the scales on her snakelike skin, her yellow slitted eyes blinking at me. There was venom in her veins, thanks to her heritage, though she hardly ever used it.

"As evident by the *two-to-one* ratio of men to women in this group," Lilith added on, her tone matter-of-fact and giving no room for argument. As if there wasn't a *reason* they were all here, by my side. "On second thought, maybe we *should* encourage him to fetch her faster. Then we wouldn't be put in this position all the time."

Talon shook his head as if amused by the two women's musings but properly kept his mouth shut.

His twin brother, Thorn, stood at his side. The two were practically mirror images of each other, and both served as my guards.

Not that I felt I *needed* either of them—I was powerful enough on my own to take down any demon in the entire kingdom. Except for one.

And once I had my queen by my side, her power joined with mine? No one stood a chance of overthrowing me or trying to take the crown that was rightfully *mine*.

But I need her here first. The thought refocused me.

"Look. You all agreed with the plan." I growled, my fist slamming down on the edge of the table. I didn't want any other distractions or diversions from the current topic of conversation. "How is *this* any different?"

"That was when *Damien* was going to bring her back," Kairos said, doing his best to appear nonchalant.

"And how long am I supposed to sit around and wait?" Baring my teeth, I did my best not to resort to my base instincts. "How long do you want me to sit here, watching the kingdom fall apart? We need her."

The statement was on the tip of my tongue, but I held it back. *I need her.* For more reasons than they even knew.

I was too unstable, my body needing to find its other half.

"Yes, you need her power," Asura remarked, "but you also need her to come *willingly*. If you are to be united…"

I gritted my teeth, anger pursing through me. "I *know*."

The bond would only work with what was freely given. Not taken. *Fuck.* Shadows darkened the room as I paced across the wooden floor. I needed to get my emotions under control before the power surging in me was set free. Before an outburst of mine led to someone getting seriously hurt.

As if I didn't need more reasons to want her here. But it wasn't an option anymore.

Damien's first mistake was finding her and not immediately surrendering her to me. Not bringing me the witch who the fates had foretold as mine.

Rubbing at my temples, I held back my groan despite no one chiming in again. "I can't wait any longer. Now. I *must* go now. I'll bring her back kicking and screaming if I have to. She'll understand in time."

She would sit on the throne next to mine, wearing the crown I had made for her, *my* ring on her finger.

I dared them all to challenge me on that. They could disagree on everything—but not on the fact that she had been made for me.

Lilith's voice was hesitant when she chimed in once again, her red eyes—the most common color amongst demons—flaring. "If I may, Zain." Holding in a growl, ignoring how feral I felt, I nodded at her. Urging her to speak. "You need to woo her."

"What?" I blinked, surprised. That was not what I'd expected.

"Win her over. Make her fall in love with you, and *then* ask her to come back with you. Her loyalty is just as important as her place by your side."

"But that takes time." I furrowed my eyebrows. "Time we don't have." I waved a hand at the map in front of me. The one that showed all the demons I'd one day rule over. "I don't need her to love me."

No. I didn't need love. I'd learned that a long time ago. Love would only hurt you.

I just needed her to be by my side. Worse case, I could give her a bargain. A demon's deal. It was tricky magic, but it could work.

"But you *do* need her to agree to come back with you. To not *hate* you." Lilith shrugged her shoulders as she picked at her pointed fingernails, which were painted a blood red shade. "I'm just saying. It's not the worst plan."

Kairos nodded in agreement. "She has a point."

If it was possible for me to glare daggers at them, that was what I would currently be doing.

As it was, I was trying to decide why I kept these idiots around.

Probably because, despite it all, they were the closest thing I had to friends. Because I trusted them, I'd recruited each one of them to my side for a reason, and I knew they were right.

Muttering, I let loose a curse under my breath. "I'm going tonight," I said, finally, not acknowledging their suggestions. We'd do it my way, and then they'd see.

Everything would be fine once I had her by my side. Once she agreed to be mine.

I waved my hand, dismissing all of them as I studied the map once more, my eyes clouding over with red.

Exhaling deeply, I tried to ignore the pent-up frustration in my veins. How long could I ignore my father's summons? He'd want a report—want to know what I was up to—but I couldn't reveal my plans.

Not yet.

* * *

She's here.

The thought struck me as soon as I stepped foot inside the bar. I could sense her before I could see her. The knowledge that the girl I had been waiting for was in the same room as me was almost *overwhelming.*

Every nerve of my body was instantly alert—*searching*.

The bar was dingy and yet somehow charming. I could sense power and magic in these humans, these witches, but it was faint—nothing like the raw, untapped potential of the demons.

But then I sensed him. The one being I didn't wish to see tonight.

My brother.

Damien was sitting at the bar, nursing a glass of amber liquid, his eyes focused on the dance floor. On the brunette witch dancing beside a blonde, their bodies pressing against each other and laughter spilling from their lips. Laughter I shouldn't be able to hear from this distance away—given I was still just inside the door, shadows cloaked around me, hiding me from view.

He wouldn't be happy to see me, either. To know I'd disrespected his request for more time. Damien had wanted until the end of the month, and this witch was the reason. His mate. He wanted more time with her.

But I needed *her*. The blonde whose entire being seemed to light up this room, her smile already warming a piece of my cold, dead heart.

She was nothing like what I'd imagined.

Not that I'd allowed myself to imagine her in all the miserable, lonely years of my existence. I'd waited centuries for her, and even in the darkest of days, I'd known that the knowledge of her was too tempting a fantasy to fall into.

To let myself bathe in her light was more than I could ever hope for.

Even if every piece of me wanted to throw her over my shoulder and carry her out of here, to sink my teeth into the creamy, tender flesh of her neck and mark her as my own.

I wanted to bury my nose into her hair, to bring her scent into my airway until I could smell nothing but her. Until I'd memorized every piece of her being.

She was real. She was *here*.

My instincts were on over-drive, my thoughts too muddled with her to think clearly. If anyone got too close to her... I growled, my lips curling over my teeth as the thought occurred to me. *No.* I couldn't let anyone else touch her or let her go home with anyone else.

She was *mine*.

So I watched her. Like a predator stalks his prey. Like a feral beast in heat.

Waiting until the time was right to swoop in and claim her as my own.

THREE

LUNA

I loved how ridiculously into Halloween this town was, and especially that our only bar did these themed nights every so often. There was a special drink menu with spooky drink concoctions, and the speakers were playing classic Halloween hits like *I Put a Spell on You* and *The Monster Mash.* For a town of witches, sometimes it was a little too kitschy. But I was happy, and after a few songs spent dancing with my sister—and the two drinks I'd already consumed making me happy and carefree—I headed back to the bar.

Willow might as well have the time alone to dance with her man. She was trying to play it off that there was nothing between them, but the way they looked at each other… it was obvious what was growing between them. It didn't take a seer to tell that.

Damien was nothing like I'd ever imagined, and yet, he was undoubtedly perfect for her. And the way he'd watched her with a heated stare and the possessive growl when someone else had tried to move in on her? *Hot.* I fanned myself just thinking about it.

He was like a hero out of my romance novels, and I was decidedly envious. At one point, maybe I'd imagined that I'd find that too.

Not that I'd never been with a man before—I was no virgin and enjoyed sex. But relationships? That wasn't something I'd ever found for myself. Maybe it was because I'd never really been interested in anyone else in town. Most of the guys here I had known since diapers. *No thanks.*

I still had time, though. At twenty-five, what was the rush? There were years left where I could have fun and mess around before I needed to think about meeting someone. Find a man I loved and wanted to start a family with.

A man who looked at me like *that.*

But if anyone deserved love and a happy ending, it was Willow.

After our parents had died in an accident, she'd graduated college and come back to town, forsaking her own dream to help me start mine. The Witches' Brew wouldn't have existed without *both* of us. Willow had always been skilled at brewing potions, and she translated that into brewing the *best* coffee drinks in our entire town. I wasn't biased, either. Everyone came in the mornings to get a drink from her.

Her recipes were magical. I'd loved our time being in business together, even if it was coming to a close. I could sense it. Willow liked to say that I was a seer, but I'd never really thought of myself like that.

All thirteen witches in my coven had a special ability given to us at birth. Mine was *Precognition.* Seeing the future in my dreams.

It should have been useful, but I rarely understood the premonitions, which made me feel slightly worthless.

What good was a gift if you couldn't use it?

And yet… I had a good feeling about tonight, like I was supposed to be here, for whatever reason.

Brushing the thought away, I turned my gaze away from the dance floor. From my sister and her dark-haired suitor, who were still dancing close together. The bar, thankfully, wasn't as loud, and it had been easy to flag the bartender over to get a drink. I'd chosen a stool in the middle, giving me an equal view of the place and both ends of the counter.

Swiveling back and forth, I took another sip of my drink. It was probably straight sugar, but it was pretty, which basically fulfilled my only two requirements for alcohol.

Only—holy hell. Goddess, I'd never seen anyone who looked like *that*. In fact, I'd never believed in the *tall, dark, and handsome stranger* stereotype before. And yet, the man standing at the other edge of the bar was equally all three. He must have been ten years older than me, at least in his mid-thirties.

He looked almost familiar in a way that I couldn't quite put my finger on. Although all it would take would be one touch…

My mouth watered, even as there was a part of me that wanted to do a one-eighty and run. That saw the beautiful man and thought, *turn around, Luna. Look the other way, and don't go over there.*

But I'd never been good at listening to my intuition. No matter how good it was. It was one thing to see the future, and it was another to let that rule my life. Anything could happen, so why worry about it? There were plenty of times it hadn't come true or had played out in completely different ways than I'd thought.

If I could foresee the ending of a fling before it even started, was it even worth pursuing it? Maybe not, but it'd been so long since I'd had an orgasm given to me by anyone other than myself. Even the battery-powered wand I kept in my nightstand drawer wasn't the same anymore. I craved the connection. Craved intimacy. Something more.

So what was the harm? I didn't have to see the future.

The man sipped from his glass of amber-colored liquid, and I slid off my stool, my feet hitting the floor before I'd even made my decision yet.

I'd always been the girl who kept looking forward. Asking myself what was next. I'd been asking that for the last year. I loved my life in Pleasant Grove, the bakery I ran with my sister, and having all of my coven at my side.

But something was missing.

Orgasms. Yes, that was definitely it.

He looked like he would deliver, too. His dark hair was cut shorter on the sides but still long enough on the top that there would be something to hold on to. And the way he stood at the bar, all cocky and assuming, spoke to something in me.

Would he like it rough? I bit my lip, letting my hips sway as I walked towards him.

I'd zeroed in on him like I was in a trance. But who could blame me? Handsome strangers rarely showed up in our town. I liked to blame the wards that the founders had put up around the town, keeping non-magical folk out of our little community, but it was more than that.

Maybe it was the realization that Willow was moving on. She was out there on the dance floor, dancing with Damien. Her something more.

That was the funny thing about fate. It hit you when you were least expecting it. Maybe I'd never see him again. But maybe… I could see where it went. Even if it would only last a little while.

"Hi," I said, adjusting my lavender colored dress. The skirt was sewn to look like a spiderweb, with each seam coming to a point.

Why come to a themed night at The Enchanted Cauldron and not dress on theme? Ghoul's Night was the quintessential spooky night at the bar, but I'd never been a witch who loved the color black or jewel tones. Pastels were more my speed.

The dark-haired man raised his eyebrow as he looked at me like he was appraising me. Just one look and a shiver ran through me. Up close, he was absolutely delicious. I'd never met a stranger I'd been so instantly attracted to, but I couldn't deny how my body vibrated as I stood next to him.

"Hello." His voice was deep—a baritone I didn't hear often from the men in this town. It was hot. Sexy, even. I bit my lip as I slid onto the stool next to him, setting my drink down on the counter.

"Come here often?" I asked, taking a sip of my poisoned apple martini.

He chuckled, the deep sound reverberating through me. "No. This is a first."

"Ah." I wasn't even trying to hide the fact that I was staring at him. "Are you just passing through?" Pleasant Grove was well-warded, after all. Since normal humans had no clue that *magic* or witches even existed, most patrons here were magical themselves.

"You could say that."

"What else could you say?" I raised an eyebrow.

"That I'm looking for something."

"And did you find it?"

He looked directly at me, those dark eyes—almost black—practically peering into my soul. "I think I did."

"Oh." I took another drink, bobbing my head. "That's good."

The handsome stranger set his glass—now empty—down on the bar. "Yes. Yes, it is." He flashed me a dazzling smile, offering his hand to me. "Hi. I'm Zain."

"Luna," I answered, putting my hand in his to shake it. Just one touch and it was like an electric shock to my system. Or maybe that was my fingertips tingling from the contact.

Just one touch… The future was hazy but warm. And maybe that was enough. The not knowing was the exciting part.

"It's nice to meet you, Luna," Zain murmured, kissing my knuckles.

The alcohol must have been affecting my system more than I thought because I *giggled*. I actually giggled. *Was I drunk?* I peered at my glass. I had a good buzz going but didn't think I'd consumed that much.

Looking back up at the Zain—my handsome stranger—I got lost in his eyes. His hand reached out, cupping my cheek as he peered at me with unabashed curiosity.

"You're beautiful," he said, the thumb of his finger tracing my cheekbone.

Maybe the copious amounts of blush I always wore would hide the flush that ran to my face, even as a part of me preened at his words.

"Thank you." I dipped my head before finishing my drink. I'd never been so bold before, but there was something about him… Something that intrigued me. Something that I wanted to get to know more about.

"Do you… want to get out of here?" I murmured, placing the glass back down on the bar.

"Yes," he agreed.

And when he slipped his hand in mine, everything just felt… right.

* * *

I'd always thought Pleasant Grove at night was magical, and the waning crescent moon in the sky was like a calming balm to my racing thoughts. That warm fuzziness in my chest hadn't faded, and whatever it was from—*him* or the alcohol—I decided I didn't care.

Shoving my hands in my pockets before I did something dumb— like let my powers free or grab his hand again—I enjoyed our leisurely pace. We passed some of my favorite businesses in downtown, places I'd spent my whole life frequenting. Most of the shops in town had the most ridiculous puns as names, but I loved it.

Where else could you find magical artifacts next door to the most recent witch fashions?

"Is this your first time here?" I asked, looking over at the man walking by my side. The streets were quiet, given the hour of the night, but our walk felt comforting and unhurried. "In Pleasant Grove, I mean." He'd said he hadn't been to our bar before, so I was guessing it was his first time here, too.

He nodded his head.

"Hm. Is it prying if I asked how you got through the wards?" I tilted my head, watching him.

"I suppose not." Zain mused, but I noticed he didn't answer my question.

His presence was unusual. But that wasn't too strange, given that most people in this town were witches. But it was different—a sort of power I could almost feel, down to my bones—something I'd never encountered before.

Except… His presence felt familiar, too. Like—

"What?" He murmured, turning his head to meet mine. "You're staring."

My heart skipped a beat in my chest. "Nothing." I shook my head, shaking off the feeling.

We'd reached the end of Main Street, and if we kept going, we'd reach the residential streets of town. A few blocks over was my childhood home, the one my parents had left to Willow and me when they'd passed away.

Turning in a different direction, I headed towards the gazebo in the middle of town. He slipped his hand back into mine.

"Where are we going?" Zain asked, keeping pace with me as we kept our fingers interlocked. I kept my powers tampered down, willing myself not to look into his future.

Our future? If we had one. For once, I didn't want to know how it would end. I just wanted to enjoy the night. Besides, the warm fuzzy was a good feeling. I wanted to sink into it.

The entire square had a faint glow thanks to the orange lights strung around the gazebo. On Halloween, the entire block would bustle with trick-or-treaters, laughing children, and families of witches, but tonight, it was empty.

Dropping our hands, I plopped down on the grass, looking up at the stars. Zain laid down beside me, his knuckles pressing up against mine.

"I've always thought this was the best spot in town for looking up at the stars," I whispered. This moment felt intimate—almost precious. "You can see so many constellations here." Cait, my cousin, loved astrology and had taught me about all of them when we were younger. I could name most of the star formations visible in our sky easily now.

When the city was upgrading to modern lights years ago, they'd created local ordinances that no lights could point up towards the sky, preventing light pollution. It was incredible because on clear nights like tonight, it felt like you could see an entire galaxy—a world beyond our fingertips. If I stretched my fingers up, I could almost imagine them.

"It's wonderful."

I rolled onto the grass so I could look at him. He'd thrown one arm behind him, resting his head on it, but kept his eyes pointed upwards, giving me the perfect view of his undeniably handsome side profile. That powerful jaw, beautiful eyelashes—it should be illegal, actually, how long they were—and I wanted to run my fingers through his dark hair. It looked soft. But I kept my hands to myself. God, he was gorgeous.

"So…" I wiggled my fingers through the grass, feeling the magic of the world all around me. "Should we ask each other questions or something?" I hoped the darkness would hide the blush on my face. "I didn't bring you out here with ulterior motives anything."

He looked amused, giving me the nod of his head. "What do you want to know?"

Everything. But I couldn't exactly say that. I traced patterns in the grass instead of looking into his eyes. "I don't know. Do you have any siblings?"

"One. That I know of, at least."

There was bitterness in his voice, and it made me frown. "Older or younger?" I asked.

"I think it's my turn to ask something now." A chuckle slipped from his lips.

"Oh. Right." Returning to my back, I looked up at the stars. "Ask away."

"What do you do?"

A laugh burst out of me. Unexpected but… exhilarating. Because he truly had no idea who I was. And in this tiny town, that wasn't something I experienced very often. A chance to be *just* Luna. Not a Clarke daughter who had lost her parents. Not Willow's sister, who needed protecting. Not the baker who smiled at everyone each morning. Just me. I was all of those things, and yet, I was so much more.

"Is that not a normal question to ask?" He was frowning when I looked over at his face.

"No. Yes. Of course it's normal. It's just that no one's ever asked me it before. Everyone knows me in town. I run the local bakery."

"Ah. And you like it?"

"My question," I reminded him, poking at his arm. It was firm. *Hard.*

I'd never taken the time to properly appreciate a man's arms before, but then again, no one had ever worn a suit quite like he did. Black shirt, black suit coat—no tie—and black slacks, and he was mouthwatering. Delicious. *Was I still drunk?*

"Older or younger?" I repeated, still curious.

"He is younger than me, but we didn't grow up together." He paused, seeming to hesitate. "There's quite a few years between us."

"Oh." I fiddled with the hem of my dress. "I'm the younger sister," I offered, even though he hadn't asked. Our insistence on who asked the next question felt more like playing than it did insistence, anyway. "My sister is three years older than me, but after our parents died, it felt like she kind of took over their role of taking care of me. She helped me open the bakery and runs it with me. Even though I know that's not really what she wants to do." A deep sigh escaped me.

Even in the last few years, it felt like she was constantly putting me first when all I wanted was for her to prioritize her own dreams. Maybe now that Damien had come into her life, she would actually do that. If I was being honest, I envied that. The having someone part.

He hummed in response. "But you like it? Your job? Baking?"

I sighed, tracing the constellation of Cassiopeia in the sky with my eyes. "Sometimes." I looked over at him, and he raised an eyebrow. *Go on,* I liked to think it meant. And I did. "I love baking. I always will. Making something from scratch—that first bite when everything has paid off, and you've made something delicious—it's my favorite thing. But lately, I feel like I've been missing something. Like maybe it's time for something new." It was a truth I hadn't offered to anyone—even Willow.

But with him, with this stranger, it felt easier to admit.

"And you want that?" His fingers brushed against mine, and I wanted him to hold my hand again. The warm tingling feeling had faded, and I missed it.

"Maybe. But I feel guilty, too."

"Why?"

"Because this was the dream that I chose. And how selfish is it for me to change my mind? Willow—my sister—she gave up everything for me. Her life. A career of her choosing. And now, I just…" I shook my head.

"I don't think she'd feel that way."

"What?" Even though his words rang true, they still felt shocking.

"Your sister. I'm sure she wants you to be happy." He moved his hand over mine and gave me a reassuring squeeze.

My body instantly relaxed at his touch.

"Maybe." I still didn't know how I'd broach the subject with her, but maybe he was right. Of course, she wanted me to be happy. I'd never doubted that. But it was the rest of it I feared. Admitting I wanted something else.

Even if I didn't know what that something else was.

"Your turn." Letting go of my hand, he nudged my side.

"What?"

Zain shrugged. "To ask me another question."

"Oh. Right." His reminder distracted me from my thoughts. I appreciated the reprieve from my emotional spiral. "If you could do anything with your life, be anyone… What would you do?" *Who would you be?*

"That is…" He blew out a breath, furrowing his brow. "Difficult."

I nodded. "Yeah. For me, too."

"Growing up, I always knew the role I would fulfill when I got older. I resented it—watching all of my so-called friends get to have fun and screw around while I was stuck in lessons to learn what I needed to know. So I guess… Maybe I never thought about what I'd do if I had a choice."

"And now?"

"Now, I think a normal, simple life is more than I could ever ask for."

I couldn't keep the frown off my face. "Doesn't everyone deserve that?"

He gave a strangled sigh. "If only."

"You do." I turned my head so I could look squarely into his eyes.

I'd only just met him, but I knew that was true. He was lying with me in the grass after just meeting me, for goddess' sake. There were a thousand things we could have been doing besides stargazing on a Friday night, but he was here. With *me*.

"How old are you?" he asked.

"Twenty-five. But my birthday's in a few months, so…"

I'd always loved having a winter birthday, and secretly, it was my favorite season. Even if Willow's favorite was fall, with All Hallow's Eve the perfect cornerstone of the month—I loved the Winter Solstice. Christmas, too, though we didn't celebrate it. I loved it when the snow covered the world in a blanket of white. That was when it felt like time slowed down, and everyone stopped rushing around to focus on what really mattered.

"What's your favorite season?" I asked, my mind on the snow.

He frowned. "Where I'm from, it's mostly just hot."

"Oh." *Where was that, exactly?* He hadn't mentioned, but I'd been to Florida before, and it was hot basically year round, so I wondered if he was somewhere in the south. "That's sad."

"Why?"

"Because I *love* the winter." I thrust my arms out like I was making imaginary snow angels. "The snow, cozying up in front of a fireplace with the person you love… It's the most wonderful time of the year." I giggled, thinking of the song.

Turning my head to look at him, I found that during our questions, Zain had turned on his side, resting his head on one of his hands as he watched me.

"Have you ever been in love?" I asked, my voice in a low whisper, unsure why that was the question that popped into my mind.

"No."

"What about you?"

"Hm?" I hummed in response, looking over at the furrowed expression on his face.

He directed my question at me. "Have you ever been in love?"

I sighed. "Maybe I thought I had been when I was younger, but… no. Just waiting for the right person, I guess."

"And what kind of person is that?"

I looked back up at the sky, imagining that life. "Someone who will be by my side, no matter what life throws our way. Someone who will dance with me in the kitchen at 3 am when I can't sleep. Who will be there for me whenever things get tough." I smiled, thinking of my parents, letting the thoughts spill out. "Someone who will be a great dad. Who will throw our child in the air, no matter how many times they laugh, because he can't bear to stop. I guess I just want someone to build a life with. Someone who will love me through all of it. Someone who feels like home." Closing my eyes, I could almost picture it. The laughter. The love. The happiness there.

But I opened my eyes, and it was gone, just the moon and the stars blinking back at me.

"You want kids?"

"Yeah. I've always liked the idea of two or three if I got lucky enough. What about you?"

He ran his fingers through his hair. "I hope so." Zain cleared his throat. "I don't know if I'd be a great dad, though. I don't exactly have an excellent role model."

I wanted to wrap my arms around him. Tell him he was wrong. That he'd be a great dad. But what did I really know about him? Nothing.

We were just two strangers who'd probably never see each other again after tonight. But I *liked* tonight. I hadn't felt this alive in so long. That happy thrumming in my veins couldn't be wrong.

My knuckles brushed against his in the grass.

"What are you thinking about?" I whispered.

"Your hair," he murmured, reaching out to tug at a strand. "It's like moonlight." His eyes flashed gold for a moment. I blinked, and they were back to normal.

I was just imagining it, like always.

"Oh." I sucked in a breath, looking away. Shivering, I sat up. It was getting late, and the temperatures were dropping—plus, the heat that had flowed through me from my alcohol buzz was fading.

Wordlessly, Zain shrugged his coat off, placing the jacket around my shoulders. I slipped my arms through the holes, appreciating how big it was on me—and inhaling his scent that clung to the fabric. He smelled like spice and musk and something absolutely delicious that I couldn't place, but I wanted to wrap my body in that smell. Bathe in it.

It spoke to something deep in my soul. Something I couldn't name.

My handsome stranger stood up and offered me a hand up. "It's late," he said. "We should get you home."

"Right." Taking his hand, I let him pull me up from the grass, briefly brushing off my backside as he kept our hands intertwined. We headed back downtown, but before we got back to the bar, I tugged on his hand, pulling us to a stop.

"This is me," I murmured, looking at the side door to my upstairs apartment and then back down at our hands.

"You live up there?" He asked.

I nodded. "Above the bakery. I wanted some privacy. It's weird to live with your sibling when you're in your mid-twenties." That was the understatement of the century. Even if I loved Willow, sometimes it was exhausting fighting over who would take the trash out or do the dishes, or to stop hogging the laundry machine.

He chuckled. "I can see that."

Clearing my throat, I looked back at him. "Do you want to come up?"

"Are you sure?"

"Yeah. We can have another drink, maybe." I had a bottle of wine in the fridge. And I didn't want to say goodbye. Not yet.

"Okay," he agreed, and I started up the stairs, pausing at the top step. *What was I doing?*

Leading this man up to my apartment? Bringing him inside, so that… what? I hesitated as I unlocked the door, and when I looked up at him, there was a frown on my face.

Zain squeezed my hand, as if he sensed the conflict inside of me. "I can go."

That was all it took. All my apprehension melted away. A reminder that this felt *so* right. Our future might have been hazy, but there was no grief in it.

"No." I shook my head, my hand wrapping around his wrist. "Come in. Please. I want you to."

He chuckled, following me into the apartment. "Okay."

I led him into the living room, slowly sinking down onto the couch. Tucking my knees underneath me, I leaned my head against the fabric. I was still wearing his jacket. Part of me knew I should probably have given it back to him sooner, but it was cozy, and I hated relinquishing it.

Zain followed me, somehow looking completely out of place in my tiny apartment.

Selene brushed up against his leg, and Zain practically jumped. "What is that?"

I giggled. "That's my cat." I picked her up, holding her in my arms as she started to purr. "She's friendly, I promise."

Zain quirked an eyebrow. "And she just lives here?"

"Have you never seen a cat before?" I frowned. Where exactly had this man been living that he'd never encountered one?

Leaning down, he brushed a hand over her white fur. "Not like this one."

"She's been with me since I was little," I said. "Every witch gets their familiar when their powers manifest."

My lips curled into a smile as he scratched under Selene's chin, and a loud purring sound emitted from her throat. "She likes you."

She wasn't the only one. I did, too.

"Huh." He kept making the motion, even as Selene emitted a few happy chirps and purred away.

Finally, he joined me on the couch, sitting on the opposite side, so the only part of our bodies that touched were our knees.

"I had fun tonight," I said, unable to wipe the smile off of my face as I bumped his knee with mine. "Thank you. It's been a while since I enjoyed myself so much." Maybe I needed to pick up hot, handsome strangers in bars more often.

The thought felt slimy. Was it because Zain was currently on my couch? Either way, I couldn't imagine this night with anyone else but him. Something about him just felt right.

"Me too," he agreed. "It was the best night I've had in a long time."

I moved closer to him, leaning in slightly, wanting him to kiss me. Hoping he'd pick up on the signals I was dropping.

"I should go," Zain murmured, brushing a hair off my forehead.

I frowned. "You don't want to stay?" As far as I was concerned, a girl inviting a guy into her apartment was an explicit invitation for sex. But maybe he didn't want to sleep with me. He hadn't even so much as tried to kiss me. How old-fashioned was he? He was acting like the perfect gentleman. As much as I loved it, I also hated it. Because I really, *really* wanted to jump his bones.

"I need to get back."

"Will I see you again?" I couldn't help the hopeful tone of my voice.

He chuckled. "Would you like that, moonbeam?"

Moonbeam. The nickname lit me up inside, filling me with a strange warmth. "Yes."

I hurried over to my counter, jotting my phone number onto a piece of scrap paper, and came back to hand it to him. "There."

"What's this?"

"My number, silly. So you can text me next time you're in town? Maybe we can have a proper date."

He picked up my hand, kissing the back of it. "Sure, Luna. I'd like to see you again."

It wasn't everything, but it was a start. Shrugging out of his coat, I handed it back to him. "Thank you for this." Instantly, I missed his smell surrounding me, already mourning the loss. "I'll be waiting by the phone."

He gave me a weird look. "Waiting?"

"Just call me," I said, laughing. Wherever he was from, it wasn't around here.

Leaning up on my tiptoes, I kissed his cheek before he slipped out my door. The prickle of his scruff was rough against my lips, but I found I didn't mind it. "Bye, Zain."

"Goodbye, Luna."

Later that night, wrapped up in the warmth of my sheets, I couldn't stop smiling, already looking forward to the next time he came into town. I didn't even realize that he'd never explained how he got through our wards.

FOUR

ZAIN

What the fuck was wrong with me?

I'd come here with a plan. And yet one look at the girl I'd been willing to do anything to get, and I couldn't carry it out. She was *light*. Pure, unfettered light. How could I tarnish that with my darkness?

But I wanted to. I had to fight every base impulse not to take her, to claim her, to make her mine down to her very soul. To control her entire being so I could ensure she could never escape from my grasp.

Except then she *smiled.*

Not at me. But I couldn't shake the thought that I wanted it to be. A grunt forced its way through my chest.

Staring down at the scrap of paper I had in my hands, I frowned. I needed a cell phone now. Though I wasn't sure how I was expected to know how to use the damn thing.

I could still feel her lips against my cheek, the way she'd leaned up on her tiptoes to be tall enough to reach. She was still too short, and I'd had to bend down to meet her. She smelled sweet, floral, citrus, and sugar, a scent I'd never found so intoxicating before. It knocked me off my feet, how my body sang with *rightness* the moment I'd laid eyes on her.

Fuck. Who was I? I wasn't a bumbling fool, ready to drop to his knees at the first sight of a woman. This was insane. It was biology, basic instincts, telling me she was *mine.*

I'd found her.

Never mind that I'd originally sent Damien to do the same, and he hadn't brought her to me.

I'd found my queen myself. Leaving the demon realm was a risk—it always was—but I'd been careful. If any demons had followed me, they hadn't made their presence known, so I figured I was in the clear.

Luna was nothing like I'd imagined, and yet she was *everything.*

When she'd come walking my way in the bar, her eyes had sparkled with determination. It had filled me with hope. But there was no recognition in her eyes.

Did she not feel our bond the way I did? There was no sign she felt *anything.* I growled at the thought. She wasn't a demon. Of course, she wouldn't feel the same.

What *had* I expected? That I was going to show up here, whisk her off her feet, and bring her to the demon realm with a snap of my fingers? I could have. I was powerful enough that it was possible.

The idea swirled through my head. Going back in there now. I'd played a part tonight, and I knew it. What would she think if I showed her the real me?

As much as the thought appealed to me, I didn't want to force her to do something she didn't want. I wanted her to choose me in the same way that I wanted to claim her. She might have been destined to rule by my side, but that wasn't enough.

Dammit, Lilith. I hated when she was right.

Cloaked in the shadows, I stood across from her apartment, watching as the light switched off in her apartment.

I needed to get back. That was the excuse I'd given to pull away. To not take her mouth in mine, to kiss the soft, pink lips that had been calling my name.

Growling, I pulled my eyes away, hating to leave but knowing I needed to.

Just a few more minutes, I thought to myself. *Just so I know that she's safe.*

* * *

"Well?" Talon was leaning against the pillar of my room as I teleported back. "Did you find her?"

"Mhm," I answered with a grunt, closing my eyes as I pictured her sweet face. Those bright green eyes. Her perfect porcelain skin. How she'd lit up when I'd called her beautiful. How much my senses had been screaming at me to kiss her, *take* her, to claim her as mine.

But I'd controlled those primal urges. It wasn't because I didn't *want* to. It was that I knew once I'd had her, I'd never be able to let her go. Demon biology didn't work like that.

"And?"

"And what?" I crossed my arms over my chest, giving him my best scowl.

He gave me a smirk like he knew something I didn't. "You didn't bring her back with you."

"Of course not," I grumbled. Not *yet*.

Despite what my brother thought—what the entire court thought, for that matter—I didn't enjoy being an asshole. Part of being the crown prince was that people respected me. Listened to me. Demons only understood that in one way. I'd only ever known violence.

But I was giving her a choice. Doing this differently.

Though I wasn't admitting that Lilith was right to her face.

"When are you going to see her again?"

Soon. I pulled the piece of paper out of my pocket. Her number. Not that a phone would work here, anyway.

"I don't know." I tucked the scrap into my desk drawer, locking it with a wave of my hand. It was my magic, so if anyone tampered with it, I could tell. "Do you think anyone noticed I was gone?"

"Your father threw an extravagant, over the top—" He grit his teeth like he was choosing his words wisely. "*Party*. Not sure anyone would have missed you, let alone realized who was there with the amount of bodies…" A full-body shudder passed through his body. "Let's just say you should be glad you weren't there."

But I would have been. When I was younger, he'd forced me to watch as he'd had women service him. As they'd all gotten drunk on demon wine spiked with aphrodisiacs. I hardly could stand to think about those memories, let alone relive them.

Moving over to my desk, I rummaged through the papers on top, reading through other minor reports of the happenings in the palace.

Growling, I threw the pile of papers to the floor. More shit for me to deal with. More things that needed fixing. If only I just had a bit more power…

"Fuck." I raked my hand through the strands of hair, pulling at them tightly.

Steady as ever, my friend just gave me a nod. "You need her."

"Yes, I am aware of that fact." I smoothed a hand over my face. I needed her for reasons that had nothing to do with biology or companionship. Things that would probably make her hightail it out of there and run away from me.

Before I'd met her, it was easy to pretend that those things weren't as important as tying her to me and obtaining the throne. Now that I had, however…

"It's more complicated than that." Because I wanted those things. Wanted her to *want* me, too. Even if love was never in the picture, it couldn't be. A demon like me didn't deserve that.

"Of course."

I waved my hand, thoughts swirling through my head. "Leave me. I'd like to be alone."

I needed to slip back into my role. The part I'd been playing my whole damn life. The broody asshole demon prince I knew so well. Some days, I hated him. Other days, I just hated myself.

Talon nodded, giving me a small bow before leaving me to my own thoughts.

How would I convince *her?* Could I dare to ask her to uproot her entire life?

If I went back and asked her to come with me, would she say yes?

Part of me didn't want to find out.

Because I didn't know how that answer would be anything other than *no*.

* * *

"Father." I stood in front of his ornate chaise, watching as two courtesans fanned him and another fed him grapes. A glass of demon wine swirled in his hand as he took a sip of the glittering liquid. He didn't acknowledge my presence, too busy ogling the demon girls in the skimpy outfits he'd forced them to dress in.

Ugh. *Disgusting.* Once, I'd thought he loved my mother. That he cared for me, too. But age had shown me the truth. My father had never loved anyone like he loved himself—and his crown.

The twisting horns that protruded from his forehead were an ever-present reminder of who he was. No one spoke his name. Sometimes I wondered if it had long since faded from memory. For hundreds of years, it was never uttered within these walls. It was always *My King* or *Majesty*, and I hated the way his lips would curl up at the words.

My father was large in stature—taller than any human, especially in his demon form.

Once, he had been called handsome. While age hadn't decayed his features, they'd been warped from years of hate, distrust, and abuse. He was a shell of the ruler he'd once been, a remnant of the past that felt archaic, holding onto power instead of letting a new age usher through.

My age.

"You summoned me?" I began, uncomfortable with this display. He'd grown too comfortable as of late, and if I had to watch him take advantage of one of the palace staff—or a female who was all too eager to please her *King*—one more time, I thought I might hurl.

I couldn't let that show. Couldn't let him see my weakness. *Pathetic.*

"Zain." His eyes tracked lazily over to me as he crushed another grape with his tongue. "Where is your brother?"

"On a mission."

I was glad that Damien and I hadn't inherited most of his traits. We shared his dark-as-night hair, and I had the golden eyes that signified demon royalty, but I was proud to be my mother's son. That I had retained even an ounce of her goodness. Even if I couldn't show it.

Both my half-brother and I had gained our abilities—his shapeshifting and my, well, *everything*—from our mothers. The shadows were the only part that had come from him—a fact he knew all too well.

He didn't need to know the truth of our current situation. What I'd sent him to do. The less my father knew of Damien's potential woman—and of mine—the better. Not until I could protect her fully.

Until she was safe—protected by the crown on her head and my guards.

"Hmm." Father didn't sound pleased with me, and I couldn't blame him. I wasn't pleased with *myself.* "When will he return?"

I grit my teeth. "He isn't your lackey, Father. He doesn't serve you." Not anymore.

As the crown prince, I'd put a stop to that. Claiming that I needed him to do my bidding was the best way to keep my brother away from our asshole of a father.

Almost three hundred years, and I still didn't feel like I'd done enough for him.

A scowl transformed his face, and I did my best to stand tall—not to cower in front of him like I knew he wanted. I'd had enough years to grow used to this.

"Everyone serves me, Zain. In case you've forgotten, I am the King."

Like I needed the reminder. I waved my hand. "For now."

"I grow tired of this," he huffed. "I expect a full report on the happenings of the palace."

Because he couldn't read them himself, he expected me to do anything he asked without hesitation. What did I have to do but please him?

"Fine. I will return tomorrow," I said, turning on a heel and leaving him behind.

I didn't want to play this game any longer. All I wanted was…

To return to Luna.

To wrap my arms around her. To let her scent fill my nostrils. To hear her laughter, to watch her eyes light up as she took in the night sky.

Fuck. I needed to get her out of my head. This wasn't me.

Was it?

FIVE

LUNA

The next morning, the bakery was empty as I kneaded my dough. My playlist in the background was playing what could only be described as angsty, in-my-feelings music. Was I being dramatic? Maybe.

He hadn't texted me yet. Maybe it was too soon.

It had only been a day, right? What did I expect? Either way, I found myself disappointed.

And I couldn't even talk about it with Willow because I'd told her to take the day off—spend it with her man. I'd been so wrapped up in Zain I'd almost missed them leaving in a hurry from the dance floor, hand in hand.

"At least one of us got lucky last night," I muttered to the dough in front of me. "Because I certainly didn't."

Even though I'd have let tall, dark and handsome do whatever he wanted to me. *Swoon.* He was hot. The kind of man women would definitely claim was their book boyfriend. Damn, was I salivating?

I finished my batch of cookies, plopping them into the oven with a wave of my hand, and stared at my locked phone as the minutes passed.

"Luna?" Eryne's voice came through the shop, the little bell I'd installed above the door ringing.

"In here!" I shouted—as if there was anywhere else I would be this early in the morning.

The smell of baking cookies filled the room—my favorite scent in the world.

"Hi." She grinned, her shoulder length ginger hair catching the light as she shuffled in, a broom behind her enchanted to sweep on its own. Her earrings today were cute little bats that matched her sweater.

"Hey." I used my magic to send all of my dirty mixing bowls to the sink. "How was your night last night?"

"Good. The boy and I had dinner and then snuggled with the cats on the couch. It was nice." Eryne yawned, and I was envious of her easy intimacy with her boyfriend. "What about you?"

"Willow and I went to Ghoul's Night at the bar. It was good to get out for once. Even if I was up way too late." With all the excitement of last night, I'd gotten *maybe* two hours after I'd finally fallen asleep. Then my alarm had gone off, and I'd hustled to get down here to start the ovens.

"That's fun, though. I keep meaning to get out more, but I'm such a homebody these days."

I snorted, thinking about how I spent most of my life in the same building. "Willow's always telling me I need to get out of here."

"You do." My friend patted my shoulder. "I keep telling you to take the day off."

"You shouldn't have to do all the opening prep *and* close. Besides, without me, who would bake everything?"

It might not have been the only reason people stopped in—plenty of folks stopped for Willow's cold brews because she made one hell of a cup of coffee—but we sold out of scones almost every morning. And when I made my pumpkin cookies, they sold by the dozen.

Still… I didn't think anyone would object too much if there was another person back here. Especially if I taught them my trade secrets.

I frowned. "Maybe I should hire another baker."

"Not a bad idea," she agreed. "I have a friend who's in college right now, but she's working part-time at a bakery up there. I could see if she's interested in starting in the spring after she graduates."

I nodded. "I'll definitely keep that in mind."

My conversation with Zain popped into my head.

About the future and how I'd been feeling unfulfilled lately. Maybe this was what I needed. Someone to share the load, so I could have days off. Or, maybe one day, we could hire a cafe manager and have someone else run the shop entirely. Would Willow be disappointed in me?

Would I be disappointed in myself?

And that didn't answer the big question… What did I want? What would I do if it wasn't this? Maybe I just needed to expand my dream. After all, I wanted more, but that was what everyone said. There was always something *more* to want. I just wanted to be content. Happy.

I worked for a few more hours in the back as Eryne took orders and made coffee. The delicious smell wafted back until finally, I gave in, getting myself a cup and sitting at a table near the windows. They looked out into downtown, letting me admire the decorated front of our store with the pastel bats and pumpkins I'd painted pink, along with lights and fake cobwebs.

The town was bustling with activity, even though Halloween was still a little over two weeks away. For a town of witches, we got really into it. I smiled to myself, thinking about all the All Hallows' Eves of the past. Ones with Willow and my parents, and then just us as we'd gotten older. They were memories I'd cherished.

Memories I hoped to one day share with a family of my own. If that ever happened.

Was that what I wanted? What I was missing?

Yes. I shut my eyes, trying to ignore how desperately that want surged through my body.

"I'm heading out," I said to Eryne as I brushed past her once my cup was empty. "You okay here alone?"

She gave me a smile and a nod. It wasn't very busy this late in the afternoon, and now that the rush was over, I knew she could handle it. The dishes in the sink were clean, now just needed to dry and to be put away later.

"Just call me if you need anything. I'll be upstairs."

Even with that, the idea of going back to my empty apartment was almost unthinkable.

Selene would cuddle with me on the couch, and we could catch up on one of my favorite shows, but that just sounded lonely. Maybe I'd curl up with a romance book for a few hours.

Even if I never found true love, at least I could experience it through someone else.

* * *

Two nights later, I once again sat at the bar, nursing another cocktail. Though this one didn't have a fun Halloween name, at least it still tasted good. And it was strong. Plus, it was as close to pink as I was going to get.

He'd never called *or* texted. Maybe he'd lost the piece of paper? The other thought that flashed through my mind sent disappointment surging through me. Maybe he hadn't felt the connection that night the same way I had.

So, I was giving myself one last night to wallow on it, and then I was moving on.

I was tough—it would be okay. I'd been alone for this long. I'd survive a little longer.

"Pretty girl like you sitting at a bar all alone makes a guy wonder," a deep voice said from behind my back.

My body warmed at his presence. I couldn't see him, but I *knew*. There was no mistaking that baritone. The little sparks that danced on my skin whenever he was around.

"Wonder what?" I murmured, not turning around.

He didn't respond to that, just slid onto the barstool next to me.

"You came back," I finally said. I was aware I was staring at his face, eyes focused on the dark hair of his trimmed beard, but I couldn't look away. He was here.

Zain was *here*.

"I told you I would." He waved over the bartender, ordering a glass of scotch. He was dressed more casually tonight, in a pair of dark wash jeans and a different black button-up.

I shrugged, trying to look casual, even though I felt like *beaming*. "I know. But you didn't call me or text me, and I didn't know…"

"Sorry." He smoothed his hand over his chin. "I had to work. Things got busier than I expected with the… company. I couldn't get away."

"Ah. I'm sorry." I shook my head, feeling guilty. He'd been busy, and I'd been… *what?* Moping? Waiting for him to come back around like a sad girl? That wasn't like me.

I'd just wanted to see him again.

"No, it's my fault. You don't have to apologize." His pinky brushed against mine, sending a jolt of electricity up my arm. Down my body. I was suddenly so aware of his presence next to me. How much larger he was.

"Okay," I whispered, not sure how to protest to that.

"I wanted to take you out," he frowned. "That's what you wanted, right? A… date?"

"I'm not opposed to it." I tried to sound cool, even though just the idea sent a rush through me. Dinner and a fancy evening with just the two of us would be *nice*. It had been a long time since I'd been on an actual date. But I was happy with this, too. "Maybe we can do that next time."

I wanted to keep him to myself for now. If we went out to dinner in town, we'd be the biggest gossip. At least at the bar, I could keep my handsome stranger to myself.

He smirked. "What have I already done to earn a *next* time?"

"Show up. Apologize." I gave him a shrug as I finished my drink. "Buy a girl a drink."

"That's kind of the bare minimum, you know?" Zain quirked an eyebrow.

I laughed, the nerves melting away. "I know. Doesn't mean most guys I know deliver it." Especially the ones in this town.

"They're fools." He had that right. Zain looked at my empty glass as he sipped on his. "So, are you going to let me buy you another one?" He spoke low, the deep timbre of his voice sending shivers down my spine.

I fluttered my eyelashes. "Of course."

After the bartender had made me a second vodka cranberry, I happily took a sip.

"You never told me what it is exactly that you do," I said. I'd told him I was a baker, but I didn't know that much about him, even after our questions game.

"I make a lot of deals. For my father's company." I watched the line of his jaw as he swallowed, fascinated by the movement of his Adam's apple.

"Business deals?" I clarified. "What type of business does he do?"

"He has his hands in a lot of different dealings," Zain muttered. Vague, but alright, I was technically still a stranger to him, too. I couldn't blame him if he didn't want to share the nitty-gritty of his life with me.

I didn't even know his last name, after all. And I'd never told him mine.

"Where are you from?"

He clicked his tongue against the roof of his mouth. "I think it's my turn to ask a question, Moonbeam."

There was that nickname again. I blushed. "Okay. Ask away."

"Did you wear that for me?"

I blushed, tugging at the neckline of the tight fitting dress. Had I? *Yes.*

Between it and the thigh-high boots, it was a little sexier than what

I'd normally wear to get a drink at the bar in Pleasant Grove. The front dipped down, showing off a bit of cleavage, and the fabric hugged my hips. I crossed my legs, pressing my thighs together.

"I mean, I'd hoped to see you again, so…" I pushed a strand of hair behind my ear, looking up at him through my lashes. It was a little insane, but I couldn't deny that I'd *wanted* him to come back.

"Me too," he said, unable to take his eyes off mine. I liked that. It made me feel wanted—seen.

By the end of the night, the bar was empty, and I had learned little more than I'd known at the beginning of the night. His favorite color— was black, he didn't have a great relationship with his dad, he'd never had a pet (though I supposed that *wasn't* that big of a surprise), and I suspected he was very out of touch with the modern world.

"I'm glad you came back," I admitted instead of asking another question.

"Me too," he murmured, interlacing our fingers and kissing my knuckles.

Last call was announced, and instead of staying until the bartenders kicked us out, he tugged me to my feet and headed to the door. Leaving the bar behind, we headed out into the darkness of the night.

I'd forgotten how tall he was. It was easy to forget, sitting side by side with him on the bar stools, but he had to be almost six and a half feet tall. Compared to my measly five-foot-five, he was practically a giant. I thought about the other night, how when he'd stood at his full height, I'd barely hit his shoulder.

"You're *so* tall," I murmured into his back, hearing his chuckle. "It should be illegal. Freaking giant." My hand flew over my mouth. *Shit.* I hadn't meant to say that out loud.

A deep chuckle came from the man in front of me.

Then we were standing on the street, facing each other.

"Can I ask you something?" I blurted out, crossing my arms over my chest as if that would keep out the cold. One day, I'd remember to bring a jacket with me.

A smirk crossed his lips. "Isn't that what you've been doing all night? I thought that was the whole point of our game."

"Yes, but…" But that was different. "I just wanted to know, the other night when you came up to my apartment… Why didn't you kiss me?" A soft murmur escaped my lips. "I wanted you to. But you didn't."

He brushed a loose strand of hair behind my ear. "You didn't ask. Maybe I was trying to be a gentleman." His lips were so close as his handsome face dipped down to meet mine. "It's been killing me that I didn't."

"And if I'm asking now?" It felt like all the air had been removed from my lungs.

I wanted it. More than I'd ever wanted anyone to kiss me, *ever*. Couldn't explain the heat in my body, the way this man garnered a reaction in me.

"Then stop talking and let me kiss you, woman," he growled, his hands coming to my hips to pull me against him.

And then the rest of the world faded away.

Because his lips were on mine, and I didn't even care if someone saw us on the street because Zain kissing me was *everything*. His lips were soft, and they moved in gentle motions against mine like he was memorizing the feel of them. I knew I was.

If I never got kissed like this again, I wanted to remember every moment. He coaxed me open for him until his tongue pushed against the seam of my lips, seeking entrance.

And didn't he know that I'd give him anything?

My hands clutched onto his shirt, needing him closer, and he must have had the same idea because he was using the hold on my hips to pull me up onto him, my legs wrapping around his waist as we continued making out like teenagers.

Right in front of the Enchanted Cauldron.

"Damn, handsome. That was one kiss." I gasped as his erection pressed against my core and pulled away, panting roughly. *Big.* Wow, he was *big.* I'd assumed he was because you didn't just have that sort of cocky confidence without being well-endowed, but… whoa.

"I think we can do better," he said, giving me a smug smirk.

"Do you remember where my apartment is?" I asked breathlessly.

There was no way I would survive him. Not when the glint in his eye promised that he'd deliver on every promise he made to me.

A chuckle. "Of course. How could I forget?"

"Let's go. Now." I ordered, because if the hardness pressing against me was any sign, he wanted this as much as I did. And I was very much trying not to grind against *him.*

And then it felt like we practically teleported back to my apartment.

* * *

I handed him my keys, not wanting to relinquish my hold on him—or the way he was capturing my mouth with his—for one second to unlock the door.

"Luna," he groaned as soon as the door was closed behind us. His hands were pressing me against his body, my legs around his waist as I rubbed against his crotch.

Desperate. Needy. Wetter than I'd ever been before. It was all *him.* What he did to me.

"I need you," I said, working my way down the buttons on his shirt, desperate to see what he looked like with nothing on at all. "Please."

"Should we move to the bedroom?" Zain murmured, helping me unbutton him as I guided us towards the kitchen.

Shaking my head, I let him tug my dress up to my waist as his gigantic hands massaged my ass. "No. Just want you."

He pinned me against the kitchen counter, his erection pressing into my hip, and okay—*yes*. I wasn't making it up earlier. He was big. Thick. Possibly the biggest I'd ever encountered, but I wouldn't complain.

"Zain," I moaned. "Please, I need—"

"*Fuck*, I like that." His voice was a growl, and then I was back in his arms. Being lifted like it was nothing. Like my weight didn't faze him at all.

"What?" I asked as he set me on top of the cold granite countertop.

"The way you say my name." His hands slid up my bare thighs, creeping towards the waistband of my panties.

"Oh." Our eyes met, and he raised an eyebrow. Like he was asking for permission. I nodded, not able to take my eyes off of him as his fingers ran up my skin. My whole body shivered from the sensation.

His thumb pressed against my clit, rubbing me through the fabric. "You're so wet," he mused, pressing a knuckle into me. My back arched from the sensation, and I couldn't hold back my whimper.

He slid my underwear down without preamble, lowering his head between my legs.

"What are you doing?" I grabbed at his hair, forcing him to look up at me. He kneeled in front of me, bringing his head to the same level as my slit.

My handsome stranger gave me a devilish grin. "Tasting you."

"*Oh,*" I squeaked, unable to hold my voice back as his tongue connected with my entrance for the first time. He plunged inside, lapping up all of my wetness.

"Is this all for me?" Zain swirled his tongue around my clit. "I think I'm going to be addicted to this after one night." His eyes closed as he kept up the motions, circling around the nub, driving me wild.

"Keep doing that," I begged mindlessly.

He slipped a finger inside of me. "You're so tight, baby. I gotta get you nice and wet for me, huh? Stretch you so you can take my cock?"

"Yes," I agreed. I wanted that. "Yes, please."

He added another finger, and I already felt so full. His hands were so big, and his fingers reached farther back than mine ever could. Making a scissor motion with his hands, he kept true to his word, loosening me up as his tongue fluttered and flattened against my clit.

"Come on, Moonbeam. Give me what I want, and I'll take care of you, I promise."

He didn't stop massaging my insides until I cried out, my eyes flying shut as my fingers dug into his shoulders as my orgasm ripped through me.

"That was... unreal," I finally said as I cracked my eyes open, watching him slide those two fingers out of me and plop them into his mouth. He licked off every trace of me from his skin before standing up and pulling me back in for another kiss.

Zain's tongue swiped across my lower lip till I opened for him, and even though I could taste myself in his mouth, I still panted into it.

"Inside," I crooned, my hands scrambling for purchase until they landed on his belt.

He chuckled against my mouth, never stopping devouring me even as we both got his belt off and it dropped onto the floor with a loud *thunk.*

Unzipping his pants, I wrapped my hands around his cock, moaning at the size. "You're so big, handsome." No amount of foreplay was going to make it easy for me to take him.

"It'll fit," he promised, kissing me again as I moved my hand up and down on his length. "You're going to take me so well."

Pulling his *cock*—because there was no other name decent enough for his magnificent length—out of his pants fully, I watched as he fisted himself a few times, swiping off the bead of pre-cum that had pooled at the tip.

I licked my lips, already ready to feel that inside of me.

He notched the head against me, pressing in slightly, and something occurred to me.

"Condom?" I said, breaking out of my haze. What was I thinking? I wasn't even on birth control. Hadn't needed to be, because the last time I'd had sex was, well… a *while* ago.

Zain froze. "Shit." He dropped his head to my shoulder. "I don't…"

"I think there's some in my nightstand." Just as I was about to get off the counter to search for them, his hand gently restrained me.

"I'll go. You stay here."

"I—" My knees were weak, so I didn't protest.

I closed my eyes as he sauntered off toward my bedroom, leaning my head back against the cabinets as I tried to catch my breath.

"Luna?" My eyes were still shut, and I just hummed in response. "What is *this?*"

"Hm?" My eyes flew open and—oh. *Goddess.* Zain was standing in front of me—holding my purple vibrator in his hands.

Was it possible to die of embarrassment? If yes, at least I'd had one last orgasm. One amazing, mind-blowing orgasm with the most handsome man to have ever walked this planet, but still.

"Can we rewind to a few minutes ago when you had your tongue buried inside of me and forget all about *that?*" Mortification flooded through me.

I'd never shared that aspect of myself with anyone before. I didn't think it was dirty or wrong, but it felt strangely… *intimate.*

"Nope." A cocky grin spread across his face as he stepped closer to me. "Let me see how you use it."

"No. That's definitely… no. No way." I knew if I'd looked in a mirror my entire face would be bright red, and I couldn't even blame all of it on the orgasm he'd just given me. I buried my face in my hands, not wanting to look at him.

He laughed, those hands grabbing mine to expose my face, bringing his back down as if he was going to kiss me again, when—

A knock sounded on the door.

"*No,*" I practically cried. It was just our luck, us getting interrupted *now.*

"Luna?" Willow's voice sounded, knocking once again. "Are you there?"

"Shit." I leaned my forehead against Zain's chest.

"You should get that." He tucked himself back into his pants and looked sheepish as he zipped them up.

"She'll go away if we ignore her," I whispered.

But Zain just kissed the crown of my head. "It's okay. Talk to your sister." He tilted his head towards my bedroom. "I'll be in there."

I didn't think about how he knew it was Willow when I was pretty sure he'd never heard my sister's voice before tonight.

"Thank you," I said, pressing my lips against his for a moment before hopping off the counter. I shimmied my dress back down my hips and found my panties on the floor. There was no time to tug them on, so I shoved them in a kitchen drawer.

I eyed the vibrator still in his hands. "Put that away while you're in there."

He smirked, saying nothing, and I walked to the door, hoping my sister wouldn't notice the sweaty sheen on my skin.

I took a deep breath and opened the door.

SIX

ZAIN

I couldn't stay away. Which was why, for the second night this week, I was here in the human realm instead of at my palace, dealing with whatever crisis was currently unfolding between demons—because there always was one.

The blood that had been pumping hot through both of our veins was cooled, and clarity had settled back in.

A reminder of what was at stake here. That I couldn't afford to mess this up. No matter how much I wanted her.

Luna and Willow's voices drifted into her bedroom, but I tried not to eavesdrop as she talked with her sister. It was after one in the morning, which begged the question—where was my brother?

Why wasn't she with him? Even if this place was hidden by witch magic, I didn't trust that it was *safe*. I could hardly bear to think about Luna living here alone.

Wandering around her room, I used the time alone to study the things she'd prized enough to keep beside her. Much like the dress she'd been wearing the first night we'd met, she clearly loved the color purple.

Her bedspread was a soft purple adorned with little white flowers, and her walls had been decorated with moons, flowers, and pastel tapestries. Sprigs of dried lilacs and lavender hung from the wall, and a collection of crystals sat on her bedside table, as well as a collection of sweet-smelling candles on her desk. There was a bookcase full of titles I was sure we didn't have in the demon realm, but they looked well-read and loved. It was nothing like I would have ever imagined for the room of a witch, and yet, perfectly *her*.

I picked up a little pink crescent moon-shaped crystal off her desk and ran my fingers over its smooth edges.

"What are you doing?" Luna asked softly, her head leaning against her door frame as she watched me take in her space.

"Observing," I said, flashing her a smile. *Learning you*. I set the crystal back down.

"She's gone. Sorry about that. I think she was just freaking out." My little queen rubbed at her shoulders. "All good now, though."

I shook my head. "Don't apologize. You two have a special bond, do you not?"

"Twin flames and all that." She nodded, waving her hand. The door shut with a click—leaving just the two of us inside.

"So you believe in it?" Maybe this would be easier than I thought. To convince her to come back with me.

Luna moved, coming to stand beside me in her room. "I believe fate guides us to where we're supposed to be. But the rest is up to us. A soulmate may be predestined to fall in love with you, but without trust and care, there's no chance of a lasting relationship."

"And do you trust me?" The words slipped out before I could think better of it.

Her eyes fluttered shut for just a moment. "Maybe I shouldn't, but I do. Is that crazy?"

"No," I murmured the word because she was close enough to hear me even if I'd whispered it. The connection I felt between us was unreal.

She kept going. "You could have taken advantage of me that first night. And I would have let you. But you didn't. Because you're a gentleman."

A gentleman who was ready to fuck you on your kitchen counter thirty minutes ago. And I would have if we hadn't gotten interrupted. "Am I?" I flashed her my teeth. I was many things, but a gentleman wasn't one of them.

"Uh-huh." Luna's hand rested over my heart. "I feel safe with you." She let her fingers creep up my chest, her voice growing deeper as she whispered, "Now... where were we earlier? Before we got so rudely interrupted?"

Putting my hand over hers, I held it in mine. Letting the rightness flow through me for just a moment. "I should go."

"Don't." Her bright green eyes captivated me, the color almost unnatural. "Stay. Please."

"I don't know if that's such a good idea." Luna groaned, but I kept going. "Earlier, we..."

"Don't care," she said, her fingers digging into my hair to bring our lips level. "I've never wanted anyone the way that I want you. Please. I just want…"

"Luna." I leaned down, my mouth dangerously close to her neck. Letting my lips ghost over her ear. "If we do this, I'm not going to be able to let you go."

"Maybe I don't want you to." She fluttered her eyelashes. "It's been a long time since I've been with anyone that made me feel alive. We don't have to worry about the rest."

Fuck.

I scraped my teeth over her bare skin, wanting to claim her so badly. Knowing that once I touched her, I wouldn't be able to stop. Her pulse point called my name, and I wanted to put my lips there, to suck it into my mouth.

"Are you sure?"

"*Yes.*"

There was no holding back after that. My lips were on hers, and heat flooded my veins. Coaxing her mouth open, I used my tongue to show her what exactly I had planned for her. It was fierce—passionate. My hands dug into her hips, desperate to push that fabric back up and bury myself inside of her.

I groaned into her mouth, thinking about how she was bare underneath. About how I'd found her toy in her nightstand drawer, and I wanted to hear what kinds of noises she'd make when she used it.

Pulling the fabric up, I cupped her ass with my hands, enjoying the feel of covering her skin with mine. Massaging her cheeks, I practically inhaled her little mewls, our tongues a tangle of pleasure. Every part of my body wanted her, and I knew I couldn't walk away. Not now—not ever.

Hoisting her up, I let Luna wrap her legs around me, her bare pussy resting over my aching cock, and carried her the few steps to her bed. She ground herself down against my length, and I groaned, finally pulling my mouth away from hers. "Luna." My voice was rough.

"Hm?"

"You're a wicked little thing, aren't you?"

She grinned, leaning in to place a kiss on my neck. "*Yes.*" Her tongue darted out, licking a line up to my jaw.

Dropping her on the bed, I tugged her pink dress up around her waist before pulling it off over her head, leaving her in a black lacy bra. Leaning down, my teeth snagged on the strap, desperate to have her naked in front of me. Placing a kiss to the swell of her breast, I dipped down before sucking her nipple into my mouth through the fabric.

I wanted to learn her body, to find out how she responded to each touch I gave her, what she liked—all of it.

Luna's fingers tangled in the buttons of my shirt as she clung to me through my pursuit, my teeth grazing over her nipple and the wet lace as I bit the peak lightly before moving to the other side and doing the same to it.

She fumbled blindly with the buttons, desperately trying to undo them once again.

"Off," she pleaded, pushing at the fabric after the last few buttons had been loosened. I chuckled, letting my black shirt fall to the floor as I towered over her.

Reaching around behind her back, I unsnapped her bra, bearing her creamy, luscious tits to my view, nipples hardened from my attention.

She laid back on the bed, that light blonde hair that looked like moonlight draped over her sheets. It pooled around her as she stared up at me, her entire body on display. For *me*. It was like she was offering herself up on a silver platter. And how could I resist?

"You're absolutely gorgeous," I murmured, unable to take my eyes off of her. Watching as her chest rose and fell, those green eyes focused on me like she was worried if she looked away—if she even blinked—that I'd disappear.

"Let me see you," Luna begged, sitting up to fumble with my zipper. My belt was forgotten somewhere on her apartment floor, and I couldn't bring myself to worry if her sister had seen it. Not when I had her in front of me like this. "All of you."

She unzipped my pants, pushing them down my thighs in one movement, and I helped her by kicking them off the rest of the way, watching as her lidded eyes flared as she ran her gaze all over my body.

I was rock hard instantly, and when she wrapped her tiny hand around my dick and leaned down to flick her tongue over the lead, lapping up the bead of pre-cum, I almost lost it.

"Luna," I groaned. She looked up at me through her lashes, green eyes twinkling with mischief as she closed her lips over the tip. That tongue of hers swirled around, exploring, tasting, and I held myself still. Letting her have her fun.

My fingers closed around her chin, pulling her off of my length. She pouted, and a deep, throaty chuckle escaped my throat. "Patience, Moonbeam. I don't want to come down your pretty little throat. Not this time, at least."

Pushing her shoulders, I guided her back down onto the bed and pressed a soft kiss to her lips. I lingered for only a moment before drawing back to my full height. Grasping her knees, I pulled them apart, bearing her slick pink pussy to me.

I dipped my fingers inside of her, pushing two in at once, my eyes glued to the spot where they disappeared inside of her. "Fuck," I muttered.

"Zain," she whined. "I want you inside of me. Please."

"Shhh," I soothed, scissoring my fingers through her wet cunt. "I gotta get you nice and wet so you can fit me, baby." The term of affection slipped out, and I couldn't find it in me to regret it.

She was practically dripping, still affected by her earlier orgasm, but I knew I was big. It came with the territory of being a six-and-a-half-foot tall demon. I was larger than the average human male, and I needed to take my time to make sure I didn't hurt her.

"Oh, *Gods*," she moaned, and I kept at it until her back arched off the bed, and she was writhing and begging under my touch. When I finally felt her convulsing around me, the force of her orgasm causing her to curl her toes and gasp, I withdrew my fingers from her, admiring the moisture coating them.

I licked them clean as Luna propped herself up with her elbows. Watching me like a cat poised to strike, ready to catch her prey.

A queen perched atop her throne. The thought came to me, unbidden, and I pushed it back down. It wasn't time to be thinking of that. Not when I ached, and all I wanted was to forget about everything else and bury myself in her flesh.

"Tell me how you like it," I said, pumping my length into my hands. "If it hurts, if you need me to stop—" Pulling the silver foil packet out of my pocket, the one I'd found in the same drawer as her toy, I flipped it in between my fingers.

"I won't," she promised. "I know you won't hurt me."

I shook my head. "I might. So you have to tell me if I do, okay? I need to hear it, Luna." My cock was desperate to be inside of her, and I had to remind myself to go slow. Not to rut into her—to claim her as my body desired.

She didn't know, and I wouldn't force that bond on her if that wasn't what she wanted. Even though I wanted to tie her to me desperately, to bring her back with me to the demon realm, even if she desired anything but.

"Okay," she agreed, the word a breathless whisper. "I'll tell you."

"Good girl," I praised, and I didn't miss the way her eyes sparked, her whole body seeming to light up at the praise. "Mmm, you like that, huh? Being my good girl?"

She nodded, a little mewl slipping from her lips. "Yes, please."

Ripping the packet with my teeth, I kept my eyes focused on Luna as I extracted the rubber from the foil, rolling it down over my erection slowly. She licked her lips, her fingers reaching down to part her folds, circling her clit as she watched me, her gaze never leaving my shaft.

Fates. She was going to kill me, and I wasn't even inside of her.

When I was fully covered, I clambered on top of her, positioning myself at her entrance.

Slow, I reminded the beast inside of me.

Luna gasped as I notched the tip inside, and I felt her stretch around me as I pushed in. I was right—she was tight, but she was also wet enough that I could enter her easily. Her fingers clutched the bedsheets as I pushed in slowly, watching my cock disappear into her entrance.

"Oh," she squeaked, her eyes widening.

"Too much?" I winced.

Luna shook her head. "You're just… so big." She looked between us at the spot where I disappeared inside of her cunt. "I mean, I knew you were, but I don't think I can take all of you—there's no way you're going to fit." She inhaled a sharp breath of air.

Leaning down, I captured her lips with mine, tangling our tongues together until she relaxed, kissing her until she was completely loose beneath me, and I thrust in the final few inches.

Luna's eyes were squeezed shut, and I kissed her eyelids. "Look how well you take me, Moonbeam. How well we fit together." Like we were made for each other. One full thrust inside, and I'd never felt anything like it. How perfectly she fit me, even with our size difference.

I was still until she groaned, her eyes fluttering open to look down between us. My thumb pressed against her clit, moving in a circle like I'd just watched her do to herself.

"Zain." She gasped. "It's too much."

"You can take it," I promised, pulling out of her shallowly to thrust back in.

She shook her head. "I don't—how is this possible?" A breathy noise came from her throat as I snapped my hips into hers. "No one's ever made me feel like this before."

"That's because they weren't me." It would never be like this with anyone else. Not for either of us. "They were too focused on their own pleasure, not on yours." But not me. Not when I would put her first every time.

Luna's head fell back, a deep moan dropping from her lips as I gave her another punishing thrust, keeping up the rhythm with my thumb as I pushed us both closer to the edge.

"Give me one more," I said against her ear, pressing my lips against her pulse point as I felt it flutter under my mouth. "Come for me again, Luna."

It didn't take much more until she shattered, pulsing around my length.

"So good," I groaned, following right behind her, the sensation of her cunt squeezing my cock too much, making me spill inside of her.

Collapsing with a contented sigh next to her, I stared up at the ceiling.

"Wow." Luna's hand pressed to her chest. "That was…"

"I know," I murmured, wishing I could calm all the thoughts running through my brain.

Because—*fuck*, had I just messed everything up?

SEVEN
LUNA

Dawn's early rays lit up my apartment, and I'd never felt so warm and comfortable as I woke up. But then again, I'd never woken up next to anyone like this. He was already awake, his thumb trailing over my naked shoulder, drawing circles on my skin.

"Hi, handsome," I murmured sleepily. My body ached in all the right places, reminding me of how roughly he'd taken me last night. How much I'd liked it.

Even if he'd been distant afterward, pulling away from me. After we'd both cleaned up, I'd almost expected him to leave. Had he gotten everything he wanted from me, and how I'd have to say goodbye? I didn't want that. Despite how insane it was, I wanted the chance to get to know him better.

And maybe do *that* again.

"Good morning." Zain leaned over, kissing my forehead.

"Yes," I agreed, stretching out with a sleepy yawn. "It is."

"It wasn't too much, was it? Last night?" His face—all those sharp lines that had first captured my attention—looked worried, and I shook my head.

"No. It was… perfect." Because there were no other words to describe it. He'd made me feel like stars were exploding on my skin every time he touched me, the drag of his fingertips on my body, the way he'd worked me up higher and higher—

Gods, it was like he knew what my body needed before I did.

One corner of his lips tilted up, and I reached up, letting my fingers brush against the scruff of his jaw. "You look good like this." My fingers ran over those beautiful lips that had explored all over my body, wanting to commit this to my memory. If this was the only night we'd have together, I didn't want to forget one bit of it.

"In your bed?" He asked.

I moved my finger over the smile lines on his cheeks. "Yes." *No. Happy.* But that felt like too much to admit.

He captured my hand, kissing my palm before bringing our lips together to take my mouth. It was a soft, lazy kiss—nothing like what we'd shared last night, but the intimacy of it all was almost too good. I sank into the warm, fuzzy feeling, enjoying the way it felt like little bolts of electricity were shooting up my skin from his touch.

"I should go," he murmured, trailing a finger over my bare skin.

"Or you could stay. Spend the day with me. I could call in sick." After all, I was already late. If the sun was up, I was normally already baking. What was a few more hours?

He raised an eyebrow. "Call in sick to your own business?"

"Sure." I shrugged. "I'll just put up a sign on the door. *Oven's broken. Be back tomorrow.*" A giggle erupted from my lips, thinking about the townspeople going without their favorite scones and muffins. But they could do without me for one day—right? There were still plenty of baked goods to put out in the display case, even if I didn't bake anything fresh today.

But Zain shook his head, standing up from the bed. "I wish I could. I have to get back." A deep sigh emitted from his throat as he reached down to grab his pants, pulling them back up over his well-toned thighs.

Goddess, the man had a beautiful physique, including that ass I wanted to dig my fingers into once again.

"Will I see you again?" I asked, trying not to sound hopeful.

But what did I know about this man? I'd let him into my home— into my bed—and if he disappeared tomorrow, that would be that. And I'd have to pretend I wasn't disappointed.

He chuckled as he zipped up the pants before flicking the button closed. "You'd want that?"

"After last night, you have to ask?" I sat up, holding the sheet to my body as I watched him dress. Covering up that body seemed almost illegal, but I couldn't complain now. Not when he was right. I had a job to do—and so did he.

Zain quirked an eyebrow as he shrugged his shirt back onto his shoulders, buttoning it with more precision than I'd ever seen a man have.

I simply nodded, doing my best not to look as overly eager as I felt. "Yes. I'd want that." Of course I did.

How could he think I wouldn't? What girl could get three orgasms from a man in one night and not want to see him again?

A wicked grin split his face. "Good."

He leaned in to place a soft kiss on my lips, and then his finger tugged at a strand of hair next to my ear.

"Tomorrow?" I asked, holding my breath and trying not to analyze why I was so quickly becoming dependent on this man.

Why I felt like not seeing him would be like the end of my world. I knew it—we'd only had two nights together, after all, and it wasn't like I had any preconceived notions about where this was going. But for once, I didn't want to worry about the future.

Didn't want to think about where things were going, because I liked how he made me feel, and I wanted more of it.

"Yes," he agreed, kissing my forehead. "I'll see you tomorrow."

"I'm counting on it," I whispered as he gave me a wink, waltzing out of my bedroom.

Selene, who must have slept on her cat tree in the living room last night instead of at my feet for once, came into my bedroom, her jingling bell alerting me to her presence.

Hopping up onto the bed, she meowed, coming over to rub her head on me and beg for my attention. I scratched her head, giving her love as she purred, and then sighed. "I should probably get up too, huh?"

After all, the bakery waited for no woman—or no witch, in this case.

* * *

The next few weeks had flown by, and now Halloween was only days away. I adjusted the apron wrapped around my waist, focusing my attention on the cookies in front of me. They were my specialty, even though by the time Halloween was over, I wouldn't want to look at orange frosting again for another year.

My thoughts kept drifting back to Zain. Of all the nights I'd spent curled up in his arms in my sheets. It felt like it was too soon, but I *really* liked him.

Our future felt bright. At least whatever was hidden behind that hazy warmth. And I trusted him. With my body, especially. Yet, in some ways, it felt like everything was too good to be true. And maybe it was.

He didn't call, and he still hadn't told me very many details about his life—where he lived when he wasn't visiting Pleasant Grove, what business he worked in, exactly—none of it.

Part of me wondered if I needed to worry that he had another family hidden away somewhere.

The thought instantly soured my stomach. I might not have known everything about him, but I *knew* him. Knew that he wouldn't do that to me. But it was more than that, too—the idea of him with some other woman made me *nauseous*. What we had, what we shared, both the powerful physical attraction and our sexual chemistry…

It was easy to see how fast I could get attached to this man if I let myself. If I let him in. But could I, when I hardly knew anything about him?

Looks like someone else had a good night, I thought to myself as Willow twirled into the kitchen.

"You look smitten," I murmured, watching my sister happily hum to herself.

She came to a stop, the dishes she'd levitated in front of her looking precariously close to falling. "What?" Her cheeks turned light pink. "N-no."

But it was so *obvious* how head over heels she was for him. And I couldn't blame her for being happy. Not one bit.

I'd wanted it for her, wished for her happiness. Had so badly wanted to see into her future for years, just to know what would come to pass." Not that she'd let me. But I got this feeling that maybe there was more to this than she was letting on.

Either way, it was good for me because she was so caught up in her own whirlwind romance she hadn't noticed *mine*. I wasn't ready to talk about Zain yet. To share him. Right now, he was all mine. The handsome stranger I shared my secrets with. Who I confessed my thoughts to in the dark.

"I… I like him, okay?" Willow dropped her shoulders as if in defeat before sending the dirty pitchers and spoons into the sink. "It's never been like this for me before."

"And he feels the same way?" I asked.

Sure, maybe I was slightly skeptical of Damien. I'd barely met the man, but the way he'd bolted out of the coffee shop during our first interaction… It felt like there was something he wasn't saying. That he was keeping from my sister, too. All I could sense from him was darkness.

"I mean, I haven't asked him for sure, but I think so." A slight smile curled over her lips.

I couldn't stop myself from pressing the matter. "What are you afraid of?"

My older sister sighed, a touch of worry coloring her tone. "That he'll leave. Decide I'm not worth it and walk away."

"Willow." My voice was soft. Reassuring. I wanted her to realize how much she was worth it. That anyone would be crazy to not want to be with her. "You don't even know how amazing you are, do you?"

"You *have* to say that." She shook her head. "You're my little sister."

"No." I said it more firmly. "I mean it. You always take care of everyone but yourself. Even me. It's time to put yourself first. Besides, if that man really leaves, he's not who I thought he was, anyway."

Willow murmured something under her breath. She turned away from me, facing the sink.

"What?" I asked, not catching what she'd said. Or maybe I had. And that was the problem.

He's a demon. Surprise flashed through my eyes.

"Nothing." My sister focused on the dishes, scrubbing at them instead of continuing the conversation. Avoiding whatever truths were in her mind.

It had to have been a joke, right? *A demon?*

Like… an immortal, supernatural being from *Hell?* She had an evil spirit living in her house? Sleeping in her bed?

But he couldn't be *bad.* He looked at her the way my dad had looked at my mom. Like he cared about her. There was no mistaking it. You couldn't fake that kind of affection.

When she finally turned back to me, I rolled my eyes. "I'm just saying. I've seen the way he looks at you." And even having my doubts, I hadn't been able to deny that after seeing them together at the bar.

"Like what?" Willow's voice was barely a whisper.

"Like you're his entire world."

Yes. He was just as smitten as her. *Head over heels.* She'd known him for a month, and yet, seeing the way his gaze was heated as he watched her…

It was how I wanted Zain to look at *me.*

"Oh."

"Yeah. *Oh.*" I pinched her arm lightly. "If you don't tell that man how you feel about him, I'll do it myself."

"*Luna,*" she bemoaned, drawing out my name. "It's still new. I don't want to ruin it." I raised an eyebrow, and she held up her arms in defeat. "Fine, fine! I'm going home now."

"Tell your man I say hello." I gave her a little finger wave as she grabbed her stuff.

"Don't stay too long yourself," Willow said, almost an afterthought. "Goddess knows you could use some time away from this place. You practically live here, I swear."

I couldn't disagree with that.

Besides, Zain would be waiting for me upstairs.

"I won't."

It was a promise I could keep.

* * *

Halloween had finally arrived, and I was closing up the bakery early before meeting up with Willow and Damien for the festivities. I wished Zain was here to see how Pleasant Grove celebrated, but he'd told me two days ago that he was going on a business trip.

I'd been pouting ever since he'd left, but luckily Willow was too busy with Damien to pay attention to how my mood had been all over the place. To how my heart beat faster every time I thought about Zain.

I loved my sister, but I did *not* need to explain to her about the *older man* I'd been seeing. Not that I'd asked him his age yet. The thought made me frown. One of these nights, I'd have to ask. Clearly, we needed to do more talking in the evenings when he came over.

It was just so hard to keep my hands off of him after that first time.

Every time he showed up, I could barely resist pouncing on him, and we ended up with our clothes off within the first ten minutes.

Evidently, I needed to clear some things up. About what this was. Were we just hooking up? Or was it… more?

Tying up the trash bag in my hands, I headed towards the back alley of the shop.

After this, I just needed to turn out the lights, and I could go upstairs and get changed for the party. I still had a few hours before it started, giving me ample time to do my hair and makeup.

Halloween night in Pleasant Grove was always incredible—when you paired the magical abilities of the town's residents with a celebration of all things spooky, people went a little over the top. Willow *loved* it. She'd been the biggest fan of Halloween for as long as I can remember, always excited when we were little to pick out her costume and go trick-or-treating together.

I smiled, thinking about the first year when I'd been learning to control my magic, and I'd levitated my plastic pumpkin alongside us until an older boy had bumped into me, causing me to lose focus—and my candy to tumble to the ground. My eyes had filled with tears, but it was Willow who jumped to my rescue, ready to fight the boy who ran into me. She'd even hexed a broom, sending it after him until he ran home crying to *mommy*.

I couldn't remember my costume or my favorite candy that year, but I remembered how my big sister would do anything for me.

She'd always been my best friend.

Was I being a terrible person by keeping her in the dark about what was going on in my life? If it wasn't going anywhere, I didn't want to tell her I was seeing someone. She would be so supportive, and it would break my heart to see her disappointment when it ended.

Sighing, I dumped the trash in the back dumpster, turning back to go inside the bakery. The sun hadn't gone down yet, but the lights were already coming on, an orange glow leaking into the alleyway behind Main Street.

"What's this?" A grating voice instantly had the hair on the back of my arms sticking up.

"Found ourselves a sweet treat, didn't we?"

I turned, finding two of them staring at me like they'd found their next meal.

At first, I'd thought they were just playing a prank on me. Some Halloween costumes gone wrong. But… it was becoming increasingly obvious to me they weren't human.

A sickly gray pallor covered their skin that stretched across a gangly, unnatural-looking frame. Claws sat in the place of fingernails. But it was their horns that told me everything I needed to know. I'd never seen one before, but there had been stories in our books about the wicked creatures that lived in the shadows.

Demons.

Willow's words echoed in my mind. *He's a demon.*

Maybe I was right not to trust him. Had he led them here, too? Unwittingly or not, I hoped Damien hadn't brought them here. It would absolutely crush my sister. Especially if they ate me.

They were close enough to rip me apart. I didn't think demons liked to *eat* humans, but my education on other species had never been that great, anyway. They were supposed to be myths. Legends. Just like vampires and wolf shifters and mermaids and the rest of them.

What were they doing here? The magical barrier of Pleasant Grove should have kept things *out*. That's what I'd always been taught, but I was second-guessing a lot of things about this town.

"Please don't hurt me," I begged, holding my hands in front of my face. All I could do was will my magic to the surface—the power that lived inside my veins.

Why hadn't I learned to defend myself when I had the chance? Even if I was terrified of it—knowing the depth. My coven didn't even know how deep my insecurities ran. I kept them all bottled up inside.

"She's the one, isn't she?" The second demon said to the first. "Our golden ticket."

"Smells like it," the first agreed. "His scent is all over her. This must be the one."

My cheeks warmed. *His scent all over me?* The thought made me dizzy.

They had to have been talking about Zain, right? Only, I hadn't seen him in days, and I'd definitely showered since then. There was no way there would be any lingering *anything*.

"I don't know who you are, but I'm no one special," I said, backing up slowly. Like if I didn't spook them, I could make it out alive. *Why had I left my phone inside?* "I'm just a baker."

"Just a baker. *Ha!*" The laugh that the creature emitted was like nails on a chalkboard. "I can see the magic that runs through your veins, witch." He spat out the word. "Your kind seek to eliminate us, to wipe us off the map."

"I'm not—" I knew nothing about that. We weren't demon hunters. A demon hadn't been seen in Pleasant Grove in decades, as far as I knew. Unless the barriers were weakened, they shouldn't have been here now.

My palms heated, the magic that sparked through my veins sizzling on my skin. Would it be effective against them? I only had one shot—maybe, if I was lucky—before they'd be on me.

I felt a presence at my back, and I inhaled sharply. Because his body heat flooded my veins like he was saying *I'm here. I've got you.* Little zaps shot through my skin where he touched my arm.

"Luna, get behind me." Zain shoved his body in front of mine, his voice practically a snarl as he turned to the creatures. "You will not touch her."

"Just let us have one taste, huh? You can share, and we'll give her back unharmed." The second creature's lips curled, exposing long canines, sharpened to points. "*Mostly.*"

I couldn't move because I was frozen. For once in my life, I knew complete fear. Nothing had terrified me before.

Perhaps I should have been more like Willow, reading our family grimoire instead of romance and fantasy books, and then I'd know what to do in this kind of situation. Maybe it was my parents' fault for not teaching me how to control this magic of mine. I knew I had power—dangerous, if wielded properly—but I didn't know *how*.

Useless. I was useless. My knees buckled, falling into Zain's back.

"No." He spoke roughly as I clutched onto him. "Don't even look at her, you worthless *trash*."

"Zain…" I curled my hands into the back of his jacket, holding onto his body as mine trembled.

"Step back, Luna," Zain barked, and I heeded the command in his voice quickly. His fingernails lengthened, turning into sharp tips. "I need you to go." Looking back, his eyes connected with mine. Shining, *golden* eyes. "Please. Go inside."

What are you? But maybe I already knew.

The wings unfurled from his back as he stepped towards the creatures, a wisp of magic curling around his body.

"*You. Will. Not. Touch. Her.*" Each word was repeated, deathly violence promised by his tone.

Trembling in fear, I pressed myself against the brick wall, feeling its rough texture against my back as he mercilessly ripped them apart.

But I couldn't look away, either. It was violent and bloody, and yet there was something graceful about the way he moved. Lethal. Dangerous. But somehow also… *Beautiful.*

Gods, I'd never been more attracted to this man than when he was tearing creatures apart for me. What did that say about me?

Devastating. He was completely devastating, standing over the corpses of the demons. My body unfroze, and I collapsed onto the ground, my knees hitting the pavement.

"What—"

"Fuck," he muttered, looking at their bodies. The blood that dripped out of them was an unnatural black. Zain pinched the bridge of his nose before waving with his hand, the carnage instantly disappearing in a glittering black mist.

Turning, his eyes swept over me, like he couldn't discern if I was okay. *But I wasn't.*

And the worst part was it had nothing to do with what had just happened. That I'd had two demons bent on using me like some sort of weird bargaining chip.

It was that I didn't even recognize the man who was standing in front of me. *Because he'd lied.* It was a shock to my core. What did I really know about this man?

Clearly, he wasn't who he claimed to be. He wasn't even human.

"Are you okay?" He asked, and I shook my head. My eyes filled with tears, but he mistook my emotions for fear. "It'll be okay," Zain promised, scooping me up into his arms.

I buried my face into the crook of his shoulder, my words failing me as he carried me upstairs into my apartment.

He set me down on my feet and I turned around, not wanting to look at him. Because I was *angry* and *upset*, and my body was still trembling as I tried not to cry.

Not to release all the pent-up emotions of the last thirty minutes. Ignoring the way I was slowly falling apart.

"Luna." His voice is soft as he slips his arms around my waist, tugging me to his front. It was all I could do to ignore how well our bodies fit together.

He's a demon. Willow's words echoed through my mind. Suddenly, the information wasn't a revelation at all as everything clicked into place.

Damien. Her *cat*.

The week after she'd adopted him, she'd been so focused on researching… something. I'd seen her in the library. And then there was the spell she'd performed.

She hadn't wanted to ask for help, even though the coven was a wealth of resources—a combined force of knowledge and unique skills.

And then Damien—human, this time—showing up on her arm. Of course, something *supernatural* was happening there. And I'd been so caught up in my thing that I hadn't even paid attention to it.

Gods, she was literally dating a devil.

And so was I.

"I trusted you," I said, the tears dripping from my eyes. "I let you into my bed, into my home, and I…"

"Moonbeam." He sounded so calm. Quiet. I hated he was collected at this moment that I was crumbling. "I never meant…"

"You lied," I murmured, stepping away from him.

Zain reached for me, but I just shook my head, wrapping my arms around myself before I collapsed onto the couch.

Over and over, that thought repeated through my brain.

He'd lied.

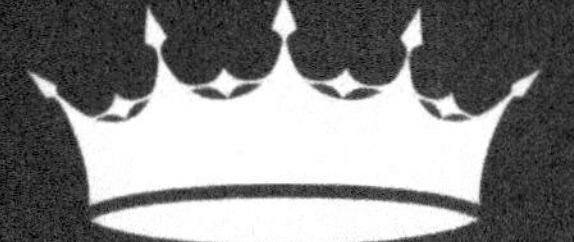

EIGHT
ZAIN

Luna was still trembling.

The bodies of the demons who'd tried to attack her were fresh in my mind. Hers, too, I was sure. Had she ever experienced that level of violence before? I hated that I'd exposed her to that.

That she'd seen *me* like that.

This wasn't how I wanted to tell her who I was.

Though I'd magicked away my wings and the blood from my fingers, my blood was pumping too furiously for me to return the rest of my human glamor.

But now… she wasn't safe here. I didn't know how they'd found out about her existence, but I supposed my recent visits to the human realm hadn't gone unnoticed.

It was the day of my deadline for Damien, not that Luna knew anything about *that*. Because I hadn't told her.

Dammit. I'd fucked everything up. Part of me had known I would because I couldn't stay away from her. She was like a drug, and I wanted more of her in my system.

As soon as I'd sat Luna down to her feet, I could practically feel her slipping away from me. Like she was building bricks between us, blocking out the bond. On the couch, she'd drawn herself in tight, her arms pulling her legs to her chest as if she could keep herself together solely with the physical effort.

"You *lied*," she whispered. Luna's eyes were focused straight ahead on the wall in front of her, avoiding my gaze. The furry beast she called Selene jumped on the couch next to her, the cat nuzzling against Luna's arm.

Sighing, I kneeled in front of her. "Believe me, I never meant to." I'd kept things from her, yes, but would she have believed me if I'd told the truth from the beginning?

"A lie of omission is still a lie." She finally looked back at me, her breath catching as her gaze caught on my irises. "Who are you?" Her eyes trailed over my form. "*What* are you?" Luna's voice was quiet as she said the words, like she was unsure if she wanted the answer.

"I think you know, love." Perhaps it was my fault. For not saying it the moment we'd met. For not getting it out in the open before we'd slept together. I knew I shouldn't have, but how could I stay away?

Her shoulders sagged.

"You're not human," she stated, a slight hesitation in her tone. "But you're not a witch, either. I *knew* that. But how'd you get through the barrier? How did the magic not keep you out? Why—" She was spiraling, all the questions I'd left unanswered coming back to the surface.

"Luna," I murmured, cupping her jaw. Moving closer, like the bastard I was, because I couldn't keep my hands off of her. Not when she looked so uneasy with the truth. But I didn't want her to fear me. "You're right. I'm not human."

"You're a *demon*," she whispered, that word not filled with disgust as I'd feared. Some of the tension in my chest eased. "That's how you could defeat them, right? They were demons, and you—"

I'd ended their sorry existences. I didn't regret *that*.

"Yes. They're a race called blood demons," I confirmed. They were demons that solely existed to prey on weak humans, who would take what they wanted without concern for other life. "Nasty things. They didn't deserve to live." I reached up to brush a strand of hair behind her ear.

The color drained from her face, and she let out a strangled sound. "Why did they come after *me?* I'm…" She twisted her hands nervously in her lap. "I'm *nothing*. No one. I'm just a baker, for goddess' sake. I'm not…"

"It's my fault," I said, cupping her jaw. Forcing her to look at me. "They came after you because of me."

"But… why? What could they possibly attain by attacking me?" Confusion painted her face.

Because of who I was. Because of who she was to me.

"They want to hurt me." I winced, knowing the next part was going to be another shock. "And we haven't been very careful. My scent is all over you."

That must have been how they'd found her so easily.

Her eyes widened. "I—what? I *smell* like you?"

"Yes." I shut my eyelids, my nose inhaling deeply. She didn't know how much it settled my instincts that she *did*. How *good* she smelled. Like mine.

"Will they come after me again?"

Tampering down the possessive flare that pulsed through my body at the thought, I smoothed down her hair, letting my fingers run through the silky blonde strands. "I wish I could tell you no. Reassure you that you'll be okay. But..."

"You can't." Her voice was hoarse.

"No." I agreed. "You're not safe here." I was angry at myself that I'd screwed this up. That I'd threatened her very existence. Even if it meant I was getting exactly what I'd wanted all along. "Not anymore. Not where I can't keep an eye on you."

"My sister is here. And her... boyfriend." She screwed up her face at the word. "I'm not alone."

But she was. She lived alone in this apartment above her bakery, and it was my stupidity that led to this incident.

Because I hadn't insisted on her coming back with me the moment I found her.

"If something happened to you, I'd never forgive myself."

Luna shut her eyes, waging an internal battle with herself. "So, what?"

"Come back with me."

"Where?" Her eyes flew open. "*Hell?*"

A deep rasp escaped my lips. "We don't actually live in Hell, Luna. Though your human views on the location aren't entirely wrong." Even I didn't want to spend time there. It was an awful place. "You can come back to my realm. My home."

"I don't want to leave my life behind." Her voice was quiet—

subdued. Nothing like the Luna from the bar. *My* Luna. The girl filled with so much energy, a smile almost always glued on her face. "Everyone I love is here. My sister. My friends. My coven… My job." She worried on her lower lip, looking away.

"In time, once the threat has passed… You could come back." I wouldn't force her to stay with me—not if she didn't want to.

I wanted her to choose me willingly. To choose us.

Luna sounded almost… resigned. "And when will that be?" Like she'd already decided to accept my offer. A spark of hope bloomed in my chest.

"I don't know." I cleared my throat, hoping I was doing the right thing. "But you'll come to enjoy living in the palace, I promise. You'd be well taken care of. Looked after."

"*Palace?*" Luna's eyes flared with surprise. "Wait. Your father's business, your…" I could see her brain working, adding up all the pieces of information in her head. "You're *royalty?*"

"Yes."

"And all those business deals you said you were making—"

"To be fair, *you're* the one who said they were business deals."

She punched my arm, though I barely felt it since her fists were so tiny. I was over a foot taller than her, and the size difference was staggering. "You didn't correct me!"

I furrowed my brow. "What was I going to say? *'I'm a demon?'* I couldn't. You wouldn't have believed me even if I had."

"Why?" Her voice was low. "Why *me?*"

I knew what she was asking. I brushed my thumb along her cheekbone. Touching her like this was abating the last of the anxiety from my system.

"You captivated me more than anyone has in a long time." The truth. Most of it.

"How long is a long time?" Luna's voice was hardly a whisper.

"A few hundred years." Give or take.

"You're *that* old?"

"That's nothing." I chuckled, thinking about how long demons could live. "To most demons, I'm still a teenager. I'm hardly a quarter of the way through my lifespan." My father was almost a thousand, and even then…

"But that's…" She shook her head. "How is this possible? Why were you even here in the first place? What business does a demon have here, anyway? "

"I was checking up on my brother." Truth enough, as it was. He was only here because I'd sent him here.

How would she feel when she found out I'd been here to snatch her away? To spirit her to my realm like Hades stole Persephone? But had he stolen her, or had she gone willingly? It all depended on who was telling the tale.

"Your brother?" I watched as something clicked in her mind. "Damien?" Her eyes widened as I gave her a nod of confirmation. "Damien is your *brother?*"

"Half, but yes."

"So, your brother is seeing my sister, and you didn't tell me?" She drew her face in, quirking an eyebrow.

I shrugged nonchalantly. "He doesn't know I'm here. No one does." The fewer people that knew, the better, actually. As evidenced by what had just happened. "But I should have known better." I rubbed at my temples.

Luna frowned, blinking at me a few times. "This is a lot to take in. Even for me."

"Come back with me," I said, offering her an open hand. "I'll keep you safe. I promise." Like a devoted knight, I still kneeled in front of her. That was what I could offer her—my body, my sword, my shield.

She smoothed her hand over her skirt. "How? We don't even know that this *will* happen again. Couldn't I be attacked just as easily—no, even *easier*, there?"

Where there was one, there were more. "I wish I could say it wouldn't happen again. But you'd never be alone. My guards would protect you, even when I couldn't be there. You just need to…" I swallowed, knowing she wouldn't like what would come next. But there was only one way I could protect her without revealing the truth. "Be my bride."

"What?" Luna froze, astonishment touching the features on her still-too-pale face. "Are you insane? You want me to marry you?"

I brushed a hair off her forehead. "No one will harm you if they know you are mine."

I'd make sure they wouldn't. They could threaten the kingdom all they wanted, revolt and pillage and burn, but they wouldn't dare to touch one hair on her head.

"We barely even know each other, Zain," Luna said, frustration seeping through her features as she pushed me away, standing up to pace back and forth across her rug. "A few nights and conversations don't equal love."

I stood, my eyes fixated on her, taking in every detail. "Yes, I know." I thought we'd have more time to get there before it would come to this. "I don't expect you to *love* me." Frowning, I let her have her space.

"What, then? It's all *fake?*" She furrowed her brows, and I was struck with the realization that it was *cute*. She was adorable, with her nose all scrunched up as she tried to work her way through it. I wanted to smooth the lines out on her forehead with my thumb.

No matter what was going on, I was constantly tampering down the urge to touch her. It was something I'd have to get better at if we were going to be spending even more time together because she couldn't know the rest. Not until… I shook off the thought.

"It can be whatever we need it to be." I shrugged my shoulders. Like we weren't talking about a marriage that would tie us together for... *No.* She'd never forgive me if she knew what I was thinking, even now.

"An act."

I merely hummed in response, watching as Luna stopped abruptly on the floor, turning to face me once more.

"Do demons make deals?" Luna quirked an eyebrow at me, crossing her arms over her chest.

"What?" I startled. A demon's deal wasn't something to make lightly. And she was just…

"Make a deal with me. That's what demons do, right? You make deals and steal souls?"

She wasn't entirely wrong, but she wasn't *right,* either. My kind of demon didn't barter with human souls.

I shut my eyes, trying to summon whatever threads of patience I had. "What sort of deal are you thinking?"

She looked up at me with those light green eyes, sparkling like peridots in the low light. Her gaze was full of such intensity that I wanted to look away. But I couldn't. I wouldn't. She'd captivated me since the first night.

"In order to protect me, you need me to be your wife, right?"

I gave her a nod, wondering where she was going with this.

Luna resumed pacing in front of me across the floor, her white furball winding under her feet. "If I'm going to—" she swallowed like she had to push out the words, *"marry you,* it should be an even exchange. What are you getting out of this, anyway?"

She turned to look at me. That pretty pink blush spread over her cheeks. *You*, I thought, *I get you.*

"I have my own reasons for needing a wife," I spoke. *A queen.* "But if you'd feel more comfortable making a deal, that can be arranged." I waved my hand, a contract appearing out of thin air.

I stepped closer, grasping her chin between my thumb and pointer finger, bringing her eyes up to meet mine. "Lay out your terms, Moonbeam." Her breath hitched, and I knew she couldn't deny the physical attraction between us any more than I could. It was intertwined in our DNA, buried in our biology. This need we had for each other overruled everything else.

What I wanted more than anything was to hoist her up into my arms and deposit her onto the counter. To take her to bed like I had so many times these past few weeks. Losing myself in her body those nights was the only thing that seemed to keep me sane.

She blinked, looking away in a haze. "My terms?"

"For our *contract.*"

Luna bit her lip in concentration. "How long will the marriage be for?"

Forever. "Until you no longer need me."

"Oh." Then she nodded. "I guess that makes sense. Once the threat is gone, we wouldn't need to be married anymore."

"Right." I cleared my throat because I hoped it wouldn't come to that. That I could win her over. That I could make her see that life with me wouldn't be so bad. That I would make every one of her dreams come true.

"I don't want to be a prisoner." She crossed her arms, a pouty look spreading over her face. Did she know how much I wanted to kiss it off her face? "I do not want to be locked up, unable to leave my room."

"Of course." I made a face. Did she really think I would do that to her? "You will have full access to the palace as long as you have a bodyguard with you."

She winced. "I don't want a bodyguard."

"You don't have an option." If someone else was with her, I would know she'd be safe.

Luna crossed her arms over her chest. "I can protect myself."

I raised an eyebrow. "Can you?" Just thirty minutes ago, she'd been trembling with fear.

"Yes." She jerked her chin up in the air. "My magic…" She twitched her fingers, gaze dropping to the floor. "I know it's there. I can feel it. But I'm just… terrified of letting it out."

It wasn't a surprise to me—I knew she had power. It called to me in her veins. The fates had chosen her for me, after all. But finding out she didn't know how to wield it was a shock. "Did no one ever teach you?"

Luna shook her head. "I didn't want to be different. The other girls in my coven had normal gifts: potion brewing, animal communication, spirit sensing, that kind of thing. And I… I got weird light powers and visions. So I forced it down and did my best to learn how to block everyone out. How to create shields around my mind."

"I can teach you." I offered, wrapping a hand around her arm to still her.

"You can?" She blinked. "How?"

I flashed her a saccharine smile. "I might not be a witch, but I am surprisingly indestructible, Luna, and I have magic of my own."

Shadows that begged to explore every inch of her. Maybe this way, they could.

Luna seemed to contemplate that for a moment, finally nodding. "What do you get out of this?" She repeated her words, a whisper in that tiny apartment. If I hadn't been so close to her, I might not have heard them.

Trailing my finger across her jaw, I tilted my face down to brush my lips against hers. "*You.*" I let the word linger with all the sexual promises it offered, tangling in the air like sin on my tongue.

Pressing a kiss to her lips, I let it say all the things I couldn't.

I'd tell her the rest—in time. She wasn't ready for the other part I required from her. Not yet, anyway. I needed her to trust me first. Needed her to realize I wasn't the bad guy.

NINE
LUNA

I'll come with you. They were the words on the tip of my tongue, yet I couldn't work them free. He said he would keep me safe, but it was at the cost of giving up the only life I'd ever known. To leave my home and my sister behind.

A deal with the devil. A shudder ran down my spine.

Even knowing the truth of what this man was, I still couldn't help my attraction to him. There was something electric between us, something that lit me up inside and threatened to swallow me whole.

His kiss made me melt against him. Like he knew I would give in to anything, he asked with the press of his lips against mine. Zain's tongue darted into my mouth, practically devouring me with each lick, each taste.

Me. He wanted me.

But what did that mean? Maybe it was just sex for him. The physical response my body had to his, and maybe there was something to trading my life and my freedom for his protection.

Was it *enough?* I'd always been a hopeless romantic. I loved those bodice rippers I found at the library in my teens, devouring every romance novel I found, imagining it was me falling in love with the devilish rake or the handsome duke.

Love.

All my life, I'd always imagined I'd marry for love. Not a marriage of convenience with a *demon prince.* A laugh bubbled free from my lips, thinking about the fact that I was living out the plot of a romance novel after all—just not one I'd ever imagined.

Gods, what would Willow think? Learning I was marrying her boyfriend's brother? Because I was going to.

I was, wasn't I? Somewhere in my freakout, I'd decided without even realizing it.

"Okay." I straightened my shoulders.

"Okay?" He raised an eyebrow.

"Okay," I repeated. "Yes. I'll marry you."

Zain smirked, the devilish expression lighting up his face. "Good." Those golden eyes were so strange—so familiar. I'd seen them before, hadn't I? Somewhere in the deepest recesses of my memory, they lingered. Somewhere between sleep and awake...

What was it about him that always had me agreeing? This was a terrible idea, and yet, here I was—agreeing to it. To marry him. To leave my life behind.

"Well, shall we?" He extended an arm towards me.

"Shall we…"

"Go?"

"*Now?*" I looked around the apartment. "What about *everything?*" Waving my arms, I gestured at my stuff. "Do you expect me to just leave all of this behind?"

He gave me a thoughtful look before dipping his face in a nod. "Alright." Zain pressed a kiss to my cheek. "I'll be back in an hour."

Like that was enough time to sort out my entire life.

"Where are you going?" I quirked an eyebrow. "I thought I wasn't *safe?*"

He gave me a smirk, crossing his arms over his chest as he propped himself up against the door frame. "You truly think so little of me, Moonbeam?" One arm was on the top, his hip leaning against the wood.

"I…" What did I think? I didn't really know him. Today had proven that. Yet I'd let him… My cheeks flushed as I crossed my arms over my chest. *I was doing just fine until you came along.* I bit back the retort. Was I? Or had this loneliness been festering inside of me for a long time, and I hadn't realized it until I met him?

"No," I finally settled on. Because despite myself, I did trust him. And I needed to show him that if we were going to make this deal work.

The demon—I was trying to remind myself of that fact because it still seemed surreal to me—let loose a sigh. "Get your stuff together. I'm just going to make sure everything is ready." He cleared his throat. "For you."

"Okay," I whispered the word.

Turning, I looked back at my apartment. What would I even take with me? *Essentials.* I needed to start with the essentials. It's not like they'd have my favorite brand of shampoo just hanging out in a demon drug store. Right? I started a mental checklist.

Tampons, lotions, and the makeup bag I always had handy. Most of my nightstand drawer.

"What do you even wear in the demon realm?" I asked, looking over my shoulder, but Zain was already gone.

I frowned, and Selene meowed at me.

"Am I making a huge mistake?" I asked her, shaking my head as I moved into my bedroom. I rubbed at my chest, but while I thought I would be filled with fear or apprehension, I just felt… curious—warm, like that first night with Zain.

My cat sat on my bed, watching me with her big eyes, that tail flicking. "Don't worry," I murmured, rubbing the top of her head. "I'm not going to leave you behind."

Pulling out a bag, I started chucking all of my bathroom stuff inside of it.

Another meow, but this one felt amused. She'd always been able to read my emotions, and I liked to think I knew what she was thinking, as well.

Of course not, her tail flick seemed to say. *I never thought you would.* She licked her paw, cleaning her bright white fur. Like snow—or the moon. Two things I loved.

"Do you think we'll like it there?" I asked her, letting the softness of her coat calm me down as I ran my fingers over her back. She purred in response, which I could only take as a good sign.

After nuzzling her for a few more moments, I stood back up, attempting to condense the rest of my life into a few bags.

And despite my head telling me to run, that it was a terrible decision, my heart beat steadily.

Like it knew something I didn't.

Like it knew I was making the right decision.

I just hoped that was true.

372

TEN
ZAIN

Fates, I needed to hire more capable staff. The last hour had been spent questioning everyone's inability to follow my directions, and I was finally back on Luna's doorstep. I'd been more careful this time—making sure not a soul was following me before I opened a portal and stepped into her world. I couldn't afford to be careless—not with her.

Just as I was about to raise my hand to knock on the door, it swung open unexpectedly.

My future *wife* stood in front of me, still wearing the same soft white dress from earlier, though the streak marks from her tears were now gone.

"What's all that?" I asked, looking at the bags by the door. Including one crate that looked a lot like a *cage*, which could only mean…

Luna crossed her arms over her chest. "You don't expect me to leave *all* of my stuff behind, do you?"

I frowned. "Of course not."

It just hadn't occurred to me what exactly uprooting my future wife meant for her. I should have been more thoughtful. Made sure she didn't need help.

Sure, I'd only left her for an hour, and that was only after I'd carefully surrounded her apartment with a magical barrier that would only let the two of us inside.

But I could have helped her, stayed with her. Instead, I'd gone back to the palace and barked out instructions to the palace staff. They needed to prepare for her arrival, and it had been a long time since there had been a woman in the palace.

Selfishly, I wanted her to feel welcome.

"It's just a few things, but…" She glanced down at the floor. The cat meowed, making her presence known.

"Right," I said, smoothing out my furrowed brow. "You can bring whatever you'd like." She'd packed rather lightly for a stay with no expiration date set. Just a duffel bag, suitcase, and her cat carrier.

Luna looked sheepish. "I wasn't exactly sure what I'd need in your… world." She hesitated at the last word.

"Nothing," I said honestly. "Anything you need, anything you desire, will be procured for you." I had to remind myself that she didn't know how demon magic worked. But she would learn.

"Oh." Her faint blush returned. "Well…" She leaned up onto her tiptoes to kiss my cheek. "Thank you."

Bending down, she put her fingers into the gaps in the crate so she could rub her creature's muzzle. "I'm sorry, baby. I promise you won't be in there too long." Luna looked back up at me. "It won't hurt her, right?"

"Teleporting?" I clarified. Though *world walking* might have been a more accurate term. Damien and I both used the shadows to do so, opening up a portal to move between realms. I shook my head. "No. It doesn't hurt." I took her in as she worried her lower lip into her mouth. "Are you… scared?"

"Not scared, exactly. I think I'm just… apprehensive of the unknown?"

"You'll be okay," I promised, leaning down to press a kiss to her forehead. "You're always going to be safe with me."

She relaxed, breathing out a little. "Okay."

And despite everything that had happened today—she seemed to trust me on that, at least.

It was a start.

Maybe I hadn't ruined everything. That sparked an ounce of hope in me. That maybe, somehow, I could still make this work despite my monumental fuckups. I didn't regret us sleeping together—could never regret the nights I'd spent in her bed—but I wished I could erase the pain from her face when she'd learned the truth.

Turning to the door to the outside world, I murmured, "Should we go?"

Luna looked back at her apartment as I waved my hand over her belongings, using my magic to send them back to her rooms at the palace. Her posture slumped a little as she looked back at the place. That bottom lip I'd spent these past few weeks kissing quivered slightly.

Then, in the blink of an eye, I saw the look of determination form over her features. She gave me a fierce nod. "Okay. Let's go."

In that moment, I could see every bit of the queen she could become. That I hoped she would be.

I held out my hand to her, a satisfied thrum flowing through me as she interlaced our fingers, and then I opened the portal.

Taking us straight into the heart of the demon realm.

* * *

Stepping out of the portal, the foyer of the palace came into view. Luna's hands still gripped at my arms from where she'd clung to me.

Her skin was pale.

"Are you okay?" I smoothed a hand down the back of her hair. "I know the first time can be… difficult." After I'd used the power for the first time, I'd vomited profusely. At least she was doing better than me.

She shook her head as I helped steady her. "I'm fine." Then her eyes widened as she took in our surroundings. "Where are we?"

"Home," I answered, my gaze landing on her. *Maybe now it would feel like it.* "Welcome to the palace."

ELEVEN

LUNA

You've got to be kidding me," I said, my jaw dropping. "This is where you *live?*"

My small apartment was nothing compared to the gleaming vision that sprawled out in front of me. Marble staircases descended to the top level, and above us was a giant, shimmering chandelier. Statues of gargoyles lined the room, and what seemed like thousands of candles lit around it.

Zain shrugged. "It's alright." Like he didn't see this place for what it was. Majestic. Beautiful. A little spooky, but not in a terrifying way.

"*Alright?*"

Another shrug of his shoulders, that casual indifference written across his face, in his posture.

But the demon realm—so far—was nothing like I'd expected. Whatever my parents had taught us about demons when we were younger, it never would have prepared me for this. Gold filigree covered the walls, down to the sconces that held all those flickering candles. It cast a warm glow across the palace in what otherwise would have felt cold and foreign.

"Toto, we're not in Pleasant Grove anymore," I muttered under my breath, looking around the room.

Zain gave me a weird look. "What?"

"Never mind." I giggled to myself, looking away. Gods, he really *was* clueless about humanity. It probably explained the whole cellphone thing.

Averting my eyes away from his, I continued to take in the details. There were paintings on the ceilings that depicted many demons—some so similar to the two who'd tried to attack me earlier. I frowned. What sorts of beings would I meet now that I was in this place full of *monsters?* He'd insisted this wasn't Hell, but I didn't know what I believed anymore.

"It's not what I expected," I finally murmured.

He hummed in response.

With a snap of his fingers, he'd shed the rest of his human appearance—now wearing a tailored black suit with a long black overcoat adorned in gold.

His gold eyes practically glittered as he turned back to look at me. "Shall we?"

I stared, dumbfounded. "Shall we… what?" I was too busy appreciating the outfit—how *right* he looked in it—to process the rest. It was almost strange how he seemed to fit here. And how natural it was seeing him like this. Like the other version of him had just been a facade all along.

"I thought I'd show you around." The subtle upward quirk of his mouth told me he saw me checking him out, and I tried not to ignore the way it sent a bolt through my system. Because even if I was still upset with him, my body didn't know that.

"Oh." I gave a small nod. "Yeah. Let's do that."

But I couldn't pull my eyes off of his bulky frame. The way the fabric rested over his broad shoulders.

How could such a sin be such an utter temptation? Clearly, I was weak. He made me want to be. Because I knew what it was like between us. How good. And that was back when I'd just thought him to be a human, passing through town. Now, everything was different.

Everything except the sparks between us.

His lips dipped low, brushing against my ear. "If you keep looking at me like that, Moonbeam…"

"What?" I said with a sharp inhale of breath.

Zain's eyes were filled with want, and he took a deep pull of my scent. "I'll have no choice but to pull that dress up and take you right here." He shuddered, his nose finally leaving that spot between my neck. "Fuck, you smell so good."

"Zain," I whimpered, the heat pooling between my legs. I wanted that, needed that. Could he smell how turned on I was?

He stiffened, and the haze cleared from his eyes. When he stepped back, it broke the connection between us. Whatever spell we'd been under.

"Come on," he said, and a wall of ice washed over me. Dousing any desire I'd been feeling for the moment. "Let's go."

"Right." I knew it was a good thing, but why did I feel rejected?

I didn't speak, just following behind him as he led me through the palace, showing me the dining room and the kitchens, the ballroom and the throne room—both with grand ceilings dripping in gold and featuring more of those magnificent but eerie demon paintings on the ceilings—and then to the library.

There were no words to convey how wonderful and insane all of it was, but I especially loved the library.

Endless rows of books beckoned me, begging to be read. I wondered what sort of secrets I could uncover in there—lessons to learn about demons, for sure. Would there be romance novels here? I wondered if a place that housed such wickedness also knew love. My eyes drifted over to Zain, who was watching me with rapt interest.

"What came first?" I mused, running my fingers along the spines as I explored the room.

"Hm?" He asked, leaning against the end of the row, never taking his eyes off of me.

I stopped on a gilded book labeled *A History of Demons* and pulled it halfway off the shelf, looking at the cover. "Humans or demons? Did you draw inspiration from us, or did we find inspiration from *you?*" I couldn't think about this race of evil creatures impacting our world, but even here, there were elements of humanity. Touches of culture that couldn't have formed independently of us.

Zain scoffed. "Who's to say we didn't influence each other?"

Shaking my head, a faint smile spread over my face. "I love this place."

"You're free to come here any time you like." He dipped his head. "It's yours."

"Oh." My cheeks were warm as I pushed the book back into its place. "Thank you."

His face seemed to lose some of the tension he'd been carrying around. "You're welcome. Do you want to see the rest?"

I nodded, letting him lead me through the rest of the palace. There was no chance I'd remember where everything was—at least, not right away—but it gave me some semblance of comfort knowing he cared enough to show me where everything was.

Peeking over at him, I watched his face, trying to read his expression.

"This is my study," he said, pointing to a room past the library. "If you need me, and you can't find me, just come here."

"Okay." I bit my lip, noticing he didn't take me inside.

Leading me up a back staircase, we wandered down a long hallway. "Those are my rooms," Zain said, motioning to a set of doors.

We walked a little farther before he came to a stop.

"And this," he said, his hand extending to swing open the door, "is yours."

"My room?" My eyes widened.

"Is that not to your liking?" He asked, brow furrowed. "I thought you'd like your own space."

Under his steady scrutiny, I looked away. "No," I said the word a little too quickly, wondering why I'd thought we'd be sharing.

Fake. None of this was real. I had to keep reminding myself of that. "It's great." I pasted on a smile, pushing past him to enter the room.

I gasped when I took it in. The room had large windows that seemed to overlook a garden outside, and a large poster bed sat in the middle, piled with white fluffy pillows—and Selene was grooming herself as she laid on top of a chaise lounge.

"Zain." My hand flew over my heart. "This—"

He cleared his throat. "Do you like it?"

"Yes," I agreed. There was a vase of flowers on the vanity. I leaned down, smelling the freshly cut lilacs. "Like it?" I choked back a laugh. "This is perfect. How did you even…"

I looked over at him, but he was still moving through the space. His back was turned to me, and I took another moment to admire his backside. Goddess, he was beautiful.

"The bathroom is through here," he said, opening a door I hadn't noticed yet. It opened into a tiled room that smelled like lemon and cleaner, every inch sparkling. "And the bathing pool is through there. You'll find if you need anything, all you have to do is ask."

"Bathing… *pool?*" I blinked. Who needed a pool to wash up? But there wasn't a tub in this bathroom, so I assumed that was my only option. I loved taking baths, even though I was normally a shower kinda girl. I didn't have a tub in my apartment, so I'd gotten used to not having one. "Sounds wonderful, actually."

He hummed in response, moving back to the main room. "Your bags have already been put away, and you'll find the closet—and your sitting room—through those other doors."

My head was spinning. "This is bigger than my entire apartment." In fact, I was pretty sure it could fit in just the bedroom here. The bathroom was the size of two bedrooms. I didn't want to know how big the closet was. I might pass out.

Moving over to the bed, I ran my hands over the white lacy curtains that adorned the sides of the bed. I'd never had a canopy bed before, even though I'd always loved them.

How did he know?

Zain snapped his fingers, and a demon girl appeared in front of us. Her skin was pale, her eyes white, and her hair was the most interesting shade of icy blue, streaked with silver. Little gray horns peeked out at the top of her forehead.

"Novalie." Zain addressed the demon, who bowed to us both.

"My lord." She stood to her full height—though even with my average height, she was a few inches shorter than me.

He turned to me. "This is Luna—my future wife. You'll be serving her from now on. I expect her to be treated with the utmost respect."

That was the first time I'd heard him refer to me as his wife, and it made my cheeks heat.

"Of course. It's nice to meet you, my lady." She curtsied, and I felt totally out of my element.

"You don't have to—" I started, only shutting my mouth at Zain's glare. "It's nice to meet you also, Novalie." I dipped my head in thanks.

"If you need anything, I'm at your service." She gave me a warm smile before disappearing before my eyes.

I frowned, looking at Zain. My future husband. Wow, that would take getting used to. "Does everyone do that here?"

"What, teleport?"

I nodded. Witches had magic, but there were limits on even our power.

He grinned. "Jealous?"

A little. "No." I crossed my arms over my chest.

"I can teach you, you know."

Opening my palms, I stared down at my hands. "How?"

He took one of my hands into his, tracing down my veins with his pointer finger. "Can't you feel the magic running through your veins?"

I shivered at his touch, but I *did*. Even with me holding my power at bay for so many years, keeping it shut behind walls, that thrumming energy lurking underneath never completely went away. It had never stopped overwhelming me, though I'd trained myself so well that I couldn't see into someone's future without focusing on it.

Though it had never stopped dreams of my own.

Closing my eyes, I focused only on the sensation of his hands on my skin.

"You just have to learn to tap into it." He squeezed my wrist before letting go and stepping back. "I'll teach you how."

My eyes fluttered open. "You will?" I tried to hide the surprise from my voice.

"I told you I would," Zain said, looking confused. "That's part of the deal."

Right. That I'd marry him, and he'd keep me safe. *Fake*. If I reminded myself of it enough, it would sink in.

"What am I to you?" I whispered, not knowing if I wanted the answer or not.

He blinked. "I don't understand the question."

"Are we… friends?" After the two weeks we'd spent together, I didn't know what to do with the distance I felt all of a sudden. Sure, the heat hadn't dissipated between us, and I still *wanted* him—always—but I didn't know what to do with that. If this was just a physical relationship… Anxiety knitted at my stomach.

Zain frowned. "Friends? Luna, we're—"

But he didn't get to finish the sentence, because a loud knock came from my door.

The demon by my side let out a strangled sound before he said, "Enter."

A man—a *demon*, I reminded myself—with dark skin and red eyes popped his head in.

"Kairos," Zain growled. "Did I not say I was not to be interrupted?"

"Sorry, my Prince." The demon inclined his head. "There's something you should know."

He made another huff of annoyance before turning to me. "I'm sorry to leave like this, but I have to…"

"Go," I assured him. "It's fine."

"Feel free to wash up if you'd like. Just shout for Novalie if you need anything." He cupped my cheek. "I'm sorry, Luna. About all of this. I really am."

"It's not your fault," I offered, shaking my head. "I'll be fine." Putting on a brave face, I did my best to smile.

"And there's one last thing," he added, his voice stern. "Don't leave without telling me."

My spine went rigid. *What?* "No. We already talked about this. I won't be kept prisoner here, Zain. I agreed to marry you, to *this*, but that doesn't mean I'll be forced into some gilded cage."

He furrowed his brows. Pressed his forehead to mine. *Please. I don't have anyone to protect you yet, Moonbeam.*

My eyes widened. His lips weren't moving, which meant he was... speaking into my *mind?* Oh, Goddess.

So I need you to stay here until I do, he continued, his intense stare boring into me. *There are wards around this room to keep you safe. Only Novalie and I can enter without express permission. Be good.*

He cupped my cheeks and kissed my forehead before whirling out of the room without another look, leaving me to puzzle over the last few hours alone.

I sank into my new bed, ignoring the pulse of emotions running through my body. My skin was still vibrating from every place he'd touched me, and I brushed my hand over my forehead.

Could he read my thoughts, too? I didn't know demons could speak through thoughts like that.

Why did it feel like the more time I spent with him, the more questions I had?

* * *

Novalie was all too happy to help me get into the bath.

The warm water was a welcome relief. I'd felt slightly grimy ever since I'd watched Zain slice those demons to bits earlier. A shudder ran through my body. Not a memory I wanted to relive.

Shutting my eyes, I leaned my head back against the tile, enjoying the blissful heat running over my body. Before she'd left, she'd filled the pool with a sweet-smelling oil and set out a fluffy robe for me. I'd never had anyone wait on me before, and it was strange, but I didn't completely hate it. Maybe it was because she was so kind and eager to help me.

It was at odds with what I'd believed in, even from the demons who had come upon me in the alley earlier.

How could anyone compare this place to Hell? No, I was pretty sure this was *Heaven*. There was no other word for it.

The bathing pool was *giant*, and it even had a water fountain that flowed in, steam billowing from its surface. I wondered if it was powered by some sort of underground hot spring, despite the water's lack of odor. I could bathe here every day for the rest of my life and not complain.

The rest of my life? I rolled my eyes, trying to make myself remember that this was temporary. Once Zain knew I was safe, he'd deliver me back to Pleasant Grove.

Back to my *life*. To my sister. To the bakery.

Oh. Shit. I hadn't even figured out what was going to happen with our shop or even texted my sister that I'd be gone. Halloween was tonight, and the coven always got together for a party. Willow would be wondering where I was. This was practically her favorite day of the year. What would she think when she realized I was missing?

I winced, sinking further down into the water so only my eyes remained above the surface. I'd practically run off with a man and not even thought about what I was going to do.

What was I going to do? I was going to marry him.

I let my body relax, the fears of the day slowly melting away.

My eyes shut, and a velvet touch brushed against my mind.

Let me in, it seemed to ask, but I couldn't.

I didn't know how.

Not yet.

TWELVE
ZAIN

What's wrong?" I whirled on Kairos as soon as the door shut behind us. He was my war general, my right-hand man. If he was interrupting… I could only assume the worst.

"Is she okay?" Kairos asked, his demon tail flicking.

"She was a bit shaken up, but—I think so." I looked back at the closed door like I could see through to her. "I just hope she can forgive me in time."

"There's always hope," he said, clasping a hand on my shoulder. He had seen so many battles in his lifetime, and yet he still hadn't become the same cynical asshole that I was. "Even in a place like this."

Rolling my eyes, I pushed him away from me, leaning against the wall. "Those demons shouldn't have been in the human world. How did they even find her in Pleasant Grove?"

"Maybe they followed you."

I frowned. "It's a possibility, but…" I'd been careful when I'd crossed between realms. Plus, the witches had wards that should have kept them out.

"Or someone sent them."

"Fuck," I cursed under my breath. There was only one person who would have stooped so low.

"He has everything to lose from you bringing her back here—and you have everything to gain. It makes sense."

I growled, the sound slipping through my lips before I could think better of it. Because maybe there was more to me wanting to keep her hidden in the human realm these last few weeks. There, I had her all to myself. Here, everyone would want a piece of her.

They would want her to prove herself repeatedly. And she didn't even know how to use her magic.

"What am I supposed to do, Kai?" There was more at play here than that. And Luna was the key to all of it. "I have to keep her safe."

"We need to move forward to the next phase, Zain. You know he can't be bargained with."

"I know. Fates, I know. That's the problem." I rubbed at the spot between my brows.

"So, let the people see their future queen."

I turned to look at him. "That wasn't part of the plan."

"If they see her, fall in love with her—it's less likely that he can cause any harm to come to her."

"But they might not accept her." I shook my head. "She's still just a *human*," I reminded him. Like he could forget. Maybe that wasn't the issue at all, though—just that she wasn't a demon.

She was strong willed, but being human here made her weak. I needed to bump my plans up, and I knew it.

"But she's a witch. And a powerful one."

I shut my eyes. "That changes nothing." Until after the ceremony, she'd be at risk.

"Are you sure?" He asked, eyes sparking with humor even as I scowled at him, shadows pooling around me. "Because I think it changes *everything*."

I grumbled, Luna's serene face filling my mind. The way her smile rocked me down to my foundation, splitting me open. There was only her.

"Fine. Plan a ball for tonight, and we'll announce our engagement there."

We'd dance and mingle, and the demons could meet the woman I was tying to me in marriage. And hopefully, they'd fall in love with her. It was all I could hope for. All I could offer her.

It could work.

He nodded. "I'll find the girls. They should be able to help."

A snort left me, thinking of Asura and Lilith in ball gowns instead of leathers. They were warriors, honed and bred. Pretty dresses? I looked forward to seeing that.

"I don't know how to do this," I admitted. "How to be everything that everyone needs me to be."

Maybe the only thing that mattered was how to be what Luna needed me to be.

Kai slapped me on the back. "If there's anyone who can figure it out, it's you. Or has three hundred years of life experience taught you nothing?"

Without another word, I left him, closing the door behind me.

I needed to head back to my future bride.

* * *

"*Oh.*" Luna squeaked, covering her breasts with her hands as I entered the bathing pool. Bubbles covered the surface of the water, keeping her bottom half covered from view. Her light blonde strands were piled on the top of her head in a messy bun.

A wicked grin spread across my face, my tongue running over my canine teeth that seemed to ache from the view of her bare neck. "You don't have to hide from me, Moonbeam." I'd already seen it all, anyway.

"I wasn't *hiding,*" she said, her cheeks flushed. "I just—"

"I'm sorry for leaving," I murmured, crouching down to the edge of the pool.

A wince escaped my lips, and her brows furrowed, concern painting her features. "Is everything okay?"

"Not particularly, but you don't have to be worried." I put on my mask of indifferent arrogance, hoping she wouldn't pry further. "I'm dealing with it."

"Is there anything I can do?" She sounded hopeful, and a knot of worry unwound itself from my stomach. This would be okay. We would be okay.

I shook my head. She was already doing it just by being here. Smoothing out my rough edges. Tempering my mood. *Grounding me.*

Something had to be done about my father before it threatened our realm's peace. Which meant I had to find a way through this. For my kingdom's sake, I just hoped she would understand.

"You weren't kidding about this place," Luna whispered

absentmindedly as she ran her hands through the surface of the water. "This is insane. I still can't believe it's *real*." She looked up at me. "I feel like I still can't wrap my brain around it."

I hummed in response, watching her. "Don't the witches have stories about us?"

She laughed, the twinkling sound seeming to bounce off every inch of the room. Filling me up with *light*. "Yeah, and we also have stories about vampires and shifters and mermaids. But no one's seen any of them for thousands of years, so… I thought the whole *don't make a deal with the devil t*hing was just a cautionary tale."

My chuckle was more of a rasp. "Just because you don't see something doesn't make it any less real." Mermaids might have been a bit of a stretch, but my future queen had no idea what sort of creatures lurked inside her world, hidden behind magical barriers of their own. One day, I'd show her everything there was to know.

"Okay, *Santa Claus*."

"What?" I raised an eyebrow.

"Are you saying you don't know who Santa Claus is?" Luna looked stunned.

I shrugged. "I haven't exactly spent a lot of time in the human world." Not until I'd gone to Pleasant Grove. "I've been a little busy here." Running my father's kingdom. Trying to keep everything in line, even in a system threatening to pull me apart.

"Right." Luna's shoulders sagged. "Until me."

Did she think she was a distraction? That for one minute, I'd ever regretted walking into that bar and finding *my* witch sitting there, waiting for me? Fates. That was a mistake I needed to remedy immediately.

"Yes," I agreed. "Until you." My hands itched to reach out, to touch her, but I kept them where they were. "But don't for one second think that I regret meeting you, Luna. Even if I had to do it all over again, exactly the same… I would."

"Oh." Turning in the water, her hands grasped the side of the pool as she turned to face me. Her green eyes held my gaze as I focused all my energy on her.

"You're not a distraction," I promised. *You're my salvation.*

Luna bit her lip. "Okay." She looked flustered, and I was trying to ignore how much I wanted to bring her lips to mine. To wring those sounds for her that had my cock stiffening in my pants. Fuck, losing myself in her body was like nothing else. And knowing her body lay a few feet from mine, completely naked and *wet…* I stifled a groan.

"Zain?" Her soft voice drew me out of my thoughts. I needed to control myself around her, which was even more apparent now. "There's something I've been wondering about." She gave me a puzzled look. "How do you… did you speak into my mind earlier?"

She still had no idea.

"It's just something I can do. As a demon."

"So *all* demons can mind-speak?"

I frowned. "Not exactly." But explaining it, explaining *why* I could share thoughts with her… that would require another conversation she wasn't ready for. Not yet.

Not until I made sure she loved me.

Her head was still resting on the edge of the pool, looking up at me with such devotion on her face that I almost broke down right then and there and told her.

"Come on," I said, extending my hand out to her. "There are some people I want you to meet."

Luna raised an eyebrow, slipping her hand into mine. "Other demons?"

A chuckle slipped from my lips. "They're all friendly, I promise." Or as friendly as they could be as warriors, spies, and trained assassins.

"O-okay."

I let the grin escape my lips. "I guess we better let you get dressed first, huh?"

"Oh." She looked down at her body. At that smooth skin. Fuck, she deserved better than me. Then some horny demon who just wanted to claim her. "Right."

"I'll be just outside," I said, standing up to my full height.

While I would have loved to join her in the baths—now wasn't the time. We'd have opportunities in the future to explore each other's bodies more.

At least, I hoped.

First, I needed to assure myself that she'd be safe here.

THIRTEEN
LUNA

We came to a stop in front of Zain's study.

It's going to be alright. I looked over at him, his lips not moving. That the sound hadn't come from his mouth. Somehow, I needed to get used to him speaking into my mind.

We'd moved through the hallways at a brisk pace, Zain clearly on a mission. He'd shown it all to me before, but all the walls of the palace looked the same, and I was relieved when I recognized the door.

How does this work? I asked, directing the thought towards him.

He cocked a head towards me. *What do you mean?*

Can you read my mind? Hear all my thoughts?

No. Only the ones you wish to share.

I raised an eyebrow. *And you can do this with everyone?*

No.

I honestly didn't know what to expect. He'd told me there were people he wanted me to meet, and so far, the only other demon I'd met—besides Kairos—had been Novalie. The rest of the palace had seemed empty earlier.

Were these his friends? Did he *have* any friends? He'd given me major loner vibes from the first time we'd met in the bar, and I wondered now how much of what he'd told me had been real, or what was embellished.

He wasn't a human. Who knew where the deception and lies ended? I needed to keep my guard up. Protect my heart. Otherwise, what would happen when my world came crashing down around me?

Zain turned to face me, his brows furrowing as a worried expression spread over his face. "If this is too much, just tell me, okay?"

"Why would it be too much?" My lips curled down as I tugged on the end of my cashmere sweater. I'd opted for comfort for this meeting, already feeling out of sorts. It was so soft, the fabric luxurious against my skin.

His eyebrow raised, and a little zap of lightning ran through his irises. *That was new.* Like he was reminding me of who he was. Where I was.

"They're your friends, right?" I asked, wrapping my hand around the doorknob.

Letting myself into the room, the large space and dark wood captivated my attention, Zain's heat warming my back as he stepped in close to me.

"I don't have friends," Zain murmured into my ear.

Right. I did my best not to roll my eyes because suddenly—all of their gazes were focused on *me*.

"These are my advisors," he said, waving his hand at the four demons standing around the large, empty table. Two females stood with two blond males—twins, I assumed, from their identical builds. Even their brown horns that resembled a goat's matched, protruding from their messy mops of golden hair. The only difference between the two was a scar that ran across one of their faces. I noticed that Kairos—the demon from earlier—wasn't here, though given how he'd interrupted before, I assumed they were close.

"So we finally meet your witch," one of the two females—with dark hair secured in a long braid and matching horns that curved from her forehead—said, a look of amusement on her face. Two wings rested on her back, like a bat.

"Took him long enough," the other said, blinking at me with snakelike eyes. She was gorgeous, and I knew I was staring, but I couldn't bring myself to look away. Her hair was green, chopped to a bob at her shoulders, and her skin was almost… scaled?

What fantasy novel did I hit my head and wake up in the middle of? I was too busy taking them in that I barely paid attention to what they said because this couldn't be real.

They were demons, and yet, they were so… *other*. There was an ethereal quality to them I'd never seen before. So completely different from the pair of demons that had been outside the coffee shop earlier today.

How had it been only hours since that? It already felt like I'd left Pleasant Grove days ago.

"This is Luna," Zain's deep voice said, causing a shiver to run down my spine. His hands rested on my shoulders, and a surety flowed through my body. Somehow, this was where I needed to be, and it was like my body—no, my *soul*—recognized that.

"Um. Hi," I said, offering a small wave to the group.

"It's nice to meet you, Luna." One of the two identical men spoke—the one without the facial scar—as he bowed slightly at the waist.

"This is Talon and Thorn. My guards. They'll be your guards now as well."

Guards? My nose scrunched up. "I thought we said—"

"I promised you I'd keep you safe, did I not?" He said the words low against my ear so the others couldn't hear, and, well… I couldn't argue with that.

That was the entire reason I was here.

"I'm Talon," the one *with* the facial scar said, a grin spreading over his face. They both had honey blonde hair, only a few shades deeper than my own, with silver eyes. "I'm the older one."

Thorn rolled his eyes. "Which you never let me forget."

"And I'm Asura," said the green-haired beauty as she shoved in front of them, peering at me with those slitted eyes. "Ignore those two. I normally do."

The twins both gave a huff, though there was no malice in the tone. They'd clearly all known each other for a long time. It made my heart ache for my sister, even though I'd only seen her yesterday. I hadn't gotten to say goodbye.

Zain kept me held tight against him.

"Come on, Z. You know we won't bite. Let us get a good look at our future queen, will you?" The dark-haired girl propped her hip against the table, her wings fanning out behind her like she was stretching her muscles.

Queen? My eyes widened.

"This is Lilith," Zain said, a little grunt escaping his lips as he disconnected himself from me, pressing his lips to my forehead before moving to his desk.

"Your wings are—" I blinked, standing in front of her. Gods, they looked completely different from Zain's but no less amazing.

"Beautiful, I know." She batted her eyelashes.

"Do you... I mean… can you fly?"

Lilith laughed, the sound erupting through the room. "I can, and I do. Often."

Careful, Moonbeam, Zain thought into my mind. *You're going to make me jealous.*

Right. He had wings, too. I wondered what that was like. My cheeks heated once again, but I couldn't help my childlike wonder at how they differed from humans and us witches.

They all shared a look, and then Asura spoke. "How much do you know about demons?"

I shook my head, my eyes connecting with Zain. "Not that much, I'm afraid."

Lilith frowned. "Zain, did you not tell her?"

"I didn't exactly have a chance." He rubbed the space between his eyebrows. "Someone sent blood demons to the human realm."

Talon's face sharped. "And we're only just now finding out about this?" He muttered something unintelligible under his breath.

"Kairos knows." Zain gave an exasperated sigh. "And anyway, we're *here*, aren't we?"

"It won't happen again, my lady," Thorn promised. "You'll be safe here."

"You don't…" I started, feeling my face warm. "You don't have to call me that. Luna is fine." I fiddled with the ends of my hair.

Lilith crossed her arms over her chest, a concerned expression painting her face. "What happened?"

"Mother of…" Zain cursed. "I don't know. *Someone* obviously found out about my unsanctioned visits. They must have sent them to figure out what I was doing."

"What were they, exactly?" I asked, my voice faint. "They mentioned my scent, right?"

More specifically, they mentioned that Zain's scent was all over me. He'd mentioned it before. It was a thought that still made me feel a little warm and tingly, even though it should have been the opposite.

"They're trackers. Once they lock onto a scent, they won't stop until they find their prey." Talon pinned Zain with a stare. "All the more reason you should have told us about them immediately. Especially if they found—"

Zain cut him off with a wave of his hand. "I took care of it. They've been disposed of." A scowl formed, and suddenly, I barely recognized him. I could see the moment his mask slid into place. Was this who he was here?

I needed that reminder of who he really was. Because despite how much my heart wanted him to be, he wasn't the human I'd been falling for. As much as I wanted to go back to those nights in my apartment, sharing my bed in the wonderful bubble we'd made for ourselves… It was all a lie. None of it was real.

Neither was this.

"What's stopping it from happening again?" Asura asked. "If someone in the palace leaked your location…"

"You are." Zain's gaze was petrifying. "And if one hair on her head is harmed…" The room grew colder and darker, and it felt like the gold of his eyes sparked like actual lightning. He shook his head, redirecting his stare. "Lilith. Evaluate all the staff of the palace. Find out who knew about my trips and if they had any cause to leak them."

She nodded. "Of course. I won't let you down."

"Talon. Thorn. One of you will remain with Luna at all times. She's free to explore anywhere in the palace as she wishes but remain vigilant by her side."

It felt a *little* like overreacting, but if it gave Zain the peace of mind to sleep at night, I supposed I couldn't protest.

"And what would you have me do?" Asura asked, running a hand through her cropped bob.

He looked away. "Keep doing what you're doing." A nod.

His fingers drummed over the desk. Like he was still silently plotting, deliberating, and making his next move.

"Zain." My voice was quiet. His eyes connected with mine, and all the malice melted away in them like he softened just for me.

"The rest of you are dismissed," he said, waving a hand. "We need a moment."

"We do?" I asked as the rest filtered out, giving me small smiles and welcoming me.

But it was hard to focus on anything other than Zain's serious face as he talked about demons tracking me. What did they want from *me?*

"Luna?"

"Yes?" I looked up, finding him staring directly at me.

"Come here, Moonbeam."

I swallowed, not sure why I felt apprehension in my gut. It wasn't like I feared him, but it felt like the entire foundation of my life had crumbled in only a day. Anyone would feel overwhelmed by that, right?

Moving my feet, I came to stand by his side, and he moved me between his legs, letting me sit on the edge of his desk.

"Are you okay?"

A lump caught in my throat. "I think so. I just…" My teeth worried at my bottom lip. "Yesterday, I didn't even know that demons were real. I thought this was just a *fling*. You and I were, well… It doesn't matter now. And now I'm here, and…" I let out a deep breath. "How much more do I need to expect?"

"Well… there's one more thing, I'm afraid," he said, before his fingers brushed over my jaw, keeping my gaze focused on him as he stared up at me. "We have company."

"Company? But we just got here. It's only been a few hours since…" I trailed off, since I'd left my life behind. My home. My sister. "Who even *knows* I'm here?"

"Who else?" He chuckled. "Seems like my brother has decided to drop in for a little visit."

"Your brother? Damien is here?" A nod. If he was here, that meant… "With my sister?"

"Yes." Zain's lips curled up in a wicked grin, and then he winced. "Though I don't think they're thrilled with me."

I frowned. "Why? And how do they even know I'm here?"

He smoothed his thumb over my forehead, brushing back a loose strand of hair. "I know I have a lot to explain to you later, if you'll let me. But for now… I just need you to stand by my side. Can you do that?"

"Of course. But, Zain… I *need* to know. To understand. You can't keep me in the dark." I couldn't live in a world of secrets and lies. Not when it felt like I didn't even know him anymore.

"I won't, Luna." His promise was the only thing I had—the only thing to cling to in this strange world.

I just had to hope he was telling the truth.

* * *

Zain left me in my room before disappearing again; with just the snap of his fingers, he could go anywhere he wanted. I really needed him to teach me how to do that.

I was trying to ignore the pull in my heart, the knowledge that Willow was *here*. Because above all else, my sister had come for me. Even if I'd seen her just yesterday, it felt like a week had elapsed in the last six hours.

Wandering through my new closet, I brushed my fingers over the fabrics—gowns of all different shades hung side by side on one wall. I hadn't even trifled through the drawers yet, but I was definitely in love with this closet. Maybe I'd never wanted for anything as a kid, but I'd never had anything like this, either.

A dusty blue one was covered in silver stars, and I touched the tulle softly before moving on. Goddess, they were beautiful. Had all of this been bought for *me?*

Novalie popped her head in. "My lady."

"Oh." I startled—too lost in my current quest to expect her arrival. "Sorry. I didn't expect…" My eyes locked on the white shimmering gown in her hands. "What's that?"

It looked like it had been embroidered with little moons, and my heart stuttered a bit in my chest.

"The Prince wanted you to wear it. He picked it out, especially for you."

"He did?" I blushed, thinking about him handpicking my gown for the evening. Instead of feeling possessive or controlling, it felt… sweet. I pushed that thought aside, not knowing to what extent I could trust him—or my own feelings. I didn't know the limits of Zain's magic. What if he was influencing my emotions, *making* me feel like this?

The demon girl nodded. "Everything in here was chosen for you."

"But—how? It's only been a few hours since I even…" I trailed off.

"We've been waiting for you a long time, Luna." Her eyes widened like she'd said too much. "We should get you dressed," she insisted, appraising my current sweater and leggings attire. "There isn't much time before his highness will be back."

Novalie produced a robe, watching as I stripped out of the soft knit sweater, letting it and my leggings fall to the ground before I slipped into the silky black material.

"Right." I let her guide me out of the closet and into the chair in front of the vanity. Watching as she fretted around my room, I couldn't hold in my questions. I was curious about Zain's friends—about her. How he had so many people who seemed so loyal to him. "How long have you worked here, Novalie?"

"My whole life," she responded as she undid my hair from the messy bun, bringing the locks down around my shoulders as she combed through it. "I was raised to serve the royal family." She must have seen the horror in my eyes because she reassured me. "It is no burden, believe me. Zain and Damien are kind despite their upbringing. All the staff here are treated well."

"Their upbringing?" I swallowed, my throat feeling unnaturally dry.

She just shook her head. "I shouldn't have said anything. It's their story to tell."

I sighed, shaking my head.

"I've been meaning to ask since it arrived in that… cage. What sort of creature did you bring with you?" Novalie asked, one eyebrow raising as she watched Selene bathe herself through the mirror.

"My… cat?" I asked, surprise filtering through my tone. "Do you not have cats here?" Zain had reacted strangely to her as well.

She blinked as if processing the word. "Not like that one. What is its purpose?"

"Selene's my familiar. Though she doesn't have a specific purpose. I mean, she can understand my emotions, and I hers. We have a deep bond. But she's also my companion. She doesn't *do* anything." My cat meowed as if in objection, then curled back up in a ball, keeping one eye open and directed at us.

Novalie brushed her fingers through my hair. "Some demons can also shift forms. So to answer your earlier question—yes, there are cats in this world, but they are *more*. Pets are a luxury that most demons could never afford." I thought that sounded a little sad.

"And there are a lot of these…. shifter demons?" I asked instead, curious to know more.

She just nodded, beginning to style my hair. "Our princes, for example, were both born from different mothers. Damien is descended from a shifter queen to the east, and she was a cat shifter."

"And… so is he," I surmised.

Another nod. I guessed it finally made sense why my first meeting with Damien had occurred when he was just a cute, snuggly black cat.

Suddenly, I wanted to know the full story. How my sister had picked *him*. If she'd known he was a demon all along.

Maybe I'd been able to sense there was something more there, something between them, but my powers weren't perfect. This was one of those instances where I'd wished I could have used my sight more, but being taught to suppress those abilities my whole life made them harder to tap into.

"And Zain?" I asked, slightly absentmindedly. Thinking about those beautiful feathered wings that he had let free in front of me. "What abilities did he inherit?"

The golden eyes.

How long had those haunted me?

"I better let him tell you."

"Oh." I tried to hide my disappointment at not learning more about the man I was going to marry soon.

But I desperately wanted to know more about him. Ever since I'd met him in the bar, I'd had the oddest sensation that I *knew* him somehow. Like my soul called to his.

I tried to think back on what Willow had asked me before ghoul's night at the bar.

"Luna, I… Do you believe in fate? In destiny?"

I'd just blinked, staring up from my mixer. "Where is this coming from?"

Willow shook her head. "No reason. Just…" She let out a deep sigh, looking as if she was trying to find the right words.

So, I offered my own instead. "I believe the Goddess gives us the paths we can follow, but the rest is up to us." It was what our parents had always taught us to believe. But even more than that, with my own abilities—I knew that the future could always change. What I saw wouldn't always come to pass.

Willow turned to face me fully. "But like…twin flames, kindred spirits, soul mates. That stuff. Do you believe there's someone out there who you're fated to be with? To fall in love with?"

I tilted my head, wondering if her new companion was the reason for all her questions. If she wanted to know… "You've always told me not to look into your future. That you didn't want to know. But now…" I raised an eyebrow.

"No!" Willow exclaimed a little too quickly as if she knew what I was implying. "I still don't want to know." She spoke the next words so softly I hardly heard her over the noise of the frosting in the mixer. "I was just wondering."

Setting the bowl on the counter between the two of us, I leveled a stare at her. "Willow, what are you really asking me?"

"When Mom met Dad, she knew, right? Do you think that's possible?"

I thought it over for only a moment before I nodded my head, thinking of what our parents had told us growing up. Sometimes I missed them so much. How much they loved us—and each other. It was hard not having them with us anymore. "I think anything's possible, Willow." Letting my magic take over, I moved the spoon in the frosting bowl as if to make my next point. "Especially in a world where magic exists."

Had she known? The moment she'd met Damien? That he was her…

I couldn't even think it. Because I wouldn't dare utter those words. To begin to imagine them as the truth.

This wasn't about love or fate. Even if meeting him at the Enchanted Cauldron had felt a lot like the latter. No, it was simply… *Lust*. Infatuation. And even if I still wanted him all the time, I couldn't help but question everything he'd ever told me.

"Luna," Novalie said gently, nudging me from my thoughts. I looked up to catch her eye in the mirror, only to find she'd finished my hair. Dozens of tiny gems were interwoven into it.

"Oh. Sorry. What?" I had the faintest idea she'd been asking me something.

"I just asked if you wanted me to do your makeup."

Giving her a nod, I tilted my chin up and let my eyes flutter shut as she worked. The time for questions was over.

"Done," she murmured a few minutes later, and when I opened my eyes, I took in the transformation.

It was still me, but my face was bright.

Sparkly eyeshadow was spread over my lids, and they were lined in kohl. I looked the same, and yet…. I touched my fingers to my face. Maybe I should have paid closer attention as she'd worked her magic, but I'd been too wrapped up in my own thoughts.

Zain was still on my mind. Watching him move, that lethal beauty, the way he'd protected me—it made desire burn between my legs. Which was definitely *not* how I wanted to be feeling right now when I still had so many questions about him.

"Let's get you changed," Novalie said, offering me a hand up from the little chair.

"Okay," I whispered, feeling like everything was about to change.

We've been waiting for you a long time, Luna. What did that mean?

FOURTEEN
ZAIN

"You look lovely."

Luna stood, facing the mirror, her fingers moving over her cheek as she stared at her reflection.

The dress I'd chosen for her looked stunning as if she were draped in liquid moonlight. It hugged every curve of her body, and with the slit in the skirt running up her leg, it left no inch of her body to the imagination.

"Thank you." Luna looked down at the floor, opening her mouth as if to say something but then closing it.

"I have something for you," I said, reaching into my pants pocket and pulling out a small velvet box. Would she like it? Gods, I hoped so. I'd figured I had more time before this, but I was glad I had it now.

I cleared my throat. "It's not much, but…"

Opening the box, I revealed a moonstone in a silver setting flanked by two diamond-encrusted crescent moons.

Luna's mouth dropped open. "Are you kidding me? It's beautiful."

I brushed a finger over her cheekbone, tucking her hair behind her ear. "You're beautiful," I murmured, unable to hold back my thoughts.

"When did you get this?"

I ignored her question, a smirk playing over my lips. "Why don't you put it on?"

Not waiting for her response, I plucked it out of the box, sliding it onto the ring finger of her left hand. *Perfect fit.*

Of course it was.

"Zain," Luna said, stepping back. She brushed her finger over the ring, looking down at it. "I just need…" She chewed on her lip. "Everything is happening so fast."

"I know." I rested my forehead against hers. If she needed a second, a minute, I'd give it to her.

Picking up her hand, I kissed her knuckles. And then the ring. "Shall we go see your sister?"

I could practically feel her heart beating in her chest. "Yes." A brief nod and the light caught on the stones Novalie had woven into Luna's platinum blonde hair.

Would she forgive me? For forcing her into this, for binding her to me? For deceiving her when all I wanted was her heart?

We came to the antechamber before the throne room, and I glanced over at Luna, her beautiful face full of worry. Looking at the doors at the other end of the small chamber, I took a deep breath.

I've got you, I said into her mind, keeping my voice gentle. *Don't forget that.*

***

Stepping into the throne room, I kept my eyes focused straight ahead—on my chair, for all that my father claimed it was still his—and waited for the show to begin.

I'd felt when my brother opened the portal, and with each step he took, could feel the emotions pouring off of him. Anger, fear, and above all—*worry.* It tasted like something I'd never experienced before, and I couldn't decide if the feeling was altogether unpleasant.

It was a perk of sharing at least one power with my brother—the shadows he commanded also reported to *me.* Our connection to our father, our powers, bound us together. I'd known the moment he opened a portal into this world just like I could use those powers to command him back. It was more of a tug, really.

"Are you sure about this?" Luna asked, as if it was *me* who needed the reassurance and not her. Not the woman who'd uprooted her whole life in agreeing to my request.

I nodded, settling into my throne, doing my best to appear calm and collected. Trying not to think about the concern etched into Luna's face.

For me. Wasn't that the most fucked up part of all of this? I knew she was still thinking about earlier—what I hadn't told her. Fuck, I was an asshole. An asshole who had manipulated the situation so she would come with me.

Damien and the brunette witch from the bar trailed in, their hands intertwined. I quickly surveyed their odd outfits, doing my best not to raise an eyebrow at the frilly shirt my brother was wearing or the pointy hat that sat on her head. Then I remembered what day it was.

Halloween. The humans celebrated All Hallow's Eve on this day, remembering the dead and wearing the most ridiculous costumes. I'd never understand it, like most of the things the humans did.

"Ah, Damien. How nice to see you." My eyes glanced at the woman by his side. I'd only seen her in the dark corner of the bar or from afar when I'd been watching Luna work at their bakery. Never up close, in the light. "I see you brought your witch."

He bared his teeth, pushing her behind his body. "Where is she?"

Willow was focused on me, her eyes darting around as she looked for her sister.

"Who?" I cocked my head as if I didn't know the answer.

Go easy on him, Luna pleaded from the shadows. *This isn't* his *fault.*

I growled to myself. It wasn't like I could just say to her *no, but if he'd have just delivered you when I asked…* Because she still didn't know the full truth. That I'd been looking for her when I arrived in Pleasant Grove's dingy bar. That our meeting hadn't been by chance.

I could almost hear her reaction, see the little scowl on her face as she said, I'm not some piece of property he needed to deliver into your lap, Zain. I grinned at the thought.

"My sister," Willow said, narrowing her eyes at me.

Luna had remained tucked into the shadows, waiting for the right moment. We were putting on a show—not just for Damien and Luna's sister, but for my entire court, who would watch our every movement. This was the first in a series of moves I had yet to play.

"Ah." I gave a lazy smile. "She's right here. Come on out, Moonbeam."

I feel like a prized cow trussed up for auction. Her thoughts infiltrated my mind once again, and damn if I didn't enjoy hearing it.

Nonsense. You are stunning.

I'd meant it when I'd said it to her earlier. Walking into her room, I'd almost stumbled, seeing her admiring that beautiful white gown in the mirror. I'd traced my tongue over every inch of that body already, and yet seeing her in this dress made my want for her burn even brighter.

Fuck. Focus, you asshole, I scolded myself. This wasn't the time to be thinking of the things I wanted to do to her.

Luna walked out onto the dais, the white gossamer gown I'd given her somehow making every aspect of her pale skin and hair stand out. But those bright green eyes didn't show one hint of fear.

Willow choked out a sob. "Oh, thank god."

"Go talk to your sister," I whispered into Luna's ear. Her eyes connected with mine for a beat before she practically flew down the stairs, colliding into Willow's arms for a hug.

As if it had been weeks that separated the two instead of less than a day.

I'd never had that relationship with my brother. It had always been tense between the two of us, mostly thanks to our father. He'd been more focused on pitting us against the other than brotherly bonding.

Gritting my teeth at the thought, I turned to him, but he was watching our females as closely as I had been.

"Are you okay?" Willow tightened her arms around her sister, like if she held tight enough, she could pretend this never happened. But it *had*.

And it was my fault. I could have prevented all of it if I'd been honest from the beginning. If I'd just asked her to come with me, instead of manipulating the entire situation.

"Brother." Damien turned to me, face stone cold as he stepped up in front of me. "We had an agreement." Those red eyes practically bore into me, and I wondered how it was I who sat up here, burdened with a power I didn't ask for, while he'd been resorted to… what? *Being my father's attack dog?*

But I had a role to play now. So I rolled my eyes, somehow both annoyed and amused. "We had no such thing."

"I said—"

I shook my head. "Damien. I don't want to fight. I…" Just wanted her.

My eyes slid over to Luna, watching her cheeks light up as she talked quickly with her sister, and I couldn't take my eyes off her. She was captivating. *Enchanting.* There was no other word for it.

"She's her *sister*, Zain." Damien spat the words.

They wounded me, and I let that sliver of remorse show, if only for a moment. "And you're…" I trailed off, looking between Willow and Damien. At the connection between them, and it was clearer than it had ever been what exactly they were to each other. But I wanted him to say the words out loud. Why he hadn't wanted to return, he'd found more than just a human to care for. He'd found…

"Yes. Willow's my mate." He chuckled. "Funny that you sent me to find *your* queen, and it led to me finding my witch as well."

The girls were still speaking in low, hushed voices, and I hoped they were caught up enough in their conversation so as not to overhear ours.

"You're not planning on returning, are you?" I knew the answer before I asked, but I still had to ask. Had to prepare myself for the genuine possibility that this newfound happiness he'd found would keep him even further away from me.

"No." My brother's eyes were filled with longing as he looked at his mate. "I want to stay with her."

"You love her."

Damien nodded. "Yes." I could feel the truth in his words.

"Will you be staying, brother? I'd love to get to know your mate." Not permanently, but at least for tonight. Because Luna might have been putting on a brave face, but I knew how much having her sister here during one of her first nights in this place would put her at ease.

"I don't—" He shook his head, but Willow chose that moment to come back over to us, sliding her arm around my brother's waist. She looked up at him, a silent conversation happening, before looking back over at her sister.

"Let's go home, Luna," Willow said, offering a hand.

But my brave girl shook her head, looking over at me. "I…" she joined me, coming back to my side in front of the throne. Luna let me take her hand in mine, and the rightness spread through me. That warmth I felt from just her touch, soothing.

"I know it's crazy, Wil," Luna told her sister, giving my hand a light squeeze. "But… I feel like I have to do this. To see where it goes." She glanced over at me.

"Are you sure?"

My witch nodded, the action loosening her blonde curls, bringing them down over the delectable white dress. "I want to do this." In that moment, I was so captivated by her bravery. All she needed was a tiara, and she would look like a princess. Soon, she would be my princess, and I'd adorn her with the finest jewels in the realm, have her practically dripping in them. "We made a deal," she finished.

Willow's gasp echoed through the hall.

A demon's deal was not for the faint-hearted. Luna's words to me, once. But what we'd bargained for hadn't been her soul. I just wanted her heart. Not that she knew that.

"We're having a ball tonight," I announced, changing the subject. "You two are welcome to attend if you want to stay. I'll be announcing my betrothal to my *fiancée*."

A bit much, don't you think? She flashed the gemstone that sat on her ring finger.

The giant moonstone that had been mined just for her. The setting that I'd had designed with her in mind. Would she flee if she knew the truth?

Willow's eyes darted to Luna, the look of surprise not abating.

Maybe I should have gotten one bigger.

You're insane, Luna said, her head shaking at me just slightly.

Maybe.

"Well?" I said, sensing that the other couple was having an internal debate of their own.

What were the odds of it, anyway? That the fates would choose two sisters for two brothers. Even ones as wicked as ourselves.

Willow's face smoothed out into a pleasant smile, even as Damien looked over at her in concern. "We'd love to attend your ball, *Prince* Zain."

I could feel my face flattening out into a thin smile. "Brother?"

"Of course. Whatever Willow wants," he promised, his eyes flaring with possession when he looked at her, a smile curving over his canines. "I live to fulfill her every wish."

Whipped already, brother? I smirked.

He just stared back at me as if resisting rolling his eyes.

"We'll see you tonight then," I offered, flicking my eyes over to my bride-to-be. She hadn't let our hands drop, and I found that reassuring.

Willow and Damien left the room, though I saw the concern flash through their faces as they looked at us before finally exiting.

His rooms had been untouched in the months that he'd been away, but I was suddenly glad they were on a completely different floor than ours.

Neither one of us said a word as I teleported us back.

* * *

I should have been getting ready for tonight—for presenting Luna in front of my people for the first time or helping prepare her for what she'd face tonight—but I was doing none of those things. Instead, I stood below the dais as my father sat on the throne—*my* throne.

"You summoned me?" I bared my teeth, a low growl emitting from my throat. "What are you doing here?" I hadn't seen him as much as lift a finger in years. Yet that immense power he wielded kept the rest of us in check.

How did you defeat someone who had an endless pool of strength?

He picked a piece of lint off his jacket like he couldn't be bothered. "What do you mean, son? It's my crown, is it not?"

For now. I gritted my teeth, biting back my retort. *So much good you've been doing, huh?* When I was younger, I would have said it. Would have taken my punishment lying down for speaking against him. But now—I was older. Wiser. At least, I liked to think I was.

Maybe I was still the same boy who would take a beating in order for him to leave my brother alone. It had never been just me I had to worry about.

And now… Luna was here. No matter what, I had to protect her. Especially when she would be my wife soon.

"Of course." I dipped my head in silent acknowledgment. "What do you need, *father?*"

"I heard you're getting married."

"I am." Folding my arms behind my back, I tried to take a stance of casual indifference. Not wanting him to pry further, to even think about touching her.

"Hmm."

"What." My response wasn't a question but a biting retort.

"Do you think they will accept her? A weak, trembling queen?"

Luna was so many things—but she wasn't weak. I'd known that since the first night we spent together, laid out on the grass. She'd survived. Persevered. Sought the life she wanted.

And you took her away from that, I reminded myself. Fates, I didn't deserve her. She deserved better than this. Better than me.

"As opposed to a demon king who hides in his palace, forcing his sons to do his dirty work? To bring down any lords who disobey you while you lead a life of debauchery?" I shook my head. "She will be my queen, father. They will come to know her as I have, and the demons will celebrate our union."

Darkness clouded his eyes, and the room grew colder, shadows rolling over us like a fog. "You think you're safe because the fates foretold you'd marry a powerful witch?" He chuckled, but the sound wasn't light. It was a thinly veiled threat. "Don't forget where you come from, *son.*"

"As if you would let me forget." A lightning bolt struck outside, rattling the glass.

He smirked. "Once again, letting your temper get the best of you. Maybe I should have groomed Damien instead. Though he's gone soft now. Letting that witch drag him all about."

Because he loved Willow. Though that was something my father would never understand—he'd loved no one but himself.

"Leave him be," I said, narrowing my eyes. "Let him have the happiness you've deprived him of for far too long."

He smirked like he knew he'd gotten under my skin.

"I heard blood demons made their way into the human world," he observed.

Testing me. "They were handled."

"Were they now?"

"What's that supposed to mean?" I narrowed my eyes.

He shrugged. "Guess you should go run along now and figure it out."

I turned, taking the dismissal instead of snipping back.

"And Zain?" My father's face formed into a smug grin as I looked backward at him. "Good luck with the *girl*."

A low snarl left my lips, and I left without another word. I'd let him have the last laugh for now.

Threats or not, I needed to get back to Luna.

Before I presented her to this kingdom as my future wife.

FIFTEEN

LUNA

How did he have time to do all of this?

He'd left me for an *hour*, if that, before teleporting us to the demon realm. There was no way he'd been able to get me a ring, right?

Except… it glinted in the light, and I couldn't help but admire it. I'd never seen such a beautiful ring. Truly, that was an understatement. It was gorgeous, yet it also felt like *me*. A giant, flashy diamond wouldn't have been my taste, but this *was*.

Honestly, it was too much. I needed to pull back, needed to not let myself get swept up by this man. Not again. I'd given him my body before, and I needed to be careful or I would do it again.

Even if he was charming and seemed to know exactly what to say to make me melt.

It's my first time showing you off to my people. His eyes flared with a predatory, possessive gleam. *I want them to know that you're mine.*

It was hard to argue with much when he said that.

Still, standing at the top of the grand, sweeping staircase in a dress that looked like literal starlight was almost surreal. It looked like hundreds of tiny stars had been interwoven together, sparkling every time it caught the light.

And then there was the tiara of crystals sitting on my head. A reminder of the vow I would take soon. Becoming Zain's *wife*.

The ballroom practically came to a standstill as we came to the top of the stairs, our hands interlaced together. Zain's face was focused, his jaw freshly shaven, which somehow made him appear younger. I couldn't decide which I liked better.

He looked over at me, and the serious expression on his face faded, warming as he gave me a once over.

Ready? He thought into my mind.

If I say no, can I go back to hiding in my closet?

He laughed, and the sound filled my chest. *Unfortunately, I think we're stuck.* I grumbled, and he kissed my hand. *I'll be right by your side.*

"Now presenting, the Crown Prince and his fiancée, our Princess-to-be. Prince Zain and Lady Luna!" The room erupted into cheers as the demon finished his proclamation, stepping back into the shadows.

Princess of the Demons. Goddess. Had the fates really predicted this? Maybe they were wrong. Or maybe Zain was. Because how could I possibly be the one they'd imagined being their queen?

I was *just* Luna—just me.

Zain squeezed my hand as he guided me down the stairs, and I was careful not to step on my dress. My new wardrobe also included dozens of heels, and though I'd never felt clumsy before, I was terrified about tripping in front of everyone.

It was like being under a giant microscope as we headed towards the front of the ballroom with everyone watching us.

I eyed the golden crown sitting on Zain's head. His tux was black, adorned in golden accents that brought out his eyes, and I kind of liked that we were each other's mirrors.

His black and gold to my white and silver.

His darkness to my light.

We reached the dais, Zain stepping up the steps first and then offering me a hand. My breath caught in my throat. Earlier today, only one throne had graced the throne room.

Tonight, two sat side by side.

His—and mine. Neither was taller than the other, just a matching set. My heart fluttered in my chest.

It was like he was claiming me as his equal.

And I didn't know what to do with that.

* * *

We danced for what felt like hours till my feet felt pinched in the brand-new pair of heels, and I begged for a moment of respite to sit down. He agreed, leaving me on my throne as he grumpily went to mingle with some of the demon lords—which was perfectly fine with me.

If I was introduced to one more person tonight, I thought my brain might explode.

I glimpsed Willow and Damien in the corner, both sipping on what Zain had informed me was demon wine. It was a gold, sparkly substance, though I'd only had a few sips of my own before I'd been swept off to dance with Zain.

Luckily, it had been easy for me to fall into step with him, to let him guide my body even through the complicated waltz. Somehow, it was like I always knew where he was going to go, how he was going to move.

Because despite everything, I still trusted him.

Zain's companions surrounded me the moment I was left alone, and even though I'd just met them earlier today, I could see the easy playfulness between them. How easily they all teased each other.

"So, how long have you all known each other?" I asked. Perhaps getting to know them would give me a deeper insight into Zain's life. The parts he hadn't told me about.

"A *long* time," Asura commented, taking a drink of her sparkly beverage. "For each one of us, Zain changed our lives when he took us under his wing. If not for him, I'd probably still be living in the slums somewhere." She'd changed into a form-fitting, one-shoulder dress, not bothering to hide the scales on her arms or the markings on her face.

"The slums?" A sickening feeling formed in my stomach. "The demon realm has a place like that?" Looking around this room, all the wealth and power displayed, I couldn't imagine anyone living in poverty here.

She sighed. "Unfortunately. But in rescuing us—"

Lilith draped an arm over her friend, her strapless crimson dress showing off her cleavage. "You're making him sound *soft*, Asa. He had his reasons for bringing us in under his wing." She winked, flaring out her left wing with the same movement.

Asura shrugged off Lilith's arm, giving her a small glare, before turning back to me.

Thorn snorted. "It's not like you can blame him. He's the product of his own upbringing." His blonde locks were styled now, brushed back with what I assumed was gel, which made the horns on his forehead even more prominent. Without the facial scar, I probably wouldn't have been able to tell the two apart.

"What was he was like growing up?" I frowned, looking down at my hands, the glass I'd hardly touched since it was given to me. "Zain hasn't told me very much about his childhood."

Talon nodded his head. "Kairos was there for most of it. He's the closest in age to Zain, though you'd never guess it. He doesn't like to talk about what it was like, though. Losing his mother. Enduring his father's punishments."

"It was *that* bad?" I whispered the words. Somehow, I knew they wouldn't be answered.

I looked over at Zain, who had once again settled into his crown prince persona. With all that swagger and self-confidence, he practically oozed power.

Was any of it real? Or was it that the person he was with me, soft and caring, was the fake? Maybe it wasn't either of those things. Maybe, just like me, he'd built up walls around himself to protect himself.

Lilith's hand rested on my knee. I blinked, securing my mental barriers. "Luna?"

"Hmm?"

"Teach him it's okay to love, will you? He needs that. More than anything else."

My palms were sweaty. "I don't…" I shook my head. "It's not like that between us." I tried to swallow the lump in my throat, but my mouth was bone dry. I took a chug of my wine, ignoring the way my head spun a little after.

"I told you," Asura said, her shoulders drooping slightly. "He didn't listen to us."

"I know," Lilith said with a sigh.

Something Zain had said earlier came to mind, even as the two seemed to share a conversation all of their own. "Can you all talk to each other?" I asked, looking between the group. "You know, mind-to-mind."

Thorn gave me a confused look. "No. That's reserved for—" The girls cut him off with a glare, but I was just confused.

More than anything, I needed a break—some air.

"I need a moment," I mumbled, standing up and gathering up my skirts so I didn't trip on the shiny fabric. They let me go, though I figured that none of them would be too far behind, monitoring me anywhere I went in this place. Sure, I wasn't a prisoner, but I wasn't exactly *free*, either.

"Luna!" I turned, finding Willow waving at me, her face bright.

I breathed a sigh of relief, practically walking into her arms and letting my sister wrap her arms around me, hugging me tight for the second time this evening.

My heart felt fuller just knowing my big sister was *here*. I loved her more than anything, and there was a part of me that wanted to go home. To take the easy way out, to go back to my life. But I meant what I said to her, too. I felt like I had to do this. To see where it went between us. Even if it was crazy.

Going back to my old life no longer even felt like an option. We'd have to talk about what would happen with the bakery before she left. It had never been her dream, after all—it was always mine. And while

I'd always loved the happiness it had brought me, it was time for a new dream. Was there a chance that I could have it with Zain?

"Wow. This is beautiful." Willow looked appraisingly at my gown.

"Thank you." Looking down, I messed with the skirts. Unlike the dress from earlier, it didn't have a slit in the leg—but it dipped massively low beneath my breasts and down my back. Suddenly, I felt like I didn't know what to say to her. "Did… Damien give you yours?"

Willow nodded. Her silky gown was a midnight blue that blended into dark purple, adorned with hundreds of tiny diamonds, which looked like a blanket of stars set against the night sky. Even more gems detailed the sweetheart neckline.

Her gaze was distant before she murmured out a, "Can we talk?" She gestured to the outside balcony with a tilt of her head, her hand occupied with a glass of wine.

I agreed.

The cool air against my skin was welcomed, and it felt like I took a full breath for the first time all night. The balcony gave a full view of the area surrounding the palace, lights from the nearby city dotting the skyline and the palace gardens spread out below us.

Out here, it felt like I could really see the place for the first time. The night was a deep red hue, a whole distinct set of constellations woven into the sea of stars.

I rested my back against the railing, watching Willow as she propped her arms against it, looking out. "This place is… Wow. Definitely not in Pleasant Grove anymore."

"Mhm," I agreed. Earlier, I'd had the same thought. And that was before I'd realized the sun was definitely a ruby hue, and whatever trick of the light made my bedroom so *bright* must have been magic.

My thoughts drifted. Hopefully no one would sneak into my room and leave the door open. Selene was always trying to escape outside, and who knew what would happen if she got loose here? It wasn't like she knew how to get home in this place. If something happened to her...

"Luna." My sister's voice was stern. "Talk to me."

I turned, looking into her eyes—bright green, the color we shared—before emitting a deep sigh. "I *am*, aren't I?" What else would we be doing out here?

Willow crossed her arms over her chest. "You were right."

As the little sister, I especially liked to hear that—because it felt like I was always losing the arguments on account of being *younger*, but I didn't feel like gloating right now.

"About what?" I quirked an eyebrow. It did also help when I knew what, exactly, she was referring to.

"Damien. Telling him how I felt."

Oh. Well, that wasn't what I'd expected. "And you told him you love him?"

"Er... Well... *No.*" Her cheeks were pink. "I only realized that *today.*"

"*Willow.*" I gave her a dramatic sigh.

"Hey. Don't sister me while I'm sister-ing *you.*" Willow tried to look stern, though the effect didn't quite work—given she was incapable of looking mean. She was one of the nicest people I'd ever met, sister or not. She nudged me with her hip. "Are you sure this is what you want?"

"So, you get to fall in love with a demon and be with him, but I can't?" I didn't mean for the words to slip through my lips or to snap at her, but I had.

"Do you?" She asked, voice soft. "Love him?"

I shook my head. "No." Though I wished the answer was yes, it wasn't. "But…" My eyes were watery, and I blinked, trying to clear them. The rush of emotion running through me was so strong that I wondered if Zain could feel it through whatever mental bond we shared. "I can't explain it, Wil. But when I saw him, my heart knew."

"Knew…?"

"That he was mine. That I was his." I indicated around us with my hands. "Maybe I'm supposed to be *here*, you know?" It was the first time I'd dared to admit the words out loud. That I felt that way, but something in him called to me, and I couldn't deny it. Not to her, and not to myself. Not when his ring sat on my finger and a crown on my head.

"But… Your bakery. Our lives. You're leaving everything behind."

I fidgeted with the ring that sat on my finger. I still couldn't believe it when Zain had given it to me, and I wasn't used to it yet.

"Lately, I've been thinking, well… I don't know how to describe it. Like I was missing something. And when he asked me to come with him, I didn't even have to stop to think about it. I just… said yes." Sure, there was more to the story than that, but I left out the demon attack. It seemed like more than enough information for one day.

"But he's a stranger. You don't even *know* him."

I blinked. "Well… That's not entirely true."

"What?"

Grimacing, I continued, knowing this wouldn't sound great—since this was the part that I had kept from her. "We'd met before. At the bar. And a few other times."

I didn't mention that we'd already slept together to her. That seemed like information I didn't need to share with my older sister.

"You didn't think to tell me you *met someone?*" She dropped her voice, though I could still hear the hurt echoing through it. It made my heart ache. "I'm your sister, Luna."

Biting my lip, I looked away. "I know. But you were all wrapped up in Damien, and I didn't want to pop your bubble. Plus, it's not like you were one hundred percent truthful with me, either."

"Right. Well, *maybe* I should have told you about his, er… *demon-ness*. In my defense, I thought I was doing the right thing. Keeping him safe."

"I don't think he needs you for that." The laugh spilled from my lips before I could help it, before I reminded myself of the severity of the situation, and my voice lost any hint of humor. But how could she have known about Zain? That we'd end up meeting?

"A witch cursed him," Willow offered. "That's the spell I did. Reversing it." It made sense. The spell she'd performed on the full moon, how she'd skirted around sharing what she was doing with me. Why she hadn't asked for help—from me or the coven. Even if it still stung.

"I didn't realize who he was to me. Not until later. But I think part of me knew I needed to help him. Maybe it was the same part of me that picked him out at that shelter." Willow blushed. "And I guess it was right. He's my…" Her fingers brushed over two little puncture marks on her neck. "My soulmate."

"It doesn't have to make sense to feel right," I said—because I knew that, understood that feeling more than I could put into words. "I thought I would hate it here," I admitted, giving my truth. "This place. I thought it would be *Hell*. But it's not. People are free to be whoever they are here. Monster and demon alike. It's nothing like Pleasant Grove."

I'd been here less than a day, and I already could feel that. Novalie had shown me that, too. She might have been a maid—a servant, not a slave—but I could sense she was speaking the truth when she'd told me she was treated well. How much she *liked* working here.

And this ball—these demons—none of them were like the ones who had attacked me earlier.

"No, it isn't," my sister murmured. She looked up at the sky—the crescent moon high in the sky, the red endless space freckled with stars. It wasn't our sky, but I found it calming.

Picking up her hand, I squeezed it tightly. "I don't know what will happen, but I can promise you I'm safe here. I'm not here against my will. I chose this... I choose *him*."

"Okay," she whispered, squeezing back. "And if you decide this isn't what you want anymore?"

"Then I'll come back." I didn't foresee that happening, though. Already, I couldn't imagine leaving him.

"Okay," Willow agreed as we dropped hands, still staring out at the palace's surroundings.

My skin prickled with recognition that could only be one thing, and a second later, Zain wrapped his arm around my shoulders.

"There you two are," he said. "We've been looking for you."

Damien stepped to Willow's side, and she relaxed into his touch.

"Hi," Willow murmured before slipping an arm around his middle.

"We were just getting some air," I shared. "It's a little stuffy in there." I tugged at one of the sleeves of my dress.

Zain chuckled. "They're just fascinated by you, my bride. Give it time." He kissed my cheek.

I sighed into his hold. "I know."

He turned his attention to Damien and Willow. "Did you two enjoy the party?"

"Oh, yes," Willow said, eyeing her empty glass of demon wine, her cheeks turning slightly pink. "It's been lovely."

"She smells like you now," my *fiancé* mused to his brother.

Willow's cheeks flamed as Damien nuzzled his nose against her neck. "I had to keep the other demons away from my mate somehow."

Zain looked down at me, humming slightly in response. If he'd expected me to be surprised at Willow and Damien's newfound status, well, he would be wrong about that.

That didn't mean I needed him to do the same to me.

"I can take care of myself," I muttered, rolling my eyes as I stared out at the gardens. Couldn't I? I had this magic in my veins. Once I learned how to use it, I could protect myself.

And go home. If I could protect myself, I wouldn't need to be tied to him, stuck in this world that was so foreign and unlike my own. *Right?*

But why did the thought of leaving feel like splitting my heart in two?

Zain frowned at me, and Damien and Willow seemed to have some sort of mental conversation of their own, punctuated at the end by a verbal "I didn't say that" from my sister.

I raised an eyebrow at her, but she just shook her head—exasperated.

It's been a long night, Zain mused into my head.

I had to agree. *A long day.*

Willow shivered, resting her head against Damien's chest. When she yawned, Damien scooped her up into his arms. "Come on, my mate. Let's get you to bed."

She nodded into his chest, giggling slightly.

"Goodnight, you two," I said, offering my sister a smile.

Willow gave me a little wave. "Night." She looked at Zain. "Don't hurt my baby sister, or I'll tear your heart out." Her eyes turned to Damien and then back to Zain. "Or turn you into a cat. Might be just as effective."

Her demon laughed. "I think you had too much demon wine, baby."

"Uh-uh," Willow argued, her eyes closing even as they walked away.

And then it was just the two of us.

Leaning my forearms against the railing, I looked out once again over the grounds. What would happen if I let my walls down? If, just for a moment, I let my power free.

I'd joked about it with Willow—peering into her future. I could do it for Zain, too. *Our future.* Something more than just the hazy, fuzzy warmth I'd felt. But what if it ended badly?

I willed the thought away. No good would come of knowing. Not yet.

"Do you think you can be happy here?" Zain asked, breaking our comfortable silence.

"I hope so," I murmured, drawing my eyes away from the flickering lights in the distance and back to his golden eyes that were brimming with so much hope.

"Me too," he agreed before offering his hand. "Shall we call it a night, Moonbeam?"

I blushed at the nickname. "Why do you call me that?" I'd been wondering that ever since our first night together.

He frowned, reaching out to tug a lock of my hair. "Your hair reminds me of the moon." Zain twirled it around his finger.

"Oh." That made sense. He'd told me that when we'd laid under the stars. That my hair was like moonlight.

He shook his head, clearly not finished. "Because you're my light in the dark. You shine so bright, Luna. I never thought… No, could have never even imagined you. How you would illuminate my entire world."

I swallowed, not expecting the onslaught of emotions.

Somehow, I suspected I'd be thinking about those words long into the night.

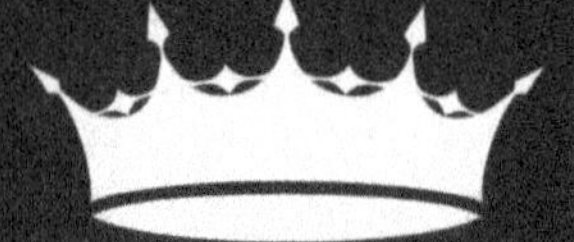

SIXTEEN
ZAIN

It was well into the night when we finally retreated to our rooms, the sounds of the party still audible from the balcony.

How had so much happened in such a short period?

This felt like the longest day of my entire life.

Sinking onto the couch, I closed my eyes, loosening the tie from around my neck and unbuttoning the top few buttons of my shirt.

"Well," I said, heaving a sigh. "That went better than I expected."

Luna turned in a full circle, gaping at me. "*Zain.*"

"Hm?"

Her eyes widened as she took in our surroundings. "These are…"

"My rooms," I confirmed. "There are eyes and ears all over the palace. We can't be too careful." If we were going to talk, I certainly wouldn't do it in the throne room, after all.

I used my head to indicate to the door on the other end of the room. "That one goes through to yours if you're wondering."

"We have… *adjoining* rooms?" She raised an eyebrow, and I nodded.

"It's customary. For royalty." Plus, it had the bonus of keeping her safe. And I wanted her right next to me. "Do you want help taking that dress off?"

"Oh. Right." Luna looked down at her attire as if she'd only just realized she was still in that beautiful gown and crown. "I can get Novalie…"

"Don't bother," I said, standing up and coming to stand in front of her. "I'll do it."

Her breath was shaky when she asked, "Are you sure?"

"Luna," I murmured, my voice low as I pressed a kiss to her jaw. "No matter what's happened today. I'm still me. We're still the same people we were in your town."

"Are we?" Her words were a whisper.

Spinning her around, I slid down the zipper—a helpful invention that we'd stolen from the humans—and let the dress fall down around her hips. She helped me wiggle the rest off, leaving it in a pile on the floor.

A strangled sound came from my throat at the little lace panties she wore.

"It was the first thing I found earlier," she said, pink rising to her cheeks as she wrapped her arms around her body.

"I see," I responded, a strangled sound coming from my throat as I summoned a robe, handing it to her. Part of me wondered why we were bothering to cover up that body I'd spent so many nights exploring. Was she uncomfortable with me now?

"Thank you," she gave a quiet murmur as she turned back to me, messing her hair.

I went to the little beverage cart in my room, pouring myself a few fingers of scotch, throwing the beverage back before pouring another. Returning to my spot on the couch, I ran my tongue over the rim as I watched her.

"I just… wow." Luna laughed, the sound a little nervous as she smoothed her hands over the black silky fabric. It was one of my robes, and the sight of her wearing it did things to me.

Fuck. I needed to be more careful.

Was she as nervous as I felt?

"What?" I rested my arm against the top of the couch.

She just shook her head, pacing back and forth as she removed pins from her hair. "I'm so in over my head here. Because at the ball, I think I just realized what marrying you really means."

I quirked an eyebrow. "Which is?"

"Do you know every little girl's dream is to be a princess? At least, for the humans." She thought about that for a moment. "Maybe it is for the demons, too."

"Oh, yeah?"

She hummed in response. "That's going to be my life. Literally, I'm going to be a *princess*. I should be ecstatic. But I think I'm a little…" Luna sighed, sitting on the couch diagonal to me, depositing her handful of pins on the side table before bringing her knees to her chest. "Overwhelmed. I just never imagined it would be like this."

Her scent hit me as she moved closer, and *fuck*, if it didn't do things to me.

"Like what?" I leaned back, my hand gripping the armrest. Did she know I could see her panties from the way she was sitting in front of me? I quickly re-adjusted myself, hoping she wouldn't notice the bulge in my pants.

She waved wildly around us. "I don't know. *This.*"

Unable to resist the temptation of being closer to her, I slid right next to her on the couch—so close that there wasn't an inch between us.

"Everything's going to be fine," I said to her, placing my hand on her bare thigh.

Though it felt like anything but.

I couldn't ignore the call in my blood that wanted to have her. Claim her. Taste her skin.

I shut my eyes, blocking out the urges. She would let me claim her without even knowing what it would *mean*, how it would tie us together for eternity.

When I opened them, her eyes were full of questions. Shit. I'd run out of time, hadn't I?

Pulling her down into my lap, her legs parted as she rested on one of my thighs.

"Ask me," I finally murmured, brushing a strand of her hair back.

Her voice was a low whisper. "Why am I really here?"

"What do you mean?" I kept my voice steady. "I'm going to keep you safe."

Luna's head shook. "No. The truth, please. I... need it. The night we first met. You were looking for something, weren't you? You said Damien would be upset with you."

Shit. I nodded my head. What the hell had I been thinking, bringing her here? I *hadn't*.

"What were you looking for?"

The truth. I reminded myself. She deserved that much. If she was going to marry me, I should at least tell her this. "You," I admitted.

"Why?"

My thumb brushed over Luna's bare leg, the one that peeked out from the opening in the robe. "I needed you." I rubbed back and forth over the skin, glad that she was at least letting me hold her like this. "No, I *need* you. That fact hasn't changed."

"But… why me?" She sounded surprised. Didn't she know how incredible she was? "Novalie said something earlier. That you'd been waiting for me for a long time, is that… true?"

Longer than you know. I nodded. "Damien was only in the human realm because I'd sent him there. To look for you." Those big green eyes widened. "A powerful witch was foretold to be my queen."

"But I'm not *powerful*," she admitted, her voice low. "Not really. I don't even know how to control my powers. I hid them my whole life." Her hands spread open, little bits of light filtering through her palms. "It's nothing more than a party trick." Her throat bobbed as she paused. "I mean, I still see things—sometimes. Brief flashes of the future. Dreams I can't explain. But mostly…" Luna's shoulders slumped. "When those demons attacked me, I froze. *Froze.* I should have been able to do something. But my legs wouldn't move."

Tracing a finger over her brow, I cradled her face with my free hand. "It's okay," I murmured softly, trying to soothe her.

"It's not." Luna sprung to her feet. She huffed a frustrated sound that seemed to echo through the empty room. "I should be able to take care of myself. I feel like I'm always depending on someone, and I'm so *over* it. First Willow, and now… you." A furrow formed in her brow like a thought had only just occurred to her. "The demons who attacked me," she started, her body trembling slightly. "Did you send them to find me, too? To convince me to come back here with you?"

I raised an eyebrow. "Do you really think I would do that? *Risk* you? After all the trouble I went through to find you?"

"I don't *know!*" She practically shouted the words at me, throwing her arms up. There was fire in her eyes, burning brighter than normal. They were almost white. "That's the problem. Because I thought I knew you, and now what? Everything's changed. And I don't even know who I am anymore." Her arms slid around her middle like she was trying to make herself smaller.

"You're still you," I said, voice soft. "My moonbeam. Nothing has changed. Not really." Luna's eyes connected with mine. Endless emotion swirled in those once again bright green depths. "Does this change anything for you?" I asked because I needed to know. If it made a difference.

"I… Just answer this first. Was any of it real?" Her face sagged, her eyes brimming with unshed tears. "I gave up *everything*. My life. My sister. My home. So I need this to be real." Tears filled her eyes. "Because if this is just a game you're playing…" She shook her head, brushing the wetness away. "Was it real? What we shared at the bar? All those nights at my apartment? Us?"

"Of course it was. All of it," I said, standing at her side and cupping both her cheeks with my hands. "You have to know that. I've always wanted you," I admitted. "Regardless of who you were to me, from the moment I saw you sitting there, all my plans went out the window."

"And now?"

I rested our foreheads together. "I want you still. In any way you'll have me. I want *you,* Luna. Your body, mind, and heart. Just as I always have."

Her eyes fluttered shut, and I watched her pulse beat in her neck.

My teeth ached. Clearing my throat, I forced out the next question. "Do you still want to do this, Luna?"

She blinked. "What do you mean?"

"To marry me. If not, I'll take you back to Pleasant Grove. We can forget any of this ever happened. You can forget about *me.*"

"But then…" Her finger fidgeted with the ring on her finger. She stared off into space for a moment before her gaze connected back with mine. "You promised to keep me safe," Luna said, though it sounded more like a question, so I nodded. Of course I would. I'd sooner die than let her get hurt.

"Yes," she answered finally. "Yes, I'll marry you."

It was a promise, the answer to a question I'd been searching for long before I'd known of her existence. It was one I'd waited a lifetime for, and I'd do my best to earn every single day.

"Thank you," I whispered, brushing my lips over her forehead. "You have no idea."

How much I wanted her. Needed her.

And that I'd never risk her slipping from my grasp—never again.

SEVENTEEN
LUNA

A knock on my door startled me out of the book I'd been reading. Trying not to get my hopes up it was him, and trying not to analyze why that was my first thought, I pulled myself out of the chair by the window. In the days I'd been here, I'd fallen in love with this little corner of my room.

It was still weird to think of it as mine. All of my stuff might have been here, and Selene seemed happy to prance around like she owned the place, but sometimes I felt like a stranger floating through this place. My home was in Pleasant Grove, and I'd left it behind.

For what? *A demon.* Maybe I was crazy. That was probably why Willow had shown up and demanded Zain let me go home. Maybe if I was here against my will, that would be a different story.

"Oh." I cracked the door open to find Lilith and Asura—two of Zain's friends, or advisors, whatever he was calling them—standing there.

"Hi." Lilith beamed at me, her wings folded in behind her. She was gorgeous, with that inky-black hair spilling over her shoulders and lips as red as blood.

Asura gave a brief nod. "Hey."

They both were beautiful—in an otherworldly way—and even though I'd barely spent any time with them, I was pretty sure I could trust them. Or, at the very least, my senses made me feel safe around them.

Whatever the reason, I hadn't expected them here.

"Did you guys need something?"

Asura peeked inside. "We thought you might want to get out of here. Do something fun."

"Fun?" I raised an eyebrow. "Here?"

Lilith crossed her arms over her chest. "What do you think we do all day, exactly?"

"I don't know." I frowned. "Demon general things?"

The two girls looked at each other and laughed. "You're mistaking us for Kairos. Zain gives us much more important work than that."

"Still, I don't want to keep you from your tasks…"

"We want to get to know you. To help you feel more at home here."

I found myself nodding, agreeing to go along with their plans. Mostly because I didn't want to be alone. "Okay. What are you thinking?"

"How's a little afternoon flight sound?"

* * *

"Stay still, my lady," Angelique reminded me for the dozenth time, a pin poking into my skin as if I needed the physical reminder.

"Sorry," I apologized—*again*. But I couldn't stop my mind from wandering even as the dress that I'd be married in quickly took shape on my body.

Somehow, that was my *least* priority. Never mind the fact that our wedding was a little over a week away now. It didn't feel real, so I was still pretending it *wasn't*.

If someone had asked me a month ago if I thought I'd be living in a Demon Palace, in a completely different realm where all the residents were demons—except for me—I would have said they were crazy.

And yet, here I was.

I'd settled into some sort of routine here already, which I hadn't expected. Even if the sun was duller—and redder than the one I was used to, I still rose with it, and without the responsibilities of the bakery, I found myself with a lot of free time.

My days were spent exploring and learning about this place, and my nights staring up at the sky as if I might memorize the new constellations that stared back at me. Like the moon could answer my questions if only I knew the right ones to ask.

The library was quickly becoming my favorite spot in the entire palace as I devoured every book I could get my hands on—the ones I could read, at least. One day, I'd have Zain teach me the demon's script, but at least I'd gained a whole slew of knowledge about demons.

Anything to distract me from the overabundance of free time I had now.

Free time that could have been used for planning my wedding, but Zain assured me he'd take care of all of it. All I had to do was be poked and prodded at by the demon who was creating my gown.

Swishing the fabric of the skirt back and forth—despite the glares I got from Zain's chosen seamstress—I took a moment to admire the look of it.

"You look beautiful," Novalie said, her hand pressed over her heart as she gave me a sympathetic smile. "Every bit a queen."

White lace covered my breasts, and the puffy tulle sleeves on my arms should have been ridiculous, yet I felt… *like a princess*. She was right. My shoulders were bare, and the iridescent white fabric glimmered like the moon.

"He's not going to be able to keep his hands off of you," Angelique agreed, stilling me once again as she continued with her alterations. She had long, reddish hair that was braided down her back and wore a pair of fitted trousers. Not at all what I'd imagined when they'd told me a seamstress was coming to make me a dress.

Looking towards the window, I watched the sun's reddish rays seeping through the glass windowpane as my fingers fiddled with my ring. "Maybe."

Despite his promises that first night—that he wanted *me*, when he'd given me the choice between returning home and being with him… we hadn't shared a bed. I missed waking up wrapped around his body in my apartment, feeling his warmth beside me at night.

If he was giving me space, I didn't want it.

There were so many things I wanted to tell him. For starters, that I'd started having visions again—flashes of what could be. Or maybe it was what had come before. I could never really tell what my premonitions meant.

Last night was *new*. A little girl with pale hair and violet eyes was holding hands with a dark-haired boy who looked around the same age. He had the same golden eyes I'd always seen.

Who was he? Who were *they?*

Those two little ones had taken my hands last night, guiding me towards something I couldn't see.

Some seer I was. I snorted at the thought, blowing a few strands of my light blonde hair off my face.

Even with everything we had shared in Pleasant Grove, the uncomplicated relationship that had developed between us in the safety of my apartment seemed to fade from my grasp. What had changed?

Teach him that it's okay to love, will you? He needs that—more than anything else. Lilith's words echoed through my brain.

But why was he holding back? He'd told me he didn't need me to love him. Assured me he needed me. It had seemed so sincere, so genuine. Maybe something had changed. I didn't know.

"All done," Angelique said, loosening the dress from my body and interrupting my train of thought.

I gave a small smile, trying to brush off my thoughts. "Thank you."

I'd chosen to stay. Knowing everything, knowing that he'd come to Pleasant Grove to find me, that he'd lied and slept with me under false pretenses—I still couldn't bear to part with him.

But I couldn't promise him my heart.

Could I?

* * *

A few hours later, after I'd read another book that I'd smuggled out of the library while curled up on my chaise with Selene, I finally gave up on waiting for him.

I was alone in a place full of strangers—demons that I knew hardly anything about. Zain didn't count since I wasn't sure I could base my thoughts about their species on just one man. Especially one that had had his wicked way with me.

My research had helped, but I wanted more. I needed a *connection.* That was one of my favorite parts about working in the bakery. Seeing the townsfolk every day, watching their faces light up. Part of me wondered if I'd made the wrong decision. Especially now.

If Zain wouldn't come to me, that was okay. I could go to him. We were supposed to be getting married, after all.

Luckily, this past week of exploring had given me plenty of opportunities to learn my way around the palace.

My knuckles rapped on the open door of Zain's study. "Hi," I murmured, leaning my head against the door frame.

He was sitting at his desk, buried under a mountain of papers. "Luna." His eyes softened as he took in my presence.

I gave my ever-present bodyguard—Talon, currently—a nod of dismissal, the door shutting behind me.

"You look beautiful."

"Thank you." It was a practiced effort not to blush at his compliment—because he always readily gave them to me. The blush pink gown was long and silky, and my hair was in a braided crown updo, showing off the plunging back.

I'd discovered rather quickly that most of the outfits in my closet showed off ample amounts of skin, but they were works of art, too. Who was I to turn down such stunning creations? It felt like a shame not to wear them, to let them sit in the closet. So. Here I was. Dressed like the royalty I was about to be in a matter of days.

"You've been busy," I observed, letting my fingers trace over the wooden edge of the desk as I wandered over to him.

He sighed. "I'm sorry. My attentions have been focused elsewhere, and I… just wanted to make sure you had some space to get used to all of this."

"I don't need space," I murmured. "I just need you."

Goddess, I wished I didn't like him this much. That would have made all of this easier.

I'd just missed his presence. I'd come here to tell him exactly that. That I missed his touch. The way it felt with his lips on mine. When we connected, it was like everything melted away, ceasing to exist. I wanted that—*needed* that. The distraction and the reminder. Especially as my world felt like it was falling apart around me.

"Luna," he murmured, his golden eyes filled with regret. "I'm sorry."

"You don't have to apologize for doing your job. I know you have responsibilities. I just thought maybe I could have you at night."

"No. You're right. There's so many things I wanted to show you." He pinched the spot between his brows with his forefinger and thumb, rubbing it slightly. "That's my fault. I wanted to help you acclimate. I did."

"Lilith and Asura have been keeping me company. They make excellent dinner companions, you know." I left out that Lilith had flown me up to the roof of the palace, and they'd pointed out things around the radius. You could see for miles up there. Though the library was still my favorite place.

A laugh. "I do. I've known them for a very long time. Talon and Thorn, too."

I hummed in response. "You know, I had a fitting for my wedding dress today."

His eyes twinkled with amusement. "Oh?"

"Only got stabbed about twenty times, so that's an improvement on last time."

Zain's whole body froze. "You what?"

I placed my hand on his chest. "Relax, handsome. They're just sewing pins." I laughed at his expression. "No one's hurt me. Everyone's been amazing, really." Novalie, his advisors, and even the palace staff had all been trying to make this feel like home for me. "But I still feel so alone."

"Luna…"

Pushing his knees apart so I could slide in between them, I whispered, "I need you. I don't know how to do this. Not without you. I wasn't born into this world. I'm not a regal-born princess. I'm just… me. And I need you to help me through it."

He brushed a thumb over my cheekbone. "I need you, too."

Shutting my eyes, I leaned into his touch. Letting the rightness of the moment flow through my body, steadying me.

"*Fuck*." The word slipped from his tongue, and then he was crowding me in, forcing me up against the wood. "I've missed you." His hand wrapped around my chin, forcing my eyes to meet his. Those golden irises held my full attention, and I couldn't have looked away if I tried.

"Do you think we can get back what we had? In Pleasant Grove?"

"Yes." He leaned in, kissing me softly. "I know we will."

I straddled his lap, already desperate for more.

"Listen, Luna," he murmured, holding onto me. "There's something you should know. Something I've been meaning to tell you. I wasn't trying to avoid you. I just needed to figure out how to say this."

"Okay."

He looked around, wincing. "Maybe… not here."

"Should we go for a walk? I still haven't explored the gardens." Though from above they looked beautiful, I hoped that he'd go with me. A romantic stroll in the gardens sounded like exactly what we needed.

His tongue darted out over his lips, and then he was standing, holding me against him as I wrapped my legs around his waist. "I have a better idea."

"Where are we going?" I murmured, my hands curling into the short hair at the base of his skull.

"My room."

Oh. Heat flooded my system. I liked that. *A lot.*

* * *

Not wasting another moment, Zain transported us back into his bedroom, setting me on my feet. He swallowed roughly as his eyes trailed down my body. Over my hardened nipples, visible through the thin fabric of the dress.

"Luna…" Zain took a few steps past me, moving into the room. "We should talk." He turned to the door, shutting it with magic before imbuing it with some sort of spell. "So we won't be interrupted," he explained. He wrapped a hand around my wrist, spinning me into him. All my bravado faded, and I was left staring into Zain's magnificent eyes.

"I missed you," he repeated, wrapping his other arm around my waist and pulling me in tight before burying his nose in my hair.

Wrapping my arms around him, I inhaled his scent, relaxing into his hold. "I missed you too," I said, the words whispered against his chest. "I thought maybe you'd changed your mind, that you didn't want me."

"Fuck." He practically growled. "No. That's not it at all."

"But you haven't touched me. Not really. Not since…" Since I'd found out who he was. Since he'd brought me here.

I'd been upset, at first, that he'd lied to me, but I was even more upset about the distance between us now. Until earlier, we hadn't had a proper conversation since the night of the ball. Then, I'd been hopeful. Now, I didn't know what I was feeling.

"So, what are you waiting for, Zain?" I whispered the words, a seductive lilt to my voice. My eyes dropped to his lips as I ran my tongue over my bottom lip.

His arms snaked around my back, pulling me in tight against his body. His hard length pressed against my stomach, the way he towered over me reminding me of the stark contrast between our bodies. Gods, he was tall—somehow seeming to appear even bigger now. He was all hard planes and sculpted body—compared to my soft, lithe frame.

Zain's head dipped down, those lips brushing against mine as I stood on my tiptoes to reach him.

I moaned at the press of his erection as he kissed me again, his hand fisting in my hair to tug my mouth up closer to his.

It was exhilarating. It was *everything*. It made me forget everything, just for a moment.

Because I wanted him. Wanted him to let loose, to take me *hard*, to give me everything I needed.

"Luna…" He warned. "Are you sure?"

"Yes." I pressed a kiss to his neck. "I don't want to think. Not anymore." I tilted my head up, rising on my tiptoes to lessen the distance between us. "I just want you."

Another groan slipped from his lips, and he hoisted me up to his waist, my gown pooling around my hips. I kissed his neck, sucking his pulse point into my mouth as he carried me towards his bed.

Dropping me unceremoniously on the black silk sheets, he whipped the thin pink gown off my body, my peaked nipples coming into full view.

"Fuck," he groaned, his eyes taking the time to fully pursue my body, all sprawled out on his black silky sheets. "No panties?"

I shook my head. The fabric was too thin, and I'd just gone without. "Zain," I begged, rubbing my legs together. "I need you."

"Shhh, baby," he said, pulling my thighs apart. "It's been too long since I've had you on my tongue."

I whimpered as he parted me, those long fingers gripping my inner thighs tight enough that I hoped he'd leave marks.

And then he pulled my hips to the edge of the bed, kneeling in front of me so his face was level with my entrance. I grasped at the sheets as he ran his tongue up my slit, a low moan slipping from my lips.

Wicked fingers. Wicked tongue. He was *wicked*, and I *liked* it. Loved it, even.

"Don't stop," I pleaded as he thrust his tongue inside me without preamble, tasting me.

"I've never tasted anything quite like you," he murmured after moving his attention from my entrance to my clit, curling his tongue around the bud. "I think I could spend forever between your thighs."

"Goddess," I cried out as he devoured me like a man starved.

"Yes, you are," he agreed. "Now, let me worship you."

With that, there were no words left. Just him, greedily tonguing my cunt, his finger finding my clit and pressing down hard enough that I almost came just from the pressure.

"Give it to me," he coaxed, moving his thumb in circles as he continued to fuck me with his tongue. "Give me what's mine."

"Zain," I whimpered.

"You can do it, baby. Come for me."

My head rolled back as I let the orgasm explode through me. The world was white. The sheets were still clutched between my fingers, back bowed off the bed as I came down from the high, looking down to see only those golden eyes peering up at me from between my thighs.

Giving me a few more languid licks, he finally stood up, running his tongue over his bottom lip before standing up, the outline of his erection clear through his bottoms.

Zain bent down to kiss me, his hips settling inside my still-parted legs.

"Don't tease me," I begged. "I need you inside me. Please."

In a flash, his pants were gone, his tip pressed against my entrance. Grasping my chin, he rasped out, "Tell me you want this. That you want me."

I nodded, feeling from the undercurrent of emotions that ran through him how important this was to him. And I needed him to know that I meant it. That I wasn't doing this just for him or for any reason other than I wanted it, wanted him.

"I do," I said, holding his golden-eyed stare. "More than anything."

"Thank fuck," he muttered, finally pushing in. The stretch was exquisite, the feeling of him bare inside of me almost bringing me to climax again.

Reaching up, my hands clutched at his shoulders, digging my fingernails into his muscles.

"You feel so good inside of me."

I cried out as he pulled out before burying himself to the hilt.

"Harder," I moaned, my hips moving in tandem with each thrust of his cock.

"Moonbeam—" He protested with a groan, but I shook my head.

"I won't break. Fuck me, Zain."

Pulling out, he flipped me onto my stomach, sinking into me from behind. His hands gripped my hips roughly, helping to pull me to my knees.

"*Oh,*" I gasped out, feeling him bottom out. "*Yes.* You're so big."

Right there, I thought, feeling him deeper than ever before. The angle made everything heightened, and I wondered if it would always be like this.

"Luna," he groaned. "You're so tight. Feels so good."

I didn't agree with words—I couldn't because all rational thought flooded my brain as pleasure burst through my body. I pushed my hips back, forcing him in deeper.

He reached around us, grabbing my hand and forcing my fingers apart, placing them on the entrance where we were joined.

"Feel us," he rasped against my ear. "Feel how good you take me, Moonbeam."

Every thrust, every movement he made as he rocked into me, sent trembles through my body. My fingers were parted around his cock, each slide inside of me brushing it up against my digits.

My moans increased, and Zain found my clit, strumming it with such precision I thought I might lose my mind. *So close.*

Stars exploded across my vision, a blinding white that overtook me without warning. My muscles clenched around him, and I could feel his cock tightening between my fingers, inside of me, even as he kept pounding into me through my climax.

"Inside me," I pleaded, not even knowing what I was asking for but knowing I didn't want to lose this feeling, this connection, yet. Pressing my ass against him further, I tightened my muscles. "Fill me up," I begged.

A deep groan escaped from his lips as he did just that, spilling deep into my body, filling me with rope after rope of his cum. I could feel the warmth inside me as his seed trickled down onto my fingers.

Zain stilled, keeping me pinned against him as his breathing leveled out.

"Damn." I panted, collapsing onto the bed. "That was…" I had no words. *How did he always fry my brain so thoroughly?*

"Thank you," Zain said, voice rough. He nuzzled his face into the spot between my shoulders and my neck, kissing it softly. Reverently.

I turned to face him. "For what?"

"For trusting me. For this." He cupped my cheeks.

Finally, he pulled out, and I whimpered at the sudden loss of him inside of me.

Our combined releases dripped out of me, and Zain's gaze was focused on his cum. He swallowed roughly.

"That's… fuck, that's hot," he muttered before using his index and pointer fingers to scoop it up and push it back inside of me.

I swallowed roughly, trying not to think about what we'd just done.

And how I knew it could change everything.

EIGHTEEN
ZAIN

Luna's blush spread down her neck as I watched my release trickle out of her body, a sight that had me half-hard again already. I willed myself to calm down, satiated enough to just share in this moment of contentment together.

Running my fingers through her blonde strands, I admired her naked form draped across mine. It finally felt like I could breathe again after *days*. Avoiding her had been hard, but it was necessary. I wanted to give her time to acclimate, to make sure that this was what she wanted. Still, keeping my distance meant I missed her, even when she was only a room away.

"You're constantly surprising me, you know," I murmured, playing with the ends of her hair.

She hummed in response. "How so?"

Where did I begin? "Coming with me. Agreeing to all of this." Her lips formed a little *o*, and I chuckled. "You could have said no, you know. Refused me. Stayed in Pleasant Grove."

Luna's only response was to nuzzle closer to my chest. "Maybe it just felt right. Being with you."

An amused sound slipped out of my throat. "Indeed." I so badly wanted to tell her why, but it was too soon.

She brought her hand up to my torso, tracing my abdomen like she was trying to commit it to memory. "You know, there's something I've been wondering…"

"Yes?"

"Maybe it's silly, but…" She crossed her arms over my chest and rested her chin on top of them, keeping her eyes focused on me. "What's your last name?"

I frowned. "I don't have one."

"What?"

"Demons have no need for last names."

"So, when I marry you, I'll be…" Her voice trailed off at the end in a question.

I kissed her forehead. "You'll be *Luna, Crown Princess of the Demon Realm.* And someday, my Queen."

She snuggled against me further. "Mm. That's going to take some getting used to."

I rested a hand on her lower back, rubbing slowly up and down her spine.

"Everything's about to change," Luna murmured.

Yes.

"I liked how it was in my apartment. Everything was so much simpler back then." Her eyes fluttered shut. "But it's never going to be just you and me again."

"No," I agreed. "It's not."

Luna let out a deep sigh.

"What?" I traced a finger over her brow, smoothing the wrinkle there.

"I know it hasn't even been a week, but… I guess I just miss it."

"The human realm?" I asked before she could elaborate. I'd taken her from her home, and asshole that I was, I'd barely even spent any time with her this past week. Her seeking me out had been proof of that.

"No." She laughed, tilting her head up to look at me. "I mean, miss parts of home, don't get me wrong. It's the only one I've ever known. I miss my coven. My cousin. My sister always being around. But what I really miss is… baking."

"The bakery?" I frowned, smoothing a hand over her bare shoulder. "What can I do?"

Because I'd build her one here if she wanted, let her bake to her heart's content, feeding the demons the delicious treats I'd been lucky enough to sneak upstairs occasionally.

"Nothing," she murmured, burrowing deeper into my side. "I just miss being in the kitchen. The satisfaction I felt finishing a batch of cookies. The way people's faces would light up when they tried something new for the first time." Her shoulders drooped, and I knew she was trying to appear casual about it. "I don't miss the bakery *itself,* though. It's strange, but…" She looked up at me. "Maybe it was time."

"Time?" I repeated, the question apparent.

"For something new."

"Mmm." Leaning down, I rubbed my nose against hers. "I can think of a better way to spend your time." I pressed a kiss to her bare shoulder, brushing my teeth against her skin.

"Zain!" Luna blushed, batting at my chest to push me away. "You're so…"

"Irresistible?" I flashed my teeth at her.

Rolling off of me, she rested her chin on her arms, leaving the bare skin of her back exposed as she adjusted in the sheets. "I was thinking of a different word."

I laughed, flicking at her nose and placing a kiss on her shoulder. "Tell me."

"*Different*. When it's just us, you're just…" She hummed, the sound filling a void in my chest. "It's different."

Everything was different with her—but admitting that was like laying my heart out on a platter. And that was something I didn't need. Had promised myself I didn't want.

This wasn't about love. That's what I'd said before. Except…

"I've never wanted anyone the way I want you," I admitted.

"So don't shut me out. Tell me what you're feeling. Let me *in*."

But could I promise her that? Could I tell her everything and trust that she wouldn't leave me? Because I wasn't a good man. I wasn't the gentleman she'd thought me to be.

Despite all of that, she was still here in my arms.

I rested my forehead against hers. "I'll try."

Maybe she would stay if I laid my soul bare to her. If I gave her all of my truths. If I let myself care for her the way I knew this was heading— words I'd given no one, not in my entire life.

But suddenly, I wanted to.

She stretched out her arms, her back arching from the motion, a little wince slipping out from her lips.

"Sore?" I asked with a wince. Maybe I'd taken her too hard. "Was I too rough?" Running a hand down her spine, I rubbed soothing circles against her skin.

"Yes, but…" Her cheeks went pink. "I liked it."

"Mmm, you did, did you?" A wicked smile covered my face.

"I'm not fragile. I told you I won't break."

No. Luna was brave, and that was her strength. Even when she'd been scared or mad, she hadn't shut down. She'd persevered. It was something I admired about her. How she'd agreed, with no hesitation.

"Come on," I murmured, scooping her up into my arms.

"Where are we going?" Luna asked, a sleepy lilt to her voice.

"I'm going to make it better," I said as I headed towards the bathing pools. *Take care of you the way you deserve.*

The baths were heated by an underwater hot spring, which was absolutely delightful, especially for sore muscles. Though I was usually sore from training and fighting, washing blood off my skin. Either way, I didn't want her to be hurt tomorrow.

Not when we'd be married within the week.

She gave a few sleepy grumbles of protest before I stepped into the warm water, submerging us deeper with each stair I took down into the pool. Those protesting noises quickly turned into little sighs of pleasure as I settled onto the bench, still keeping her in my arms.

"Better?" I asked, getting a nod in return. Her silky hair brushed up against my torso. I wanted to wash it for her. To take care of her, do things for her I'd never done for anyone else. It wasn't just a want, though. I longed for it.

I wondered if the man I'd been a month ago would even recognize me now, with all the sweet things I was doing for this woman. Part of me felt repulsed by my actions, even if I didn't understand them. I'd never wanted to do any of them before, not until her. Now, I wanted to take care of her, to make her feel *worshipped*.

She looked up at me with those big, captivating eyes, and I was lost.

Luna shifted, sitting up and resting her head against my chest like she was using me as her own personal chair. My fingers rested on her hip, helping to keep her in place with my grip as she relaxed.

"Open your legs for me, Moonbeam," I instructed, reaching behind me with the hand that wasn't holding her to grab the soap. "Let me clean you up."

She separated her thighs, draping a knee over each of mine, and I trailed my hand down her stomach, inching slowly over her bare skin.

"Zain," she breathed, sucking in a quick breath as I lathered up my hand.

"Shhh," I soothed. "I'll take care of you."

I held my hand there, only a featherlight touch as I cupped her sex. Bringing my other hand down into the water, I used the soap to rub gentle circles on her thighs, cleaning up the sticky mess we'd made earlier. When I'd been bare inside of her. Fates, nothing would beat that feeling. Of her accepting me into her body. Of painting her womb with my seed.

I pressed the tip of my middle finger inside of her just an inch, my cock stiffening between us as I slowly explored her body.

My teeth ached, and I leaned down, pressing my nose into the crook of her neck, placing open-mouthed kisses to her soft skin.

It'd be so easy. One bite, and she'd be tethered to me. She wouldn't even know. I ran my sharp canines over that point, desire pulsing through me to puncture her skin.

Luna shifted, leaning back to press against me more, even as she wiggled like she was trying to get closer.

Closer. *Closer.* Clicking my tongue in warning, I brought my lips to her ear. "*Careful.*"

She turned her head, brushing her lips across mine. "What if I don't want to be careful?" Bright green eyes shined up at me, and one corner of my mouth tilted up.

"Tell me what you want," I instructed, moving my fingers slowly over her skin.

Squirming against me, she finally gasped out, "Touch me. Please."

I hummed into her skin, finally pushing my finger all the way in as a reward.

Thank the fates that no one would interrupt us here. That these were our private rooms, and the servants would only come when called for.

Because I didn't want anyone to see my bride like this. Unabashedly riding my hand, her head tipped back onto my shoulder as she let out a series of small, breathy noises that only spurred me on, encouraging me to continue as I coaxed her body into another orgasm. I slipped a second finger inside of her, pumping into her as my other hand moved to rub at her clit.

"That's it," I said as she let out a long moan. "So good for me."

Her body slumped against my chest as her muscles relaxed, her wet heat clenching around my fingers, still inside her.

"Better?" I asked, kissing the top of her head.

"Mmm," was her only response as she nestled against my skin, content and sated. "That was—" She tilted up her head to look at me, her eyelids fluttering. "How am I ever going to leave when you do that to me?"

"You won't," I said, leaning down to suck the skin of her neck into my mouth. "That's the idea."

Because, selfishly, I wanted to keep her—forever.

Tie her to me, mark her, make it so she could never leave me. Fuck, I was an asshole. That I'd do it all and not regret a single moment of it, as long as it gave me *her*.

Luna twisted around, pressing her bare breasts to my chest as she straddled my lap, arms winding around my neck.

Her lips met mine as she kissed me—sloppily, hungrily, before one hand wandered down my body, tracing down my chest and abdomen before wrapping around my cock.

"Luna—" I protested as she moved her hand up and down.

She moved her lips down my neck, kissing towards my pecs. "It's your turn," she said, flicking her tongue over my nipple. "I want to take care of you, too."

Wrapping my hand over hers, I stilled her hand, gritting my teeth from the sensation, how good it felt to have her touching *me*.

"That was just for you," I protested, raising an eyebrow. "I don't need you to reciprocate."

"But—" she protested, and I clicked my tongue.

"We're not trading favors, Moonbeam. If I want to fuck you with my tongue, then you don't have to give me anything back." Because I was desperate to have her taste on my tongue again, to bury myself in her sweet cunt every day, but I had to rein myself in. I wasn't a beast in heat. I could practice some control.

"You…" She looked away. Her face was red, and I wondered what combination it was from—her orgasm, the heat of the pools, or the adorable blush she often got when talking about *this*. "But what if I *want* to taste you?"

Fuck. She was going to ruin me. "You do, hm?" I let her hand resume its motion, both of us working my length in tandem. My voice was a rasp when I choked out, "Next time." I'd let her do whatever she wanted to me as long as she kept touching me like *that*.

She hummed, her eyelids drooping as I got closer, feeling myself harden further in her grasp, my balls tightening.

"Luna." My teeth clashed together as I forced out the words in warning, but she didn't stop. "*Fuck*," I groaned, grabbing her by the hips and lifting her out of the pool.

"What?" She frowned. "Was it not—"

I kissed her forehead. "You're perfect." Grabbing a towel, I kneeled in front of her, taking the time to dry her legs, moving up and treating each inch of her body with the same attention. A light moan slipped from her lips as I moved the fabric over her nipples, and she pressed against me, only the towel keeping our skin apart.

"We're just going to get dirty again," Luna whispered in my ear, tracing a finger up my abs.

Her damp hair spilled down over her skin, drawing my attention to the little freckles dotting her shoulders.

"You're going to be the death of me," I groaned, trying to focus on my current mission.

Once she was sufficiently dry, I moved to repeat the process on me, but she stole the towel from my hands.

"That looks painful," she continued, her eyes narrowed in on my weeping cock. "Why don't you let me take care of it?"

"Luna," I clicked my tongue, letting her drop the towel to the floor between us.

And then I hefted her into my arms, carrying us back to bed, eager to finish what we'd started.

* * *

She'd finally fallen asleep after I'd lost count of how many orgasms I had given her. With my tongue, my fingers, my cock. After I'd filled her up with my seed, coated her skin with my scent, so there would be no question whose she was.

Good. I felt smug, like a preening peacock. I had to make up for lost time, the nights I'd spent apart from her. Now, my girl was in my arms, and it was everything.

And in a few more nights, she'd be my wife.

Her leg was thrown over mine, our naked bodies intertwined, when she let out a whimper. I frowned, smoothing over the skin on her forehead. I knew I should sleep, but I couldn't help but feel like the moment I did, I'd wake up and find out this had all been a dream.

"Zain," she groaned, hand clutching around my biceps. Her nails dug in, slicing tiny half-circles into my skin.

Her body spasmed, thrashing back and forth with her eyes open wide—like she was *seeing.* Whatever it was, it was more like a nightmare.

"Luna." I rested my hand on her forehead. "Wake up, Moonbeam."

Her skin was cold, and I scooped her up in my arms, cradling her to my body as she shook, silent tears spilling from her eyes.

"No, no, no," she sobbed, curling her hands against my chest. "I'm no one. Please."

"Luna." I pressed a kiss to her forehead. "It's just a nightmare. I'm here."

Was she seeing the demons who'd tried to attack her that night?

"I need—"

Shaking her shoulder, I tried my best to wake her up, but whatever vision she was seeing seemed to have her in a vise.

"Zain." More tears came from her eyes. "I can't lose you."

"You won't," I promised her, kissing her tears away. "It wasn't easy to find you. I'm never letting you go again."

She whimpered slightly, her hands clutching onto my shirt.

"You're mine, Luna."

It was a promise I'd never break.

* * *

"Well?" Talon raised an eyebrow, perched against my office door as he watched me work. If he was here, it meant that Thorn was with Luna, who I'd left sleepily curled up in the sheets of her bed.

I resisted raising one right back. "What?"

He just grinned. "How's it going with your…" He trailed off. "Witch?"

"Fine." Though I couldn't help but think about Luna's trembling body as she'd cried for me. What had she seen? I wanted to take her fears away. Ease her worries. Prove to her I'd never leave her. That no one would take her from me.

The other parts of last night, however… I didn't want to share *those* details with anyone else. The way my body heated just thinking about what we'd been up to. That she'd taken me bare. How it had been after, in the bath together.

I'd never been one for cuddling after sex. It hadn't appealed to me but with Luna… I couldn't stand to be parted from her after our couplings. Though I wouldn't dig too deep into why that might be.

Everything was… amazing. Until her nightmare.

Running my thumb across my lip, the skin caught on one of my canine teeth.

"You haven't claimed her yet."

"No." My eyes squeezed shut. It was taking everything in me not to.

"Why not?" He crossed his arms. "Her scent is all over you."

A statement that made me feel like a possessive animal. If she smelled like me, no one would dare to harm her.

"It's too soon." Leaning back in my chair, I crossed my arms over my chest. "She's not ready for that."

"Are you sure?" He whistled, like he knew something I didn't. "Do you know what your future wife has been doing every day?"

I frowned. "What do you mean?"

"Ever since you put Thorn and I on babysitting duty—"

"*Guard* duty," I corrected. Someone had to keep her safe on the off-chance someone tried to hurt her.

"Yes, yes. That." He waved a hand in dismissal, and I scowled. "She's been in the library."

I blinked. "So?" I knew Luna loved books—she had a stack of them on her nightstand in her apartment, a color-coded stack that somehow just looked like it belonged—but we'd never specifically discussed her reading habits.

"Do you know what books she's been reading?"

I shook my head. "No." A bookcase sat in her living room of her apartment—what were the contents? Did she miss having those things here? Maybe I should take another trip to the human realm. I could ask Willow what things would make her feel more at home here.

A smirked curled over his face, red eyes shining with mischief. "You should ask her."

"Alright."

I put down the stack of papers I was working on.

They could wait.

Checking on my bride could not.

NINETEEN
LUNA

Yawning, I stretched my arms, feeling sore in all the best places. The past few days had been good. Great. It felt like Zain was opening up to me, and I was just happy to spend more time with him again.

This morning, I'd finally gathered my pride and asked if I could use the kitchen, wanting a distraction from all the bustling about the palace. I didn't have to lift a finger, which felt strange, considering it was my wedding, too.

It was rather easy to commandeer the kitchen, especially given I was marrying their *beloved* Crown Prince. Though sometimes I wasn't sure if they worshipped him or were terrified of him. Maybe both. When he was with me, he was like a little puppy, but I saw how broody he was with everyone else.

Either way, I had a kitchen, and thanks to a little begging to Zain, I had access to all of my ingredients from my bakery in Pleasant Grove. He'd opened a portal for me, though I'd barely had enough time to grab all my supplies before he closed it again.

The smell of baking cookies instantly made me feel at home.

All I needed was a cup of my sister's legendary coffee to feel better.

I wished I could call her. If only my phone worked here. In so many ways, I wished this world wasn't a realm away from my sister.

Tomorrow, I was getting married. I would be someone's wife.

My world was changing right before my eyes.

I'd dreamt about the two little ones again last night. And when I woke up, my surroundings still strange to my eyes, I couldn't get those golden and lavender eyes out of my mind.

So strange. Because they felt so familiar. Like I *should* know who they were. Was I seeing the past—Zain's past? But who was the little girl? I'd never met a single witch with eyes of a purple hue.

What would he think? Maybe he'd be like the others—brush it off, tell me I was just making it up. But I didn't think so. He'd always seen me, listened to me, in a way that I knew he wasn't faking.

Suddenly, it all felt so real.

I cared for him—I knew that in the depths of my soul—and even with everything that had happened, I still felt a rush of anxiety and apprehension. Maybe it was that my family wasn't here. A rush of sadness passed through me, thinking about our parents.

Would their spirits be able to find me here, looking over me as I said my vows? Or was that just the hope of a naive girl?

"Somehow, I knew I'd find you here," came a familiar voice.

My head whipped around, though I couldn't find any words as I saw the head of light brown hair come into view.

"I heard someone needed an older sister," Willow said, a grin spread over her face.

Happiness pooled in my chest, and my heart felt full.

My eyes instantly flooded with tears. She was *here*.

Before I realized it, my feet were flying, and I met her halfway across the room.

"Hi, Lune," she whispered, wrapping me up in her arms.

"Hey, Wil," I said back, burying my face in her shoulder. How did she know all I wanted was to have her here with me?

"What's wrong?" Willow frowned when we finally pulled apart, wiping at the wetness that had collected on my cheeks. "Why are you crying?"

I shook my head. "They're not—I'm not sad. They're happy tears."

Because she was *here,* and the last few weeks had been surreal, to say the least. I was still trying to adjust to this life, surrounded by demons and beings I'd barely known. Meanwhile, my support system was back in Pleasant Grove.

Her green eyes stared back at me as she cupped my cheeks. "I couldn't miss my sister's wedding." She gave me a warm smile.

"Is Damien with you?" I asked, peeking around her but not seeing her dark-haired demon. I knew one of Zain's bodyguards was outside—the constant protection never faded unless he was with me.

"He went to check on Zain," Willow said, her nose sniffing the air as she smelled what was baking. "Did you make pumpkin chocolate chip scones?" They were her favorite.

"I was feeling a little homesick," I admitted. "And when I told Zain about missing baking, he helped me out." And now I had enough supplies for at least several dozen different desserts. Plus, the pantry here was stuffed full of new ingredients I was already coming up with ideas for.

"No complaints here. You know I'll never turn down one of your scones."

"Do you have your dress?" I asked, changing the subject. I'd been dying to see all the details of the wedding. Zain insisted it was a surprise.

"Oh." My sister looked down at the deep plum dress she had on. It was nothing like the gown she'd worn to the ball, but it was pretty. The color somehow made her eyes even brighter, the silhouette making her curves stand out. "Right. Damien mentioned…" she trailed off, looking over at me.

"Don't look at me. I just showed up." I held my hands up in the air. "He barely let me help with anything."

She giggled. "He asked Damien about human weddings and our traditions as witches. If there was anything specific that we did for our ceremonies."

"He did?" Oh. That was… sweet. For a demon, he was constantly surprising me. No one could really be this thoughtful, right? Though it no longer felt like an act. Maybe it never had.

"Yeah. Turns out explaining the concept of a *best man* and *maid of honor* to a demon is… really fucking weird."

"So is marrying one," I snorted.

"How are you feeling? About all of this?"

"Fine," I answered, staring down at my nails. I wasn't apprehensive about Zain—it was the rest of it.

"Yes, that explains the tears," Willow snorted. "I still can't believe you're getting married. Before me, no less."

"Shut up," I muttered, though there was no malice behind it. "I'm only three years younger than you, anyway." And knowing how possessive Damien was of her, I was sure it wouldn't take long till they were walking down the aisle, too.

She hopped up on the counter across from the stove as I went back to check on the scones.

I propped my hip against the opposite side as I faced her. "Lately, I've just been feeling like… something was missing in my life. And then you went and adopted a cat, and he turned out to be your soulmate, and I'm just… I don't know. Everything feels different now."

A sly smile touched her lips. "Because of Zain?"

"Maybe." A flush spread over my cheeks as I looked at the floor. "But even before that, I'd been wanting more. And don't get me wrong, I still love baking, but there's so much about myself that I've never learned. That I never really got a chance to, but now… I want to know how I fit into all of this."

"It's okay to admit that you like him, you know." Willow grinned. "You are marrying him, after all."

"I just… How did you know?" I asked her, fiddling with the crystal on my necklace. "That Damien was the one? That you…" I couldn't quite say the words.

Because as much as I liked Zain—and had since we'd first met—I couldn't quite say that I was *in love* with him. Not yet. The way it was going, though…

"That I love him?" My sister's warm smile lit up her face, and I could tell she was thinking about the demon who had the other half of her heart.

I nodded, suddenly feeling like a naive girl all over again.

"It would be easier if there was any one thing I could point to. But he makes me feel safe. Loved. *Treasured.* He gave me back a part of myself I hadn't even known was missing. Part of me had been scared, though. That I'd let myself love him, and he'd leave. That it had been too good to be true. But…"

"But he stayed."

"He did. And we chose each other. Soulmates or not, I'd never found someone who felt like home before. Who saw every piece of me and loved all of it. Someone who'd do anything for me." She shook her head. "Damien's not perfect—not by a long shot. Learning he kept things from me—about his brother, about *you*… That was hard. But I forgave him because I loved him."

"I was okay," I said, my voice low. "You know that, right? That I'm fine here?"

"But what if you hadn't been? What if he'd been keeping you here against your will? I just—"

"I would have told you. Asked you to take me home with you. If I didn't trust him, I…" The words were on the tip of my tongue. That I *never would have come.*

Willow reached out to squeeze my hand. "I know you're okay now. And I love you. But more importantly, I trust you. And either way, I'm always gonna be here for you, Lune. Even if you decide that all this is too much."

"I know," I whispered back, squeezing just like we always had as kids. "And maybe that's why I can do this. Because I know you've got my back."

"Always will." She winked.

"I love you so much, Wil. I don't think I say that enough. Truly, I don't know what I would have done without you." Willow waved me off, but I continued. "You gave up your life for me, and I don't know if I ever really thanked you for it. The bakery—moving back to Pleasant Grove—*everything* you did for me. You're the best sister a girl could have ever asked for."

"Oh, Luna. I didn't give *anything* up. No part of me that regrets any of it. Working together all of those years was the best thing I could have asked for. Speaking of the bakery, though…" Willow twirled her finger in the air. "I might have hired a manager. I hope that's okay with you."

"You did?" I was shocked.

"After we talked last time, I hired the new baker. And I guess I'd been adrift for a while, too. Not knowing what I wanted to do with my life. So I decided it was time for me to step back, too. And with Damien, I just…" she trailed off, a breathtaking smile taking over her face.

"You're happy?"

"I've never been happier."

"Good."

That was all I could hope for. A joyful life. Love.

And maybe that was the dangerous thing about dreams.

They always left you wanting *more*.

* * *

A bouquet of violet and light lilac flowers was placed in my arms as I stared at the large doors that opened to the ceremonial hall.

"I'm getting married," I whispered the words like I was tasting them on my tongue.

My makeup was flawless—eyes lined with kohl, a shimmer over my eyelids—and Novalie had loosely curled my hair, not a strand out of place. Somehow, she got the curls to hold, a feat I was attributing to magic instead of whatever tool she expertly wielded.

The masterpiece of a dress Angelique had designed fit me like a glove, the fabric shimmering no matter how the light hit it.

It was the same face that I'd seen in the mirror for the last twenty-five years that blinked back at me. The same light blonde hair, bright green eyes—like Granny Smith apples—and the same porcelain skin and rosy cheeks. I was me. And yet, I was someone completely different, too.

Stronger. Eyes brighter. I looked every bit the role I was filling. *Ethereal.* They'd truly made me feel like a princess.

My pale blonde strands flowed behind me, and a long, shimmering veil draped down my back. Then there was the crown that sat in my hair, a large moon sitting in the center, dozens of tiny gemstones and crystals spreading out from around it.

Today, I'd become his wife. And one day... his queen. A shiver ran through me at the thought.

Despite all my extensive research and the amount of books I'd read on the subject over the last week, I still had no idea what to expect from today.

Zain had been tight-lipped about the whole thing. Even though he hadn't been vocal about what exactly it would entail, he'd at least been present with me *physically*. I'd spent the whole last week wrapped in his arms every night.

I could tell something was bothering him, and he hadn't shared it with me. It seemed like stress above and beyond one could expect from a wedding—especially from an immortal, three-hundred-year-old demon.

"Are you ready?" Lilith asked at my side, dressed in a red one-shoulder gown, her wings tucked in behind her, the long black hair braided thickly over one shoulder. Somehow, her horns completed the look, making her look sensual—beautiful.

It was strange how quickly I'd gotten used to everyone's appearances around me. How different it was here than Pleasant Grove, and yet… I *liked* it here. His friends had made me feel welcome. Like I could rely on them if something went wrong.

And I liked it when Asura or Lilith—sometimes both—would sneak into my room and take me on an adventure. They'd become my friends, and I was so grateful for that.

When I answered, there was not an ounce of hesitation in my voice. "Yes."

"Then let's get you married," Willow said, a twinkle in her eyes. Pride filled her voice, and I resisted throwing my arms around her again.

Hugging her tight like I had so many times since yesterday. We'd spent the entire night talking, catching up on what we'd missed in the last two weeks. Zain and Damien had been close by like neither one of them could let us out of their sight.

We'd both ended up with overprotective men, but I secretly didn't mind. His hand rested on my thigh—possessively, and I couldn't help but wonder if this meant something to him the way it did to me. If he felt like his heart was going to burst out of his chest like I did?

Worse. The thought flickered into my head, and I blinked suddenly. I still wasn't used to being able to talk with him like this—mind to mind.

Are you spying on me? I said, scowling at the thought.

I could almost feel his smirk. *Spying? Is that what we're calling it now?*

Zain—

I'm waiting, he said, the thought like a caress against my mind. *Don't keep me in suspense for too long, Moonbeam. A man can only be so patient.*

I took a deep breath. Rolled my shoulders back.

Willow stood in front of me, dressed in her floor-length lavender gown. "Shall we?"

Then I was walking in, about to swear vows of love and loyalty to the Prince of the Demon Realm.

I thought back to Zain and our conversation in bed. *Princess.*

My eyes connected with his, standing there in a gilded black suit adorned with lavish details and the crown that sat on his head.

Warmth spilled through my chest, but I still couldn't help but wonder… Was I making the right choice?

TWENTY
ZAIN

"Thank you for coming," I said, clearing my throat as I stared at my brother, who looked completely human standing there in his three-piece tuxedo, which was so at odds with the ceremonial suit I'd pulled on.

"You're getting married," Damien said, shrugging his shoulders with that nonchalant air he'd always had. "Of course I'd be here." An eyebrow raised high. "Plus, you asked."

"Right." I dipped my head.

"Does Luna know?" My brother asked, shoving his hands in his pockets.

"Know what?"

"Everything you did this week."

"Of course not."

Willow was with Luna, helping her get ready, which I supposed was part of it. I'd taken a trip to the witch town, seeking her sister's help with my *other* surprises.

"You should tell her. All the secrets…" Damien shook his head. "There were other ways."

"I didn't kidnap her if that's what you're implying. She came willingly." I gave her a choice.

She'd *always* had a choice. And she always would have one. If she didn't want to be here with me, I'd let her go. It would hurt, but I'd do it. No matter what I'd said.

Because her happiness was the most important thing to me. She was my light in the dark, even if I'd grown accustomed to living in the shadows all these years.

My brother clenched his fists. "You went behind my back, even though you *assured* me I had until the end of the month—"

"I couldn't wait." Huffing out a breath, I interrupted him. "Fuck, but I needed…" *Her.* Couldn't he see that? My desperation? "Time was running out."

His fists balled up in his hands. "You didn't see Willow's face when she realized her sister was missing. She was terrified. That look of devastation, not knowing if I could fix it…" Damien ran his hands through his shaggy black hair. "If she hadn't forgiven me for the role I played… I don't know what I would have done. She's my *everything*, Zain. Truly, I…" He looked away, voice rough. "I never expected to find her."

I knew that. Because finding your mate wasn't guaranteed in our world. And finding them was a bit like learning there was another half of your heart living outside of your body. No matter what happened, you had to keep them safe.

"Then you understand why I needed Luna."

Damien sighed, his blood-red eyes flashing with resignation. "Yeah. I guess I do."

"I don't want to fight. Not today." The day I was marrying the woman who would become my queen. The one the fates chose for me. "Would you ever consider coming back?"

My brother's red eyes connected with mine. "You know that I never asked for this. Any of it."

I narrowed my gaze at him. "And I *did?*"

"You're the Crown Prince. This is your legacy. I'm nothing more than a bastard child who's been dragged around on his leash his whole life. Now that I have Willow… I don't know." Damien shoved his hands in his pockets. "I don't want to force her to uproot her entire life."

He wasn't wrong, and maybe that was the worst part of all of this. If I didn't have this obligation, this role, would I still choose to be here? Or would I have also run away to be with my mate?

"You don't have to. But once he's gone…" I looked over at the crown that sat on my desk. "One day, when the kingdom is mine, I hope you'll come back."

Damien nodded. "Willow wants to live in Pleasant Grove for a while yet. But eventually, I think we'd be back. After he's gone." He sucked in a sharp breath, violence clouding his eyes. I knew he shared my thoughts about our father, and it was easy to see where his mind had gone. "That asshole doesn't even deserve to breathe the same air as her." He slammed his hand on the wooden desk. "Bringing her here…"

"I know," I agreed. "But now I can end this. Take him down." My voice shook as a bolt of lightning struck outside. "It's time."

He looked over at me in surprise, red eyes meeting my gold. "You mean…"

"Now that I have her, there's only one thing stopping me."

Damien hummed in response, leaning against the edge of my desk. "How much longer?"

"Soon, I hope. Once she's ready." That was all I could offer until the final puzzle pieces were slotted into place.

My brother nodded, and I changed the subject. Not wanting to dwell on the topic, even if this room was guarded with magic and the chances of us being spied on were low.

"What was it like? Claiming her?" My canines ached even now, the delayed mating driving me mad with need. "I know what they all say, but…"

"It's nothing like when you experience it," my brother offered, his tongue darting out to swipe over his lower lip as if he was thinking about it. "The need, the want—it feels like you're blinded with lust. But after…" His hand slid over his chest, resting over his heart. "You feel whole."

"And it was… pleasant? For her?"

My brother pinched between his eyes as a strangled sound left his throat. "I cannot believe we're having this conversation right now."

I thrust my hand into my hair—probably messing it up, but fuck if I cared about that. "I don't want to hurt her."

"You won't." He shook his head. "If you love her…" Damien paused, giving me a look. "You do, right? Love her?"

Did I? Love wasn't something I deserved. Besides, she might have been fated for me, but it wasn't like she loved me, either.

I cleared my throat. "It's been a month."

He shrugged. "I knew after those first two weeks. Even if she hadn't been my mate, I still would love her. She makes me feel alive in a way I never did before. And all those silly human things she makes me do…" His lips tilted up in a dopey grin, and then he cleared his throat. Refocused. "You'd know."

"I do care for her. More than I've ever cared about anyone else."

"That's a start." My brother slapped a hand on my shoulder. "Just focus on her—making sure she feels pleasure and not pain." A fang popped out over his lip. "And I don't just mean with your teeth."

I groaned. Of course, I'd always known that it was sexual, but the desire had been practically blinding the last time I'd taken Luna to bed. I couldn't wait any longer.

Which meant it had to be *tonight*.

"Are you worried she won't accept you?"

I ran a tongue over my canine teeth. "No. Before, maybe, but now…"

She'd been so eager the last few days. Asking me questions about demons, our culture, and traditions. Neither one of us mentioned Damien and Willow's mating, but I knew she was aware of it. Would she be open to it? The bond would connect us even deeper, and while I knew I could never complete it without her consent, it was getting hard to wait any longer.

"Then what troubles you?"

That I won't be able to keep her safe. I couldn't voice the words, even though they were right there on the tip of my tongue. *That she won't want to stay.*

I rubbed my hand over my smooth jaw.

How would she react when I brought up my need for an heir? A child that looked like the two of us. We hadn't talked about a child between us, and yet…

I found it was all I wanted. Desperately.

To keep her by my side, no matter the cost.

* * *

I'd been waiting for her for a lifetime, but the moment she entered the hall, I knew I would have waited for the rest of my existence for her. For just a moment in her light.

Her moonlit colored curls tumbled around her shoulders, dressed in a gown of stark white, my crown resting on her brow.

There she is. I could see Luna's mouth tilt up with just the hint of a smile as I stood at the front of the room. Damien stood by my side as my only groomsman—one tradition I'd borrowed from the human world for the evening.

Demon weddings weren't the most elegant of affairs in nature, but this was our future queen. I wanted her to be respected and admired, for them to worship her like I would. There would be more onlookers outside, waiting to get a peek at my queen, but that would come later.

And just as I'd calculated, all eyes in the room were focused on the beautiful woman coming up the aisle. A long, tulle veil trailed behind her like a sea of stars spilling from her back.

My wife.

"Hey, handsome," Luna whispered as she reached me, the bouquet in her hands featuring dozens of purple flowers, including some small sprigs of lavender and lilacs nestled among the white lilies and roses, as well as flowers that didn't exist in the human realm. It felt representative of us—demon and human.

I'd had them all picked from the palace gardens specifically, thinking of the dried flowers that had previously hung on the wall of her apartment. The one I'd cleared out this week.

She wouldn't be going back, after all, not after this.

"Beautiful," I murmured, brushing a stray curl back behind her ear.

Luna beamed, her green eyes filled with such hope, and I hoped that spark would never fade. She turned slightly to hand her sister the bouquet before looking back at me.

"So… We're doing this?" Her eyes strayed from mine for a moment to survey our audience. Except for the horns and tails and wings of the demons in the audience, I liked to imagine this place could have passed for a wedding hall on earth. It was what I'd asked for, after all.

"If you still want to," I chuckled, though the sound felt more like a rasp as I took her hands into mine.

She nodded, and that was all the confirmation I needed. Signaling to the demon in charge to start the ceremony, the words flowed over us, the magic of the ceremony binding us together for eternity. Light flowed out of us, forming two overlapping circles on the floor beneath our feet— symbolizing connection, unity, and balance.

Our bond, in corporeal form, was visible for all to see.

It wasn't a long, drawn-out affair—unlike some of the human weddings I'd made Willow describe to me. We repeated the ceremonial words when asked, the ancient demon tongue sounding clumsy on Luna's tongue, but she didn't falter. Though we demons spoke the languages of humans now, we still used our own language for ceremonies, like coronations and weddings, but also to celebrate birth and death.

"And now, the two will drink from the ceremonial cup," our officiant announced to the room. There was no religion in the demon realm—unlike the humans, we didn't pray to Gods—but there was training to carry out important rituals such as these. "An offering to the fates, for guiding them through this next stage of their lives."

Luna eyed the goblet suspiciously. "I don't have to like, drink your blood or something, do I?"

"Don't be silly. We're not vampires."

"Wait." Her eyes widened. "I thought they were just a myth."

I grinned, my lips dipping down to brush against her ear. "Are they?"

But now wasn't the time to talk about the other creatures that lived in our worlds, hidden behind their own veils and wards.

My hands closed over hers, guiding the cup into both of our grasps before I bent and took a long pull of the dark wine. It wasn't like the sparkling demon wine she'd tried at the party—but something deeper.

Holding it out to her, my hands remained wrapped around hers as she tipped the cup to her own face, drinking it deeply just as I'd done. I watched her throat as she swallowed, the line of her neck begging for my tongue.

Careful, I thought to her mind. *Too much will make you sick.*

Her tongue darted out to catch a stray drop. *What's in it?* Her eyes widened as she scrunched up her nose. *It's almost... spicy.*

I didn't bore her with the list of ingredients. *It's believed to deepen the pathways between the souls.* Maybe it was all just a pretense, some romantic fabrication, but it was a tradition I would not squander. *Or so they say.*

She hummed in response, and then the goblet was taken away, our hands clasped once again. Now that my people's traditions were fulfilled—mostly—I had another tradition to complete.

The demon officiant nodded at me to continue. I'd filled him in on my somewhat unconventional plans beforehand, wanting to keep all of it a surprise from her.

"I, Zain, take you, Luna, to be my wife. My queen. I promise to be true to you in good times and in bad, in sickness and in health. I will love you and honor you all the days of my life, for as long as the fates shall allow us. Till eternity do us part."

It was a declaration. An intention. Me claiming her as my everything.

I pulled the wedding band out of my pocket, slipping it on over her moonstone ring. Another human tradition, but one I was happy to comply with.

Luna's face softened as she held up her hand, admiring the diamond-encrusted eternity band. "Zain, I…" Her breath caught. "This is too much."

I raised an eyebrow as if to say, *look where we are.* "Nothing is too much for you, Moonbeam."

She blinked at me. *Your turn.* I gave her a small mental prompt.

My bride inhaled roughly before letting out a shaky breath. "I, Luna, take you, Zain, to be my husband. My… King." Fuck, I liked that word on her lips. Maybe I could get her to say it again later. "I promise to be true to you in good times and in bad, in sickness and in health. I will love you and honor you all the days of my life, for as long as the fates shall allow us. Till eternity do us part."

Willow nudged her, placing a dark band in my bride's palm. This time, it was me who was surprised. I hadn't mentioned rings to her. When had she had time to get this made?

"It's tungsten," she explained. "The strongest metal on earth. And it has obsidian inlaid in it, which the witches say is good for protection."

"Did you get me a ring that would help keep me safe?" I rasped in her ear.

Her cheeks were pink as she slid it onto my ring finger before her hand slid back into mine.

"You made me a promise," she said. "We have a deal. So you can't go getting yourself hurt and go back on that."

An appreciative hum vibrated in my throat. I liked that she worried about me. Though I couldn't find a single thing I didn't like about the woman standing in front of me.

The one who had just become my wife.

"An eternity wouldn't be long enough with you," I said, voice low so only she could hear. And I meant it. I meant every word. Thank the fates that they'd brought her to me.

She squeezed my palm in response, her eyes rimmed in silver.

The officiant cleared his throat, distracting me from our moment. We'd been in our own little bubble, truly not a care about the rest of the beings in the room.

"I now pronounce you, Prince Zain and Princess Luna, as husband and wife. You may seal your vows with a kiss."

My hands wrapped around her waist, pulling her body in tight to mine before dipping her. Our faces were only inches apart as she cupped my face, holding me there.

"I'm going to kiss you now, wife," I whispered against her lips, and then the rest of the world faded away as we came together.

As I kissed her like no one was watching. Like no one else existed in the world.

Nothing would ever feel as right as this.

TWENTY-ONE
LUNA

My husband looked down at me, those golden eyes shining bright, and I wondered if my entire life had led to this moment. To meeting him.

Everything felt sharper now like someone had applied a filter to the world. My senses were all working in hyper-drive, but all I could see, feel, and hear was *him*.

"How did I get so lucky to find you?" he murmured against my lips before kissing me again, and I'd forgotten that there were hundreds of people watching us, that we were in the middle of our wedding because the entire world ceased to exist except for him and me.

The entire room exploded into applause, and the cheers finally brought me back to reality. Willow handed me the bouquet, and my free hand slipped into Zain's as we faced the hall, the aisle looking much shorter than it had when I'd walked up it.

I expected us to walk back down the aisle together, but Zain had other plans. He scooped me up into his arms and carried me out of the wedding hall, dress and all.

Heading out, I'd expected us to head into the ballroom, but he went up the large staircase and out onto the balcony. The entire palace courtyard was spread out below us, filled with demons.

"Zain," I blushed, poking at his chest. "You can put me down now."

He lowered me to my feet, keeping hold of one of my hands. My husband brushed a hand over my cheek before pressing his lips to my forehead.

The demons were cheering, screaming our names. I wasn't even sure how anyone outside of the palace knew who I was, considering I'd been behind the palace walls.

"What's going on?" I gasped.

He brushed his knuckles under my jaw. "I'm presenting my queen."

Zain kneeled before me, kissing my knuckles.

"But I'm not the queen yet," I said, swallowing a breath of air. Suddenly, it felt like I couldn't breathe.

"You will be."

I sucked in a breath. It was still hard to believe. Even if I'd just vowed to live an eternity by his side.

Somehow, he projected his voice, and the entire courtyard quieted as he spoke. Still, the moment felt as intimate as it would have alone in our bedroom.

"I vow my never-ending allegiance to you. That you and you alone shall wear my crown. My undying fealty is yours, my queen. There is no other in the worlds who should have it."

"What am I supposed to say?" I whispered back.

His voice was only a murmur. "Accept my vows to you, Moonbeam."

"Okay." I nodded, taking a deep breath before I stood tall. "I accept."

A grin split his handsome face, and he stood, towering over me with his full height. Even the heels I was wearing didn't bring us to the same level, but that didn't matter.

I cupped his face, feeling his freshly shaven jaw. I liked the beard, but I didn't mind this. He looked younger, somehow. Lighter. It also showed off his incredibly sharp jaw and structured cheekbones.

Swoon. He would always be the most handsome man I'd ever seen. Demon or not.

"Thank you." He murmured, bringing his lips down to meet mine.

"For what?" I asked.

But all he said was, "*Everything*."

We waved to the demons below, and then he scooped me back into his arms again, continuing further into the palace. I knew the floor plan well now—I'd spent the last weeks exploring every nook and cranny. Part of me still couldn't believe a wedding to this scale had been planned in two weeks, but I guessed for demon royalty with magic, anything was possible.

Either way, I knew exactly where he was headed. Our bedrooms.

"Isn't there a reception?" I asked, meeting his stare. "Like… a feast? Or a ball? Some sort of party?"

He smirked, leaning down to nip at my ear. "I don't think they're going to miss us, wife." Zain pressed a kiss to my pulse point. "Besides, the festivities will last for days. We can rejoin the party later. First, I need to take my time with my *wife*."

A slight moan slipped from my lips as his lips met my skin again, and then we were in his room, the dark furniture and black sheets making the entire room feel almost… *sensual.*

He set me down on my feet, slipping an arm around my waist to steady me. His scent filled my lungs, the intoxicating aroma making me burn up with want for him, and my core was already needy.

Dropping my bouquet on the side table, I turned to look at him. With a wave of his hand, Zain lit a handful of candles placed throughout the room, bathing us in a warm, flickering light. He slipped the black and gold overcoat off, draping it over the chest at the foot of his poster bed.

Gods, he was handsome. And he smelled like my personal brand of temptation like someone had mixed everything deliciously musky and spicy and bottled it up. Plus, in that get-up? I was a goner.

I'd always been attracted to a man in a suit, but in this princely attire, he looked like he'd stepped right out of the pages of one of my favorite historical fantasy romances. A prince ready to bed his wife. That shouldn't have increased the wetness between my legs, but it did.

My teeth dug into my bottom lip as I watched him remove the crown from his hair, and it joined the coat in the same spot. *Fuck.* I took the veil out of my hair, brushing my fingers through the curls and letting them spill down my back.

A wicked smile spread over his face as he caught me watching him. "You know… a demon marriage ceremony isn't finished until it's consummated." He rolled up his sleeves, revealing those thick forearms I'd daydreamed about.

And then, all six feet and five inches of him towered over me. In my heels, the top of my head was level with his chin. His body was unreal, and now he was *mine.*

"Oh." My thighs rubbed together, and my body was heating. Like I was growing progressively more aroused by the second.

"*Zain,*" I whimpered.

"It's okay," he soothed, kissing down my neck. "I'll make it better."

What was in that wine?

I wasn't sure if I'd asked it out loud or in my head, but Zain responded anyway. "It's an aphrodisiac."

"It's a—*what?*" I was achingly aware of how empty I was, and my skin itched. "I need—" I tugged at the dress.

Off. I needed it *off.*

"I know." Zain spun me around so fast I barely even had time to blink. He brushed my hair off to one side and pressed a kiss to my shoulder before turning his attention to the row of pearl buttons on the back of my dress. His fingers worked at them, pushing them through the loops. Slow. This was torture for both of us. He made a frustrated growl, and I heard little plinks on the ground, and then my dress was loose around my waist.

I blinked. "Did you just… *rip* the buttons off?" Pushing the dress over my hips, I let it flutter to the floor.

His liquid golden eyes burned into me, full of lust. "You weren't going to wear it again, anyway."

Zain looked like a satisfied predator, the way a cat would when licking his paw. But he was still a beast, and he was on the prowl for *me.* "I'll buy you another dress. And another. However many you want, as long as you let me take them off of you."

His eyes were fixed on the white lacy corset I was wearing, complete with laces down the back and a set of matching underwear I had absolutely no hope for.

"Wait," I said, placing a hand on his chest to stop him. "What do you mean the wine is an aphrodisiac?"

Zain frowned, a bit of the fog disappearing from his gaze. "It was—" He groaned as I ran my hand down his front, feeling the rippling muscles under his shirt, down lower—

His hand caught mine, stilling me. I pouted, wanting to cup the bulge in his pants that was painfully clear.

"It assures that the ceremony is completed. It doesn't impact your ability to consent, but it forces you into a heat-like state. You can't stop until it's been satisfied." He turned my hand over and brought it to his lips, kissing my wrist.

"Why?" I let out a little gasp when he ran his teeth—those sharp, pointy canines—over my veins.

"To assure the bond is complete."

He kissed a line up my arm, and I tilted my head to the side, giving him full access to my neck.

"I won't hurt you," he promised. And I believed him. There was nothing he would intentionally do to hurt me.

"I know." And maybe I sensed this was the most important part because I took his face in between my hands. "You never have. I feel safe with you. I need you to know that." I'd give him every piece of me before we were done—willingly. Gladly.

I could feel his fingers tangling with the laces of the corset, and I wondered if he'd rip them just like the buttons, but he worked deftly, those fingers freeing me from the fabric. Facing him, I didn't move to cover myself as he dropped the garment to the floor.

It wasn't like he hadn't already seen all of me.

I wasn't feeling shy anymore.

Zain swallowed roughly before lifting me into his hands and carrying me over to the bed.

My heels fell to the floor in loud clunks, and then I was sprawled out on the bed, my hair spread out around me. The tiara was still pinned in place, and I reached up to take it off, but Zain growled, his hand pinning me down.

"Leave it on. I want to see it when I fuck you. Nothing but *my* crown." He lifted my hand. "And my ring." The possession in his voice was clear, but it was hot.

Was it weird that I liked it? I wasn't sure there was anything Zain could do that I wouldn't like. He knew my body like the back of his hand—how to turn me on, how to bring me higher and higher.

He kissed the tops of my breasts, his tongue swirling over each of my nipples for just a moment before moving lower—lower. Then he was kneeling at the edge of the bed as his fingers slid into the waistband of my lace panties.

The sound of fabric ripping filled the air, and he looked up at me with a wicked grin as he tossed the scraps aside. Leaving me bare, spread out in front of him with nothing but his crown on my head. His eyes did a slow perusal of my body, the pure lust in them leaving nothing to the imagination.

Zain pried my thighs apart, positioning his head in between my legs before taking a long, languid lick at my entrance.

"Oh," I squeaked, because no matter how many times we did this, I didn't expect how good it would feel.

He stayed there for a moment, sucking on my clit and driving me wild, but stopped before I could come. A low whine slipped out from the back of my throat, but Zain silenced me with a sloppy kiss, letting me taste myself on his tongue.

"I need to be inside of you," he groaned. "It won't be soft or sweet. I—"

"You can be rough with me," I said, meaning it. My fingers fumbled with his buttons, helping him push his shirt off, and then his dress pants quickly followed, and he was climbing on top of me on the bed, giving me exactly what I wanted. "Break me. *Ruin me.*" The words were uttered against his mouth, our faces barely an inch apart.

"You're the one who has ruined me," Zain said, pulling my body to his so he could plunge into my mouth deeper, our tongues tangling.

Gently pushing me onto my back, Zain pushed inside me with no warning, and my eyes practically rolled into the back of my head from the fit of him. My hand splayed over my stomach, feeling the warmth of his cock nestled inside of me.

And everything else faded away. I let myself drown in the sensations of his body thrusting into mine, fast and hard, as he fucked me. It was primal, and my hips couldn't stop rising, moving to meet his as he plunged into me.

"I'm close—" I gasped. When had I been able to come like this?

Maybe it was the aphrodisiac in the wine. He wasn't even touching my clit, but the stretch, the rapid pace, all of it was bringing me right up to the edge quickly. Too quickly.

Gripping the sheets, I shattered, his name on my lips as I came, feeling like I was having an out-of-body experience even as Zain followed behind me a few moments later.

Breathing heavily, he moved off of me carefully as if he was trying not to crush me with his weight, pulling out of me once our erratic heart rates had calmed.

My body should have been sated, but I still wanted more. I turned to face him, but he was already looking at me, an expression of surprise on his face.

"Luna," Zain said, *mesmerized.* "You're glowing."

"I—" I blinked a few times, but there was an incandescent sheen to my body. I wouldn't go so far as to say I was literally glowing, but it was hard to deny the truth. "This has never happened before."

Removing my hands from the sheets, I looked at my palms. "Is this… my magic?" I worried my lower lip into my mouth. Why had it never manifested this way before? I couldn't help but feel grateful, though. At least no one else had ever seen this. If every orgasm made my skin light up, I would have *died* of mortification.

"Appears so," he chuckled. "Look at you, so fucking beautiful. You shine so bright. Brighter than the moon."

His words made me melt. Zain bent down to kiss me, his hips settling inside my still-parted legs. The brush of his cock—already hard again— against my core sent a jolt through my body, and I squirmed against him. I didn't care if it was the spiked wine talking. I'd take everything I could get tonight.

He shifted, resting his back against the headboard, and I straddled his lap, my arms wrapping around his neck. I ran my fingers through the back of his head, combing through his hair as I rocked against his length, enjoying the feeling as it ground against my clit.

"Luna," he murmured, throat swallowing roughly. He brushed a strand of my hair off my shoulder, exposing my shoulders, dotted with little freckles, my collarbones—my neck. "Fuck, you look like…"

"What?" I batted my eyelashes.

"*Mine*," he growled, the motion exposing his teeth. Those two extra sharp canines. He ran his tongue over them, and I wondered how it would feel if he used them on me. "You look like mine."

"I am," I agreed. "I'm yours."

He kissed my neck, taking a deep pull of my scent. "Will you let me mark you?"

I pulled away, looking down at him. His eyes raised to meet mine from underneath his gorgeous eyelashes—it was really unfair that men got such nice ones—and his expression didn't waiver.

"Mark me?"

His nose nuzzled against the soft skin between my shoulder and throat, and he hummed, the vibration going straight to my clit. "Mhm. It's what we do to claim our mate. So everyone knows that you're mine."

I froze. *Mate?*

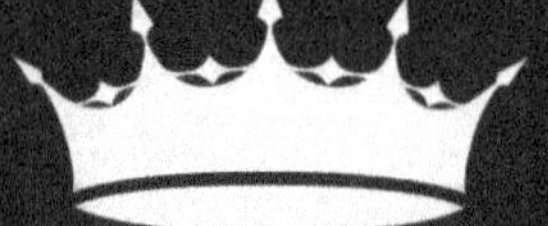

TWENTY-TWO
ZAIN

She had to know who we were to each other, didn't she? Why I'd been unable to get her out of my thoughts since the moment I'd laid eyes on her. Why I'd come for her in the first place.

You know me. Just like I've known you. Maybe my whole life.

"Luna. You're my mate." Reaching for her hand, I interlaced our fingers.

I wondered if she'd sensed it. What was going through her mind?

Demons knew what the signs were. We were taught from a very young age what it was like to find your fated mate—the person who was born for you. I'd never imagined that fate would have brought me to the human realm. To Pleasant Grove. To her.

My queen. My mate.

"You were made for me. You're everything I've ever wanted," I said, voice low against her neck. "Everything I've ever needed."

I wanted to mark her, to claim her, to *breed* her, to take everything I wanted and never let go. But only if she wanted that, too.

"You're… we're…"

"Mates."

"Right." Luna's breath was ragged. She couldn't say the word. Still. Even knowing what was between us. "Is that… why we can speak mind-to-mind?"

"Yes. Did you not suspect?" I asked, wrapping my hands around her waist to bring her tighter against my body.

"I…" Luna shook her head. "I mean, I knew there was something between us… Something more than lust or the physical connection, but I…" She glanced up to the ceiling. "Willow told me about how it was with her and Damien. I'd only guessed."

"I should have said something earlier," I said, gritting my teeth.

"Why didn't you?"

"I didn't want to ruin this. If there was a chance you didn't want me, that you wouldn't stay…" Then I wouldn't have forced her to.

But now, she couldn't run. We were tied together inexplicably. If we didn't complete the bond, it would be painful for both of us.

"Oh." Her hands tightened in my hair. "Did you think I would leave you?"

"I wanted you to choose me, not to be forced or without a decision. But I'm a selfish bastard, Luna. You deserve so much better than me."

"No." Her voice was quiet, and she moved her hands to cradle my cheeks. My eyes drifted shut, savoring her touch.

My *mate's* touch.

Her forehead rested against mine. "How do you do it?"

"The claiming? I'd bite you. Here." I brought my hand up to her neck, tracing over the veins. "Marking has to do with scents, but it merges ours together." A simplified version.

"Does it hurt?" Luna's eyes were wide.

"Maybe at first. Damien told me it's pleasurable, though. He said—"

Luna held up a hand, scrunching up her nose. "I do *not* need to hear about your brother and my sister."

I chuckled. "Fair enough. I won't suck your blood. But it will make me…" I resisted rocking against her, the feeling of her bare pussy sliding over my dick making me half mad already. "Unable to stop."

"Haven't I already proved to you I don't *want* you to stop?" She kissed me softly. "That I need you as much as you need me?"

"Impossible," I groaned. "There's no way that you feel like this. Like—" Like nothing mattered but her. That I'd forsake the whole damn kingdom just for her. She was my *everything*.

I kissed her again so I didn't spill my entire soul, a strangled curse slipping from my lips as she squirmed on top of me.

Fuck, the effects of the wine were strong. Was it always like this?

But maybe it was just her, the very essence of her thrumming in my veins, needing to get closer, closer. Our powers merging, strengthening both of us.

"Luna," I moaned. "Need you. Need *this*."

She bared her neck to me in invitation. "Then claim me," she whispered, guiding my mouth to her neck. "*Please*."

Parting my lips, I let my tongue run over the spot, sucking it into my mouth lightly. "I'll never give you up."

Luna let out a low moan as I scraped my teeth over the spot, my fingers moving down to her clit, making sure she was ready for me again. I circled the spot as I teased her neck, little nips without breaking the skin.

"Don't tease me," she begged. "I need you inside me. Please."

I couldn't say no to her. "My mate," I muttered against her skin as I guided my length inside of her, relishing in the tight fit.

When I sank my teeth into her at the same moment, she cried out my name. We were so loud, I wondered how the entire palace didn't hear it. Not that I cared.

Let them hear me making my wife scream in pleasure. No one else would ever touch her again.

Her arms were wound tight around me, my hands tight on her hips as she rocked against me slowly. My mouth was still planted on her when she dipped her head down to mine, kissing the same spot on my neck.

But I couldn't let go. Couldn't focus on anything but her moans as she worked her hips, nestled in my lap like she belonged nowhere but there—her throne.

"Zain," she cried out, and I released my grip on her neck, running my tongue over the mark to seal it with my magic.

She dropped her head back, eyes squeezing shut as she moved her hips faster, grinding on top of me, those hands moving to grip my shoulders, her nails digging in. In that moment, I didn't care if she marked *me*, if she drew blood, because she was mine and I was hers, and nothing else mattered.

"My mate," I groaned. "My wife."

"Yours," she agreed, and I brought our lips together, kissing her deeply as we both chased our own climax.

And she shattered, light spilling out of her—truly a star in her own right.

I was close behind, my instincts urging me to pour my seed inside of her, to fill her up till she was completely full of my cum. "Fuck." I splayed my hand out over her stomach. "I want to see you swollen with our child."

Her hips stilled like her entire body was frozen. "You, ah—what?"

"Shit." I buried my head in between her breasts, nuzzling my nose against her soft, porcelain skin. "I know we haven't talked about it, but… you do want children, right?"

We'd talked about it that first night, looking up at the stars. I knew she wanted to have kids, but I didn't know if she wanted them with *me*.

"I do." She ran her fingers through my hair. "Do you?" Her words were soft.

"I'll need an heir," I choked out. But that wasn't my answer, not really. "Before I met you, I'd never let myself even dream about this. About what our future might look like. I figured the likelihood of me having any kids was small." I ran my hands up her back, a light touch that had her shuddering under it. "But I can't stop thinking about what it would be like. To have a little girl who looks just like her mom."

"Zain." When I looked up into Luna's eyes, they were filled with tears. "That's—"

"We can wait if you want. You can start on the herbal tea that some use to prevent pregnancy tomorrow if you're not ready. But…"

She shook her head. "I don't want to be on anything. Besides, I think the time for that has passed." Luna pressed a kiss over my heart. "So what are you waiting for, husband?"

Pulling out, I moved us till she was on her back, her head cushioned by the pillows. Before I could second guess it, I added another one under her, helping angle her hips.

My hand rested over her stomach. "Are you going to be a good girl and let me put a baby in you, Luna?"

"*Yes.*" She whimpered, nodding as I nudged her knees apart with mine before throwing one of her legs over my shoulder.

I plunged back inside, squeezing my eyes shut as I tried not to focus on how good it felt inside of her. How deep I was at this angle, like I'd found fucking paradise, and I didn't want this to be over. Not yet.

Luna ran her fingers up my spine, distracting me. "Your wings… Can you summon them at will?"

"Yes," I grunted the word as she squeezed around my length. "Why?"

"Let me see them," she whispered. "Let me see *you.*"

"You…" My voice caught in my throat. I'd never bedded someone with them out, period.

They were a reminder of who I was—what I'd lost. Sometimes it was easier to wear the face of the asshole crown prince without them looking back at me. The son of the Demon King and the bride he'd stolen—a fallen angel.

Her face was filled with so much emotion that I couldn't help but obey.

I let the magic ripple out of me, my dark wings unfurling from my shoulder blades as shadows spilled around me. They were as much a part of me as any of my physical features—the powers I'd inherited from my father.

Luna's fingers ran over the feathers, her face completely mesmerized. "Gods." Her tone was reverent. No one had ever touched me like this before, the underside of my wings extra sensitive.

"My name." I rasped, thrusting *hard*. "You say my name when I'm fucking you." My hair fell onto my forehead, sweat dotting my brow, but I couldn't be bothered to stop to brush it off my face.

The feeling of her touching my wings, her expression, looking at me with so much tenderness… all of it made me shudder. But maybe it was just *her* touch that lit me up inside, that brought me into the light like no one ever had before.

She gasped as I filled her to the hilt, the sound of our flesh and her cries the only thing you could hear in the room. "*Zain.*"

"I know, baby. *Fuck.*" Her legs wrapped around my waist, forcing me in deeper. I dipped my mouth down to her ear, capturing an earlobe with my teeth and tugging it. "Do you think you can come again?" The words were a rasp, but I needed it. Needed to feel her squeezing my cock, milking me for everything I was worth.

"I—" She shook her head, her breaths coming out in pants as she searched for words. *It's too much.*

You can take it, I said against her mind.

The feeling of being connected to her like this, feeling the bond flowing through us—it was more than I could have ever asked for. I pushed all of those feelings through it. Did she feel our connection the way I did? I fucking hoped so.

Give it to me, Moonbeam.

My magic wrapped around her like a caress, invisible hands running over her body, teasing her nipples, a brush over her clit—and then she shattered, glowing brighter than all the stars in the night sky.

Fuck, if that wasn't satisfying. To know that I could do that to her. To know that she did the same thing to me.

"That's my girl," I said against her forehead, continuing to fuck her through it. "My wife. My queen. My mate."

Her hand splayed over her abdomen. "Fill me up, my mate," she begged. "I want your cum."

Fuck. Hearing those words from her lips was almost too much. I leaned down, taking her mouth with mine.

"Does my little wife want me to breed her?"

Kissing her again, our tongues meeting in an endless war of pleasure, and I was lost to the sensation. The feeling of her tight cunt milking my cock. Begging me for it.

Lightning crackled outside, the thunder shaking the room as I roared my release, emptying inside of her, painting her womb with my cum.

Rolling her onto our sides, I shifted our positions so that I wouldn't crush her with my weight, my wings folding behind me.

She blinked, looking out the window. "Did we just…"

I smirked, kissing her softly. My body was still wrapped around hers. "Looks like we need to see what those powers of yours can do, hm?"

"Maybe tomorrow." She yawned.

I moved to pull out, but Luna tightened her legs around my waist, keeping me in place. "Can we just stay here like this?" Her words were a soft murmur as she nestled into my arms.

We were a boneless, sweaty mess, but I couldn't complain. She peeked up at me, those big green eyes, and fuck. I was a goner.

Because I had the girl—right where I wanted her.

My cock was already hardening again inside of her, but I burrowed my face in her neck, inhaling her citrusy, floral scent. Lemon and lavender. I couldn't get enough of it. It soothed me down to my soul.

She took every jagged edge of me and made me want to be whole. For *her*.

And I wanted—*Fuck*, I wanted *everything*.

With her. Always with her.

Even if I knew I didn't deserve it.

TWENTY-THREE
LUNA

My fingers ran over the bite mark he'd left behind. It almost felt like I could see the bond between us, that shimmering cord of moonlit silk.

Mates. Maybe I'd known all along, but I'd been in denial. Because how could a man this powerful—this wonderful—be my soulmate? He was a prince, a *demon,* and I was just… a witch who didn't even know how to control her powers.

My *magic.* I could feel it thrumming through my veins, even now. Letting Zain mark me, dropping my barriers—it had unlocked something inside of me. That much, I was sure of.

Maybe I could move forward now—to find out who I was. What I was made for.

My wife. My queen. My mate. I was all of those things, but also I was still me. Luna Clarke, daughter of witches. Baker. Hopeless romantic. Avid reader.

I would learn to love this part of me, too.

Just like I was learning to love him.

Though maybe I'd never needed to learn. There was always a part of me that knew—from the moment I'd met him at the bar, and we'd lain side by side together in the grass under the stars—that if I let him into my life, I could love him.

Terrifying parts and all. The demon parts of him should have scared me, but he was beautiful. Like my dark angel. He'd done nothing but show me, over and over, that he would keep me safe. That he would protect me.

I swept my eyes over Zain's face, taking in his sleeping features. His chest rose and fell steadily. And maybe that was why, for the first time, I reached out. Let my walls down, my mind unguarded.

And I cupped his cheek. Pushed forward with my magic.

Golden eyes. Dark hair. Wings. A little boy that looked just like Zain. A little girl that looked just like me. Lavender eyes. Laughter. There was happiness. Sadness, too. But that didn't all have to be bad.

A future. *Ours,* if it came to pass. I practically cried at the thought. I'd been seeing our future all along, and I had shut myself off from the idea.

"You're awake." He blinked up at me, reaching out a hand to brush through my hair. Zain frowned, as if taking in my face. "Are you okay?"

I nodded, trying to force the tears away. "They're good tears."

His thumb swiped underneath my eyes, catching the unshed emotion. "Are you sure? Last night wasn't…"

"It was perfect," I answered, feeling the truth of my statement with every part of my being.

Zain kissed my neck. "Do you want breakfast?"

I didn't know if it was the wine, but we'd been unable to keep our hands off of each other since yesterday. I wasn't sure how we'd gotten any sleep at all. Every time we'd finished, it had only taken a few moments before we were both all over each other again.

I was ravenous. Hungry, but not for food.

"I can think of something else that sounds even better," I murmured, straddling his lap.

During the night, his wings had disappeared, and disappointment flowed through me. I liked the reminder of who he was. How powerful yet soft he could be. It was a dichotomy, just like him.

"Down, girl," he murmured as I pressed a kiss to his bare chest. "I need to feed my wife."

My cheeks were warm. "I can't believe we're actually married." But the rings still sat on my finger. I raised my hand to look at it, and Zain put his hand on top, interlocking our fingers. So I could see his ring, too like we were claiming each other.

"Was it everything you ever imagined?"

I laughed. "Honestly? No."

Zain frowned. "Really? But I thought…"

I took his hands in mine. Squeezed them. "It was wonderful. Beautiful. I promise. I can tell you put a lot of thought into it."

"Then what was wrong?"

A snort escaped me, which turned into a full-body laugh. "Nothing was wrong. I loved every minute. But I never pictured getting married like this, and certainly not to a *demon*. It's been a whirlwind." Incredible but *crazy*.

Zain looked sheepish as he admitted, "Willow helped me, you know."

Nodding, I drew circles over his bare chest. "She told me about it when she got here. When did you even have time to do all of this, though?"

"It was last week. After we talked. I realized I hadn't been present enough and didn't want to be that kind of husband to you. And also, I didn't want you to regret this, so I stopped in for a visit." He rolled his eyes. "Damien wasn't pleased."

"Oh." My eyes grew damp. "Thank you."

"It was nothing."

Except, to me, it was *everything*.

I shook my head. "You don't even know how wonderful you are, do you?"

"Only for you," Zain said, wrapping his arms around me and burying his head in my neck. I burrowed in, savoring every moment of the bear hug. Gods, there was no feeling quite like being in his arms.

"I have another surprise for you," Zain whispered. "*After* you eat something."

"Bribery, on day two?" I gasped. "But fine. I suppose I've worked up an appetite."

He grinned. "I'll go get the food." Untangling himself from me, he stood up—stark naked. He stretched his arms, giving me an eyeful of the muscles in his back flexing—and his bare ass.

Gods, it was a nice ass. I wanted to sink my teeth into it.

"Luna."

"Hmm?"

"Stop salivating over your husband." He turned, winking at me. "And you might want to put something on before anyone comes in here."

I flushed, looking down at my body, at all the marks he'd left on me last night. Without seeing it, I knew the little bite mark was visible on my neck.

Grumbling, I went to his closet to slide on one of his luxurious black robes, embroidered with a small golden Z.

I was claiming them all as mine now.

Happy to see he'd put on some pants before disappearing, I sat on the chaise lounge and waited for him to return.

Did he have to be so *distracting?*

He reached over the table and fiddled with my hair as I took a bite of the egg dish. My eyes trailed down to his bare chest. He'd pulled on a black shirt but left it open, giving me a full view of the abdomen that seemed like it was sculpted by the Gods themselves. Damn, how was he my *husband?*

Zain smirked like he'd caught me checking him out *again*. Damn demon husband and his fast senses. Though if I was being honest, mine also felt sharper than before. Heightened. Maybe it was the power in my blood.

"Are you going to tell me your surprise yet?" I asked, raising an eyebrow and setting my fork down.

Zain's head bobbed in a nod. "Yes. I actually meant to take you there last night, but one thing led to another, and…"

"You couldn't keep your hands off me?" I sassed, but there was no bite behind the remark. Not when I'd *liked* it.

When I'd let him claim me. *Breed* me. The mark thrummed, even under my soft robe, as if in a reminder of what he'd done.

He cleared his throat. "Something like that. I want to take you somewhere."

"Okay." My answer was instant. "Like a… honeymoon?" Maybe because I'd barely seen this world besides the palace, but going somewhere else sounded amazing.

Plus, if we were alone together, I wouldn't have to worry about anyone overhearing us. Heat flooded my cheeks at the thought.

Zain's rough chuckle ran a shiver down my spine. "Something like that."

"Let's go," I answered, not even bothering to finish my food.

He frowned, scooping up my fork and putting another bite on it himself before offering it to me. "Finish eating first."

I closed my lips around the fork, watching his satisfied expression as I ate, feeling the purr in his chest. Did he think I was a baby bird that needed to be fed?

"I'm not that hungry," I murmured, quickly finishing my food and gulping down the liquid at my side. Part of me wished I had one of Willow's amazing mochas and a scone.

My fingers itched to bake. Hopefully, his surprise had a kitchen.

"Can we go now?" I asked after my plate was cleared.

He looked me up and down, heat burning in his gaze. "Maybe let's get you dressed first, wife. No need of anyone else seeing what's mine."

I looked down at the robe. I hadn't bothered to put anything else on underneath, after all. A smirk crossed my lips. "Possessive, much?"

Zain made a low noise in his throat, and I practically leapt from my chair. The laughter that bubbled out of me as I ran to my closet, with Zain hot on my heels, couldn't be contained.

It was joyous and *free* in a way I hadn't felt in years.

* * *

"What is this place?" I removed my arms from Zain's waist, allowing him to steady me after we teleported out of the palace to another, *smaller* palace.

I'd changed out of my robe and into a surprisingly soft sweater and leggings since Zain insisted I didn't need to wear any formal clothing or dress. Being comfortable was perfectly fine with me, especially after last night. I was sore all over and trying not to wince.

"I come here when I want to be alone," he said with a shrug. "You didn't think I spent all my time in the palace, did you?"

Part of me wondered if he'd come here in the last few weeks to escape. Did he feel like he needed to hide from me? The idea didn't sit well with me, so I tried to brush it off. I liked this happy bubble we were in—I didn't want it to burst.

"Hey." He tilted up my chin to bring our eyes together. "It's home now. For *both* of us."

"Please don't leave me alone again?" I choked out the words, unsure why I was suddenly so emotional.

"Never." He dropped a kiss to my lips. "Want to see it?"

I nodded. With a grin, Zain swept me into his arms and carried me in a bridal hold over the threshold.

Our tour wasn't very long—despite the outward appearance, it wasn't much larger than the house I'd grown up in.

We reached the bedroom—singular, which made sense—we *were* married now. And *mated,* if the mark on my neck meant anything. What did it mean to the demons? Witches didn't place that much weight on soulmates because the chances of finding yours were small.

But it was different between us. More sacred.

Looking around the room, I had to blink a few times before the sight registered. A gasp slipped from my lips. "What's all my stuff doing here?"

Everything from my apartment was here: my blanket collection, my crystals, and even my collection of romance books.

He did his best to look a little bashful. "I brought it all here."

"You did? When?"

Zain looked away, mumbling something under his breath.

"What was that?" I poked at his chest.

"Last week. When I went to see Willow." He ran his hands through his already messy hair, avoiding eye contact. "I hoped, well… that you wouldn't want to go back. That you'd want to stay with me. Did I overstep?"

"Zain." I took his hands between my face. "I said yes too, you know. Even if we went into this for different reasons, I'm *here*. I'm not going to leave you."

Because deep down, the feeling that he was my home was settling in my gut. How could he expect me to give him up when I finally had him—all of him?

He inhaled deeply through his nose like he was doing his best to gather my scent. "Fuck." He growled. "You smell so good."

"Yeah?" I bit my lip, looking up at him. "What do I smell like?"

"Mine."

I wrapped my arms around his neck. "So, did you have specific plans for us sneaking away from the palace, or can we spend the next weekend in bed?"

His breath was hot against my neck as he said, "I promised to put a baby in you, didn't I?"

"Mmm." I hummed in response. "Did you want to get started now, or…"

I laughed as he threw me over his shoulder, carrying me over to the bed and doing just that.

TWENTY-FOUR
LUNA

Part of me never wanted to leave this bed. Because it felt like *ours*, and it was the most comfortable thing I'd ever laid on. Except…

"Do you want to learn how your powers work today?" Zain asked, interlacing his fingers through mine. "There's a field past the back gardens here. I thought we could *experiment* there."

"I…" I hesitated. Why did I feel so weak admitting this? "I'm a little scared," I whispered, doing my best to avoid his gaze as I exposed my deepest shame. "What if I hurt you?"

"You can't. And besides, did I not tell you I would protect you?" My husband said, his soothing tone doing everything to calm my beating heart. "If that includes from yourself, I will do it."

"Zain…"

Instead of responding, he brought our lips together in a soft kiss.

"You were born to be mine," he said, rubbing his nose against mine. "My queen. My equal. I believe that. And whatever powers the fates gave you, even if your only parlor trick is iridescent skin, I don't care. I just want you."

Nodding, I let my eyes flutter shut. "I know."

I could feel that.

Now, if only I could figure out exactly how to wield my magic, everything would be perfect.

* * *

"Show me what you've got," Zain instructed an hour later, after we'd bathed, had a quick lunch, and re-dressed. The room smelled like sex—our scents mixed, his spicy one overwhelming my senses with need—which was another reason we needed to get outside. We were insatiable, and it didn't even have to do with the wine anymore. No, that was all him.

I'd pulled on a pair of pants and a loose-fitting blouse—because there was no way I was attempting to use my powers in any of those pretty dresses that hung in my closet. There were more here, all seeming to be perfectly my size. He really had thought of everything.

"You're thinking too hard," Zain called, crossing his arms over his chest. He'd thrown on a black, billowy shirt and black pants, and I was trying really hard not to compare him to all the romance heroes—my guilty pleasures.

And yet, Zain won every time.

"Am not," I protested, though I had to bite back my snarky reply that I was thinking too hard about *him,* and the delicious soreness between my legs was an all-too-constant reminder of how many times he'd taken me last night. We'd fall asleep and then wake up and do it all over again.

I didn't know if his stamina resulted from the wedding, but I hadn't complained. Not when I'd lost track of the amount of orgasms he'd given me or from the lightning strikes lighting up our window as he relentlessly poured into me.

Or how I'd begged him to put a baby in me, over and over. I'd never thought I had a breeding kink before, but when a man like him asked you to have his child, why would you ever say *no?*

"Luna."

My cheeks were warm, and I turned away, staring up at the reddish sun.

If I'd ever thought this place was hell, I was truly wrong. Demons lived in a mostly civilized society—though there were still some races that liked to go rogue. Like the ones who'd been in Pleasant Grove that day. I still had nightmares from that night, watching them drag Zain's lifeless body away from me, dozens of them overpowering him—

"Sorry. What?" I whipped my head back to meet his gaze.

"We don't have to do this now, you know. If you're not ready."

"I want to be strong enough. To protect myself." He opened his mouth, and I finished before he could start. "I know you said you'd keep me safe. And I lo—" I stopped myself before the word could slip out. "—appreciate that. But my whole life, someone else has always kept me sheltered. Even Willow gave up her own life for me. So I have to take control of my destiny now."

I didn't want to cower in fear if I ever ran into one of those demon monsters again. Because that was what they were. *Monsters.* They didn't have the same cognitive functions as demons like Zain and Damien or the countless other residents of the palace.

"I don't want to be scared anymore."

A small grin lit up his face as he saw my resolve. "Then let's see what you can do."

I nodded, looking down at my palms. All I'd ever succeeded at doing was making light appear in my hands. How did I do that again?

"Even if you fail, no one's watching you, Moonbeam. It's just us out here." Zain rubbed a hand down my spine in encouragement. "Close your eyes and picture the magic flowing through your veins."

I did as he said. It was easier after last night, somehow. It felt like I'd awoken a different side of me. Visualizing the pathways in my body that the power flowed through. All I had to do was let it out, right?

Zain's presence brushed up against my mind—a reminder that he was here.

Shape it, he said, his thoughts like a caress against my spine. *Turn it into whatever you desire.*

Was it that easy? Sure, I'd been using my magic my whole life. I'd levitated bowls and stirred spoons, all without ever blinking an eye. I knew how to do those things like the back of my hand. It was natural.

This power felt foreign. It was mine, but it was also... *his.* The glimmering thread of white stretched between us.

"Do you feel that?" I whispered as if it was something I could grab onto and tangibly hold.

"Feel *you?*" He practically purred. "Open your eyes, Luna."

I did, and in the center of my palm was a white ball of light. Tiny— maybe nothing more than a parlor trick, but... it *was* a tangible, physical manifestation of my power—more than just light filtering through my skin.

"What do I do with it?"

Zain raised an eyebrow. "What do you *want* to do?"

"I don't know." I rolled my eyes, the power flickering out. "A little sphere isn't very helpful." Maybe if it was bigger…

A smirk crossed his face, and he summoned two shadowy forms. "See if you can hit them," he said, stepping aside.

Training dummies. He'd just used his power to make me *training dummies.*

"What if I miss?" I swallowed roughly.

"The gardens will regrow," he said with a laugh. "And if you hit someone, then we'll know what you can do."

"Zain!" I exclaimed. "I'm not trying to hurt your people."

He was across the field in a second, pressing our hands together against my heart. "*Our* people, Moonbeam. And you won't." A wicked gleam sparkled in his eyes. "I was assured no one would bother us."

"Okay." I gulped, and he stood at my back, his warmth bleeding into my body, washing away my apprehension.

I focused on the little ball of light in my palm, feeding it with more of the power that ran through me. What were my limits? I'd never done this before, and I was already curious how *much* of this magic I could use at once.

Feeding it more, it grew larger, to the size of a baseball, and then—a large, floating ball of light. *Moonlight.* Despite its appearance, it wasn't hot, but was almost… *cold.*

What was I supposed to do now? *Throw it?* Could you even throw a ball of light?

If Zain was listening to my thoughts, he didn't comment, but he mimicked me, gathering an orb of shadows—pure darkness—in his hands and then practically hurled it with lethal precision, crashing against one of the shadowy figures.

I did my best to copy him, though I didn't have any of the grace that his demonic body possessed. Maybe because he'd had three hundred years to perfect this while I'd spent the last twenty-something years burying it deep inside of me.

The orb missed, fizzling out on the grass. *Damn.* My cheeks heated, but this time in mortification. I'd never been a very good shot.

He made a circular motion with his finger. "Try again."

I nodded, repeating the process. Over and over and over again. Until finally, my blow landed, the shadowy form dissipating where my light hit it.

"Hm," Zain mused from my side. "*Interesting.*"

"What?" I blinked.

He shook his head. "Think you can try something different?"

I shrugged. "Worth a shot, right?"

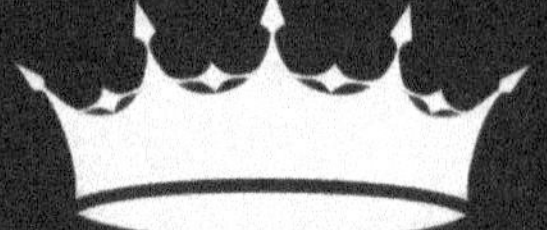

TWENTY-FIVE
ZAIN

She was magnificent. Her teeth gnawed on her lower lip, and her brow furrowed in concentration as she attacked the shadow dummies I'd summoned repeatedly.

The sweat formed on her brow as she worked on creating a beam of pure moonlight in her hands, directing it towards the shadows. There were a few patches of dead grass—iced over—from where her shots had missed, but I was fascinated by the light that poured out of her.

It was iridescent; the sheen containing a magnitude of colors like a rainbow, and yet, in the right hands… *Utterly lethal.*

This was why the fates had chosen her for me. Not only to rule by my side, to be the other half that brought me back into the light… But to be a power in her own right.

I didn't need to fight her battles. She could do that herself. She'd been fighting for the chance her whole life. Who was I to stop her?

No. I wouldn't hold her back. Not from fulfilling her destiny.

The destiny that we would fulfill together once we got back to the palace. If she was ready, and if I was. I felt stronger now—did I stand a chance?

"I think that's enough for the day," I said, watching as she panted, sweat soaking the thin blouse she'd worn. "You don't want to over-exert yourself."

"One more," Luna said, a look of concentration in her eyes.

All I could think was my mother would have loved this woman. *I* loved this woman.

My fierce, dedicated queen, who'd never shied away from whatever life had thrown at her. Every time I thought she'd draw the line or pull back, she'd surprised me.

Fuck, I loved her ferocity, the intensity with which she loved her sister. Every bit of her.

I watched as she let another bolt of light hit the shadowed form square in the chest and then wrapped my arms around her.

"Good job." I kissed her cheek.

She scoffed. "I think I hit the lawn more than anything else."

"It's a start." That was the important part. "And the lawn will grow back."

Her eyes twinkled as she looked back at me. "Thank you."

I scoffed. "You don't have to thank me. Don't forget, I forced you to come here with me." My tone was playful, even though I still doubted myself sometimes.

Luna whirled on me, wrapping her arms around my neck. "Don't say that." Her voice was soft. "I *wanted* to come with you."

"You did?" I raised an eyebrow.

She nodded, though the gesture was subdued. "Do I seem like the kind of person who does something that she doesn't want to do?"

"No."

"Exactly." She kissed me softly before adjusting our positions so she could interlace her hand with mine, leaning on me. "What's next?"

* * *

Even though I knew we needed to go back—to return to my responsibilities as crown prince and to all the different issues facing me at present—I couldn't bear to leave the peace that we'd found here. It finally felt *right*.

Like maybe things were working out exactly the way they needed to.

Could she love me?

Sometimes it felt like she did. When she looked up at me, with the brightest smile on her face, I let myself hope.

It wasn't something I'd ever considered before finding Luna. Ever since I'd lost my mother, I'd practically shut out the idea of falling in love with someone. No woman was worth the time or energy, not until her.

My mate.

We were walking back into the small palace from another round of lessons in the outside garden the next day.

I was delighted, feeling like a teenager holding a girl's hand for the first time. And in some ways, I was. Had I ever done this before? Holding someone's hand for no other reason than because I wanted to.

She was my first in every way that mattered.

"What?" Luna asked, looking over at me with that beautiful blush on her cheeks. "You're staring."

I smiled. "I'm *happy*. For the first time in my life, I'm just..." I shook my head. "You came into my life and burrowed your way into my heart. I don't think I can get you out."

She stood on her tiptoes to press a kiss to my cheek. "Then don't."

"Mmm." I tightened my grip on her hand, leading her further into the house.

"Where are we going?"

"I thought maybe you could show me what you've been getting up to in my library every afternoon." Of course, there was a unique set of books here, but I'd be happy to help her learn anything she wanted to know.

"Oh." Luna blushed. "You heard about that?"

I nodded. "Oh, I heard." Dipping my head down, I nipped at her neck. "I know about everything that goes on in the palace, wife."

"Maybe I just wanted to know more about you."

Unable to resist, I scooped her up into my arms, carrying her the rest of the way into my own private library. The one in the palace was where I'd taken solace growing up, losing myself in books. It'd been the only place my father wouldn't bother me.

"You can always ask," I said, chuckling as she giggled into my hold.

"Put me down," she laughed. "I can walk."

"Apparently I didn't fuck you good enough last night then, hm?" The words were low, muttered against her ear.

"Zain!" she scolded, like I'd scandalized her.

"There's no one around, Moonbeam." A wicked grin spread over my face. "Perks of the private house, huh? Besides, a husband has to satisfy his wife. The king has to take care of his queen."

She shook her head incredulously, but a little smile crept over her face.

I sat us down on one of the little sofas in the library, leaving Luna sprawled out over my lap.

"So... What is it you wish to know about me?"

Luna hummed in response. "I want to know *everything*."

"That's a tall order," I said, furrowing my brows. "You know how old I am, right?"

"Well..." She worried her lower lip into her mouth. "Will you tell me about your childhood? Your mother? Your friends, they mentioned some things, but..."

I nodded, my throat growing tight. "I lost her when I was young."

"Who was she?"

"She was a queen in her own right." My mother's face filled my vision. "You remind me of her, actually."

"I do?"

I brushed a hand over her hair. "She brought light into this place, too."

She'd been too good for this kingdom. Maybe that was why she hadn't thrived here. I always knew she loved me—that hadn't been a doubt in my mind, but she shriveled under my father's hand. Though I could never prove my father had lain a hand on her, the signs were all there.

He'd taken her power and left her to rot.

I'd do everything in my power to be nothing like him.

"You learned about different demons, right?" I'd seen the pile of books left on the desk one night and had looked over the titles.

"Yeah. I never knew how many types there were." She shifted her gaze away from mine. "In the modern world, witches aren't taught much about demons. It's not really a problem anymore, I guess. That's why I thought you were all tricksters, trying to steal our souls." Luna's cheeks flamed. "But you're not."

I laughed. "Well, there are still some who make deals, trying to swindle humans, but I do my best to provide for them, too." Luna's eyes shut as I ran my hand up and down her spine soothingly. "It's what my mom would have wanted. My father…" I struggled to find the right words, thinking about the last time I'd spoken with him. "The title of Demon King has a bloody history, and it's safe to say he didn't gain the crown by waiting for his father to give it to him. He took it." My teeth ground together. "And he took her."

"Your mother." Luna's voice was soft. Soothing. Grounding.

"Yes. She was too good for this place." I massaged the spot between my eyebrows. "She was never supposed to be here at all, actually."

"She wasn't a demon?" Luna's voice caught.

I chuckled. "No. The opposite, really." My wings unfurled behind me, and she ran her fingers over the feathers. I normally kept them hidden with my magic, but when she'd asked to see all of me, something had healed inside of me. "Have you not wondered? Why no other demons are like me?"

"Damien's a *cat*." Her face worked into an adorable little squint. "I suspended my disbelief in reality a *long* time ago."

"Shapeshifter," I corrected. "His mother could also shift into cat form. He inherited that from her."

"Right. They mentioned that. And yours was…"

"An angel. A rarity, especially for here. No demon had ever dared to take one for their queen before."

Luna's eyes widened. "She was *forced?*"

"Taken," I amended, though I wasn't sure my wife was wrong, either. "Though I believed she cared for my father in her own way."

"That's awful."

But had I not planned to do the same thing with her? To force her to my side, bind her to me as my queen, watch her swell with my child so she couldn't leave? It might have been the way things were done in the past, but I would make sure it wasn't how it continued in the future.

"They were mates." I shook my head. "But he didn't deserve her. He's not a good person, Luna." That was the understatement of the millennium.

"Then why is he still the Demon King?" She asked, her gaze meeting mine. "Has no one challenged him?"

"No." A rough sound emitted from my throat. "Because they can't."

"Why? You said it was a bloody history…"

A knot formed in my throat. "It's complicated." Because it was my crown to take. Because they weren't strong enough, just like I wasn't. Or… hadn't been.

"So help me understand. If I'm going to be by your side, I can't be left in the dark, Zain."

"What if I'm not a good person, either? Will you still stand by me?"

"I don't believe that's true."

Shaking my head, forced the words out. "It's my birthright. No one else can take it from me. I've given up everything for this kingdom. My father is the worst sort of demon, but the only person who can see the life drain from his eyes is me." I rubbed a spot on my forehead. "He knows that I'm the only one who can end his sorry existence. So he fights me at every opportunity, with every decision. Knowing that I won't back down. That I care too much."

"What did he do to you, Zain?" The softness in her voice startled me, and Luna cupped my cheeks, bringing our eyes together.

Those beautiful eyes shone into mine. Like she *believed* in me. Like I hadn't just told her I wanted to gut my father.

"You don't want to know." Flashes of my childhood flew through my mind. Abuse. Neglect. Memories I never wanted to relive. Memories I didn't want to give her because I knew the pain in her eyes was for me. "I had to be *perfect*."

I tried to explain it to her then. How Damien didn't get the brunt of it because he wasn't our father's heir. Because he always treated him like a bastard, as if it was Damien's fault that he'd gotten his mother pregnant. That the affair had resulted in a child.

My father had known no shortage of women. Had never wanted for anything. He'd bathed the world in blood before he took the crown, and everyone had been terrified to cross him. Because he was powerful—too powerful, and that was before he'd kidnapped my mother. Before he'd used the same mating ceremony, we had to marry their energies together.

And then he'd done nothing, watching the light slowly fade from her body. Her goodness had protected me—until she was gone, and I found out how cruel the world was.

When I finished talking, Luna brushed her hand against my face. "Sometimes people leave wounds, and even if the scars aren't visible, it doesn't mean they're not there," she said the words as if she could see them—the bruises, the scars, the way I'd bled. It felt like a bandage over my scarred heart.

"I heal fast," I muttered, the emotion on her face too much to bear.

"So why don't you end it?" She cupped my face. "Take the crown for yourself." Her eyes were burning with a ferocity I'd never seen before, like she was angry—for *me*.

"*Ruthless*," I muttered, dipping my head down to meet hers. "I didn't know my queen was so bloodthirsty."

"I don't like the idea of anyone hurting you," she admitted. "Even if he is your father."

I brushed a piece of hair behind her ear. "What if I told you there is a way to stop him? But I need your help?"

Her response was immediate. "I'll do it."

"Are you sure? I haven't even told you *how* yet."

"Have I not already proven that I'd do anything you asked?"

I leaned my forehead against hers. "I don't deserve you."

"Except you do. Because you're *good*," Luna insisted.

"No. But I'm trying to be. For you." My thumb rubbed over the marks I made on her neck, and her eyes flared.

"Zain." She whispered my name so softly that I wasn't sure I'd have heard her if not for the empty library. "What can I do? Where do I come into all of this?"

"I need you," I offered, the words never having been empty. "I've always meant that. I can't do this without you."

"You don't have to. I'm here."

That meant more than she could ever know. It was everything.

"When we married, a ceremony was performed."

She nodded. "Obviously." Luna held up her hand, wiggling her ring finger.

"No. I mean—it tied our life forces together. Our power."

"Our…" she blinked. "*Life forces?*"

I nodded, tracing a finger over the veins on her wrist. "Yes. It serves two purposes. For one, your power has lived dormant inside of you for all these years. But now, we share."

"How? I don't feel you… like, *inside me.*"

I quirked an eyebrow. Couldn't control the smirk that spread across my face. My little queen punched me in the shoulder. "I didn't mean it like that and you know it!"

Dipping down my head, I nipped at her lower lip. "If you wanted me inside of you, Moonbeam, all you had to do was ask."

Her cheeks were pink, but I cleared my throat. Refocusing my thoughts was hard, and not just because I was. "It's not like that, anyway. You can't use my powers, and I can't use yours. But being bonded, being *mated,* it changes our strength. Think of me as your backup source. An endless well of energy flows between us."

Luna scrunched her nose. "And this matters… how?"

"Only true mates can perform the ceremony successfully. Accepting the mating bond by letting me mark you—that cemented it even more. Now that we share our energies, I'm more powerful. And you are, too. I suspect that's why your powers are easier to use now. Alone, it still might not be enough to defeat him. But with you by my side…"

"You're asking me to help?" Her eyes widened.

I cupped the back of her neck. "Yes. I want your help. I need it, too. But if you don't want to, I can find another way."

"I'll do it. Of course I will."

I sighed, not liking what I had to say next. "We should go back soon, then. If we want to stop him…"

A sigh slipped from her lips. "I know."

But I couldn't help drawing her closer, holding her against me with everything I had. "But let me be selfish for a little while longer. To enjoy this bit of peace, if it's all we ever have."

Luna squeezed my hand. "We'll be okay, though, right?"

I wanted to say yes, but part of me was afraid to promise her something I didn't know. "You're the seer. You tell me. What's in our future?" I kissed her knuckles. "Everything's going to be different after, I promise."

Once the crown was in place on my head, when I ruled the demon realm in his stead…

Everything would be different.

TWENTY-SIX
LUNA

One afternoon turned into a day, and then two, and then I'd blinked, and a week had passed in this cozy little paradise of ours.

All I knew was I didn't want to leave. Didn't want this to end. Even though we both knew it had to. After our conversation in the library, the gravity of the situation had settled into me. But he'd been helping me train each day, and we lost ourselves in each other's bodies each night.

Selene was curled up on my feet as I rested my head on Zain's chest, content not to move out of bed.

He leaned over, brushing the hair off my shoulder and kissing my neck softly.

Especially with his ever-hardening erection underneath me. Maybe straddling his lap in the morning was a bad idea, which brought the other idea that had been pinging around my brain.

Zain pinched my hip. "What's going on in that head of yours?"

"There's something I want to try, but…" I blushed. "It's embarrassing."

"What, my queen?" His eyes flared, and I knew he could sense my arousal. "Asking for what you want should never be embarrassing. You know I'll always give it to you."

"I want you to wake me up by…" I shook my head. My face was on fire. Maybe my whole body. How far down could a blush go?

"Yes?" A smirk covered his face, but I knew he was just as interested as I was. Those golden eyes were pooled with desire, like liquid lust. "Use your words, wife."

I looked down at our hands, which were still interlocked. Maybe he was right. Maybe it didn't have to be embarrassing to ask. "I've always found the idea of being woken up with sex to be… really hot." Not that I'd ever tried it with anyone. I'd been too embarrassed to ask.

A low grumble sounded from his throat. "Is that what you want, then? Me to wake you up with my cock?" His hips jerked, the motion bumping against my clit. "Slide inside this wet pussy while you sleep?"

I moaned. "*Yes.*"

"But we're not asleep now," he said, a devilish expression on his face. "So, what do you want?"

Leaning down, I pressed a kiss to his collarbone. Trailed my tongue over his nipples, and let my hands explore his firm chest. Those abdominal muscles that could never be obtained at a gym. No, he was bred for strength, that lethal power he gave off in spades.

And he was soft, caring, and loving only for me. Something sparked in my chest, but I pushed it down. It was too soon, wasn't it?

"I want you," I said instead, helping him guide himself into me.

"And who am I?"

"Zain," I cried out as I slid down his shaft, impaling myself on his cock.

His hands captured my nipples, pinching them lightly. "Who am I?" My hands rested on his chest, the wedding ring sparkling up at me.

"*Husband,*" I moaned. Feeling too good.

"Good girl," he praised, like he enjoyed hearing the title slip from my lips as much as I liked saying it.

Fuck, that would never get old.

Did I have a praise kink, or did I just like it when *he* praised me? I couldn't think of any time when it had been like this. Thought I couldn't think about any other men when Zain erased the very thought of all of them in my mind. He'd ruined me for anyone else.

"You've ruined *me*," Zain said, hearing my thoughts. "There's no one but you."

"Good." Using my knees, I picked myself up before dropping back down on his shaft. Zain's large hand possessively sprawled over my stomach, like even now, I could be carrying something precious.

My eyes squeezed shut, only able to focus on the stretch, how deep he was, how he hit my womb with every thrust. His colossal size should have been impossible, but my body accepted him like I was made just for him.

"Mine," I muttered, completely mindless as I worked myself closer to my orgasm.

"*Yours,*" he agreed, and when my eyes found his, there was pure love shining in them.

Neither of us had said the words yet, but I knew I felt it. Was pretty sure he did, too.

And when I slipped over the edge, Zain following right behind me, I thought if this was what married life would be like…

I could have done a lot worse than marrying the prince of the demon realm.

* * *

"*Zain*." A breathy moan slipped from my lips as Zain's hands slid up my thighs, parting them to bare myself to him.

"*Fuck*," he groaned, inhaling deeply before running his tongue up my slit. "*You're so sweet, Moonbeam.*"

"*Yes*," I agreed, throwing my head back and clutching the sheets tightly as dream-Zain buried his tongue inside of me, lapping at my cunt. He was so talented with that godsdamn tongue. "But I need you inside of me," I begged.

"Luna." His tip pressed against my entrance. Zain slid inside of me, the stretch of his cock as he sheathed himself inside of me, the grip of his fingers on my thighs as he spread me apart—all of it was too good. "Fuck, Luna. You're always so tight."

Wicked. Filthy. I'd never had such a dirty dream, but I liked it.

His breath was warm against my ear. "Wake up, Moonbeam. See how well you're taking my cock."

"Zain," I whimpered. My eyes were still squeezed shut because I so desperately wanted to stay in this moment. I didn't want to wake up—not yet.

"Luna," he groaned, thrusting harder. "I need you to wake up, baby."

Then his lips were on mine, and I let my eyes flutter open, kissing him with restless abandon—not caring about morning breath or my current appearance. All I could focus on was how good it felt waking up to him sliding inside of me.

"Oh, *fuck*." I gasped as he rocked his hips into mine, sending bolts of pleasure down my spine.

"Good?" He asked, keeping up that steady rhythm.

"So good." I mewled. My hips rose to meet his, and then he was shoving a pillow underneath them, burying himself deeper inside of me.

I cried, my mewls filling the room.

Zain kissed me softly. "Shh, baby. I'm going to fuck you until I can make sure that you're pregnant." His eyes were full of lust as he nipped at my neck. "Until you're growing my baby inside of you. I want you all round and swollen for me."

Yes. Yes, I wanted that. To be connected to him this way, to know his child was growing inside of me—our child.

How had I ever thought this could be temporary? From the moment I'd agreed to marry him, I should have known it would end up like this, with me so desperate to give him everything he asked for.

"Give it to me," I begged. "Give me your cum. Fill me up." I dug my fingernails into his shoulder as I wrapped my legs around his waist, forcing him in deeper.

His tip kissed the top of my cervix, and I was so impossibly full. No one had ever done the things to my body that he could. To work me up so fast, coax orgasm after orgasm out of me. From the first moment I'd laid eyes on him in the bar, every inch of him had screamed out to me. *Mine.* That tiny possessive voice in my brain had been there all along, hadn't it?

"So deep." A whimper slipped from my lips. "You-you're *so* deep." The stretch I felt from his cock was like nothing else in this world. He was big, impossibly so, and it would never feel like this with anyone else. Like he truly was made for me.

Fuck, why was it always so good? Zain could build me up and break me over and over, and I wouldn't care. Wouldn't complain. I clenched around him, and he groaned.

His body poised over mine, sweat dotting his brow as dark strands fell across his forehead. "*Fuck,* you're so tight. I can't wait to pump you full of my seed."

He rested his forehead against mine like we had to be as close as possible together.

I nodded, letting out a string of incoherent words and breathy moans because all I could feel, all I could see—was Zain.

My husband. My mate. The only man I'd ever loved.

Because, *fuck.* I loved him. Didn't I? There was no other way to explain the warmth in my chest—the vise grip he had around my heart. I'd never known I'd needed him, but now I couldn't imagine life without him.

Just that thought was enough to get me close to the edge, just a little more, and I'd be there.

"Need you to get there first," he said, nipping at my ear. "Gotta feel you clenching around my cock."

"Zain," I cried. "I need—"

Lightning sparked in his golden eyes as he gave me a wicked smirk. "I know. I know what you need." He pounded into me relentlessly. Bringing me closer to that edge with each stroke. Zain reached down, brushing his thumb over my clit, sending little sparks into me with his power.

Oh. *Oh. Fuck, that was—*

"My wife," he growled. "My mate. Mine."

"*Yours,*" I agreed, letting out a deep moan as Zain kept rubbing circles over that bundle of nerves. Each shock of electricity was too much, and I couldn't hold myself back, letting my climax burst out of me like a shooting star.

Warmth flowed into me as he spilled inside of me, pouring his seed into my womb as promised.

How many times had I let him come inside of me since we'd begun this? What were the chances I wasn't already pregnant?

"Mm. Zain." My eyes fluttered shut as he wrapped his arms around me, holding our bodies tight together, staying buried deep inside of me.

"What did I do to deserve you?" He murmured into my ear. "You're too good for me."

"Oh. Handsome." I reached my hand up to brush his cheek. "You don't think that's true, do you?"

He nodded, our foreheads rubbing together. "You're light, Luna. So pure." Zain reached his hands up, running his hands through my tangled hair. "And I'm just..." A rough laugh came from his throat. He shook his head. "Fuck. I don't know how to do this."

"Don't think that way," I said, voice soft. "Ever since we met, all I've ever felt is safe. All you have to be is yourself, Zain. That's all I want. Not the scary demon prince I see you pretend to be, or anyone else. I just want you to be comfortable to tell me whatever you're feeling."

He leaned down, kissing me softly, our tongues tangling lazily.

"Zain," I protested, feeling him hardening inside of me already. "We should really—"

"Mmm," he hummed, ignoring me and kissing me again. "Let me have this."

He coaxed my body into another orgasm, dragging me down with him into pure bliss.

Finally, after carrying me into the bath, we got ready for the day.

I was practically floating on air, feeling that same warm feeling in my chest whenever I thought about Zain and his early morning confessions, how he'd listened to me, to what I wanted.

But was it enough? Or was I just deluding myself into thinking I could be happy here?

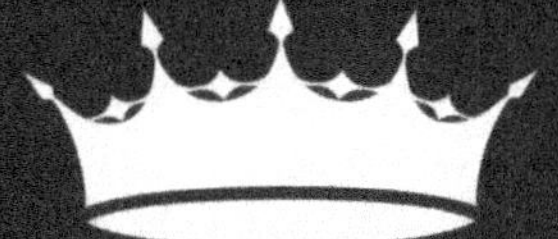

TWENTY-SEVEN
ZAIN

We left the next morning, saying goodbye to the lovely estate we'd spent a week relearning each other. It was like those first nights together in her apartment in Pleasant Grove, where we asked each other anything and everything.

It felt like maybe this was going to work. That even when everything fell apart, I'd still have her by my side.

Immediately after teleporting back, I was pulled into meeting after meeting, and all the work that had piled up over the last week needed to be done. Truly, ruling was a lot of monotonous decisions, as I tried to put our people's interests before my own.

We attended dinners with the court officials and the demon dukes and lords who controlled the surrounding lands. Luna sat tall with a crown on her head and a different pastel-colored ball gown on her every night. It felt like she belonged there, like she'd always been a part of this world.

She was a goddess. I truly didn't know what I'd done to deserve her. Every night, she slept by my side, looking so angelic, all curled up in my sheets.

My beautiful, brilliant mate. The one who would wear my crown, rule at my side. Fates, but I loved her.

My father had no idea about the fire in her eyes. I thought about the way her lips had curled over her teeth, the way she was so quick to jump to my defense as if I hadn't done horrible things. But she wasn't worried about that. *No.* She wanted to know how he'd hurt me. And those bright green eyes burned with revenge.

I needed to end it. Once and for all. *We* needed to end it.

What was I waiting for? She'd gotten better with her magic, but was it enough?

As if I'd summoned her with my thoughts, Luna padded into the throne room, wearing a white nightgown that ghosted the tops of her thighs, a cloak draped around her shoulders.

"Why are you awake, Moonbeam?" I asked, uncrossing my legs as I watched her move towards me.

"You're awake," she murmured, like that answered everything. Her voice was still groggy with sleep, as if the first thing she'd done when she'd woken up was come to find me. I liked that more than I could possibly express.

I quirked an eyebrow as she clambered onto my lap, wrapping her arms around my neck. "Can't sleep without you," she murmured in response. "You're like my personal furnace."

I hummed back, burying my nose in her hair, inhaling that floral, citrus smell I loved. Scenting her calmed my senses. Every fizzled part of my brain shutting down at my mate's presence.

"What's on your mind?" She asked, tracing a finger up my chest.

Where did I begin? I pulled back so I could look into her eyes. "I don't want to burden you with all of my problems."

"Didn't we discuss this earlier?" She frowned, moving her finger to smooth the worry lines on my face. "Your problems are my problems, are they not?" Her forehead rested against mine. "That's what happened when you married me."

"Yes." I shut my eyes. "I just need time."

"Sort of the perk of being an immortal demon," Luna said with a smirk, her fingers curling into my hair. "All you have is time."

I rested my hand on her thigh. "Yet it never feels like enough." I slid my fingers up, creeping toward where that tiny nightgown ended. There was a little bow between her breasts, and I wanted to pull on it with my teeth.

Her fingers brushed over the spot on her neck where I'd claimed her, marking her as my own. Merging our scents together so that no one would doubt that she was mine.

Just as much as I was hers.

"What?" I asked, tracing her cheekbones with my pointer finger.

"Can I…" Her cheeks deepened. "Can I bite you?"

I smirked. "Does my queen want me to wear her mark, too?"

Luna nodded, and I rubbed my thumb over her lip.

"That way, everyone knows you're mine," she said, the possession clear in her tone.

Kissing the mark that graced her neck, I bared mine to her. *I have always been yours.*

"Are you sure?" she mumbled the words as though she didn't already have all of me. Heart and soul.

"*Yes*. It would be an honor to wear your mark."

Humming in response, she ran her tongue over her canines.

"My possessive, ruthless little moonbeam, hm?" I eyed my mark on her neck. "Do you really want to?"

"Yes." Her voice was breathy, and with a wave of my hands, I infused those canine teeth of hers with magic, sharpening them so she could leave a mark.

"Oh." She ran her finger over the razor-sharp tooth. "Are these…?"

"Temporary," I laughed. "But if you ever want them again, all you have to do is ask."

"Mm." Luna seemed to consider the idea before leaning into me to press her face against my neck. She inhaled deeply. "How do I do this? I don't want to do it wrong."

"You couldn't."

"And it won't… hurt?"

"Did it hurt when I bit you?" I asked, raising an eyebrow.

"Well… no." She turned a beautiful shade of pink. "But…" I could tell she was thinking of that night. How the claiming had also been *sexual*.

Without her having to ask, I confirmed her thoughts. "It will be like that again. The wanting. The *needing*."

"Oh."

"I won't be able to stop once I start. It's a primal need built inside of us. To fuck and *claim*. To make sure that our intended is *ours*. Like prey."

"Prey?" Her eyes widened. She was so sweet and naïve, like a little white bunny. Fuck, I could never tire of it. Not when every bit of my soul responded to hers.

"Mhm," I responded, a hum that had her giggling as she placed her lips over my throat. She kissed a line down the sensitive skin, from right under my jawbone to over my pulse point and down to the crook of my neck.

Luna's nose inhaled deeply, taking a drag of my scent.

And then, quick as a flash of lightning, she struck. Those teeth I'd given her buried into my skin, and she let out a small moan. Her bite wasn't painful, but it sparked something in me—in my very being. Primal and possessive.

A grunt slipped from my lips before I could stop it. My blood burned hotter as she released my neck, her tongue running over the marks like I'd done to her. The saliva helped seal the claim, keeping the small marks visible on our skin.

"Zain," she whimpered, even as her mouth remained poised over the same spot she'd just marked. Luna's free hand drifted down between her thighs, parting her folds.

Her scent permeated the air, the thick aroma of arousal robbing me of the ability to think clearly. Lifting her up, I swapped our positions.

Luna, sitting on the throne, me kneeling below her. The only woman I'd ever kneel for—my Queen.

She didn't have to tell me what she needed. We were one soul, one heart, living in two bodies. Her thoughts were my thoughts. Her wants were my wants.

Prying her knees apart, I buried my tongue between her folds, licking and sucking and devouring. I was dying of thirst, and her taste was the only thing that could quench it. In fact, I could get drunk off of it.

"Fuck," she cried. "You're so good at that. Don't stop."

Her hands buried themselves in my hair, trying to push me down deeper, and I flicked my tongue against her once in warning. "Luna, what do you want?"

A pant left her mouth. "To come."

"Is my good girl going to come on my tongue and let me lap up all of her sweetness?"

"Yes. Please."

My shadows wrapped around her wrists, pinning them to the arms of the chair before I did the same to her ankles, keeping her cunt slick and open for me.

"Now let me feel you clench around my tongue," I instructed before going back to lapping at her clit. Once I'd given it ample attention, I put my mouth back onto her, plunging my tongue into her center. *Fuck.*

I reached down, squeezing my cock. Just tasting her made me hard, and I was desperate to be inside of her, but I wanted her to come first. I was obsessed with getting her pregnant, and from what I'd read, it was easier if she had already climaxed. Maybe I could relax once my baby was inside of her. Once I knew she could never leave me.

Luna. I flicked her sensitive nub with my thumb, moving her clit in circles as I fluttered my tongue inside of her. *Come for me, wife.*

"Yesss," she cried, her orgasm ripping through her.

Luckily, after practicing with her powers, she didn't seem to glow after she came as much anymore. I almost missed it. The glow made her look ethereal, like a moon goddess.

Pulling my cock from my pants, I let it spring free.

"Let me touch you," she begged. "Let me taste you."

"My little queen wants to suck my cock?"

She nodded, her eyes glazed over with lust. "Yes."

I let the shadow restraints free, and she pushed me into the chair, moving between my legs.

"So big," she murmured, wrapping one hand around my dick, her fingers not meeting on the other side. "So thick." Luna leaned down, her tongue lapping up the pre-cum that oozed out.

"Do you think you can fit me in your mouth?" I asked, rubbing her lower lip with my thumb.

She didn't respond, too busy giving my length attention. She traced the veins with her tongue, all while moving her hand up and down at a slow pace.

Like she knew she was torturing me.

"Luna." I grit out. "Put me in your mouth. I want to feel you suck on my cock, Moonbeam."

"Mmm," she said, circling the head like she was licking a lollipop before finally—finally, her lips closed over it. She increased her pace on my shaft, sliding up and down as her head bobbed, alternating between taking me in a little deeper and sucking deeply.

"Fuuuck." I pulled her off, and she frowned, running her tongue across her lips.

"Did I not do it right?" Her cheeks flushed. "I don't have a lot of experience."

"Baby." I groaned. "If you'd kept going for one more minute, I would have spilled down your throat. And that's not where my cum goes, is it?"

"No," she shook her head, still kneeling between my legs.

"Where do you want it?"

"I-inside." She let out a rough breath. "In my womb. So you can give me a baby."

"Mmm." I fisted myself, squeezing roughly. "Come here, Luna. Come sit on my cock."

She scrambled onto her feet, straddling my lap and guiding me inside of her.

Her wet warmth welcomed me into her body as she sank down on me, inch by inch, as her hardened nipples brushed against my chest through her nightgown. I bent my head down, pulling the bow with my teeth and exposing her nipples to the air.

"Oh," she gasped, bottoming out, taking all of me inside of her. I nipped at her breast, biting down before soothing it with my tongue. "*Yes.*"

"Made for me," I groaned. "Your perfect pussy, just begging for my seed."

I helped her ride me, moving her hips as I sucked on her tits. Luna threw her head back, eyes squeezed shut as she came, her orgasm setting off mine.

Surging up, I pumped into her, releasing all of my seed into her desperate cunt, all of my effort focused on putting a baby inside of her.

"I hope…" Luna's hand spread over her abdomen. She didn't have to finish her thought because I already knew what she was thinking.

"Me too." I kissed her lightly before lifting her up into my arms and pushing her thighs together. "Don't let any leak out."

"Can't waste it," she agreed, letting her head rest against my shoulder as I carried her up to bed.

Perfect. She was perfect.

And all *mine.*

Forever, if I had my way.

TWENTY-EIGHT
LUNA

When I'd gone looking for Zain and found him in the throne room, I certainly hadn't imagined *that* was how it was going to go, but I wasn't *upset* with the outcome.

Not in the slightest.

I giggled, thinking about how ridiculous it was when Zain froze.

What—I started to ask, but a voice interrupted us before I could.

"Son."

Zain gently settled me down onto my feet and pushed me behind him, hiding me behind his large stature. I'd been glad for the late hour—figuring no one would see us leave or find out what we'd been up to—but this was an unforeseen development.

An unwelcome one, if Zain's body language had anything to say about it. My gut was filled with an unsettling feeling, nausea churning.

"So this is her." His father's voice made an uncomfortable shiver run up my spine. "The human you went to such lengths to keep from me." He spit out the word like it was foul-tasting.

Never mind that I was a witch with powers of my own. That he'd bonded with me, mated with me—that we were stronger together. That we both had deep feelings for each other.

"She's my *wife*," Zain snarled. "And you will treat her with respect."

I peeked over his shoulder, catching sight of his father.

If I'd thought Zain was tall, his father was even taller, towering over me. Maybe seven feet with a pair of curling black horns coming from his forehead, but those unmistakable golden eyes. It was obvious where Zain had gotten them—and his looks.

"Curious little thing, aren't you?"

Stay behind me, Zain ordered into my mind. *I won't let anything happen to you.*

Sliding an arm up his back, I held back my unchecked anger. I knew he wouldn't, but I also remembered what he'd told me back in the countryside house. But I was more worried about Zain's emotional state than my own. Even if I'd lost my parents younger than I would have wished, and the ache was always there, I had always known they loved me.

Zain had never had that. He'd lost his mom when he was young. When was the last time anyone told him they loved him? Showed him any care?

I didn't want him hurt, either.

"What are you doing here?" My husband's voice was low. I slid my free hand into the one that he had behind his back, keeping me in place.

His father chuckled. "Just thought I'd check in on things. You haven't given me a report in the last few days."

"I've been a *little* busy."

"Bedding your new wife? Because you think that once you have your heir, you can finally be rid of me?"

I scrunched up a face. *Zain.* I squeezed his hand to get his attention. *What does he mean?*

Never mind, he thought back, giving me no explanation.

But—

Luna. His voice was stern in my mind. *Now's not the time.*

Fine. But what game was his father playing?

Zain told me he needed to have an heir, but I hadn't thought twice about it. But was that truly why he wanted me to have a child? So it could be in line for the throne?

I bit my lip. What role did I even serve here? It had been weeks since I came to the demon realm, and all I'd done was comb through the library, bake cookies, and learn how to control my powers. That, and sneak off with Zain whenever we had a spare moment, him always as desperate to get inside of me as I was to have him.

But that wasn't enough.

He'd asked me to help. Had confided in me about his dad. It was everything I'd asked for. I couldn't hold it against him if there was more. Could I?

His father reached out like he was going to touch me, but Zain batted his hand away. "Don't touch her. Don't even look at her. I swear, Father, if you do—I will end you. It will be the last decision you ever make." The ground rumbled under my feet, and I stumbled, my body colliding with Zain's.

He whirled around, not saying another word, pulling me behind him, but I could feel his father's chuckle echoing through my bones.

It was a foreboding sound, one that felt like a bad omen for the future.

* * *

Zain slammed the door to his room shut behind us and wasted no time before stripping me down. Both of our clothes were shed in a pile on the floor, and I could almost feel the way his anger was a palpable energy.

Then I was on the bed, face down on the pillows, his large body poised over mine.

"I need you," he said, voice hoarse. "And I'm not going to be gentle. It's going to be hard and rough."

I nodded, and he pushed into me from behind without preamble, rutting into me like a beast in heat. Like he couldn't stop.

Fuck, he was big. Thankfully, I was still wet from his earlier release, his cock slipping inside me easily. This time, I felt him *everywhere.* He was so deep inside of me in this position.

"Zain," I cried out.

His hips rocked into me, over and over, the sound of our skin slapping filling the room. Zain grunted, his cock hardening further inside of me. He had a hold on my waist with one hand, and the other fisted my hair, arching my back towards him.

Normally, his sole focus was on my pleasure. But tonight, I could sense there was something more... *animalistic* about his need. Like whatever control he normally had on his desires had *snapped.*

I was the prey. Just like he'd said, he needed to *claim* me. To make sure I was his. That need was overriding his brain. Lately, it hadn't felt like *fucking* when I'd let him inside my body. But that's what this was. Hard and fast. My orgasm hit me the same way, like a burst of electricity in front of my eyes.

My fingers clutched into the pillows as his fingers dug into my hips even tighter, a snarl ripping out of his mouth before he buried his cock in me *deep*, a warmth spreading through my stomach.

But he didn't stop—he just kept fucking me through it, moving in and out even as he came inside of me, filling me with his thick cum.

I sat up, pushing myself off of him, knowing I was a mess. That my hair was probably in knots from his hands, and my hips ached from his grip, his cum dripping down my legs, but I needed the distance.

"Are you feeling better now?" I didn't turn around to see his face. I couldn't.

He didn't answer, and finally, finally, I forced myself to look at him.

"Are you okay?" I whispered the question. "Will you tell me what happened tonight? Why *that* happened?"

He shook his head. "No."

I wrapped a robe around myself, tears filling my eyes. I was okay with him using me like that, but not with him shutting me out. Sometimes, it was easy to forget who he was. What he was. When he was so kind to me, winning me over with sweet words and endless praise. When he made me feel better than any man ever had before.

Right now, though, I just felt *dirty*.

But this was a reminder of the demon underneath. The man I'd *married*.

"Maybe I should sleep in my bed tonight. I think I need some space."

"Don't go." He wrapped his arms around me. "Fuck, baby. I'm sorry. I didn't want to hurt you."

"You didn't. Not like that." Sure, I was sore, and I knew there would be bruises tomorrow, but what was hurting was my *heart* because he wouldn't talk to me. "I can't do this. I can't be your wife and have you shut me out. You have to *trust* me with all of it."

"I do trust you."

"With what? I don't even have anything to do here. A *purpose*. I need to do *something*." Helping him take down his father didn't count. I would do that happily, but what would be left once it was over?

Zain furrowed his brow. "You *have* a purpose."

"Do I? Because being with you can't be my purpose. Having your child can't be my purpose. There has to be something *more*." A deep sigh heaved from my lungs. "In Pleasant Grove, I had the bakery, and it fulfilled me. Gave me a reason to get up each morning. Seeing people's faces light up when they ate things I made brought me joy. A reason for being. Here, I'm just…"

What? What was I? I'd told him when I agreed to all of this that I didn't want to be trapped, but I couldn't help but feel that way, anyway.

"Luna." His voice was soft as he cupped my cheeks, forcing my eyes to meet his. "You can do whatever you'd like."

"Can I?" I raised an eyebrow. "Because the bodyguards following me around wherever I go seem to point to the opposite. Why are you so afraid of him, Zain? You said we could end it. Together. That we could do this." He said nothing, looking away. "Why are you hesitating?"

"It's complicated." He pinched between his brows. "I just…"

"Okay." I sighed. "You know where to find me when you need me." My heart hurt as I walked away from him.

As I curled into my cold sheets, unable to remember when the last time I slept in them was. They didn't smell like him, that musky scent that soothed my frayed nerves.

I let the tears fall, not caring if anyone heard me cry.

Because he was here, and he was still breaking my heart.

TWENTY-NINE
LUNA

A week passed without mention of Zain's father or what we were going to do about it. Zain had been attentive and yet distant, always checking in to see if I needed anything, but his head seemed like it was a million miles away.

Even when I spent the night in his arms, it felt like there was a wall between us that had never been there before.

"Luna?" Zain called, his voice groggy from sleep.

I wiped away a bit of flour that clung to my cheek as he padded into the kitchen. Humming at him in response, I kept mixing my dough.

"What are you doing?" He asked, watching me work.

"I couldn't sleep."

So I'd come down to the kitchen to make a batch of cookies to calm my racing mind. There was a book open on the counter I'd stolen from the library, too. Not that I was doing much reading. I hadn't been able to focus on the page all morning.

A yawn freed itself from my lips. I'd been feeling extra tired lately. Maybe it was from the dreams that kept me up at night. The visions all involved his father and the crown. Something bad was coming, and I was completely at a loss for what it was.

Zain wrapped his arms around me, clearly not caring about my mess. "Come back to bed, wife," he murmured in my ear.

"Hmm?"

He frowned, curling a finger around my ear to push a strand of hair back. "What's wrong?"

"Nothing." I shook my head, forcing a smile onto my face. "Everything's fine. But… has something happened?" My voice was subdued. Quiet.

Because if that future came to pass, this entire realm would be bathed in blood.

"Nothing you have to worry about," he insisted.

"But—"

Maybe I needed to worry him. Tell him about what I'd seen. As my magic got stronger, so did the visions I was seeing. How many of them were real?

Zain kissed my forehead. "How are you feeling?"

I blinked up at him, surprised by his sudden change of subject. "Fine, why?"

He swallowed roughly. "No reason."

"Okay… Well, how's everything with your dad?"

After running into him in the hallway, I was even more cautious about bringing him up around Zain. It instantly made his body go on edge, and the tension that ran through his enormous frame made me worry. "The bastard won't step back. Even though I've been practically running this place for years, he just... I didn't want this to end in violence. And if he succeeded, passed down the crown, then it wouldn't have to." A deep sigh came from his throat.

"So we should do it." I was ready. I felt more confident in my powers than I ever had before. And I'd been studying spells in the library, which had given me an idea. "I told you I'd help." I placed my hand on his shoulder. "I feel like I'm just sitting around doing nothing." Looking down at my feet, I stared at my ring. "As your wife, I feel like I should be doing more for you."

Zain shook his head, wrapping a hand around my neck and pulling me in closer. "You're doing exactly what I need. Being here for me. Just letting me hold you is all I need." He took a deep pull of my scent.

"If you're sure..." I whispered, still wishing I could do more to calm him.

"You smell so good today," Zain groaned, running his tongue along my neck. "What's that smell?"

I blushed. "I might have commandeered the kitchen to make scones and cookies. There's still some left, actually." I grabbed the bowl, unwrapping the cloth that was covering them. "Do you want one?"

His eyebrow raised. "Do *I* want one?" Had I ever seen him eat sweets besides mine? *Not really.* But he smirked, reaching over and grabbing one out from underneath the cloth. Zain took a bite. "Mmm. What's in this?"

"Lemon and lavender scones. They're my favorite." Comfort food. The floral and the citrus surprisingly balanced each other out, and I loved the result. Plus, I'd made the icing from scratch that I drizzled on top.

"Like you," he mused.

"Huh?"

"You should make them more often," he said, taking another bite. He didn't offer further explanation for his other comment.

"I guess I should," I said, humming as I popped one into my mouth, too. I felt more like myself when I was baking as if I was figuring out who I was now. It had been a long time since I'd felt content. Even before leaving Pleasant Grove, I'd been... unsettled. Wanting something more.

I'd told him I needed a purpose, and that was true. I couldn't be his broodmare or just some pretty trophy to sit on a throne. But maybe what I really needed was him. Knowing he loved me.

I might not have had something to do every day, but deep in my bones, I felt... *alive* like I never had before. Happy. All of that had to do with one thing. *Zain.* I rested my head on his shoulder.

I'd just let my eyes drift shut for a moment, and then I'd get back to it.

Just a moment...

* * *

Blood. There was *so much* blood.

Zain. Where was Zain?

Lifeless bodies surrounded me. Weapons discarded on the ground where they'd fallen. Kairos's dark skin, Lilith and her beautiful wings, Asura's eyes open and lifeless, and even Thorn and Talon are together in life and death. They were all gone.

My knees gave out, and I fell to the ground, screaming in agony.

"Zain," I begged. "Please. You said you wouldn't leave me. You promised."

I couldn't control the tears that dripped from my eyes. The power felt like it was flowing out of my body until not a speck of that beautiful light I'd grown so used to was left.

And what remained? Nothing. Chaos. Destruction. *Death.*

This was Hell—the demon realm—on fire.

The Demon King sat on his throne, laughing, as the bodies continued to pile up around me.

"You'll pay for this," I said, cursing him with everything I had. But it wasn't enough, not without my mate, not without Zain, not without—

"Luna," Zain's voice sounded murky like it was far away. Like I was underwater. "Luna, baby. You have to wake up. Come back to me."

"Zain?" I mumbled, my hand clutching his shirt in a death grip. My eyes opened, and I was in his lap, being rocked and cradled like an infant.

"Thank the fates. You scare me half to death when you do that."

I blinked. "That wasn't the first time?"

Zain pressed a cool cloth to my forehead. "No. I don't know what sets them off, but I can never get you to wake up. You're always stuck in these trances, and I—"

"What?" The concern in his voice filled me with fear. "What's wrong?"

"Luna. You're bleeding."

"Oh." I looked down, drops of blood soaking through the front of the nightgown. "I—" My throat choked up. "I'm probably just starting my period." My eyes squeezed shut. It would be fine. I'd get through this, just like I did everything else. I would not cry over this, too.

"Do you need anything? I'll go get Novalie and—"

I grabbed the sleeves of his jacket. "Don't go. Please. I can't lose you."

"What do you mean?" He frowned. "I'm not going anywhere. I just want to take care of you."

"No." I shook my head, blinking away the tears. "Listen to me. I saw—" What good were my powers, my abilities if no one listened to me? If he didn't take me seriously? "Destruction. Death. And blood. There was so much blood." I choked. "Zain, please. You can't leave me alone. You promised." All I knew was in all the nightmares, I was alone. He'd gone without me.

Why was I so weak? *Worthless?* I'd promised myself that when I came here, I'd learn more about my powers. That I'd get stronger.

And maybe I had, but… it wasn't enough. I'd never be enough, would I? A sob worked its way free.

He scooped me up in his arms, cradling me to his chest. "I won't leave you. If I could, I'd never let you out of my sight again."

"I know what you're planning," I said, because it was obvious. "You're going to do it alone." Zain swallowed before giving me a tiny dip of his head. "You *can't.*" I felt like I was fighting for my future—*our future.* "You can't do it alone. He'll kill you."

His hand closed over mine as he kissed my knuckles. "Moonbeam. I would destroy the world for you. Forsake any plans I'd ever made just to keep you safe. To give you everything you've ever wanted. A happy life. The one you deserved. But I—" His voice cracked. "I have to keep you safe. If anything happened to you…"

"I know." My voice was soft. Subdued.

I hated it, but I knew he was right because I felt the same.

If anything happened to him, the world would be bathed in blood.

And it would be *me* at its helm. The power in my blood thrummed at the thought, at the idea that I would do anything to avenge my mate if he was harmed. If something took him from me.

"Luna," he murmured, brushing his hand over my cheek. "Your eyes are glowing, baby."

"Huh?" I blinked a few times, feeling the rage clear from my system.

"There's my girl." His golden eyes were warm—full of love, and more tears dripped from my eyes. "My mate."

I nodded because if I opened my mouth, I would lose it.

"I love you," he said, not a hint of hesitation in his voice. "And everything I've done—everything in my life—it'll all be worth it. As long as I have you."

"You do," I choked out, letting the tears fall freely from my eyes. "You *do* have me."

I knew he couldn't abandon his people. His world. He was their protector as much as he was mine.

"I—" I wanted to say it, but the words were stuck in my throat. What was I scared of?

He cupped my cheek. "You don't have to say it back. I just needed you to know."

"Okay," I whispered.

But if he loved me, why did it feel like he was slowly slipping away from me?

* * *

Normally, the food here was incredible. But tonight, something on the table smelled rancid. I couldn't tell what it was, but my stomach wasn't tolerating it. Covering my mouth and nose with my hand, I did my best not to breathe too deeply.

"I'm so sorry," I announced, standing up without preamble, giving a small nod to those sitting around us. "I'm not feeling well, so I think I'm going to retire early." Pasting a fake smile on my face, I bid them all a good night.

Zain frowned, grabbing my hand. "Want me to come with you?"

I shook my head. "No. I'll be fine. Just stay here." I brushed my hand over his shoulder. Leaning down, I pressed a kiss to his cheek.

"I won't be too long," he promised, though I waved him off. Even if he didn't enjoy it, when he was schmoozing, sometimes he would lose track of time for hours.

I didn't mind as long as I was away from the *smell*.

Pulling the door open, I headed towards my room, wishing I had Willow here to give me advice. Suddenly, I was feeling so alone.

Talon followed behind me all the way back to my rooms. Ever the loyal guard dog.

"I want to be alone," I announced when we were in front of my door.

"Of course." He dipped his head.

"Thank you," I whispered back before slipping into my room.

I let myself sag against the door for only a moment before seeking out Selene. I might not have been able to hug my sister, but at least I could snuggle with my familiar. At least she always seemed to understand what I was feeling.

I needed something to calm my stomach. Grabbing the pillow off Zain's bed, I inhaled deeply. It smelled like him, that scent helping to settle my nerves.

Sliding on top of the covers, I sat upright and thought about everything he'd said last night as I cradled his pillow in my arms. *Why hadn't I said it back?*

I was scared. Scared to admit how attached to him I was. Even now, his scent was the only thing that could calm my racing heart. Scared that he was slipping away from me, and even love wouldn't save us.

"Luna?" Novalie repeated, like she'd been calling for me for some time.

"Huh?" I turned, toying with the pendant around my neck.

"How are you feeling?"

I wished everyone would stop asking.

"Fine," I said through a yawn. "Just a little tired."

Luckily, the nausea had abated some, though my worry had not. I hadn't been able to stop worrying about Zain. It was taking a toll on my body. I'd thought I was starting my period, but there had been no more blood today, so I couldn't even blame it on that.

Novalie hummed, moving around the room and dusting. "Would you like me to help you get undressed?"

Frowning, I looked down at the gown I was still wearing from tonight's banquet, before looking back out the window.

It would be winter now in Pleasant Grove. Had the first snow of the season happened yet? We were well into December now. I always loved the winter, when icicles hung from the eaves of our house and the snow glittered in the sun. But the demon realm was the same as when I'd gotten here, hardly even a slight nip to the air.

"Maybe later," I mumbled, adjusting the pillow.

"My lady, forgive me for asking, but…" She hesitated, like she knew she was overstepping, but couldn't help but ask. "Are you…" Novalie trailed off.

"Am I?" I looked up at her, and then my cheeks warmed. "Oh. I—"

It was too soon to tell. *Wasn't it?* I could do the math. Maybe I just hadn't wanted to. Hadn't wanted to acknowledge the changes, the truth that was going to change everything. I was exhausted. My breasts were tender. I'd peed more in the last week than I could ever remember.

When *was* the last time I'd gotten my period? I tried to rifle through my brain. Truthfully, I'd never been great at keeping up with my cycle, and that, plus all the added stress, meant I hadn't kept track. But I definitely hadn't touched the box of tampons I'd brought from home.

I touched my stomach, wondering if it could be true. Somehow, the idea hadn't felt real. Not till right now.

I'd agreed to it when Zain had brought it up, and couldn't believe how much I enjoyed begging him to put a baby in me. But it hadn't even been two months since I'd left my home. I'd expected it to take longer.

"I think I'm going to take a bath now, Novalie. And then I'd like to be alone for a while."

She gave me a small bow. "Of course, my lady. Just call for me if you need anything."

I nodded at her, though I was hardly listening to a word she said as I left the cozy bed, Zain's pillow forgotten as I padded into the baths.

All I needed was a moment to clear my mind. To process.

My robe and nightgown were quickly shed, and I stared at my naked form in the mirror.

When had I become the woman looking back at me? I didn't even feel like the same person I'd been before I came here. Before I found out that demons were real.

Before I'd learned that my soulmate was the heir to the demon throne. I wore his ring on my finger—his mark on my neck.

I stared at my belly, still flat. And yet…

Could I really be…?

"Hi," I whispered, smoothing a hand over my stomach. A little jolt ran through me, and a smile curved over my lips. "If you're in there…" The idea had just sprung into my mind, but *Goddess*, I wanted it to be real.

Was there a demon realm version of a pregnancy test? This place wasn't that far behind the human world in technology—after all, there were electric lights and running water—but the idea of asking for one made my cheeks heat. Or maybe it was something that Zain could sense?

Maybe I could go visit Willow. It could wait, right? I'd wait until Zain got back, and then I'd tell him. Then we'd find out. Together.

My eyes shut as I dipped my toes into the bath. Sinking down into the warm water, I let a small moan slip from my lips at how good it felt against my skin.

I needed to wash my hair, which was already getting greasy and stringy, but all I wanted to do was soothe my aching muscles.

A knock sounded at the door, and I frowned. I knew it wasn't my husband because Zain's presence always gave me that fuzzy warmth, which I knew now was because of our soulmate bond. Plus, he would have just teleported himself to wherever I was.

"Talon?" I called out, wondering who else would interrupt me. I'd told Novalie I wanted to be alone. No one responded. Standing up, I pulled a plush bathrobe on.

"Novalie?" I asked, a rush of apprehension running through me. Zain had promised me I was safe here. Protected.

My eyes squeezed shut. *Zain.* I searched for him, the call of his senses responding to me down our mental bond. No one else should be in here. Not with the wards Zain had created. Not when—

Peeking open the door, I found the butler standing there, a tray of food in his hands.

"I'm sorry," I said, gagging at the scent. "I didn't ask for any food."

He appeared unbothered by my statement. "I was told to bring this to your room since you'd left dinner early."

"By whom?" I went to close the door. Something didn't feel right. Every sense I had told me to get away from this demon.

"I'm afraid I can't tell you that, my lady." His foot kicked in the door, and I tightened my robe around myself.

"You need to leave." I felt my power surging up through my hands, and I held them up, wondering if a sudden burst could stop him enough for me to flee.

To find Zain. Talon. Where was my guard? And why had I told him he could go?

I winced as something sharp poked into my arm—my eyes widening as I looked at the demon in front of me. His devilish grin.

"*No,*" I whispered.

And then the world went black.

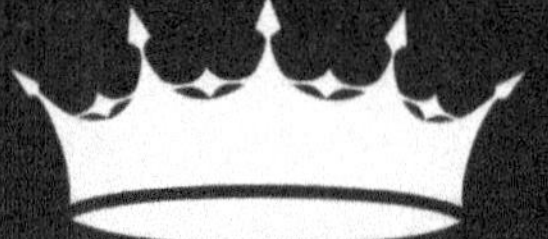

THIRTY
ZAIN

"If you'll excuse me," I murmured, pushing out of the table, eager to follow Luna upstairs to check on her. *Shit*, she'd looked extra pale tonight—was she not feeling well? I cursed under my breath, ignoring the look of surprise the surrounding demons gave at my sudden outburst.

Her scent had changed recently, and I had a feeling I knew why, but I hadn't confirmed it yet.

Lilith stood outside the door, flicking her dagger into the air and then catching it.

"Everything okay?" she asked, her wings keeping her slightly above the ground, sheathing the dagger in the belt at her side.

"Yes. No." I shook my head. "I don't really know. Luna just… I need to check on her."

"You can talk to us, you know? We're more than just your advisors. We're your friends."

I closed my eyes, taking a deep breath.

She was right. I'd spent the last two centuries surrounded by them, and part of the reason we didn't have these conversations anymore was it felt like we knew everything there was to know about each other.

Besides my brother, they were the only family I had, even if I'd built it myself. Bringing each one into the fold, training each one of them to unlock their powers, learning to trust them with every fiber of my being.

"She's good for you," Lilith added. "I've never seen you so happy as you are when you're with her."

"She's my everything," I confessed.

"But?"

"Why does there have to be a but?" The words were barely more than a grunt. "I told her I loved her."

"So?" She raised an eyebrow. "I'm not hearing an actual problem here."

"She put two and two together. That I didn't want to risk her." I looked around us and pulled her into my study. You could never be too careful. "And she didn't say it back."

I'd told her I loved her, and she hadn't said it back.

Her eyes widened in surprise. "So you—"

"Yes," I growled. Shoving my free hand into my hair, I tugged on the loose strands. Why hadn't I told her sooner? Because I was scared that she wouldn't feel the same?

Lilith raised her hands up. "I'm just trying to get a grip on the situation here, Zain. What did she say back? Do you think she doesn't love you?"

You do have me. But that wasn't the same as *I love you, too.*

"I can't risk her. She knows that."

"You're an idiot." She snorted, punching me in the shoulder. "But at least you listened to my advice. It was looking dicey there for a bit." Lilith shook out her hand, wincing like it hurt.

"Hey." I frowned. "That's not—"

"Whose bright idea was it to kidnap the girl and bring her back here?"

I crossed my arms over my chest. "But I *didn't.*" She gave me a look. "Fine. You were right. About all of it." I shut my eyes, breathing out through my nose. "But don't tell Asura. She'll never let me hear the end of it."

"The end of what?" The demon herself asked, popping out from behind the door.

"Nothing," I muttered, rolling my eyes. *Women.*

Asura leaned into Lilith's space, the two exchanging hushed whispers, which I was sure were about me. And Luna.

Fuck. *Luna.* I shouldn't have waited so long to tell her. Have made her think of a plan where risking herself was worth it. It wasn't. How could it be?

"Do you think she's okay?" I looked up at the ceiling. Even if I couldn't see her, it still felt like my heart was searching for her.

Asura placed her hand on my forearm. "She has Talon. Of course, she's okay. He won't let anything happen to her."

Safe. I steadied myself with the knowledge. *She was safe.* I'd meant what I told her—I wouldn't be able to focus if I thought about something happening to her.

"She said if I did it alone, something bad would happen."

Lilith nodded. "Sounds about right. We all told you it's foolish to even try."

I looked around, shaking my head. "We should finish this discussion later." Where there was no chance of prying eyes. With Luna present. "I just need to go check on her, and then I'll bring her down to my study."

* * *

Zain. Luna's voice filtered into my thoughts. I could feel the terror running through her. *Where are you?*

Hold on. Was something wrong? *I'm coming, Moonbeam.*

But she didn't respond. My body moved faster than it ever had before, teleporting at once towards the bedroom we shared.

One of the twins was normally stationed outside at all times, but Talon was missing. Fuck.

A meow slipped from the room, and I wrenched open the door, finding it in perfect order: bed made and everything in its place. But it was empty. Quiet. Her laughter normally filled the space, her warmth soothing that tattered part of my soul.

"Luna?" I called, hoping like hell everything was fine. That she was here, where she was supposed to be.

Her fluffy white cat gave me another sullen chirp. Scratching at her head, I frowned. "Where'd she go, Selene? What happened to our girl?" The cat didn't answer me. Of course not. She was nothing more than an animal, after all.

Moving through the room, I entered the bathroom. The steam fogged up the mirror with Luna's discarded nightgown at the edge of the baths. Her scent still clung to the air, overriding my senses. I shut my eyes, letting out a long string of curses I wasn't proud of.

She'd been here and now… She was gone. I was too late.

There was a discarded tray of food in the corner, but it looked like she hadn't even touched it. I frowned. Luna had left dinner early, not feeling well—had she asked for food to be sent up? I hadn't ordered anything to be sent to her.

"Zain?" Talon's voice was rough as he peeked inside the door.

"Talon." My voice was clipped. "Where is she?" He looked guilt-ridden, and my heart sank. *No.* "Tell me she's okay. That something hasn't happened to her."

His dark blonde hair was dotted with blood like he'd been knocked out. "I—I was drugged. It was like they'd known I was watching her tonight and slipped it into my food. The kitchen staff must have been in on it. And Novalie…" He shook his head, a shaky breath coming from Talon's lips. "They knocked her out, too. We were completely blindsided. I—" He rubbed at the scar on his face.

One he'd gotten when the twins were twelve, attacked by blood demons in broad daylight. Something my father had let happen. Luckily, I'd brought them back here. Welcomed them into our circle.

But I'd never forgotten what they'd done to him, what my father allowed to continue. He was involved in this, too. I knew he was.

"Where's my wife? Where's Luna?" I slammed my hand onto the marble countertop, staring down at one of the men I'd trusted more than anyone else in the world. To keep the woman I loved safe. *My mate.* "*Where is she?*"

I couldn't feel her down the bond. Our link always allowed me to sense her, to teleport to her side with barely a thought. But now, it was just darkness. Like a cold, empty cavity remained in the space of my heart.

"I didn't see this coming, Zain. Otherwise, I never would have left her side. You know that."

I growled, cutting him off. "How did they get through the wards? How did they *take her?*"

"I don't know. This power..." Talon wrung his hands. "It's *strong.* There's only one being that could do this."

My father. *That fucker.* I was going to bleed him alive after this, to make him wish he'd never even *looked* at her.

"How long were you out?"

"Maybe fifteen minutes? When I came to, the door was wide open. Luna was gone, and Novalie was tied up in the closet." He winced, rubbing at his wrists like he was the one who'd been bound.

"Fuck!" I pulled at my hair. I tried to tell myself that it could be worse. Fifteen minutes wasn't that big of a lead. But with his power, where would he take her? He could go anywhere. Do anything.

"Gather everyone—all the staff. Lock the palace down. No one leaves until we know who did this." Until I knew which of my father's lackeys was going to lose his life tonight.

He nodded. "Of course." Talon spun on his ankle, moving back out of the bathroom, but then turned back to me. "We'll find her, Zain. I know we will."

I just had to hope that he was right.

* * *

Two hours later, we were gathered in my office. Lilith, Asura, both of the twins and Kairos. We'd swept the palace grounds. Anyone who was involved with the kidnapping plot was currently locked in the dungeon.

Kidnapped. Fucking hell. They'd kidnapped my wife, and I didn't have a single lead on where she was.

My hand closed over my chest. Our mental bond was still blocked, and I couldn't get through to her, no matter what I did. I could still *feel* her, but her heartbeat was faint. Every so often, I felt her pain, and I had to grit my teeth.

What were they doing to her?

They must have given her something to affect her like this.

Lilith shook her head. "Zain, I don't think…"

"Clearly not." Thunder rumbled outside, and I couldn't control my anger. "You're clearly not thinking, or else we would have already found her."

I needed her here to calm me. Her scent, her touch. And until she was back in my arms, I would feel this way. It was like I was completely off-kilter, adrift in the darkness without her light.

"One job!" I exclaimed. "You all had *one* job. And you failed. You failed *her.*" My throat was choked up. *I'd failed her.* From the beginning, I'd promised to keep her safe, and I hadn't even done that. "I failed her." The words slipped from my lips before I could think better of it. To show weakness in front of them… Normally, I would have hated it.

But right now, all I could focus on was Luna.

She was supposed to be here. Making this plan *with* us.

Lilith made a noise in her throat, and I looked up to find her face full of emotion. "Your father—"

"He knows. That's the only reason he would have taken her. *He* has to know what I've planned." I scowled.

Asura's eyes narrowed to slits. "You think he would hurt her?"

"Yes."

Why? Because he wanted to put me in my place. Remind me who the *actual ruler* was. Luna had been right. She'd warned me, and I hadn't listened to her.

"But this is *cruel,* even for him."

"If he had a heart, I've never seen it. Even when my mother died, he never so much as shed a tear. He took her power, his *mate's* power, and then he let her *die.*" I looked away, thinking about if I ever had to say goodbye to Luna. The pain of losing my mate—it would destroy me. "He wouldn't hesitate to end the life of my wife just to ensure I couldn't overpower him." I spit the words out. "That's my father for you."

You left your wife behind, defenseless and alone. A voice in the back of my mind said. *This is your fault for not protecting her.* Running my fingers over the place where she'd left her mark, I tried to take solace in the fact that I could still feel her at the end of our bond.

Luna, I thought, hoping that the bond between us was strong enough to reach her at this distance. *Please be safe.*

"Fuck." I rubbed at my temples. "I need to get her back. Before they hurt her even more."

"How?"

"Can you follow the bond?"

"I *could,* but they did something to it. She's unconscious. Weak. All I can feel is darkness." Normally, there was only light. But I could still feel that she was alive.

"They must have drugged her. But if you can still feel even a trace of her, then there's a chance."

I nodded, running my hands over the fresh stubble on my chin. It was weak, at best, but *maybe.*

"Is there a chance this is a trap?" Thorn had unfurled a map of the palace, studying it intently. "That he's going to ambush you, to kill you?"

"I'm sure it is," I said, rubbing my eyes. "He'd love to put me six feet under. He's wanted to my whole life." After all, I was never good enough. Never strong enough. Powerful enough. And I'd let that affect everything. The way I saw myself. How I acted.

Until Luna. Seeing the trust in her eyes—how much she loved me, even if she hadn't said it yet—I knew it was true. I was more than enough.

"He never did before because he knew Damien would forsake his birthright. So what changed?"

"She did," I said honestly. She had changed me, made me softer. Made me see how love could transform everything.

"We'll take care of the situation here," Kairos insisted, laying his hand on my shoulder. "*Go*. Make sure your wife is safe. We need our future queen after all, don't we?"

I nodded, my wings sprawling out from behind my back. Ready to take me to my home. Because it wasn't a place, it was a person.

My mate. I'm coming back to you, Moonbeam. Just hang on.

THIRTY-ONE
ZAIN

"Where is she?" I demanded, throwing the door open to the throne room.

My father sat there, crown on his head, with a smirk on his face. "That's no way to greet your father, now is it?"

I pulled the sword from its sheath at my side, a growl on my lips as I stalked forward. "What did you do to her? Where's my *wife?*"

The power pulsed through my veins, and I wanted to unleash it. To destroy everything he'd ever touched. But I kept myself in check.

Because I needed her.

"You can't kill me," he said, running his fingers over the elegantly carved chair, tracing the wood. "Not without her. And how can you when you'll never find her? They already scented her once, you know…"

A flash of a canine tooth and his claws dug into the throne. "You know how they like their blood."

I froze, his threat filling the air. Except—he was wrong. Because I *could* feel her. Which meant there was still hope. That she was close enough for me to reach.

"Why?" I asked, not expecting an answer, but demanding it anyway.

He laughed. "I'm the demon king. I think the better question, my son, is, why *not?* Either way, the answer is simple: I cannot allow you to undo everything I've done over the last thousand years."

"I'm going to find her," I growled. "And when I do, I'll be back to end your sorry existence."

"You can try."

It was a promise—one I'd pay in blood.

* * *

Luna.

I could feel—hear—her pulse nearby, the bond in my veins guiding me to her. As if she was waking up, it was gradually getting stronger.

Thank fuck.

I might have had the ceremony tying our life forces performed without telling her about it first, but I couldn't find it in myself to be sorry now. Not when it was the only thing that tethered me to her completely. The mate bond was there, too, but it was her power that called to me.

I'd left a trail of blood in my wake. Demons hiding in the woods on guard, as if my father had wanted me to find her.

They'd underestimated how much my powers had grown, though. With Luna's life force joined to mine, I could have leveled the entire forest to the ground.

A scream rang out ahead, and then I was flying faster, wings beating furiously behind me to reach the sound of the noise.

Her heartbeat was louder now. Closer.

Another demon bared his fangs at me, but I threw my sword, impaling him in the heart without blinking as I marched forward. With my magic, I summoned it back to my hand before plunging it through the chest cavity of yet another demon, black sludge spewing out onto the dirt.

And then there was nothing—no one to stop me from claiming my mate.

"So this was where they hid her?"

They'd thrown her in an old wine cellar at the edges of the palace grounds. This was too easy—a *trap*. Hair rose on the back of my arms.

But my feet were frozen in place as I entered the dirt cellar and saw her below. It was hardly more than a pit now. There was no ladder to climb out with.

"Baby," I whispered the word, staring down at her limp form. My wings carried me down slowly, like the entire world existed in between each heartbeat.

She was bound and gagged, wearing nothing but a loose, bloody shift. It looked like it had been torn. Like she'd put up one hell of a fight. Her body was shaking like a leaf, as if the dampness of this dirt cell had seeped into her bones.

I reached down, pulling the gag from her mouth and slicing the bindings from her wrists.

Her eyes raised to meet mine, but it wasn't the stare I knew and loved. The bright green gaze that had looked up at me each morning was gone. They were *white*, pulsing with energy as it swirled through her.

Like they had the night she'd seethed with anger. But this was different. Like no life was behind her irises.

"What did they do to you?" I asked, brushing a hand over her skin. It was shimmering, just like that night in bed right after we'd been bonded. We'd lost ourselves in each other, in the pleasure of how right it was together. Though there was no pleasure in this. She felt no comfort, only pain.

Her body was ice cold.

"*Luna*." Beams of light nestled in her palms. "Who did this to you?"

Whoever it was, they'd be dead if they weren't already.

"Moonbeam," I begged, nestling her against me as if I could bring some warmth back to her freezing body. "Come back to me."

Her hand reached up, and she ran her fingers over my jaw. "Zain." Her voice was a croak. She tilted her chin, her gaze finally meeting mine. "I don't know how to stop it. Whatever they did to me, I—"

It was why they'd shoved her in here. Because they feared her, they should have. But they'd been even more scared of me.

"They're all gone," I promised. I didn't want to think about the blood I was wearing. How many lives had been lost tonight? I lost count. "I took care of them. Let's go home."

"No," she protested weakly, scooting away from me even as I tried to wrap her up in my arms. A sob worked free from her lungs. "Zain, there's something wrong with me."

I shook my head. "There's nothing wrong with you. There never has been, baby. Just breathe."

"*Stop!*" she screamed, the light flaring brighter. "I don't want to hurt you! I can't—" Her power shot out of her hands like two beams of light, baring holes into the dirt floor.

"You won't." Even as tears streamed down her face, I ignored her worries, pulling her into my arms and soothing her with calming words. "You *can't*, Luna." Wrapping my arms around her, I rocked her back and forth as she cried. Her magic was still haywire, but she couldn't hurt me. I didn't know how—maybe because of the darkness that lived in my veins—but ever since she'd attacked my training dummies, I'd suspected there was something different about how my powers reacted to hers.

Her light should have burned my eyes, my skin. Instead, I wrapped her with mine. My shadows covered her light as I held her tight against me. As I kissed her forehead, letting the warmth of my body seep into hers. Burying my nose in her hair, I inhaled her scent, the only thing that could calm me right now.

"I killed them," she cried. "My attackers dragged me out here, and I-I killed them. I ran, but t-the branches were so thick, and they caught me, and I-I—" I could barely understand her through her tears, but I heard enough to understand.

The light in her eyes was dimming as she burned her way through whatever magic-amplifying drug they'd given her. Slowly, they were turning back to that brilliant shade of light green.

"Luna," I soothed. "You're okay. You're safe now, I promise." I kissed the top of her head as she buried her face into my chest, her hands gripping my shirt.

The sobs wracked through her slight frame, her chest heaving from the motion as she cried.

"Your father, he—"

"I know." Cupping the back of her head, I pushed down the apprehension in my gut. "I know. I know everything."

This wasn't over.

He'd pay for this.

Creating a portal, I stepped through the shadows, not wasting a single second before taking her home.

* * *

"Are you sure about this?" Kairos asked, all of us crowded around my office. Luna was wrapped up in a blanket and sitting on the small couch.

As soon as she'd stopped shaking, I'd taken her back to our rooms. Bathed her and cleaned each of the nicks where branches snagged her skin. Where teeth and claws had bloodied her perfect porcelain complexion.

It was all I could do not to go on a violent rampage.

I was so angry I was practically seeing red. But I couldn't leave her alone. She wouldn't let me out of her sight. Like she knew what I wanted to do as well.

"It's what we have to do," Luna said. Her voice was hoarse from screaming, and it made me sick. Knowing that this was my fault. "Our powers, combined… that's the only way this ends. I've seen it all. And I know what we have to do."

"Okay." I took a deep breath. "But I need you to stay hidden until the last possible moment. Can you do that?"

My wife—my beautiful, enchanting wife—nodded.

"Asura and Lilith will be with you."

The two demons agreed, Lilith's fingernails already pointed, sharpened into weapons of lethal destruction. *Ready.*

"If anything goes wrong—" I said to them, ignoring Luna's protests. "You have to get her out of there. Keep her safe. Do you hear me?"

"I won't let you sacrifice yourself for me," Luna said, an angry pout on her face. "Either we die together or not at all. You hear me?"

"Neither one of us is going to die," I said with a growl. "Don't even think that."

Tell me you love me. My thoughts were a plea in her mind.

Her eyes narrowed and then softened.

I need to hear it. Just once.

No. Her thoughts were a soft caress against mine. *I can't say it like this. So you have to win. We have to beat him.*

My forehead pressed against hers, my hands tangled in her hair as we carried on our conversation mind-to-mind, no one else moving in the room. Like they all knew exactly what was happening. But this wasn't the end. This wasn't goodbye.

I will, I promised her, pressing a soft kiss to her lips. *For you, Moonbeam, I'd do anything. For our future, I'd tear down the world and rebuild it, even if it just meant one more day with you.*

She nodded, silver rimming her beautiful green eyes, but she didn't let the tears fall.

"Ready?" I asked the room.

Luna answered by summoning the moonlight in her veins, and I knew we'd never have a moment like this again.

* * *

My father was right where I'd left him, the picture of calm as he lounged in the throne.

"So, you found her."

I crossed my arms over my chest, scowling. "It wasn't hard."

He smirked. "Who said anything about that?"

"Why did you take her?" I asked again. "What is so dark and twisted inside of you that you'd do this? That you can't bear for me to be happy?"

"*Happy?*" My father snorted. "You truly think that witch will make you happy? She has you wrapped around her finger, son. You're one of the most powerful beings on the planet, and you're acting like her little guard dog."

"No." I narrowed my eyes. "You're wrong. She's everything, father. I love her."

"You think you love her? *Ha.*" He laughed, the booming sound filling the empty throne room. "You don't even know what love is."

"Maybe not. Because I didn't exactly have an excellent role model for it, did I?" I sneered, pacing closer till I was right in front of the throne. "You paraded around a different female every night. You didn't even care when my mother got sick. When she *died,* I was the only one who mourned her. What do you think *that* taught me?" Shadows surrounded me, licking up my boots, but I didn't bother trying to brush them off.

We were equally matched now, my father and I—with Luna's life force running through my veins. His shadows versus our *light*. Luna's moonlight and my lightning.

My mother had given me the key all along, and Luna had unlocked that part of me, made me whole. Light would vanquish the dark.

And I knew what love was.

I saw it every time Luna spoke with her sister. How she treated everyone with kindness and compassion. It was the way she looked when she sat on that chaise lounge in the library, curled up under a blanket with a book in her hands, lost for hours. The way she smiled when she bit into a fresh cookie. The way she cared for me and my feelings. How angry she'd been when I'd shared my past with her.

I let my wings spread out behind me.

"From the time I was young, I vowed to never be like you. That was your first mistake. Forcing me into a role, beating me into submission. I never asked for this, Father." Rage filled my body. "But I will not back down now."

"You and your brother are both too soft. I should have been harder on you. Maybe then you wouldn't both be such disappointments."

Lightning crackled around me as I stepped onto the first stair, ignoring his comments. "Your second mistake was assuming you were still in charge around here." A bolt of lightning hit the floor, cracking the tile behind me and sending it flying. "Because this isn't your palace anymore, old man. It's mine."

"Do you think I fear you?" Fire burned in his eyes, the color reminding me of molten lava. "That I'm scared of *you?* You forget your place. I *made you,* son. And I can just as easily destroy you."

Another step. Thunder rumbled the windows. I didn't care if I left destruction in my wake. Not now. "Now, your third mistake... that one I can't tolerate. Not when you threatened my wife." The electricity covered the blade of my sword, buzzing with energy. I curled my lips up over my teeth. "When you hurt my *mate.*"

"*Tsk.* Did you think I didn't know?" He clicked his tongue against the roof of his mouth. "She makes you weak. Foolish."

"Is that how you felt about my mother? Is that why you forced her to marry you, to *love* you, and then let her *die?* She didn't deserve that. And Luna deserves so much better than me. But that's where you're wrong." I took the last step up, coming directly in front of him. Staring down at the man who'd fathered me but had never been a *father* to me. My shadows wrapped over his hands, strapping them to the arm of the chair as I loomed over my father. "She doesn't make me weak. Luna never could. She makes me *strong*. Every single piece of her makes me want to be better."

My power sparked in my eyes.

"You—" His eyes grew wide. "How can you—"

Magic circles had formed on the ground. Much like the ones from the wedding ceremony, the bonding. Except these were runes.

Cast by the witch who I'd been cloaking with my magic. Luna appeared by my side, her eyes flaring with white power—pure, unfettered moonlight.

"You see, it was never about being strong enough to defeat you. It was always being stronger together."

White runes formed over his body. The ancient demonic text that I'd taught Luna on our honeymoon proved *extremely useful*.

"You see, father. She might not be a *demon*, but she was made for me."

Luna slid her hand into mine, both of us sharing our endless depths of strength with each other. As she finished the intricate sealing curse, bringing my father completely under her control.

"And she's going to look damn beautiful with the crown on her head, the queen of the demons."

"She'll never—" my father narrowed his eyes.

That was the moment we struck his heart with a concentrated beam of both our magics, lightning, and pure moonlight twining together. The spell Luna had suggested wrapped around him, binding him in ropes of white.

"How?" He asked, his dark eyes wide, looking up at me. Once, we'd shared the golden eyes that denoted demon royalty. That could only be born of a mate match. Now, his were black, just like his soul.

"Her," was all I said as Luna's grip tightened on my hand.

His skin was *melting,* which shouldn't have been possible, but the longer the magic touched him, the more he screamed. His horns caught fire, and I pushed free every bit of magic in my system, knowing my mate was doing the same.

"Just a little more," I grit out, looking over at Luna, who looked increasingly pale. It had to be now. A roar ripped free from my lips, and then it was over.

My father's form disintegrated into ash, the throne seemingly untouched by the display of magic.

Gone. How was it possible that, after all that, he was *gone?*

The glow faded from her eyes, and she gave me a hesitant smile.

"We did it," I said, pulling her in for a kiss. "You're magnificent."

"Zain…" Her skin was ghostly white, her pulse weak as she collapsed into my arms.

No. Not now. Everything was supposed to be perfect now. "Luna. Please. You can't leave me. Not now."

Luna's voice was hoarse. "The baby…" Her eyes met mine as she curled a protective hand over her stomach. "You have to make sure the baby's okay."

The baby.

Her eyes fluttered shut, and she passed out in my arms. Blood soaked through the front of her nightgown.

No. I couldn't lose her. I couldn't lose—

"Lilith!" I shouted, knowing she was the only person who could get there in time as I cradled Luna's limp body into mine, carrying her out of that horrible place.

"Find the healer. Bring her to me."

THIRTY-TWO
ZAIN

He was gone. It was done.

But she wasn't with me.

I sat next to Luna's bedside, where I hadn't moved since bringing her back to our rooms. There was more to take care of, but I wouldn't leave until I knew she was going to be fine. So I'd watched the healer work, tearing away the bloodied dress, her hands moving over Luna's body.

She used too much power. I never should have let her, never should have—

I worried my hands in my lap, unable to focus on anything else.

"They're okay," the healer finally said, cutting off my line of thought. She stood up straight, done with her examination.

"Luna and the—" My throat was dry. "The baby?"

She tipped her head. "It might take some time before she wakes up. Using that much power seems to have weakened her significantly, and her body needs time to repair itself." She looked over at Luna's sleeping form. Too still and still so pale. "But she's strong. And, luckily, so are the babies." The healer gave me a small smile.

Time stood still. "Babies?"

"You didn't know? They're twins."

Shaking my head, I could barely drag my eyes away from my wife. "I'd suspected she was pregnant—her scent had changed, but I…" I trailed off. I'd never imagined. *Twins.*

Fates, she was strong.

"She's six, maybe seven weeks along. My powers in this area are limited, so I can't tell you the exact timeline, but I can definitely sense two souls. Twins are rare in demons, so you can think of this as a gift from the fates." The healer reached out, squeezing my shoulder before giving me a small bow.

"Thank you," I said, swallowing roughly as I tried to keep my eyes from filling with tears. I reached out, grabbing Luna's hand and squeezing it tightly.

Her warmth was coming back, which I took as a good sign. Once the color returned to her body, I'd feel better.

"I'll leave you alone now, Your Highness. Let her get some rest. She needs it."

"Okay."

I sat holding her hand until nighttime fell, watching her chest rise and fall as she slept, and then I kissed her forehead, promising to exact the vengeance we both deserved.

Grabbing my sword, I let the door close softly.

* * *

"It's done," I said, the door shutting behind me. I wiped my hand over my face, letting the events of the evening sink in. "It's over. It's all over."

"You look like absolute shit," Asura muttered, running her hands through her chopped green bob.

"Ha. Thanks," I huffed, rolling my eyes.

"How's she doing?" Lilith asked.

Six demons stood outside the doors, hardly a breath to be heard. Talon and Thorn, their blonde heads pressed together, Kairos and even Novalie. All of them just waiting to hear how Luna was doing.

"She'll be fine," I promised, keeping the other nugget of information to myself for now. "The magic just took a lot out of her. The healer said after some rest, she should wake up. She'll be okay."

Sighs of relief went through all of them.

"Thank you." The words were a struggle to get out. "For staying by my side all these years. I don't deserve your loyalty, but I'm damn glad I have it."

"You deserve *all* of this, Zain," Lilith said, a little twinkle in her eyes. Was she… crying? "But don't stay out here with us." She pushed me back towards the bedroom. "Go wait with Luna."

I dipped my head in a nod, unable to say anything else.

Luna was still laying in *our* bed, sleeping, her hair spread out over black satin sheets that made her look like the moon. So bright. So beautiful. And all mine.

Slumping into a chair next to her bedside, I finally closed my eyes.

The effects of today—all the energy used, of being awake for so many hours—had taken its toll on me, too. Even though I was powerful, even my body had its limits.

All I needed was a moment of rest, and then I'd be right as rain.

That was what I told myself as I succumbed to sleep, letting it take me under.

* * *

Daylight's reddish rays streamed through the window when I cracked my eyes open, stretching my arms and neck from the uncomfortable position of sleeping in the chair.

But she was awake. In a clean dress. Like someone had helped her bathe.

"Zain," she whispered, her hand resting over her heart.

"Luna." I stood, unable to stand another minute apart from her. "You're awake."

"I have been for a little while, but you looked like you needed it more than me."

I let out a huff of air. She had no idea. "How are you feeling?" I asked her, sitting on the edge of the bed and taking her hand so I could kiss her knuckles.

"I should be the one asking *you* that." Luna reached out, brushing her thumb over my cheekbone. "Are you okay?"

I shut my eyes, relishing the feeling of her touch. "Honestly, no. But I will be. He deserved his end. I just wish I'd been awake when you woke up."

She shook her head. "Novalie helped me. I didn't…" Luna swallowed roughly, sliding her hand into mine. "I'm sorry if I scared you. I didn't know that would happen."

"It's my fault. I dragged you into all of this. I told you I'd keep you safe, but I couldn't even do that. I never should have tied you to me." I looked up at the ceiling, unable to make eye contact with her. "If you want to go back, I can take you." My heart was in my throat.

"To Pleasant Grove?" She sounded shocked. "Why?"

"It's your home."

Luna's grip tightened on my hand. "No, Zain. My home is here. With you." Her voice was soft, so full of love, as she slid her other hand down to my chin, pulling my face down to hers. "I never want to leave your side, ever again."

"Are you sure?" I played with her fingers. "You deserve so much better than me, Moonbeam."

A small smile curled over her lips. "I think you're exactly the man I deserve, handsome. Even if you're ruthless and a little terrifying at times, I love that about you."

"You do?"

"Mhm." She adjusted her position so she could cradle my head in between both her hands. "I love you, Zain. I think I've loved you since you laid on the grass with me, looking at the stars. Since the first time I saw you. I was just scared. Honestly, I'd never felt like this before. I've never been in *love* before."

"Me either," I breathed, leaning over to kiss her forehead. "I didn't know it could be like this." That I could have so much love in my heart, that nothing would matter to me except for her.

"I thought something happened to you. That you'd…" I couldn't bring myself to even suggest it. All I knew was that if Luna wasn't in this world, I didn't want to be, either. An eternity without her seemed like the worst kind of punishment.

"I'm sorry," she said again, shaking her head as tears sprung loose.

I brushed them away with my thumb, letting our foreheads rest against each other. "Don't cry, baby. It makes me want to burn the world down when you cry."

"I can't help it," Luna murmured, "I just…" She blew out a breath. "I'm a little overwhelmed, is all."

"Understandable."

"What happens now?" She asked, moving the covers off her body and coming to sit on my lap.

"Now we get our happy ending," I promised her. "And they'll put a crown on your head, so everyone else will know what you are. What you've always been."

"And what's that?"

A smile curled over my face. "My queen."

I kissed her softly.

"I love you. Fates, but I do. You taught me what it was like to love someone and what it was like to be loved in return. No one's ever cared about me, not like you do. I've spent the last three hundred years wondering what it might be like when I finally found you, but my dreams pale in comparison to the reality of you. You're my moon, Luna. Even when you're not around, I can feel my pull to you. You're the brightest thing in my night sky. The thing I always look for to know I'm home. And if I had to do it all again—struggle through every hardship—I would, knowing you were waiting for me at the end."

"Zain." She was crying again. I brushed them away from her cheeks with my lips, kissing each side softly. "How is this my reality?"

"Believe me, Moonbeam. I've been asking myself the same question since I walked into that bar and laid eyes on you. Since you asked me to come up to your apartment. Since you told me you'd marry me." I kissed the ring on her finger. "But I'm the luckiest demon alive, even if I don't deserve you." I rubbed our noses together.

"You do," she said, her voice full of conviction. "You deserve all of this. I just need you to believe that, too."

"I'm working on it," I promised. "I just might need you to remind me every once in a while."

"Mmm," Luna murmured, her eyes fluttering shut. "I think I can do that."

"Good." I kissed her forehead. "I love you." Now that we'd said the words, I couldn't stop them because it was so sweet.

"I love you too." Her lips curled up in a small smile, but then she bit her lip. "And the baby's… okay?" Her hand rested on the small bump—hardly there—of her stomach.

"They're totally fine. Healthy."

"They?" She looked confused.

"The babies."

Her eyes were wide. "Two?"

THIRTY-THREE
LUNA

Two. I blinked.

"Two?" I looked over at Zain. "There's *two?*" Maybe them knocking me out had caused me to hit my head a little harder than I thought because I couldn't seem to process the word.

I'd only just come to terms with being pregnant with one, but two was even crazier.

He grinned. "Twins. It's—" His forehead rested against mine, that deep voice of his all choked up. "We're having twins."

"Twins," I repeated, the information still processing before it finally settled in. There were two babies growing inside of me. "Wow. I never expected—"

His hand rested over top of mine. And I could see them, clear as day.

A little boy with dark hair and golden eyes. The blonde baby girl with violet eyes.

Never us. Always *ours*.

"Oh." And then I was crying again.

"What?" He pinched my side lightly.

"I should have told you before," I whispered. "That I loved you. That I suspected…" I took a deep breath. "I just… I've been dreaming of these two kids for so long. I thought maybe it was you when you were younger." There was a lump in my throat when I tried to swallow. "But maybe I've just been dreaming of them for so long, I couldn't see the truth of it."

"You've dreamed of *them?*"

I nodded. "And you. Ever since I was little."

He puffed up at that. "Oh, yeah? What did you see?"

Tracing my finger up his back, I whispered in his ear. "Your eyes. Golden, always searching for me. Your beautiful wings. Powerful. Like they were going to pick me up and carry me off somewhere." A brief laugh escaped my lips. "I guess they did."

"So they did." His smile lit up my heart. "Is it weird that satisfies some possessive, primal part of me? That while I was here, waiting for you, you were dreaming of me?"

"Yes." I laughed. "So glad I was worth the wait."

He brought our lips together. "Every single moment."

I rested my head on his chest, eyes growing heavy with sleep once again. Whatever they'd given me to knock me out, whatever they'd done to me upon kidnapping me—it had taken all of my energy.

Though growing two half-demon, half-human beings inside of me probably didn't help either.

"Zain?"

"Yes?" He asked, smoothing his hand down my back. His lap was so comfortable, and I was pretty sure his arms were the best place in the world.

"Can I ask you something?" I fiddled with the loose opening of his shirt.

"Of course."

"When you said you needed to have a child—an heir to secure your line—did you mean that?" That was what had started our frenzy. We'd been able to keep our hands off of each other, and I'd been content to let him breed me. Because deep down, I wanted it more than anything.

A baby. A family. All of it, with him.

"No."

"Oh, so…"

"It was selfish." Zain chuckled. "And I'm afraid it doesn't exactly paint me in the best light."

I poked at his arm. "Tell me."

"I wanted you to have a reason to stay here. With me. Even if you were safe, I wanted…" He shut his eyes. "*More*. But I remembered what you said that first night. About your dreams. The kind of man you wanted to be with. And for the first time… I wanted that, too. To be everything you'd dreamed of. The father of your children. The one I'd never had growing up."

My eyes softened. "You're going to be such a wonderful dad."

"How do you know?" He looked so vulnerable, so close to breaking, and it hurt to know anyone had inflicted scars this deep on such a strong man.

"Because you care. Because you have so much love in your heart, you're just scared to show it to other people." I kissed that spot on his chest as if in demonstration. "And you didn't have to get me pregnant to get me to stay with you, dummy. I would have done it if you asked."

"But you're happy? With this? With everything?"

"Could have gone without the kidnapping," I mumbled, getting a soft swat on my ass.

"Sass."

"You like it."

"Yeah. I like you."

"That's good," I murmured, "because you're stuck with me now. Jokes on you."

"Luna?"

"Mhm?" I hummed in response, letting his scent fill up my nose.

"Thank you." His hand slid over my stomach. "For this. For everything."

I yawned, burying my face in his neck and rubbing my nose over the spot where he'd let me mark him weeks ago. "For you? Anything." I meant it, too. "I love you."

Snuggling against him, I thought about everything that had happened over the last few days. About everything that would need to happen now that his father was gone.

"Do we have anything we need to do now?" I asked, resting my head against his shoulder and letting my eyes flutter shut.

"For now?" Zain wrapped his arms around me before picking me up and then settling us both down on the bed. "Just sleep."

"Promise you'll be here when I wake up?"

"I'll never leave you alone again." A promise.

And he didn't break his promises.

That night, curled up in his arms, tucked away where I was safe… I slept better than I had in a long, long time.

* * *

"Happy coronation day," Zain whispered in my ear, his fingers brushing over my face as my eyes fluttered open.

It still didn't feel real.

A month had passed since his dad's death. Since the night I thought I'd lost everything.

"Five more minutes," I mumbled, curling into his chest, letting his scent fill my nostrils.

He tucked a piece of hair behind my ear.

When I looked up, he was smiling at me.

"What?"

"This is everything I've ever wanted."

"Mm." Snuggling back into him further, I kissed the spot over his heart. "Getting sappy on me now, are you, husband?"

"I can't help it. You bring it out of me." He scowled. "People used to take me seriously around here."

A giggle escaped my lips. "You're just a grade-A simp."

"What's that supposed to mean?" I sat up, shaking my head. He'd never understand all the human colloquialisms I used, but I was totally okay with that. Mostly because it gave Willow and I something to laugh about with our husbands.

Giving him a kiss on the cheek, I slid out of bed, heading towards the restroom.

After using the bathroom, I stood in front of the mirror, inspecting my reflection as I brushed my teeth. It was crazy how much had changed in the last month. How much we'd accomplished.

If I'd doubted myself, my abilities, and my place here in the demon realm before—I had no reason to anymore. We'd spent the last several weeks traveling around the demon realm, helping rebuild and passing out supplies to those in need. Zain had made sure I didn't stay on my feet all day, being overbearing and protective as usual, but at least this time, he had two excuses.

I'd brought baked goods with me everywhere, introducing myself to the people I'd help rule over. Though I'd been apprehensive about meeting so many demons, I was surprised how many had no issues at all with a human witch being their queen.

Though I wouldn't be *quite* human after tonight. Still a witch, but something… *other*.

We'd tied our lifespans together, ensuring that I'd live as long as he did. Apparently, it was common with demons who mated with other races. I realized how much we didn't know in Pleasant Grove, how in the dark we'd been as a magical race. There was so much out there in the world that I had no idea about, and I wanted to see it all.

But that last part would have to wait.

In tight-fitting clothing, my bump was beginning to be obvious, though it was easy enough to hide it from almost everyone around the palace. Novalie knew, of course, as she helped me dress every morning, and so did Zain's advisors—who were like a second family here. Lilith and Asura had adopted me like sisters, something I desperately missed.

"Are you excited to see your sister?" Zain's arms wrapped around me as I stood in front of the vanity, brushing my hair. It was like he'd read my mind, but I knew how strongly our emotions were tied these days.

I rested my head against his shoulder as he took the hairbrush out of my hands.

"Yes. But I'm nervous, too."

"To tell her?"

I nodded, sliding a hand over my stomach. "I already know she feels like we rushed into this marriage, and maybe we did, but… I wouldn't change it. Part of me feels like everything happened the way it did to bring us together. Like the fates knew we needed that little push."

He buried his nose in my hair. "Sometimes I wonder what would have happened if I'd told you that first night. Asked you to come with me then."

"I'd probably have laughed in your face," I said honestly. "Or told you that you were insane."

"What about the second night?"

"Before or after you gave me a mind-blowing orgasm?"

Zain kissed my neck. "There were at least two."

"Mmm. Maybe. I think I would have had to be convinced."

His fingers pushed the straps down of my nightgown, baring my shoulder to him. "What about if I gave you another one? Would that help?"

"Perhaps…" I breathed as he ran his nose over my skin. "We should find out." I tilted my head to the side to give him access to the crook of my shoulder, wanting him to sink those teeth into me. To feel the pleasure of our beings merging as one.

Zain's hands cupped my breasts, and a low moan slipped out of me. They were already more sensitive and tender, and it felt like I could come from him playing with my nipples alone.

"Luna," he groaned, his erection pressing against me. "You're going to be the death of me one day."

"I hope not," I said, turning around so I could wrap my arms around his neck. "Especially since I tied my life to yours." I could feel the satisfaction that ran through his body.

"You're mine," he said, pressing a kiss to our mark. "My moonbeam."

"I'm yours," I agreed.

A knock on the door had us springing apart—though I knew there were few people who would interrupt us in here. Which meant it was probably time to get ready for the day, unfortunately ending our quiet moment. And any chance for an orgasm.

"Guess we don't have time for you to prove your theory," I murmured, dragging my hand up his chest.

He caught it, kissing my palm. "Later," Zain promised. "I'll make good on every single one." His eyes sparkled with a challenge, and I couldn't wait. A shiver ran down my spine.

I rubbed my thighs together, doing my best to ignore the needy feeling.

Novalie's voice called out, "My lady. I have your gown here if you're ready to dress."

"Just a moment," I responded, not wanting to extract myself from my husband's arms.

"If you don't want me to put you on the counter and show you exactly how much I want you, I suggest you go now." He nipped at my ear.

"Okay, okay, fine!" I turned like I was heading for the door, but he spun me back in, dropping a kiss on my lips. It quickly turned heated. His tongue brushed over my lower lip, seeking entrance, and I moaned a little as it slipped into my mouth. He slipped his hands up the slit in my thigh, grazing over the skin there, closer and closer—"Zain," I whimpered.

He kissed the tip of my nose. "See you soon, Moonbeam."

Finally pulling away, Zain headed towards the baths as I pushed my straps back up, straightening the gown before going to the door.

Novalie wore a knowing smile when I opened it, moving into my bedroom.

"Sleep well?"

I nodded, though the morning sickness that had hit in the last few weeks certainly hadn't been making it easy on me. Though the healer had assured me it was perfectly natural—especially with a twin pregnancy—it still didn't make it any easier on my body.

She guided me to the vanity, grabbed a comb, and began to brush out my hair the rest of the way. I watched her work through the mirror, thinking about how it had been over three months since I'd arrived here.

Everything was different. My life was changing. But that was okay. Because I had a purpose now, and I was happy, and everything had unraveled just the way it was supposed to.

Sure, maybe I was only twenty-five, but I was married to a man who cared about me. One who did everything in his power to make sure I was happy.

And I knew that no matter what trials came our way, I would have done it all over again to get here.

The future was ours.

And that was everything.

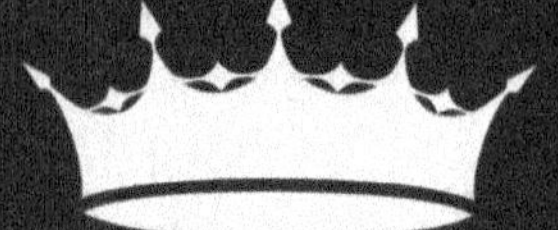

THIRTY-FOUR
ZAIN

Luna's hair shined like moonlight, adorned with those tiny little crystals I loved. A gown of lavender hugged her breasts before spilling down around her in layers of tulle. It was fashioned not to hug her belly, even though she'd insisted she wasn't *that* far along and a regular dress would be fine. Still, the empire waistline was beautiful—even if it hid her bump from me.

The skirt glittered like the stars, each tier dotted with its own set, and a bejeweled belt sat below her bust. The neckline had also been inlaid with more gemstones, and her cleavage spilled over the top, already larger from pregnancy.

Beautiful. She was the most stunning thing I'd ever laid eyes on. A tiara sat on the top of her head, a cloak of pure white velvet draped around her shoulders.

Her big green eyes looked up at me like she was memorizing my face the same way I was currently taking in hers. Like she never wanted to forget this moment. I knew I didn't.

My Queen. It felt like my whole life had built to this moment. The crown was mine, but more importantly, so was she.

I wanted to remember the moment forever when she'd said her vows to my kingdom, to serving at my side. Somehow, it meant more than our wedding.

Maybe because we knew how we felt now. Because I got to go to sleep every night with the love of my life in my arms, my entire world. Even if everything descended into darkness, I knew I'd still be able to find my way.

Because I had my light. My moonbeam. My mate.

"And now we get our happy ending?" Luna murmured, interlacing my fingers through hers as we walked to the ballroom together.

My cape draped behind me, the black fabric a mirror of Luna's, and a large golden collar rested against my chest.

"Yes." I leaned down to brush my nose against hers. "Now we get to be happy."

I guided her outside onto the balcony. Thousands of demons were collected below, all of them cheering for us as we waved hello, but that wasn't what I wanted to show her.

Luna blinked as her eyes took in the view, her hand reaching up to capture the small flakes floating down from the sky. "It's… snowing?"

"Do you like it?" I grinned, watching with rapt attention as she stared in childlike wonder.

"*How…* Did you do this?"

"I had help." Magic.

The snowflakes collected in her hair, dotting her pale skin before melting. She closed her eyes and inhaled the crisp scent.

"I love the snow," she murmured. "Willow always loved fall best, but I'm partial to winter."

"I know." I grinned, brushing the snowflakes off her cheeks. "Don't forget, I listen, wife."

She blushed, "But I thought it didn't snow here. The climate is…"

I shrugged, not wanting to ruin the wonder.

Rustling came from the open doors, a blur of activity, and when I turned, I found the two people we most wanted to see.

"Willow!" my wife exclaimed as her sister hurried over, dressed in a dark green gown and wrapped in a dark fur stole. Damien's hand was tight in hers like he couldn't bear to let her go.

A feeling I understood now all too well.

"Hey, Lune." She let go of my brother to wrap her arms around Luna. "I missed you."

"You have no idea." Luna rested her head against Willow's shoulder. "I think you need to visit more."

She smiled. "I think that can be arranged."

Damien held out his hand for me to shake. "You did it," was what he finally said, his voice deep.

"I did." We hadn't held a funeral for the bastard we called our father, though there was no body to burn, anyway. He didn't deserve it. In the last month, I'd come to terms with my role in my father's death. Part of me had always known someday I'd be responsible for his end, but I had hoped it wouldn't play out the way he did. But harming Luna, risking our unborn children—that was something I couldn't forgive.

"I'm only sorry I wasn't here to help."

"No." I couldn't help the shake of my head. "I'm glad you didn't have to see it. It was my burden to bear."

"It shouldn't have been." Damien placed a hand on my shoulder. "You take on too many burdens, brother."

Probably, but that wasn't what I'd come here today to discuss.

"I'm glad you have Willow."

"I know I was worried when you basically kidnapped her sister, but… I am happy you found your mate, too. Luna seems happy."

"She is. We are. Speaking of that…" I slipped my hand back into Luna's, addressing them both. "We have something we want to tell you."

The tip of Luna's nose was pink, but the smile that covered her face was dazzling. *Breathtaking.* Just like she was.

Willow leaned her head on Damien's shoulder, an eyebrow raised in intrigue.

Luna didn't leave them waiting for long. "I'm pregnant." My wife looked up at me, happiness filling her eyes.

"You're… what?" Her sister's jaw dropped. Those eyes—just a shade darker than Luna's—were wide.

"You're gonna be an aunt!" She exclaimed, throwing her arms around her sister again.

"And an uncle," I said to Damien.

"Oh my gods. You're serious." The smile spread over her face. "You're really having a baby? And this is… good? We're happy? Excited?"

"Very happy," Luna confirmed. "And, well… two babies. That's what the healer said. I'm hoping to come to the doctor in Pleasant Grove to get an ultrasound." Luna scrunched up her nose. "Technology here isn't quite what it is back home."

"You can say that again." Willow laughed.

"Congratulations, you two," Damien said, playfully bumping his fist into my shoulder. "Twins. Wow. Overachiever, much?"

I shrugged, shoving my hands. "That's what it's like when you're the insufferable older brother, you know. Always gotta do my best to one-up you."

Damien smirked. "Let's just wait and see how that turns out, huh? Besides, you're not the insufferable crown prince any longer."

Huh. "No. I guess I'm not." The golden spiked crown on my head proved that.

Luna rolled her eyes at the two of us. "Now, if the two of you are both done being insufferable…"

I held back my grin at her feisty attitude. I wanted to fuck it right out of her. An idea for later.

"Never." Both of us grinned as our mates gave a little huffed sound, then laughter.

We stayed out on the balcony like that until Willow was shivering, and Damien draped his jacket around her shoulders.

"Should we head back to our rooms, Wil?"

"Mmm. Yes. I've missed that bathtub."

He chuckled. "I know you do."

"I can't believe my little sister got married *and* is pregnant before me," Willow bemoaned as they walked away.

"We can remedy that, you know."

She punched him in the shoulder. "Patience, *Padawan*. We're not ready yet."

A fang popped out from Damien's lip. "Are you sure? And don't think I didn't catch the Star Wars reference."

"At least you're learning." Willow patted his arm. "We've still got a lot of pop culture to catch you up on, demon."

"Little witch, you so enjoy torturing me, don't you?" He leaned down, pressing a kiss to her forehead.

"You know you like it."

Damien leaned down, whispering something in Willow's ears that had her turning bright red.

"Goodnight, you two!" Luna called after them.

"Finally alone," I said, snaking an arm around Luna's waist to pull her in closer to me. She ran her hands down over her bump, her small belly poking through the fabric as she held them there.

"This feels familiar," she mused, wrapping her arms around my neck. I swayed us slightly to the music I heard from inside.

I thought about that night all those months ago. When I'd first brought her here, and she'd been like a single lone star in the sky—my beacon of light.

"Do you remember what I asked you that night?"

She furrowed her brows as if deep in thought. "If I thought I could be happy here?"

"Yes."

Her eyes softened. "I am. You know that."

The clock on the wall struck midnight. Bringing us to a new day.

I leaned down, dropping my voice to a whisper. "Happy Birthday, Moonbeam."

Her lips curved. "You knew."

"Of course. I have my sources."

"Willow has to stop giving out all my secrets," Luna muttered. "Besides, it's not even that exciting. I'm twenty-six."

"It's important to me." Because it was the first one we'd spent together. Because it was the first year of the rest of our lives. "And I know the perfect present for my newly crowned queen."

Lifting her up into my arms into a bridal carry, I headed back towards our bedroom.

I had an earlier promise that I still needed to deliver on, after all.

* * *

"Zain…" she panted, her thighs spread wide across my face as I thrust my tongue inside of her, my magic curling around her clit with little vibrations, bringing her right up to the edge and then stopping every time. "*Please.*"

But I was taking my sweet time devouring her, enjoying the taste of her on my tongue, letting her ride my face as she rocked her hips, trying to get enough friction.

As soon as we'd gotten back, I'd given her the present I'd gotten for her—a diamond pendant. And then I'd stripped that beautiful dress off of her, desperate to be inside of her.

Fates, she was gorgeous. And all mine. That primal urge was satisfied, knowing she carried a piece of me inside of her. That I could see the visible swell of her small belly, slightly rounded as she grew our babies.

Fuck, but that was the only present I'd ever need.

I kept fucking her with my tongue, letting her squirm all over my mouth, lapping up her juices with each stroke.

"Let me come. *Please.* I want to come so bad."

Luna, I scolded, flattening my tongue against her clit. But as much as I wanted to keep teasing her—edging her until she was crying for release—I wanted to be inside of her even more.

I was already rock hard, fisting my cock to keep from spilling just at the taste of her.

"So sweet," I muttered, pulling away. "You always taste so sweet for me, my queen."

She thrust her fingers into my hair, forcing me back against her. Luna whimpered as I flattened my tongue, lapping at her slowly.

"You want to come?" I asked, letting my powers rub slow, steady circles over that bundle of nerves.

"*Yes.* I need it," she whined. "Need to come."

Another languid lick up her slit as she moaned, rocking her hips faster. *Then come for me, Moonbeam.*

As if on command, she did, her orgasm bursting through her, pulling on my scalp almost to the point of causing me pain.

I lifted her off my face, and she moved to straddle my hips.

"Fuck. That's never going to get old." I leaned up, brushing my hand through her hair till I could cup her cheek, pulling her face down for a kiss, letting her taste herself on my tongue.

She let out a small groan as our tongues met. We kissed lazily, without a care in the world. Like we were the only two beings in this entire universe.

"I need you," Luna murmured, planting her hands on my chest and pushing herself back into a sitting position. "Inside." Her ass rested against my cock as she ground down on me. "Please."

"Look at you." I flicked my tongue against her nipple. "Naked and begging for me. Are you going to be a good girl and do what I say?"

She whimpered. "Yes."

I helped her lift her hips up, allowing me to position my tip with her entrance before she sunk down on me.

"Oh, Gods." Her head was thrown back as she worked herself down onto my length. "You're so thick. You always fill me so full."

My hands rested on her belly, that small curve that spurred me on even more. Knowing that I'd done that to her, bred her, that she was mine… It satisfied that primal instinct inside of me.

She moved up and down, working my cock further inside of her until I was buried to the hilt.

"So tight. Feels so fucking good."

Fates, she was a sight.

Her tits bounced as she rode me, the two of us moving in tandem. I couldn't keep my hips from thrusting, fucking up into her, from giving her everything she wanted. Even when I was in charge, she still had a grip on my heart.

"I love you," I murmured, closing my mouth around one of her breasts, swirling my tongue around a nipple.

She let out a series of breathy noises that went straight to my cock. "They're so sensitive," she cried, biting her lower lip as her nails dug into my chest.

I looked up at her, smirking as I switched attention to the other side, bringing her closer to the edge.

"I'm so close already. *Goddess*."

"My goddess," I agreed, popping off her breast. "I can't wait till they're filled with your milk." I nipped at them lightly, letting my teeth pinch at the little pink buds. Running my tongue over her nipples once more in a soothing motion, I wondered what it would taste like.

"You're wicked," Luna gasped, and I moved my attention up, brushing my teeth over that mark on her neck.

"Yes." I'd never disagreed with that. "Wickedly yours."

"Oh. *Bite me.* Please." Luna begged, and I couldn't tell her no. I ran my tongue over the bite mark before puncturing her skin, a low moan slipping from her lips.

As soon as I sank into her, she came, her cunt squeezing around my cock. My balls tightened as I continued thrusting up inside of her, her climax pulling me into mine.

It didn't take long for me to follow right behind, pouring my cum inside of her like she was milking me for all that I was worth.

She collapsed onto my chest, kissing the spot above my chest before I shifted our position, rolling her onto her side. Luna threw her leg over mine, keeping me in place.

"Happy Birthday, baby," I murmured.

She gave me a lazy smile, curling into my side. "Best birthday ever." Her eyes fluttered shut, tucked into me, my cum leaking out of her body, my babies safe in her belly, and I'd have traded a thousand birthdays for the rest of my life to look just like this.

"I love you," I said, kissing her forehead and playing with her moonlit strands of hair.

Luna peeked her eyes open, looking blissfully content and totally sated. "I love you, too."

"Thanks for doing life with me. By my side."

"I wouldn't have it any other way."

Life with my fated mate, the woman who'd been destined to be my queen?

That was the greatest gift anyone could have given me—ever.

614

EPILOGUE
ZAIN

Six months later…

You're kidding me," Luna whispered as she took in the nursery.

I leaned against the door frame. "It's not too much, is it?"

I'd been working on the room in secret, not letting her in here until I finished the entire thing. Everything down to the wallpaper had been done by me, carrying in piece by piece as it was delivered by carpenters and craftsmen from the villages nearby.

When she turned back to look at me, her smile lit up the room, those soft strands of icy blonde hair spilling down her back. She was wearing a thin, pale, pastel lavender shift dress, which exposed her large belly.

Carrying twins wasn't easy, especially on her small frame, and the healer expected it could be any day now.

I also really didn't want her on her feet. She'd had a hard time during the pregnancy, between horrible morning sickness in the first trimester to being unable to get comfortable now. Luna's human doctor insisted everything was fine and it was normal, but I still hated to see her discomfort. I wished I could take that away from her.

"Too much? How did you even…" Luna's eyes were watery as she shook her head. "You did all of this?"

Taking her hand, I kissed her knuckles.

A goddess. She was everything, and she was mine.

My queen. My wife. My mate.

"Yes." Urging her into the rocking chair, I helped her take a seat. "I didn't want you to have to worry about it."

I leaned down to kiss her belly before resting my hand over her bump and feeling them kick. "They're so active this morning."

"Tell me about it," she groaned, her hand settling on top of her belly. "And I think baby girl's sitting on my bladder. I've had to pee constantly. There's not enough room in there if they get any bigger."

I frowned. "Are you sure you don't want to be in Pleasant Grove for the next few weeks? Deliver at the hospital?"

"No," she said with a sigh, rocking slowly in the chair as she looked down at that belly. "I want to be here. In our home." She gave me a small smile.

We were at the one I'd taken her to on our honeymoon, our escape from the palace, and all that came with running a kingdom. Ruling over the demons was never easy, and sometimes, it was nice to just get away.

"This is beautiful." Her fingers traced over the white wood of the rocker. "All of it is."

The room wasn't as ornate at the palace, though I hadn't spared an effort in here. The wallpaper was a neutral striping, with gold detailing decorating the walls. Two gilded bassinets rested side by side in the corner, as well as a changing table and a large dresser.

That and the closet were both filled with gifts we'd gotten from everyone. There were hundreds of tiny baby outfits. I couldn't imagine how they could wear them all. But the demons had come out in droves, offering their well-wishes to us, and when we'd gone back to Pleasant Grove for Luna's baby shower—hosted by Willow, of course—her entire coven had brought even more gifts.

I'd been introduced to all of them, including Luna and Willow's cousin, Cait, whose gray cat followed her around everywhere, though I was surprised at how accepting they all were of me.

Especially for a demon who had kidnapped their youngest member, spiriting her away into the demon realm. Even if the rest of the town just thought we lived overseas. I wouldn't correct them.

Maybe it was because they all knew about Damien. Either way, I was grateful.

Thorn and Talon had insisted on coming along, both of them wearing a human glamor, and so, of course, Kairos, Lilith, and Asura hadn't wanted to stay behind either. They wanted to see where Luna had grown up. The place that turned her into the woman she is today.

Giving me her hand, I helped her out of the rocking chair, pulling her up as she wobbled on her feet.

"It's perfect." She sighed. "I can't believe they'll be here so soon."

"We built one in the palace, too. Though that one's much grander." I gave her a lopsided grin. "The girls insisted." Lilith, Asura, and Novalie had been thick as thieves, working around the clock while Luna had been on bed rest.

"I love it." She leaned up to kiss my cheek. "Thank you."

"Of course. Anything for you."

Placing my hand on her lower back, I guided her into the little living room and onto the couch. I sat down first, letting her slide in between my legs, resting her back against my chest as I cradled her in my arms.

"Have you thought of any names?" Luna whispered, tracing circles over her bump.

We'd been talking about them for weeks but hadn't settled on anything yet. Part of me felt like we wouldn't end up deciding on any until we met them. At one ultrasound in the human world, we'd found out the genders of the babies, though Luna had known we were having one of each from the beginning.

"A few. Maybe Estelle for the girl. It means star." I brushed a strand of hair off her face.

"I really like Orion for the boy. Or maybe Xander. Though Xaden is cute, too."

"Hm. Not Zain the II?" I asked, smirking.

She scrunched up her nose, tilting her head up to look at me. "You have a big enough head without us naming our son after you."

I laughed. "Fine. What about Iliana or Elena?"

"Hmm. I don't know. I'm not feeling it." She patted her belly. "Neither is she."

I rolled my eyes, covering the other side of her bump with my hand. "We'll know when they get here, right?"

"Hopefully. We can't call them baby boy and baby girl forever." She laughed. Little feet kicked at my hand as if in agreement with their mom.

Maybe they just liked hearing the sound of her laughter as much as I did.

I could have stayed there like that for hours, just holding my wife, our fingers interlocked over the miracles we'd created.

"Zain?" Luna whispered the words, nudging at me with her elbow.

"Mm?"

"I love you."

I rested my head against the crook of her neck, inhaling her sweet smell. That floral citrus with just a hint of sugar. Like no matter how long it had been since she left the kitchen, she always smelled a bit like the bakery.

"I love you too, Moonbeam."

My little ray of light. No matter what, I knew that with her by my side, I'd make it through anything life threw at us.

She winced slightly. "Also… I think my water just broke."

"Are you sure?" My eyes widened.

"I'd like to retain some dignity because if not, I definitely just peed myself, and that's embarrassing. *Gods.*"

I sat up, the reality of the situation sinking in. "You're in labor."

"Yeah. I've been having small contractions all day, but they were pretty far apart, so I didn't want to worry you—"

She looked so small. So breakable, even as she cupped her stomach. Blew out a breath through her mouth.

"Fuck. Okay." I was terrified of something happening to her. "I'll go grab the healer," I said, already ready to teleport back to the palace.

She was on standby, but I should have been more prepared. What had

I been thinking, bringing her here when she was so close to delivering?

"Wait." Luna grabbed my hand, squeezing lightly. "Can you help me into bed first? And I think I'd like to change." She wrinkled her nose at the damp spot between her legs. "Maybe take a shower. It'll probably be a while till I'm in active labor, anyway."

I nodded, holding her hand and helping her to our bedroom. And when the contractions got worse, coming even closer together, I didn't stop holding her hand—even when I thought she was going to break mine.

* * *

Orion Zayden was the first to enter this world, fifteen minutes before his sister, Raelynn Elena—the newest prince and princess of the demon realm.

"Your mom is a warrior," I whispered to the two sleeping babies, wrapped up in blankets as I held them both in my lap.

They were so beautiful. It was amazing to think that just an hour ago, they'd both been inside of her and now they were in the world, fully formed beings.

"You're going to be so loved," I promised. "We already love you so much."

I'd worried a lot—about whether I'd be a good dad, especially with a role model like mine. But the second they'd been placed in my arms, I knew I'd do anything to protect them. That seeing harm done to them would cause *me* pain.

It was love at first sight. Just like with their mom.

Luna's eyes fluttered open, yawning after her quick nap. "Hi."

"Hello." I looked down at our babies' sweet faces. "Do you want to hold one?"

"Uh-huh." She nodded, extending out her arms.

I placed the little blue bundle there, and she softly stroked down his nose with her finger.

"They're so small," Luna whispered the words like she was afraid to wake them up. "But so precious."

I cleared my throat. "The healer said you could try nursing now if you wanted."

Luna nodded, unlacing the top of her gown, the movement causing a small cry to slip from Orion's lips.

"Shhh," she murmured, bringing him to her breast, trying to get him to latch on like she'd been shown. She gave a small grunt of frustration.

"You want to try with her?"

"No, I—" she gave a little gasp. "I got this." Her eyes closed, and I watched our son's mouth work.

"Look at my boy. He's a natural. So strong."

Luna adjusted him into the crook of her arm, and I settled our daughter on her other arm, her mouth widening in a tiny yawn.

"Hi, sweet girl," she cooed, repeating the motion until both of them were feeding from her breasts.

"You're a miracle," I said, standing over her and watching in awe as she fed our children.

Luna looked down, unable to take her eyes off of them. "Do you remember what you felt the first time you saw me?"

"Yes." Of course. I did. Like nothing would ever be the same again. I nodded, resting my forehead against hers. "That I'd never seen anyone so beautiful in my entire life. You lit up the room, melting my heart."

Happy tears streaked down her face as she murmured. "It's the same with them. One look and I knew everything was *better*. Like it wasn't possible for something more perfect in the universe to exist. My heart is just overflowing with love for them."

She adjusted the pillows on the bed so I could slide in behind her, letting her rest against my chest, helping her hold them, staring at the wonder of life that we'd created.

"Do you know what Raelynn means?" I asked, tracing a finger over her little, tiny fingers.

"No."

"It means *beam of light*. That's what she is." A little dusting of blonde hair coated her tiny head—just like her mother's. And when her eyes blinked open, I knew what color would be shining back at me. Violet, just like my mother's. "Just like you are."

A smile curled over her lips. "Orion means *heaven's light*." She brushed a finger over Rion's cheek. "It's fitting, really."

"That we both picked names that meant light?" I chuckled.

Luna nodded, a dreamy sigh escaping her lips. "It's perfect. They're perfect."

"You're perfect," I said, pressing a kiss to her cheek. "I love you, Moonbeam."

"Till eternity do us part," she whispered.

I chuckled. "Till eternity do us part."

I hoped I never had to see a day without her, but I knew that even forever wouldn't be long enough to be with her. To love her. To love the lives we were creating together. The little bundles of us that rested in front of us.

Our future was as vast as the night sky, unfurling in front of us. All we had to do was reach out and take it.

Between her light and my dark, we were a match made in the stars. Two beings, perfectly balanced. *Harmony.*

And now, there wasn't just one light in my life anymore—there were three.

EXTENDED EPILOGUE
LUNA

"What do you think, Luna?"

"Hm?" I looked over at my sister, Willow, who was bouncing their one-year-old daughter on her knee. Opal giggled her dark head of hair just like her dad's bobbing with the movement.

She poked my arm. "You're distracted again."

"Well, who can blame me?" I leaned my head on my sister's arm, filling my nose with her pumpkin and coffee scent that always felt like a warm hug.

It wasn't unlike the way Zain's scent calmed me, brought me back to earth, and instantly felt like home.

As if I'd summoned him in my thoughts, my husband looked over at me, a grin spreading over his face as the little black-haired toddler climbed into his lap with a yawn. The guys were on the couch while we'd been sitting cross-legged on the carpet.

We were all gathered in the living room of the house I'd grown up in—now my sister's house—Willow, Damien, and their little one, Opal. My family. In some ways, Pleasant Grove still felt a little like home, and it was always a breath of fresh air to come back and visit. Domestic, in ways that living in the palace was decidedly not.

Don't look at me like that, he said into my mind, his voice soft like a caress.

Like what? I thought back, doing my best to look innocent.

Like you want another one.

I only hummed in response. It wouldn't be the worst thing, would it? Blowing him a kiss instead, I ignored it as Willow giggled at my side.

"Mama," a little hand tugged on my sweater. "Up."

Given that it was early December in Pleasant Grove, we were all dressed for warmth after playing outside in the snow this morning.

"Oh, my sweet girl," I said, scooping her up in my arms before kissing all over her cheek.

My daughter rested her head over my heart as she cuddled against me.

"So sweet," Willow murmured, putting Opal down, who crawled away to play with her blocks. "Gods, I can't believe how big they've gotten."

"You say that every time you see them."

She pouted. "Maybe because I don't get to see them every day." It felt like months in between visits, even if it was only weeks.

But in truth—she was right. The twins had gotten so big, turning into toddlers right before my eyes, and sometimes it felt like I could blink and they'd be completely grown up right before my eyes. I just wanted to savor these moments with my babies.

I leaned in, kissing the top of Raelynn's head. She'd fallen right asleep on top of me, just like she'd always done since she was born.

Gods. It had been two years now since I'd found out I was having the twins, and I'd found out a few months later that Willow was pregnant with hers and Damien's first child as well.

Now, my little ones were big enough to walk on their own. They got into more mischief than I could have ever imagined at the palace, and sometimes, it was nice to just get away.

"You could come visit more, too," I said, looking over at our husbands. With Damien next to Zain, it was like seeing triple. My son, Orion, was practically my husband's little clone, all three of them sharing that mess of black hair.

Never mind that I'd carried him for nine months and then gave birth to him—he didn't have a lick of me. Down to those bright golden eyes, just like I'd dreamed about.

Willow stretched her arms out before standing. I followed, getting up and heaving my daughter onto my hip as she moved into the kitchen.

My sister sighed deeply, and I watched out of the corner of my eye as Opal tugged Selene's tail, my cat meowing in protest.

Any time we left the demon realm for too long, we brought her along with us and would stay in my old apartment over the bakery. Even if we'd hired a manager and a whole bakery staff, it still felt like ours.

"What's on your mind?" I asked, nudging her with my elbow.

"I've just… been thinking," Willow murmured.

"Yeah?" I leaned my head against the wooden cabinets as she moved around the space, doors opening, cups flying around without being touched, and then two cups of coffee sat on the counter.

She picked it up and then took a sip before turning back to me. "About what I want."

I raised an eyebrow. "If you're about to tell me you're going to run off and join the traveling witches, I have news for you." I used my head to indicate the people we'd left in the other room.

Willow laughed so hard she had to place her hand over her chest. "No, no. Nothing like that." She gave me a small smile. "I love our life. And Opal's perfect. Everything's great, really." She looked out the window that looked into the big backyard. "But I never really figured out what I wanted to do with my life."

"And it's time?" I asked because I truly wanted that for her. To follow her heart, to find her passion. She helped me follow my dream, and I'd always have her back to find hers.

Her face brightened. "Yeah. I know someday we'll leave the human realm entirely, but I've been thinking about going back to school. Do something for *me*."

"Oh, Wil." I nuzzled the head of my fast-asleep toddler. "That sounds like a great idea. Have you decided on what yet?"

"No." She shook her head. "But I know it'll come to me. What about you?"

I shifted Rae. "What do you mean?"

"Do you ever miss it? Having a purpose?" I'd said that to Zain once—that I needed to have a purpose. A reason for being. Something that brought me joy.

"They're my purpose now," I admitted, burying my nose in her hair. "That, and running an entire kingdom. Taking care of our people.

Sometimes, it feels like I'm exactly where I'd always dreamed I'd be."

That my life would end up just like this. Happy. In love.

Still baking whenever I could.

I sighed happily as I held Rae tighter. At least she resembled me, with her blonde hair and curious demeanor. And those lavender eyes—just like Zain's mom. It made me feel closer to her, even if we'd never met. I wished I could thank her for giving me her son, for the man I'd fallen in love with. The same way I'd wished my parents could have met the men we married.

My husband came in from the living room, scooping a sleeping Raelynn out of my arms.

"How are my girls doing?" He leaned against me, pressing his nose into my hair as he inhaled my scent. Did he suspect…?

"Good." I peeked into the living room and found Rion playing with a black cat on the couch. "Looks like your brother's at it again." I playfully rolled my eyes.

Willow smirked. "One day, that trick is really going to bite him in the ass."

Little toddler feet padded across the tile floor, and then a tiny pair of hands tugged at the bottom of my jeans. "Up! Up, Mama!"

"Rion," I laughed, lifting him up into the air like a plane. "Did you have fun playing with Uncle Damien, buddy?" He nodded, babbling incoherent words to me, a conversation no one could understand but his twin sister.

Then Damien was there too, their little one riding on his shoulders. He wrapped an arm around Willow, my sister instantly relaxing into his hold.

"Want me to start dinner?" Damien asked her, passing off Opal, who didn't seem to want to let go of her dad's thick locks.

"That'd be great," Willow said, carrying their daughter into the little playpen. I set Rion down with her, and he immediately started playing with a set of toy cats.

You good with her? I asked Zain, who was now leaning against the doorframe, rubbing smoothing circles on our daughter's back. *I can take her back.*

We're great.

"Should I pour you guys some wine?" Willow asked, grabbing a bottle out of the cabinet now that her hands were empty.

"Sure," my husband said, looking towards me.

"Oh, no. I'll just stick to water, I think."

Zain raised an eyebrow at me. *Have something to tell me, Moonbeam?*

Not yet. I gave him an innocent look.

She flicked her fingers, using magic to pull three wine glasses out of the cupboard, filling two of them with red wine, and then handing them off to the guys.

Hm. Maybe I wasn't the only one with a secret.

Rae stirred in Zain's arms, and he put her down in the playpen, placing a little kiss on her forehead before she moved to play with her cousin. When he came back into the room, he slid into my side, sipping from his wine glass.

"So, what are the chances we can actually get you to spend the holidays in the palace?" I asked, changing the subject.

I knew neither of our demons cared about the holiday—they'd never celebrated it, of course—but we'd grown up with a tree in our living room, and I wanted to keep the tradition alive for our kids. Plus, who needed an excuse for presents?

Willow popped her hip against the counter, sipping her glass. "Pretty good, I think. But… wait." She narrowed her eyes. "Will it be decorated?"

"You forget, I'm the *Queen*. Of course, it'll be decorated." I shot Zain a look like, *bite me*.

He popped a canine tooth out over his lips. *If you want me to, all you have to do is ask, wife.*

"We'll be there," Damien promised, still hard at work at the stove. "It'll be good to be home."

Home. The word made my heart feel full.

Truthfully, it didn't matter where we were—as long as my family was around me.

* * *

"They're all tuckered out," I said from the couch in my old apartment. We'd stayed at Willow and Damien's until both kids had fallen asleep and then carried them back here.

I couldn't convince Zain to learn to drive a car, and he hardly tolerated *riding* in one, so we normally walked when we came to Pleasant Grove unless it was to a doctor's appointment in the next town over when I'd been pregnant.

"Yeah." Zain scooped Raelynn up in his arms, kissing her blonde forehead.

Then he took Orion out of my arms, tucking them both into the toddler beds we'd built in the living room.

"This place is getting a little cramped with the four of us, isn't it?" I sighed.

And it would be even more crowded soon.

"Yeah. We could always find a new place. Maybe on the outskirts of town? Somewhere with a big backyard?"

I pouted. "I *like* the apartment, though. It reminds me of when we first met. Like it's a little magical." I knew I was being totally irrational, but I was attached, dammit. And hormonal. "Besides, we don't come here enough to justify a house. It's not like we can't stay with Willow and Damien. They have plenty of rooms."

"But then I don't get you all to myself," Zain protested, pulling me into his arms. He took a deep pull of my scent. "Your scent changed, you know."

"Hmm?" I fluttered my eyelashes, pretending not to know what he meant, wiggling out of his arms to find the little box I'd hidden earlier.

"It's extra sweet. Just like—"

"Zain," I blurted, cutting him off. "I know this trip was a little impromptu, but…"

"I already know," he murmured, pulling the box from my hands. "But tell me anyway, Moonbeam. I want to hear it from your lips."

"It's really early. Like *really* early. I technically haven't even missed my period yet. But I sensed it with my magic, and I wanted to be sure."

He pulled open the box.

"I thought I'd be sure, so…" I fiddled with my fingers.

The pregnancy test inside had two little pink lines.

"You're pregnant." His voice was reverent, and he lifted me up, spinning me around. "This is the best surprise ever."

I laughed. "Ready to do this all over again? Though I'm pretty sure there's only one this time."

Zain just nodded, kneeling down to press a kiss to my flat stomach. "Boy or girl?"

"I don't know." A smile curled over my face. No visions had come to me, and besides being able to detect the tiny life in me… I sort of liked not knowing. "Guess we'll find out together, huh?"

He stood up to his full height, towering over me before cupping the back of my neck. "You're the greatest thing life has ever given me. What would I do without you?"

"Be a moody, insufferable crown prince, probably."

His chuckle went through my body, straight to my core. "But I'm not a prince, am I?"

"No."

He started walking, forcing me to take little steps backward toward our bedroom. "What am I?"

"My husband." My knees hit the edge of the bed.

"My king." I let my body drop onto the mattress.

"My mate."

He kneeled in front of me.

"And what am I?" I breathed out as Zain placed a hand on either side of the bed like he was holding me in place.

His head dipped low. "My wife."

He placed a kiss on my collarbone. "My queen."

His hands sneaked up underneath my shirt, cupping my breasts. "The mother of my children."

"*Yes.*" I let my eyes flutter shut as he brushed his thumbs lightly over my aching nipples.

"The love of my life."

"Mmm," I said, as his hands trailed lower. "I like that one." I flicked open the button of his pants.

"*My mate.*"

I nodded when he dipped his fingers underneath the waistband of my jeans.

"My moonbeam."

"Yes," I agreed, wrapping my arms around his neck. "Yours."

"Mine." His voice was low, a growl against my skin.

It was a love some people went through an entire lifetime without finding. And it was worth it. Every minute. Because through him, I'd found out exactly who I was. And I was exactly where I was supposed to be.

Here, with him and the little family we'd created.

All because I'd gone and fallen in love with a demon.

A wicked demon prince who was determined to call me his.

But that was the funny thing about fate, wasn't it?

It was all worth it in the end.

"Forever?" I asked, my lips closing over his.

"And always," he responded, kissing me back softly.

BONUS EPILOGUE

Zain

It was a meow that woke me from my peaceful slumber. And then a delicately placed paw, standing on my chest.

"Wife," I groaned, reaching over in bed to wake her up. "Your beast won't leave me alone."

All I found was cold, empty sheets.

"Luna?"

Even after all these years, the panic flared in me at finding her missing. A side-effect of my newly-pregnant wife having been kidnapped and trapped underground.

Sometimes, I still got nightmares, but then I'd wake up and find her sleeping next to me, her moonlit blonde hair sprawled across my black, silky sheets. It was enough to calm me, to soothe that ache in my soul.

She'd been sleeping so much lately that I couldn't imagine what would have dragged her from our bed. Though she'd probably just gotten up early, and I'd find her making a batch of scones in the kitchen. Just like always. No matter what changed, her love of baking never did. I loved that about her. How she always smelled sweet, like sugar and lemons and lavender.

I ran my fingers through my hair, eager to seek out my mate. I tugged at that shining golden cord that tied us together, feeling her love at the end of it.

Fates, but I loved her. How could I have ever imagined my life—our life—as anything but this?

Getting up from our bed, I pulled on my robe, heading toward the bathroom.

We'd come to the smaller manor in the countryside for a few weeks of peace. I'd left Kairos in charge, figuring a little delegation certainly wouldn't have the entire demon realm collapsing around us.

I did a double take, rubbing my eyes at the words written on the bathroom mirror. *Happy Birthday, Daddy!* was written in… *icing?*

Running my fingers through it, I brought them up to my lips. The taste exploded on my tongue. *Chocolate.* A smile spread over my face. I'd forgotten the importance my wife placed on the day of my birth, probably because I'd never really celebrated before her.

Pulling on a black shirt and a pair of gray sweatpants, I hurried down the stairs. Luna had bought them for me last year in the human realm, insisting I wear them around the house.

Watching the heat spark in her eyes whenever I did made it worth it.

Something about the heroes in her book also wearing them?

I didn't care—if it made her happy, I'd do anything she asked.

Figuring I'd find my family at the source of the icing, I padded into the kitchen. Leaning on the door frame, I watched the scene unfold in front of me.

My wife and our five-year-old twins were crowded around something on the massive counter, giggling to themselves. Luna had our three-year-old daughter on her hip, attempting to stick her hands in whatever they had been working on.

I chuckled, the sound attracting the attention of my little demons.

"Daddy!" Rae and Rion shouted, hopping off their stools and running over to me.

"Did you get up early to surprise me?" I asked, bending down as they both wrapped their arms around me in a hug.

Rion nodded. "Mommy said we could help for your birthday."

I hoisted them both up in my arms. They were both getting bigger by the day, and I was grateful for the power coursing through my veins that allowed me to still carry them like this. I already knew I'd miss these days when they were gone.

"Happy birthday, Daddy." Rae cuddled against my neck, and I kissed her little blonde forehead. So much like Luna's, even though she'd gotten my mother's violet eyes.

"Thank you, little star."

"Morning, handsome," Luna said as I walked over to her, pressing a kiss to her lips. "Happy birthday."

She was wearing a pretty, flowing lavender dress that cut off at the knees and had left her light blonde waves tumbling down around her.

"Thank you." I rubbed my nose against hers. "They just keep getting better."

A grin lit up my wife's face. "Good. That's what I'm going for, after all."

Luna was only thirty, compared to my three hundred plus years, and sometimes it felt like I wasn't really living before I met her. Like I'd just been going through the motions. I'd been surviving, just waiting for this.

A life full of love, warmth, and happiness. A life with a family of my own.

"So what did you all make me?"

"A cake, Daddy!" Rion beamed up at me from my arms. "It's chocolate, and we helped Mommy!"

"So that's where the frosting came from, huh?"

Luna's lips curled up, a small smile lighting up her face as she adjusted Lia on her hip.

I hummed in response, setting them both down and ruffling my son's hair. "Good work, bud." I looked at the cake. I could definitely tell they'd helped, even though it still had all the charm of Luna's baking. I was sure it would taste just as good as normal.

No, better. Because they'd all made it with love.

"And how's my sweet angel?" I asked, tugging at a strand of our youngest daughter's dark hair. Liana had Luna's bright green eyes and features, her light coloring in stark contrast with her jet-black hair.

She held out her arms for me, and I took her from Luna.

"Careful," she warned, wiping her hands on her apron as Liana stuck her fingers in my face. "She has some frosting on her fingers." My wife giggled.

I grunted, taking our baby girl—though she wasn't all that little anymore—over to the sink to wash off her hands. "You just wanted *me* to deal with that, huh?"

Maybe. Luna sent the thought to me and winked as I dried off Lia's hands, adjusting her pretty dress that thankfully came out unscathed.

Blowing raspberries on her cheeks, she erupted into laughter, and I threw her up into the air. "More, Daddy!" she cheered, throwing her hands into the air.

"Later, Princess." I kissed her cheek. "Let's check out this cake your mom made first, hm?" Sure, I'd just woken up, but cake sounded like an excellent idea.

I reached out, but Luna swatted at my hand. "Breakfast first."

I frowned. "So you're tempting me with a *delicious* cake made with love by my family, and I'm not even allowed to eat it?"

"Yes." She stuck out her tongue. "Because I also *made* breakfast. Your favorite."

Quirking an eyebrow, I held her gaze. *I can think of something else I'd rather have for breakfast. My favorite meal. I'd happily eat you—*

Zain! Her cheeks turned pink. *Not with the kids around.*

I waved her off. *Later, then.* My lips turned up in a wicked grin. Later, indeed. I knew just what I wanted for my birthday this year.

Two little hands wrapped around my free one, and I was tugged towards the balcony door. Raising an eye at Luna, she gave me a sly smile as the glass doors opened in front of us—magic. *Her* magic.

I was constantly in awe of her, how with just the flick of the wrist, she could summon items to her, the way she gave her full attention to baking even while being the queen of the entire realm.

Magnificent. Never mind that I had my own magic. She was incredible.

"You did all this?" I finally choked out as I surveyed the patio. She'd spread out a picnic blanket, and there was a basket of freshly baked scones and other assorted breakfast items laid out for us.

"Mhm." She slid an arm around my waist. "The kids helped a little."

"Oh, I bet." I eyed our children, who were eagerly staring at the chocolate filled pastries in front of them. "Thank you." I kissed the top of her head. "Now, let's dig in."

* * *

Luna

The birthday cake sat on the counter, half demolished by the three little hellions who ran around here like they owned the place. In a way, I supposed they did. They were Princes and Princesses, after all.

Though we wouldn't be raising them like that. And unlike some royals, *we* were raising our own kids. Thankfully, the demon realm had been peaceful after his father's death. Everyone seemed to be happy with our rule, even if I was a witch and originally mortal. Though these days I wasn't quite human any longer.

Sometimes it still felt strange to me that I had an eternity to live now, but I also knew that we'd do it together.

Me, Zain, and whatever brood we raised. Plus Willow and Damien and their kids. A smile lit up my face.

Some days, I was extra thankful that we'd managed to fall for a pair of demon brothers.

A prickle of awareness trailed down my spine, and I didn't have to turn around to know who was standing there.

I'd been cleaning the kitchen as Zain ran around the palace with the kids, getting into countless shenanigans, I was sure. Though the twins were still small, they'd already started coming into their own magic, and they wreaked havoc all over the palace grounds.

Zain slid behind me, wrapping his hands around my waist and pressing his body tight against mine. "Thank you, Moonbeam." He pressed a kiss to my cheek. "Today was…" He exhaled roughly. "There aren't enough words. I love you."

I turned in his arms to press a kiss to his jaw. "You deserve it, Zain. Every bit of happiness." I cupped his cheek.

He shut his eyes, nuzzling into my hand.

When his eyes opened, they were shining with heat. Molten, liquid gold, swirling around in those beautiful eyes I'd spent so much time staring into. How had I ever thought those dull, muted brown eyes he'd glamoured had been anything but a farce?

This was the real him. Demon and wicked and all mine.

"I love you," I murmured, kissing the corner of his mouth.

"You know, the kids are all tuckered out now…" Zain's hands wandered, slipping up under my skirt to grab my ass. He squeezed lightly, sliding his fingers under the thin line of my panties even as his lips found mine. His tongue swept along the seam of my lips, seeking entrance, and it didn't take much for him to coax them open. Our mouths were locked together, devouring each other like it had been ages since we'd last tasted each other instead of hours.

My husband hummed slightly, playing with the waistband of the scrap of lace. He could probably scent the arousal pooling between my thighs, but I was long past being embarrassed with him.

"What?" I bit my lip, holding in a gasp as he snapped the fabric against my skin.

"Was thinking I liked it better when you weren't wearing these all the time." He rubbed my clit through the material.

My cheeks were warm. "*Zain.*" I couldn't hold back a small moan as he rubbed me over the thin fabric, my wetness already soaking them.

"I know what I want for my birthday this year," he said, his deft fingers continuing to drive me crazy. I was so empty, and all I needed was for him to slide them inside of me, to fill me up.

"Hmm?" I mumbled, blinking at him through the haze of lust. "But you already got your presents." We'd opened them after dinner. Though what did you *really* get a demon king who had magical powers and owned everything he could ever desire?

"What do you say we have another one?" Zain asked, resting his free hand on my flat stomach.

I gaped at him. "What?"

"A baby." He rubbed his nose along my neck.

I let the sleeves of the soft purple dress slip down my arms.

"What, three isn't enough for you?" I laughed as he pressed kisses along the sensitive skin there, taking extra care to press one over the mark he'd left all those years ago.

"Liana's three. The twins are five. Doesn't it seem like a good time?" He let his teeth scrape over my skin, and I already knew what my answer would be. *Yes.* "Let me get you pregnant again."

"You're insane."

"You like it."

"Yes," I confirmed. "I love it. And I love you. My wicked, wicked demon husband."

He hummed, a devious expression covering his face, before he crooked his fingers into the fabric against my hip, tearing it from my body in one movement.

I shot him an incredulous look. "Zain."

"What?" A wicked smirk covered his face. "I like you bare for me." He ran his knuckle over my slit. "Just like that."

"I liked those," I pouted, ignoring the way his fingers teased my entrance, how desperate I already was for him. How much our conversation had flipped that switch inside of me.

"Haven't I already proven to you that I'll buy you more?" He brushed a piece of hair off my cheek.

"Still. Those were pretty."

Zain chuckled, hoisting me up onto the counter, his arms boxing me in. "What do you want, my queen?" His eyes flared, that bright golden color looking like liquid metal, little bolts of lightning surging as he took me in.

"You," I admitted, running my tongue across my lower lip. "But today's supposed to be about *you*."

"This is about me," he said, lowering onto his knees. "And right now, I want to taste my mate on my tongue."

Using his hands to part my thighs, he dipped his head down, his face stilling for a moment as he inhaled my scent.

"Zain," I murmured, burying my fingers in his hair and tugging him further against me.

The first swipe of his tongue against my clit made my body jolt, though that may have been the spark of lightning that surged through my body.

Fuck, it never stopped being amazing between us. He thrust his tongue inside me, lapping up my arousal. "So sweet," he muttered, swirling his tongue inside of me before sucking on my clit.

Zain feasted on me like a man starved, working me higher and higher until I was about to shatter.

Though I'd learned to control my magic, sometimes it still found ways to burst out of me when he caught me off guard, overwhelming me with powerful orgasms.

He pushed two fingers inside of me, and that was all it took. Between his mouth and the way he knew exactly what spots inside of me would make me come, it was a wonder I could last as long as I did.

Though I enjoyed it equally as much when he had me crying and begging on the edge, never quite letting me tumble over.

He stood up, still fully clothed—though he'd changed after breakfast out of his sweats and into a black silky shirt and black trousers—and stepped in between my thighs. His hardened length pressed against the front of his pants, and I reached out, tracing a finger up his shaft.

He clicked his tongue, pushing my hand away. "It's my birthday, isn't it? That means I'm in charge."

"Yes," I whispered, feeling my pulse fluttering in my throat. I liked it when he took control, reminding me exactly who he was. My husband, the demon king.

"Take this off," he ordered, running a finger between my breasts. "I want to see you."

Obeying him, I pulled my dress off over my head, letting the garment fall to the floor.

"Good," he murmured, placing a kiss to the top of each breast—still held up by my lacy bra that matched my now ruined panties. "And this."

I unhooked my bra, and it joined my gown in a heap. My cheeks warmed as he surveyed me—completely naked, sitting on the kitchen countertop—while he remained fully clothed.

After giving birth to three children, I wasn't as slender as I'd been when we first met, but Zain never made me feel anything less than beautiful. He still called me his goddess, and the way his eyes heated as he took me in made it hard to deny that. Stretch marks or not, he was still just as insatiable for me as I was for him.

"The perfect present," he murmured. "Spread your legs for me, Moonbeam."

Doing as he asked, I parted my thighs, giving him a full view of my bare pussy.

"Good girl." Zain's croon filled me with satisfaction, making me feel bolder—empowered.

I cupped my breasts, running my thumbs over my hardened nipples as he watched me. Biting my lip, I hid a smile as he groaned, palming his cock through his pants.

"Zain," I whispered, running a finger through my wet folds as he freed his erection—long and full and *thick*—and pumped himself as he watched me slide a finger inside.

"Luna," he groaned. "You drive me absolutely wild, you know that?" Wild was an understatement. He was a feral beast when he unleashed himself, driven purely by his demon mating instincts. The way I had been after our wedding—drunk on demon aphrodisiac wine.

"Come here," I begged. My fingers weren't enough. I needed him to quell this aching need inside. I was so empty, desperate and needy for him. Only him. Only ever him. "I need you inside of me."

"Do you need me to fill you up, wife?"

I whimpered, nodding as I circled my clit with the finger that had just been inside of me. "Yes. Please."

"Need me to flood that sweet pussy with my cum over and over, hm? Until you're all good and bred for me?"

A moan slipped from my lips. "*Yes.*" Before I could beg again, he was in front of me, his fingers digging into my thighs as he pulled my legs further apart. Without warning, he pushed inside of me, filling me to the hilt with one thrust. Stars exploded in my vision.

"Fuck," he groaned. "You feel too good."

I let my head fall back, exposing the crook of my neck to him. "Zain," I begged. "Bite me."

He complied, sinking his canine teeth into my flesh, the sting quickly turning into mind-melting pleasure.

Wrapping my legs around his waist, I curled my fingers around the cool stone countertop, digging my nails in to keep myself in place as he fucked me harder. The sound of our bodies moving together filled the room and was sinfully delicious.

Each stroke of his flesh against mine, the way he filled me completely—it was all too much. I cried out as another orgasm ripped through my body, my insides clenching around his length.

"That's it," he praised, releasing my neck. "My good little wife." Zain licked at the bite marks on my skin, sealing them with his magic.

He pulled out of me, and I blinked up at him. "But…" He hadn't come yet. Even if he normally put my pleasure first, I wanted to feel him come inside of me.

For him to fill me up, just like he'd promised. Instead, he released my thighs, massaging them lightly to counteract the sting of how he'd kept them pulled apart, and guided me down off the counter.

"What—" I murmured, but he silenced me with another rough kiss against my lips. "I thought you were going to fill me up," I muttered when he released my mouth, leaving one last kiss on the corner of my lips. My fingers fiddled with the buttons on his shirt, attempting to divest him of at least one piece of clothing.

The corner of his mouth tilted up. "I promised I would, didn't I?"

Then Zain spun me around, bending me over the counter so my nipples pressed against the cool stone. His knee wedged between my legs, pushing them apart. His hand traced down my back, down the ridges of my spine, before swiping down my exposed slit.

"So wet for me, Luna."

I let out an unintelligible string of words as he pushed his fingers inside me, not giving me what he knew I needed.

Straining my neck to look back at him, I found he'd shed his clothes, those magnificent black wings spread out behind him. Powerful, yes, but also beautiful. And to know that I was the only one he let see him like this made it even more meaningful.

A satisfied hum left my lips as he gripped my hips, pressing our bodies tightly together so I could feel how hard he was for me.

"Fuck me," I gasped, pushing back against him and rubbing my ass against his cock.

His tip pressed against my entrance before he pushed inside, stretching me fully with his size.

"That's it, baby," he muttered, pushing inside as I let out a series of short, gasping breaths. "Look how well you take me. Made for me."

A moan of agreement spilled out of me. "I was."

Nothing had ever felt as right as being with him. As his wife, his queen, his mate—I knew it was true that the universe had made us for each other. And even if he'd had to wait three hundred years for me, at least we had each other now.

And I never wanted to let him go. Not when I'd found so much happiness here. A purpose, a *meaning*. Everything I'd ever done had led me here to this life. Though I'd never imagined I would be a queen, my family was everything to me.

Zain wrapped one hand around my neck, the other still on my hip, keeping me pressed tightly against him as he moved with short, punishing thrusts. He worked me higher and higher, electricity sparking through my body with each push of his body against mine.

"I'm so close," he grunted in my ear.

In response, I squeezed my thighs together, tightening around him.

"Fuck." He buried himself even deeper inside of me, and I tightened my grip on the countertop. "I need you to come again."

My back arched as a shadow touch ghosted over my clit. "*Zain.*" Gods, he knew me too well. When his powers melded with mine, it was enough to override all my senses. He massaged my clit with his wisps of shadow, tightening his grip on my neck, and that was it.

I came with a scream of his name, light flooding from my fingertips, and he followed behind me with a roar as lightning cracked outside, thunder rumbling as he poured his seed inside of me.

Warmth unfurled in my belly, and I moaned as he did just what he'd promised—filled me up.

"See?" Zain whispered in my ear as he pulled me upright, sliding a hand over my stomach. "I always keep my promises, don't I, wife?" He released his grip on my neck, pressing a kiss to each side. "Are you okay? I wasn't too rough, was I?"

I laughed, pressing my ass against him. "No. But haven't we well established that I *like* it when you're rough with me?"

A rough chuckle vibrated through my body, reminding me that he was still buried inside of me, though I was content to stay just like this for a bit longer. "You're perfect."

His fingers guided my chin to the side so he could press a soft kiss against my lips, and then he pulled out of me. Our combined releases trickled out of me, and he swiped a finger through the mess we'd made before pushing it back inside of me.

"Caveman," I muttered, rolling my eyes.

Zain gave a hum of satisfaction as he pulled on his pants, tucking himself back inside before picking up my dress from the floor. He guided the garment over my outstretched arms, letting it fall over my naked body before he wrapped me up in his embrace.

We stayed like that for several moments, swaying back and forth in the quiet of the kitchen, his head resting against mine as he held me tight.

"Thank you," he murmured.

Turning in his arms, I rested both hands on his cheeks. "For what?"

He shook his head. "Everything you've given me. For every moment since you agreed to be mine." He took one of my hands in his, kissing my palm.

"I love you," I murmured, knowing the words weren't enough to describe the depths of my feelings for him. Luckily, we didn't need words. I could feel exactly what he felt for me, too.

"You're my everything, Moonbeam. I love you so much."

A grin spread over my face. "I know." I stepped up onto my tiptoes and pulled his neck down so I could whisper into his ear. "Now take me to bed, husband. We're not done celebrating yet."

He smiled wickedly before throwing me over his shoulder and carting me up to our bedroom, where he showed me exactly how much he liked that idea.

THE END

ACKNOWLEDGEMENTS

When I finished writing this, it was the seventh book that I typed *the end* on. When you're reading this, I'll be finishing up my ninth. It feels surreal in so many ways.

Spookily Yours was a surprise in every way, and I felt those expectations *so* hard while writing this one. Every so often, I'd be writing and would remember that someone was going to *narrate* this book. Out loud. That was paralyzing.

I finished writing it, and then shoved it aside for two months, because the thought of editing it made me nauseous. What if everyone hated it? What if I couldn't replicate Spookily Yours?

But somehow, despite all that, what was supposed to be another silly little demon book turned into a 92k word, 350 page book. Way longer than the 60k I'd ever planned for this story.

I'm so thankful for each and every one of you who has taken the time to read my books. Your support of this series, especially, changed my life.

Thank you to Katie W, who's been cheering me on from the very beginning.

To Katie D, who reads every book I write and never goes "Jennifer what did you just make me read?"

To Olivia, for putting up with me every time I said "but what if it's bad?" and then assured me it, in fact, did not.

To Drew & Jessi, my loves who both scream to me about how much they love Daddy Zain—often.

ABOUT THE AUTHOR

Originally from the Portland area, Jennifer now lives in Orlando with her dog, Walter and cat, Max. She always has her nose in a book and loves going to the Disney Parks in her free time.

Website: www.jennchipman.com

FIND ME ON:

Amazon: amazon.com/author/jenniferchipman
Goodreads: goodreads.com/jennchipman
Instagram: instagram.com/jennchipmanauthor
Facebook: facebook.com/jennchipmanauthor
TikTok: tiktok.com/@jennchipman

ALSO BY JENNIFER CHIPMAN

Best Friends Book Club

Academically Yours - Noelle & Matthew

Disrespectfully Yours - Angelina & Benjamin

Fearlessly Yours - Gabrielle & Hunter

Gracefully Yours - Charlotte & Daniel

Castleton University

A Not-So Prince Charming - Ella & Cameron

Once Upon A Fake Date - Audrey & Parker

Witches of Pleasant Grove

Spookily Yours - Willow & Damien

Wickedly Yours - Luna & Zain

S.S. Paradise

A Love Beyond the Stars - Aurelia & Sylas

A North Pole Christmas

Elfemies to Lovers – Ivy & Teddy

www.ingramcontent.com/pod-product-compliance
Lightning Source LLC
Chambersburg PA
CBHW060706010826
48977CB00007B/490